IMAGE COMICS, INC.

Robert Kirkman • Chief Operating Officer
Erik Larsen • Chief Financial Officer
Todd McFarlane • President
Marc Silvestri • Chief Executive Officer
Jim Valentino • Vice President

Eric Stephenson • Publisher / Chief Creative Officer
Jeff Boison • Director of Sales & Publishing Planning
Kat Salazar • Director of PR & Marketing
Drew Gill • Cover Editor
Heather Doornink • Production Director
Nicole Lapalme • Controller

IMAGECOMICS.COM

DEATH OR GLORY, VOLUME 2: I STILL MISS SOMEONE. First printing. September 2020. Published by Image Comics, Inc. Office of publication: 2701 NW Vaughn St., Suite 780, Portland, OR 97210. Copyright © 2020 Rick Remender & Bengal. All rights reserved. Contains material originally published in single magazine form as DEATH OR GLORY #6-11. "Death or Glory," its logos, and the likenesses of all characters herein are trademarks of Rick Remender & Bengal, unless otherwise noted. "Image" and the Image Comics logos are registered trademarks of Image Comics, Inc. No part of this publication may be reproduced or transmitted, in any form or by any means (except for short excerpts for journalistic or review purposes), without the express written permission of Rick Remender & Bengal, or Image Comics, Inc. All names, characters, events, and locales in this publication are entirely fictional. Any resemblance to actual persons (living or dead), events, or places, without satirical intent, is coincidental. Printed in the USA. For international rights, contact: foreignlicensing@imagecomics.com. ISBN: 978-1-5343-1251-7.

DEATH OR GLORY

WRITER **RICK REMENDER**

ARTIST **BENGAL**

LETTERER **RUS WOOTON**

EDITORS **BRIAH SKELLY & WILL DENNIS**

PRODUCTION ARTIST **ERIKA SCHNATZ**

LOGO **VINCENT KUKUA**

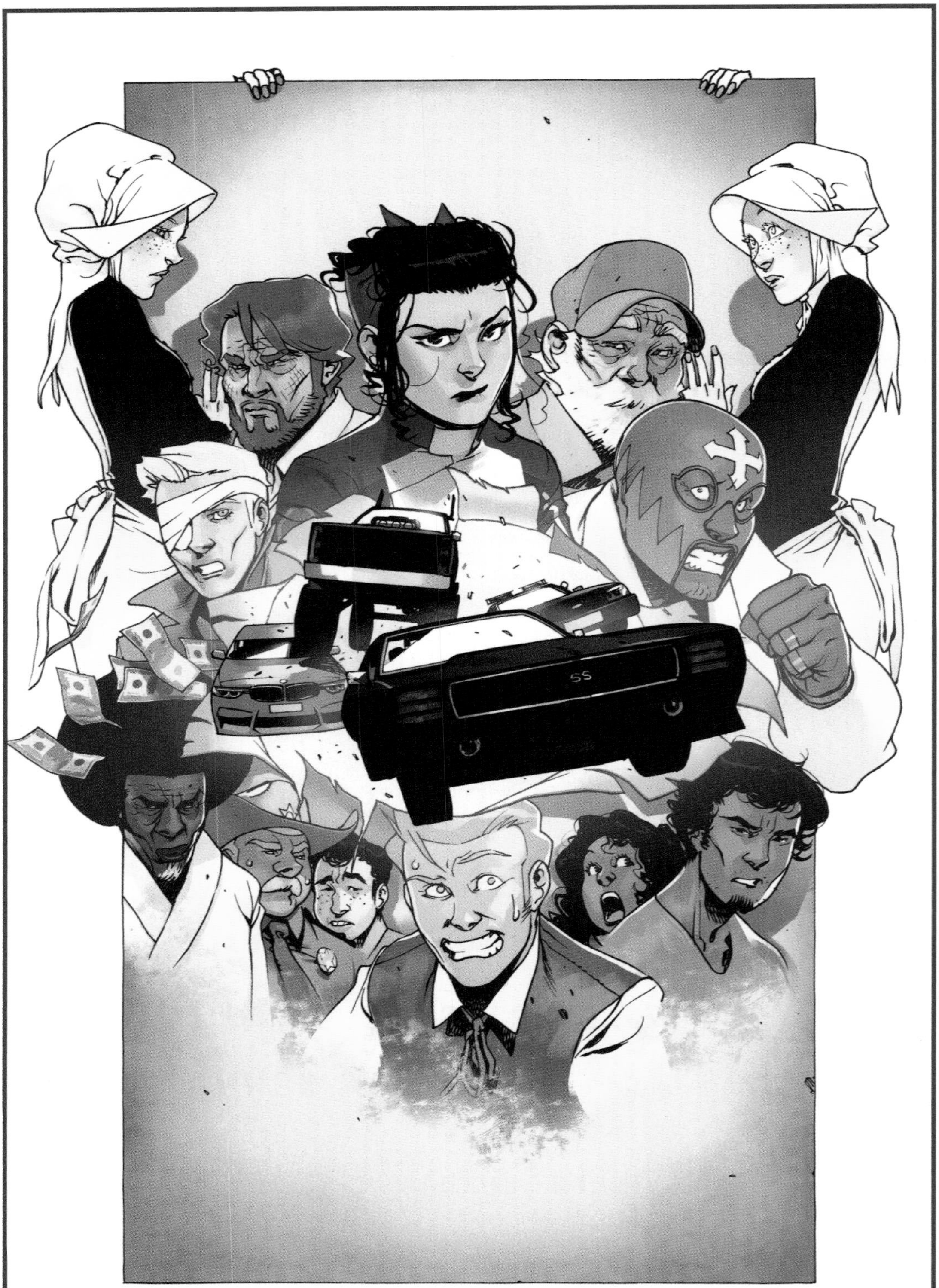
SS
B.

SIX

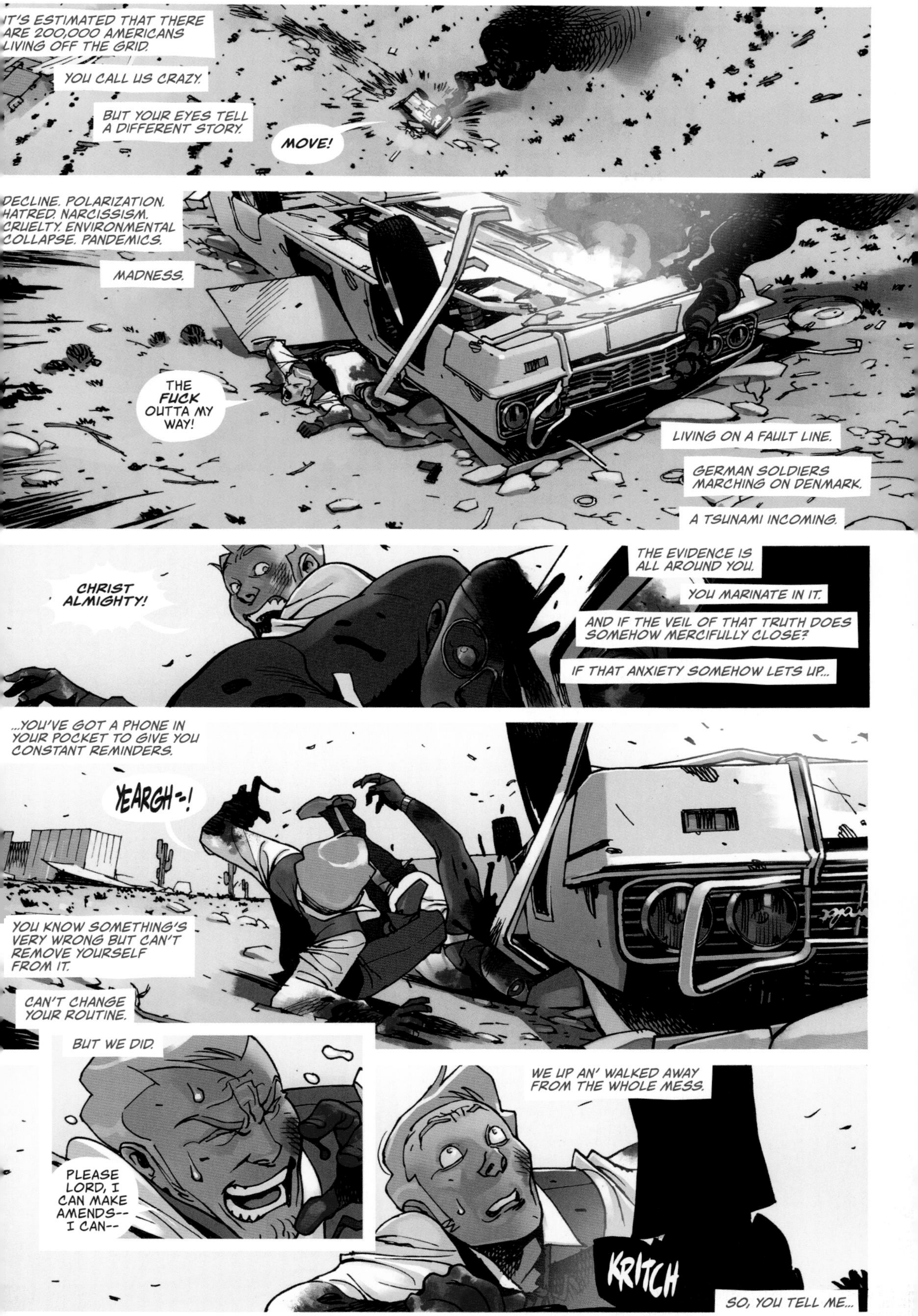
IT'S ESTIMATED THAT THERE ARE 200,000 AMERICANS LIVING OFF THE GRID.
YOU CALL US CRAZY.
BUT YOUR EYES TELL A DIFFERENT STORY.
MOVE!
DECLINE. POLARIZATION. HATRED. NARCISSISM. CRUELTY. ENVIRONMENTAL COLLAPSE. PANDEMICS.
MADNESS.
THE FUCK OUTTA MY WAY!
LIVING ON A FAULT LINE.
GERMAN SOLDIERS MARCHING ON DENMARK.
A TSUNAMI INCOMING.
CHRIST ALMIGHTY!
THE EVIDENCE IS ALL AROUND YOU.
YOU MARINATE IN IT.
AND IF THE VEIL OF THAT TRUTH DOES SOMEHOW MERCIFULLY CLOSE?
IF THAT ANXIETY SOMEHOW LETS UP...
...YOU'VE GOT A PHONE IN YOUR POCKET TO GIVE YOU CONSTANT REMINDERS.
YEARGH--!
YOU KNOW SOMETHING'S VERY WRONG BUT CAN'T REMOVE YOURSELF FROM IT.
CAN'T CHANGE YOUR ROUTINE.
BUT WE DID.
PLEASE LORD, I CAN MAKE AMENDS-- I CAN--
WE UP AN' WALKED AWAY FROM THE WHOLE MESS.
KRITCH
SO, YOU TELL ME...

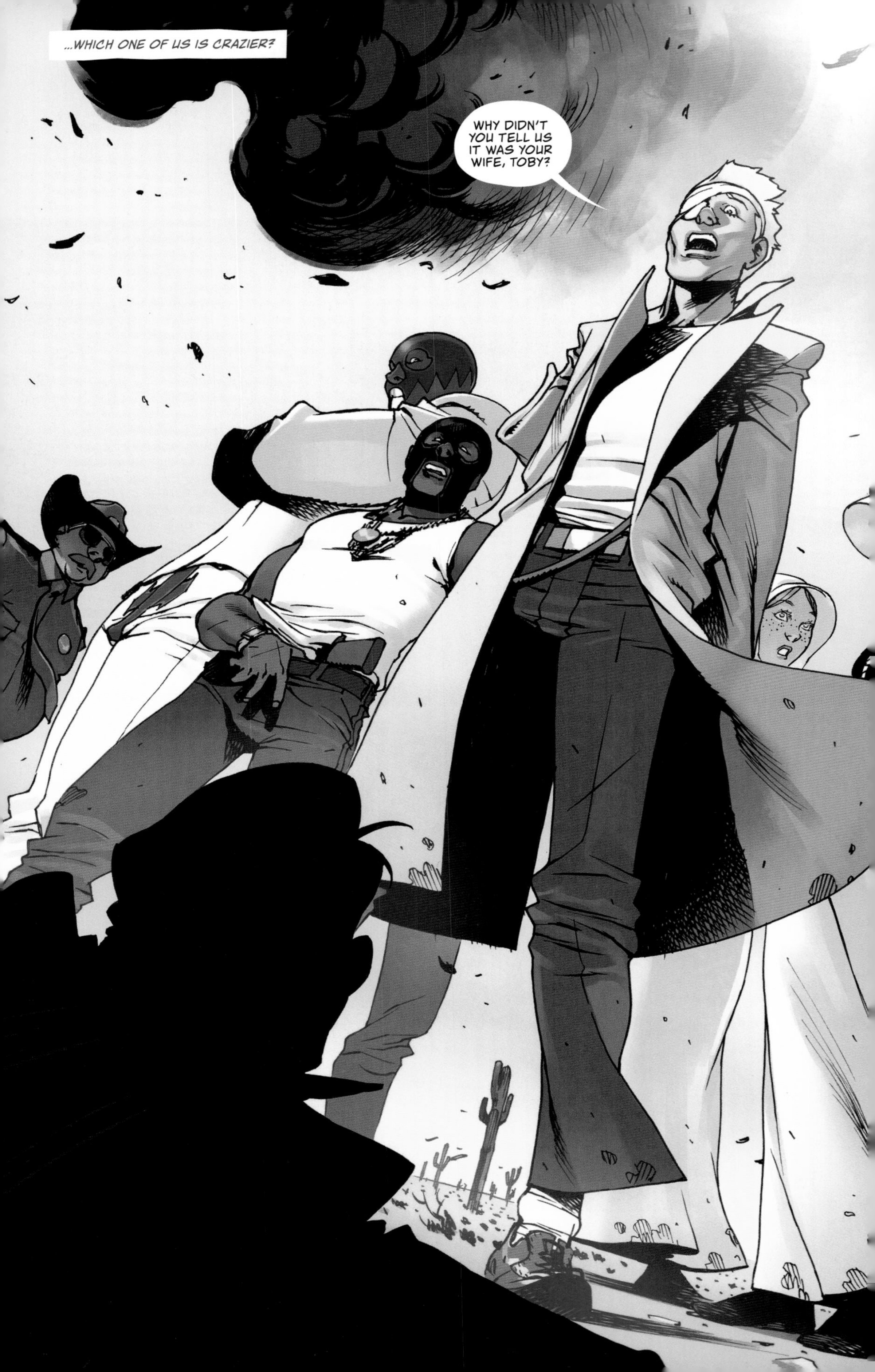
...WHICH ONE OF US IS CRAZIER?
WHY DIDN'T YOU TELL US IT WAS YOUR WIFE, TOBY?

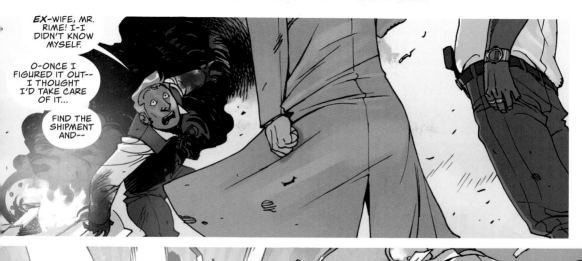

EX-WIFE, MR. RIME! I-I DIDN'T KNOW MYSELF.

O-ONCE I FIGURED IT OUT-- I THOUGHT I'D TAKE CARE OF IT...

FIND THE SHIPMENT AND--

CRADWOOM

OH...

FILTH!

I-I'M SORRY--

GET IT OFF! GET THE FILTHY FUCKING BLOOD OFF ME!

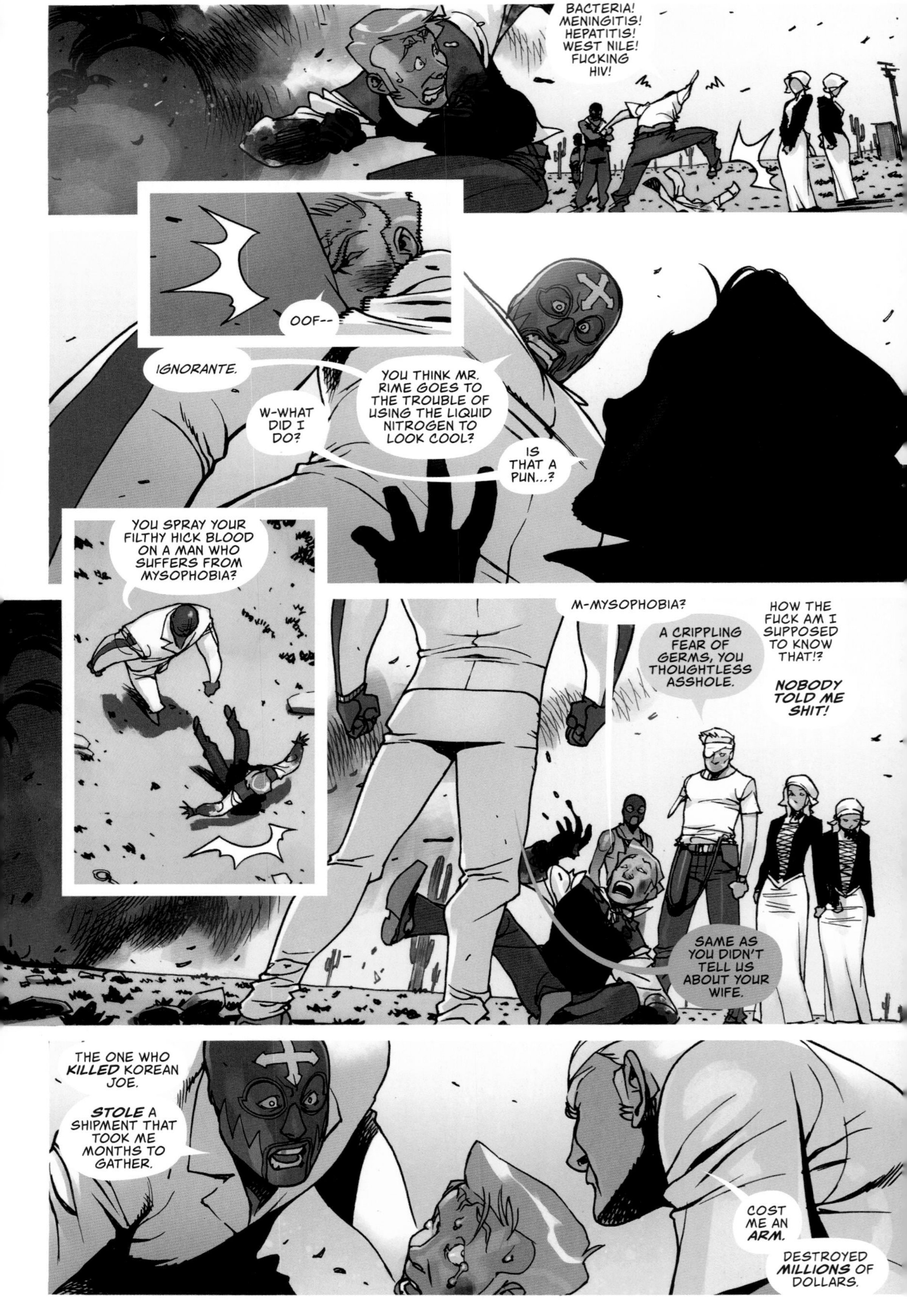

BACTERIA! MENINGITIS! HEPATITIS! WEST NILE! FUCKING HIV!
OOF--
IGNORANTE.
YOU THINK MR. RIME GOES TO THE TROUBLE OF USING THE LIQUID NITROGEN TO LOOK COOL?
W-WHAT DID I DO?
IS THAT A PUN...?
YOU SPRAY YOUR FILTHY HICK BLOOD ON A MAN WHO SUFFERS FROM MYSOPHOBIA?
M-MYSOPHOBIA?
A CRIPPLING FEAR OF GERMS, YOU THOUGHTLESS ASSHOLE.
HOW THE FUCK AM I SUPPOSED TO KNOW THAT!?
NOBODY TOLD ME SHIT!
SAME AS YOU DIDN'T TELL US ABOUT YOUR WIFE.
THE ONE WHO KILLED KOREAN JOE.
STOLE A SHIPMENT THAT TOOK ME MONTHS TO GATHER.
COST ME AN ARM.
DESTROYED MILLIONS OF DOLLARS.

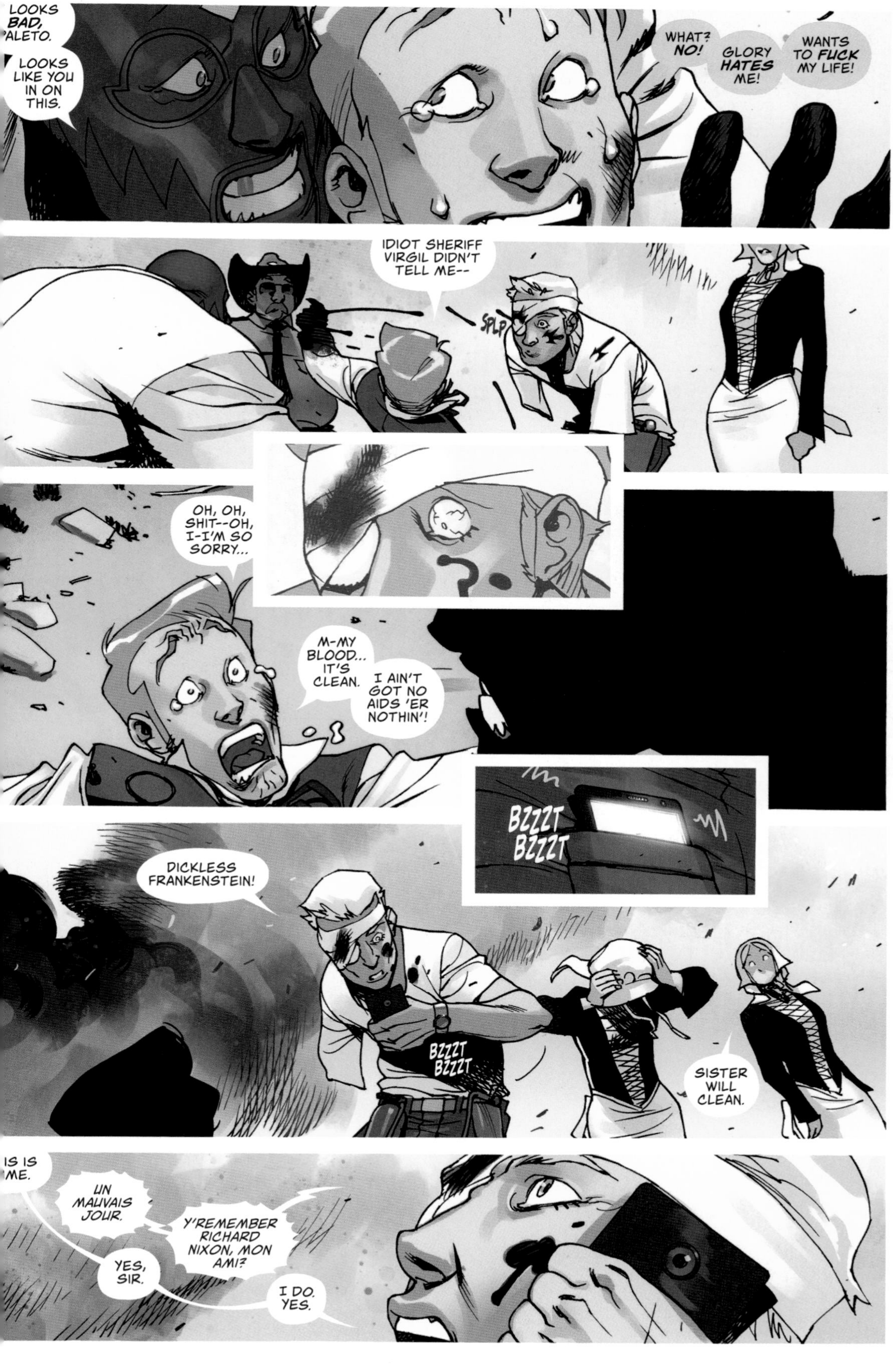

LOOKS BAD, PALETO.
LOOKS LIKE YOU IN ON THIS.
WHAT? NO!
GLORY HATES ME!
WANTS TO FUCK MY LIFE!
IDIOT SHERIFF VIRGIL DIDN'T TELL ME--
SPLP
OH, OH, SHIT--OH, I-I'M SO SORRY...
M-MY BLOOD... IT'S CLEAN.
I AIN'T GOT NO AIDS 'ER NOTHIN'!
BZZZT BZZZT
DICKLESS FRANKENSTEIN!
BZZZT BZZZT
SISTER WILL CLEAN.
IS IS ME.
UN MAUVAIS JOUR.
Y'REMEMBER RICHARD NIXON, MON AMI?
YES, SIR.
I DO. YES.

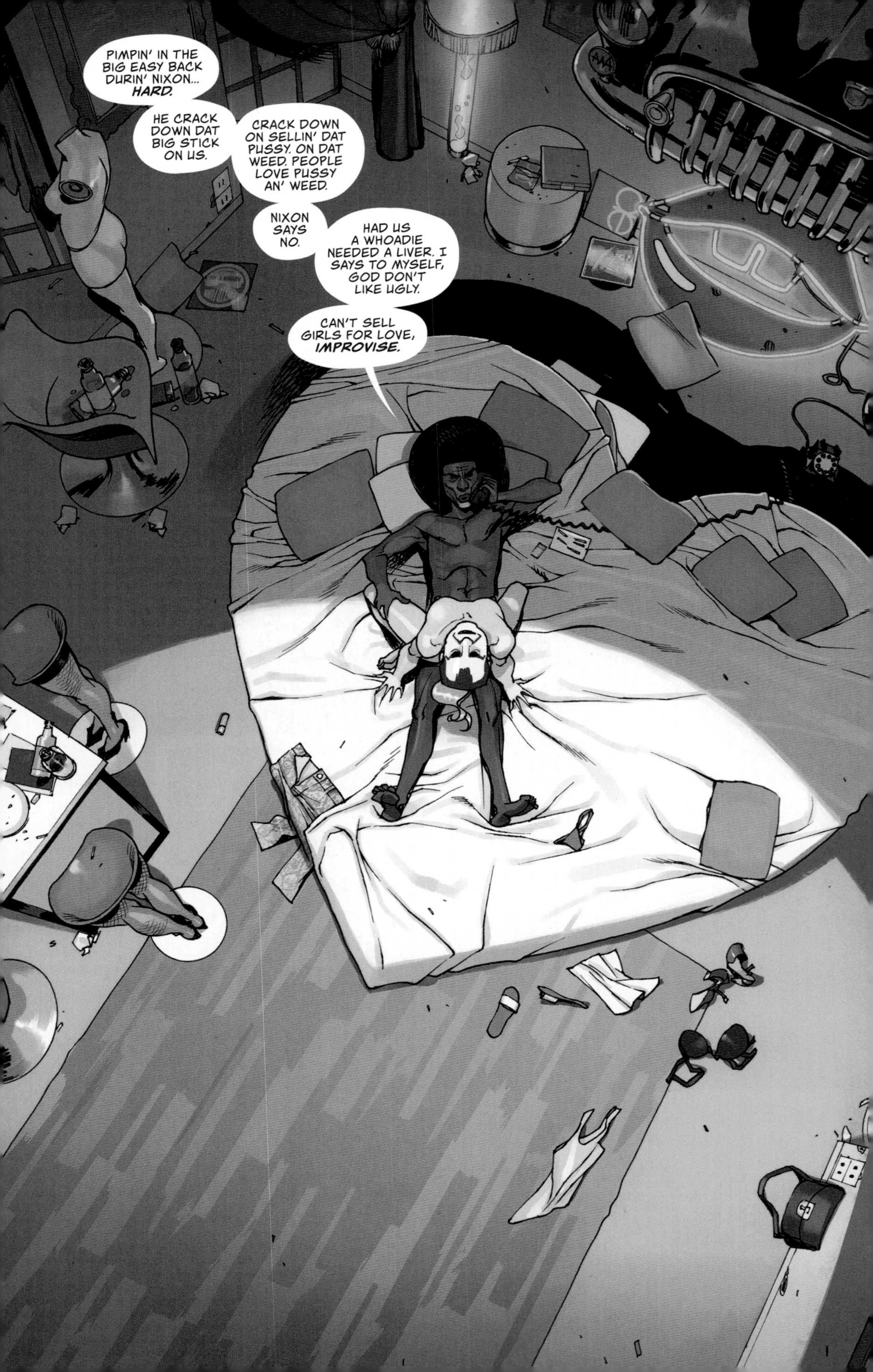
PIMPIN' IN THE BIG EASY BACK DURIN' NIXON... **HARD.**
HE CRACK DOWN DAT BIG STICK ON US.
CRACK DOWN ON SELLIN' DAT PUSSY. ON DAT WEED. PEOPLE LOVE PUSSY AN' WEED.
NIXON SAYS NO.
HAD US A WHOADIE NEEDED A LIVER. I SAYS TO MYSELF, GOD DON'T LIKE UGLY.
CAN'T SELL GIRLS FOR LOVE, **IMPROVISE.**

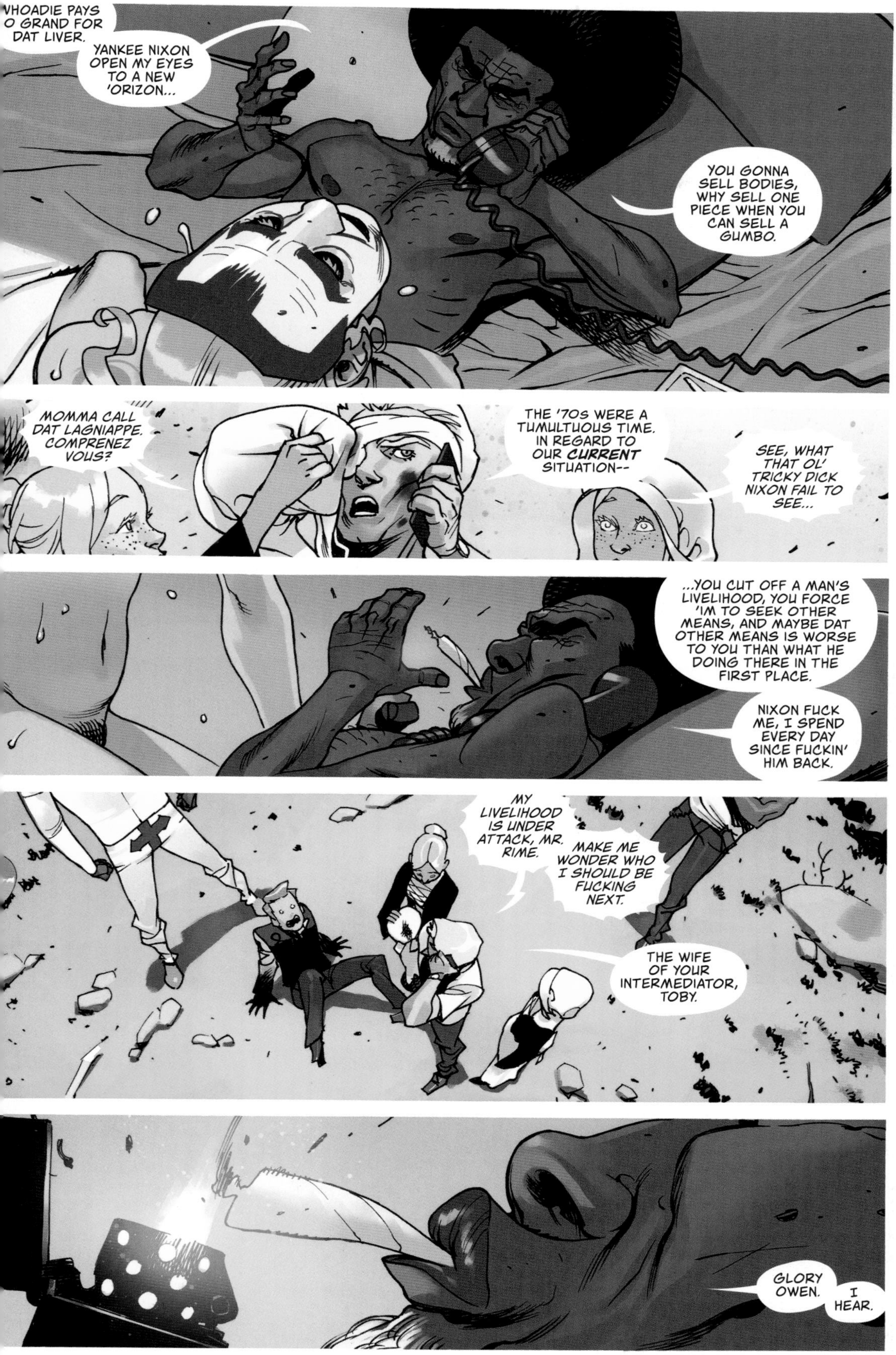
VHOADIE PAYS
O GRAND FOR
DAT LIVER.
YANKEE NIXON OPEN MY EYES TO A NEW 'ORIZON...
YOU GONNA SELL BODIES, WHY SELL ONE PIECE WHEN YOU CAN SELL A GUMBO.
MOMMA CALL DAT LAGNIAPPE. COMPRENEZ VOUS?
THE '70S WERE A TUMULTUOUS TIME. IN REGARD TO OUR CURRENT SITUATION--
SEE, WHAT THAT OL' TRICKY DICK NIXON FAIL TO SEE...
...YOU CUT OFF A MAN'S LIVELIHOOD, YOU FORCE 'IM TO SEEK OTHER MEANS, AND MAYBE DAT OTHER MEANS IS WORSE TO YOU THAN WHAT HE DOING THERE IN THE FIRST PLACE.
NIXON FUCK ME, I SPEND EVERY DAY SINCE FUCKIN' HIM BACK.
MY LIVELIHOOD IS UNDER ATTACK, MR. RIME.
MAKE ME WONDER WHO I SHOULD BE FUCKING NEXT.
THE WIFE OF YOUR INTERMEDIATOR, TOBY.
GLORY OWEN.
I HEAR.

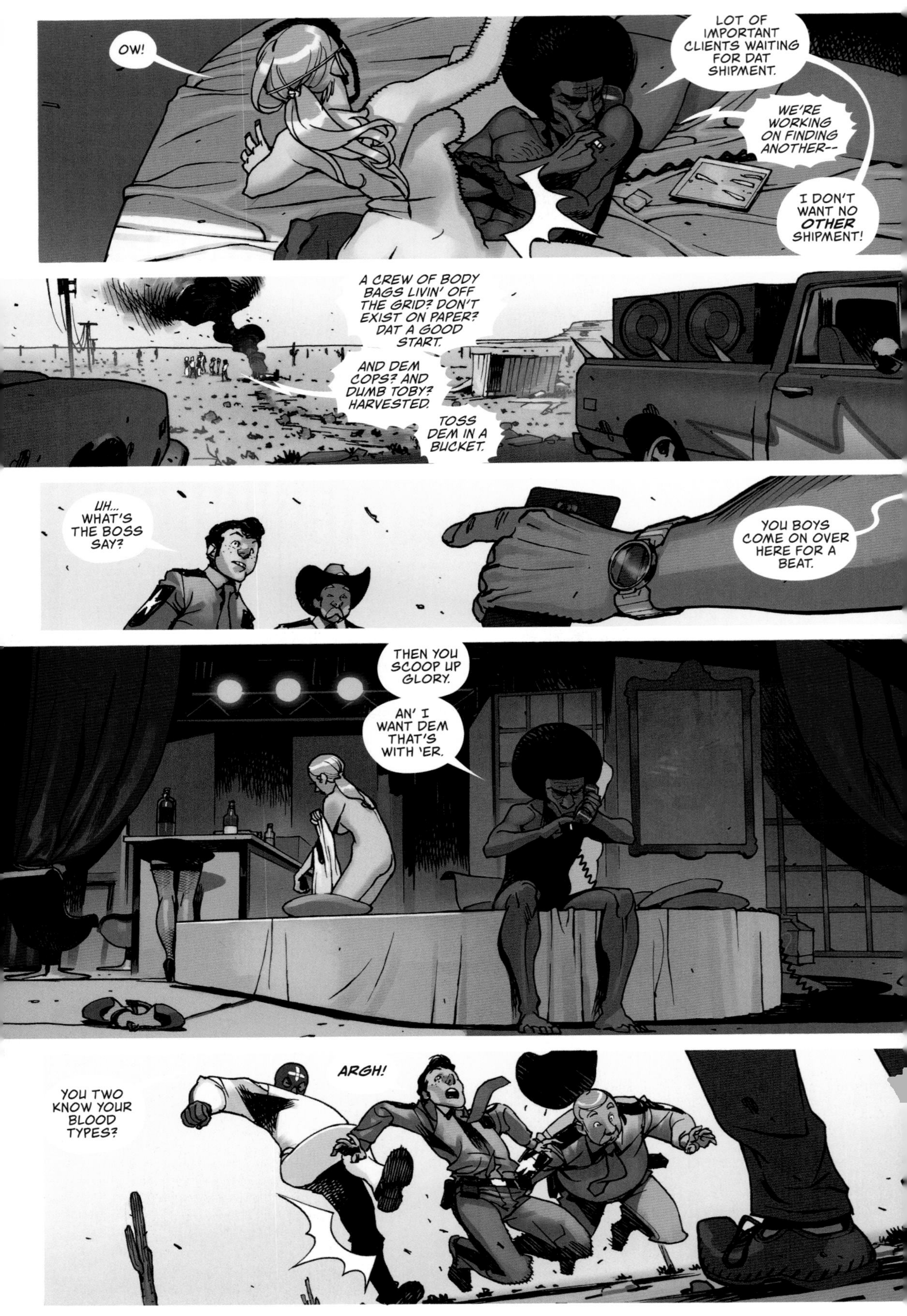
OW!
LOT OF IMPORTANT CLIENTS WAITING FOR DAT SHIPMENT.
WE'RE WORKING ON FINDING ANOTHER--
I DON'T WANT NO OTHER SHIPMENT!
A CREW OF BODY BAGS LIVIN' OFF THE GRID? DON'T EXIST ON PAPER? DAT A GOOD START.
AND DEM COPS? AND DUMB TOBY? HARVESTED.
TOSS DEM IN A BUCKET.
UH... WHAT'S THE BOSS SAY?
YOU BOYS COME ON OVER HERE FOR A BEAT.
THEN YOU SCOOP UP GLORY.
AN' I WANT DEM THAT'S WITH 'ER.
YOU TWO KNOW YOUR BLOOD TYPES?
ARGH!

WHERE'S TOBY?

SISTER SEES HIM.

LISTEN CLOSE, NOW.

Y'ALL DOUBLE HUSTLE.

MORE THAN JUST GOOD PEOPLE WAITIN' ON IT...

THE BRAZILIAN NAMED AFTER THE PAINTER?

HE HAS **SPECIAL** REPLACEMENT PARTS.

PARTS I WANT.

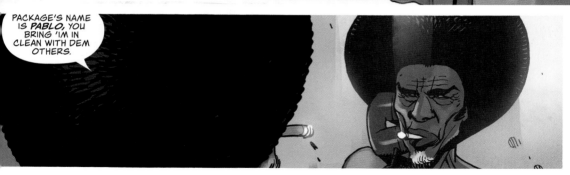

PACKAGE'S NAME IS **PABLO**, YOU BRING 'IM IN CLEAN WITH DEM OTHERS.

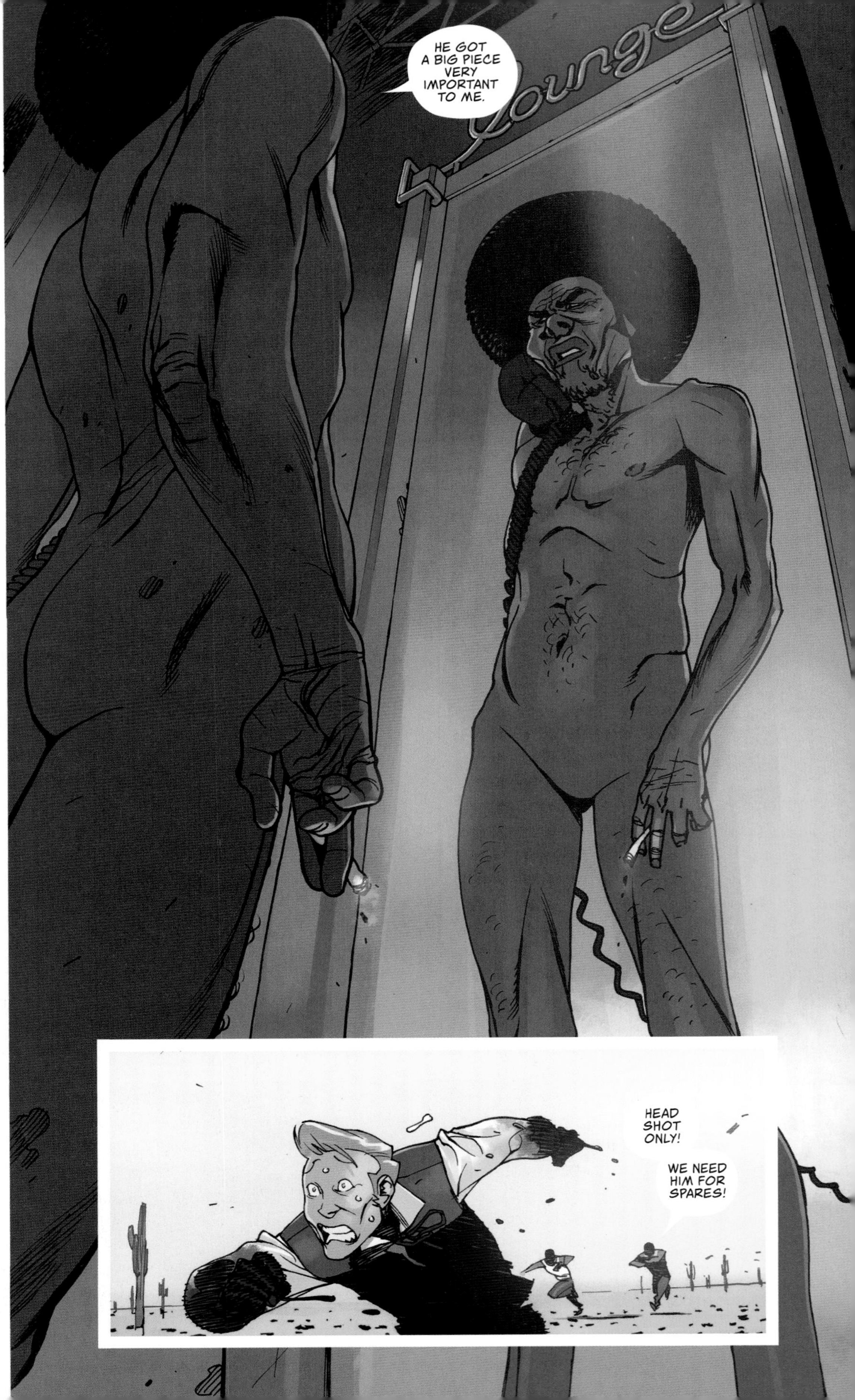
HE GOT A BIG PIECE VERY IMPORTANT TO ME.
Lounge
HEAD SHOT ONLY!
WE NEED HIM FOR SPARES!

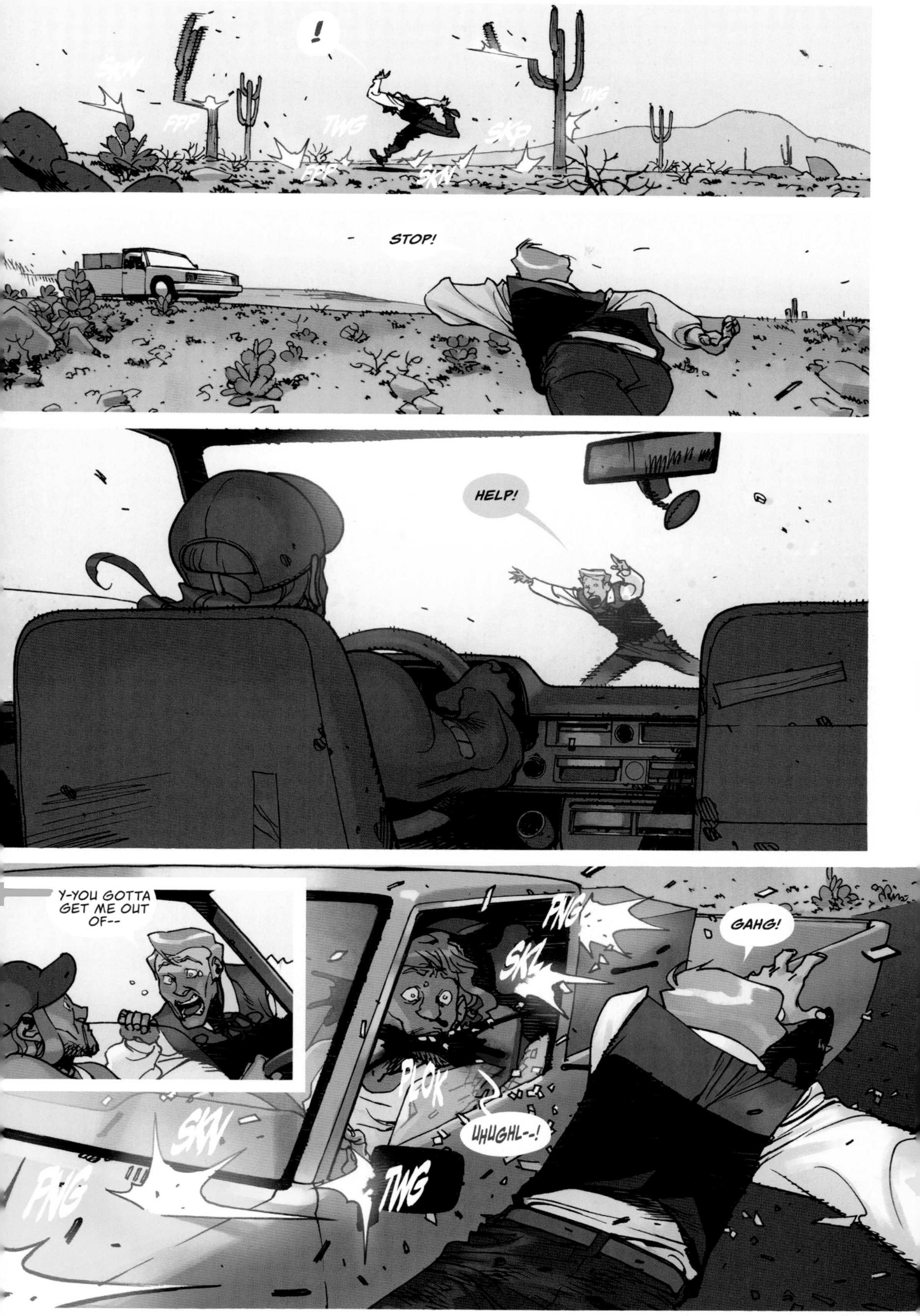
!
SKN
FPP
TWG
SKP
TWG
FPP
SKN
STOP!
HELP!
Y-YOU GOTTA GET ME OUT OF--
PNG
SKL
GAHG!
PLOK
UHUGHL--!
SKN
PNG
TWG

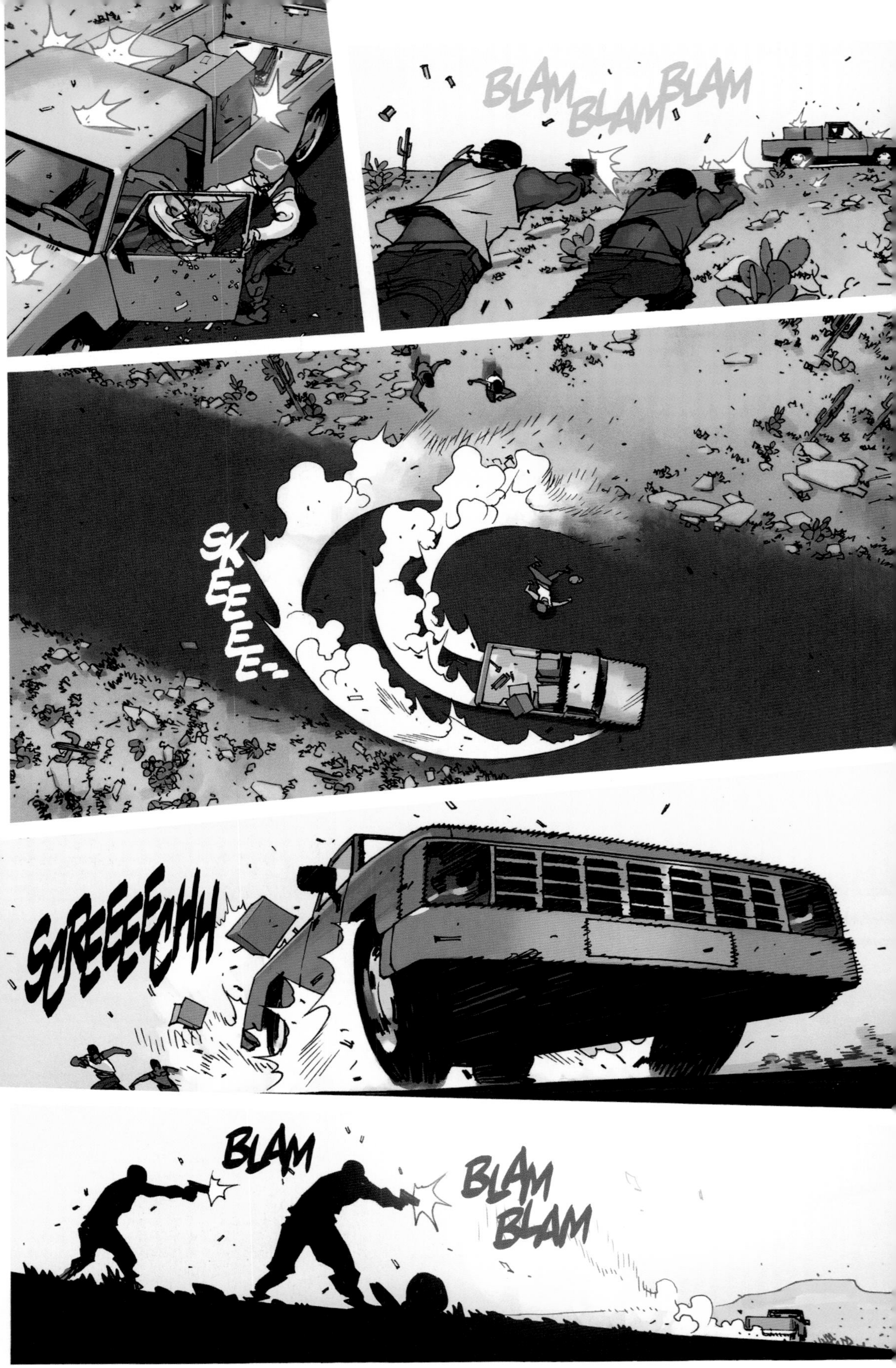
BLAM
BLAM
BLAM
SKEEEEE--
SCREEEECHH
BLAM
BLAM
BLAM

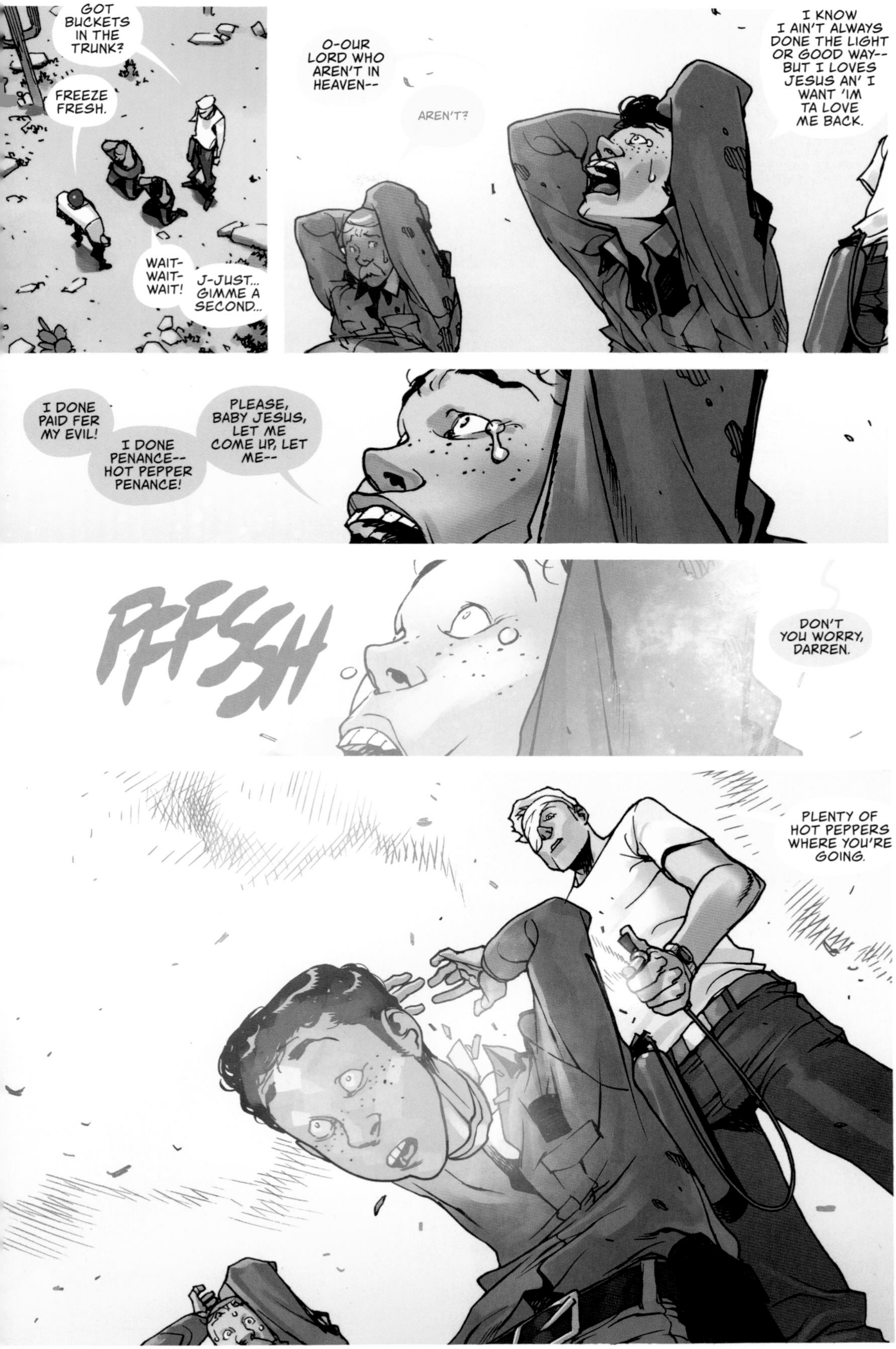
GOT BUCKETS IN THE TRUNK?
FREEZE FRESH.
WAIT-WAIT-WAIT!
J-JUST... GIMME A SECOND...
O-OUR LORD WHO AREN'T IN HEAVEN--
AREN'T?
I KNOW I AIN'T ALWAYS DONE THE LIGHT OR GOOD WAY-- BUT I LOVES JESUS AN' I WANT 'IM TA LOVE ME BACK.
I DONE PAID FER MY EVIL!
I DONE PENANCE-- HOT PEPPER PENANCE!
PLEASE, BABY JESUS, LET ME COME UP, LET ME--
PFFSH
DON'T YOU WORRY, DARREN.
PLENTY OF HOT PEPPERS WHERE YOU'RE GOING.

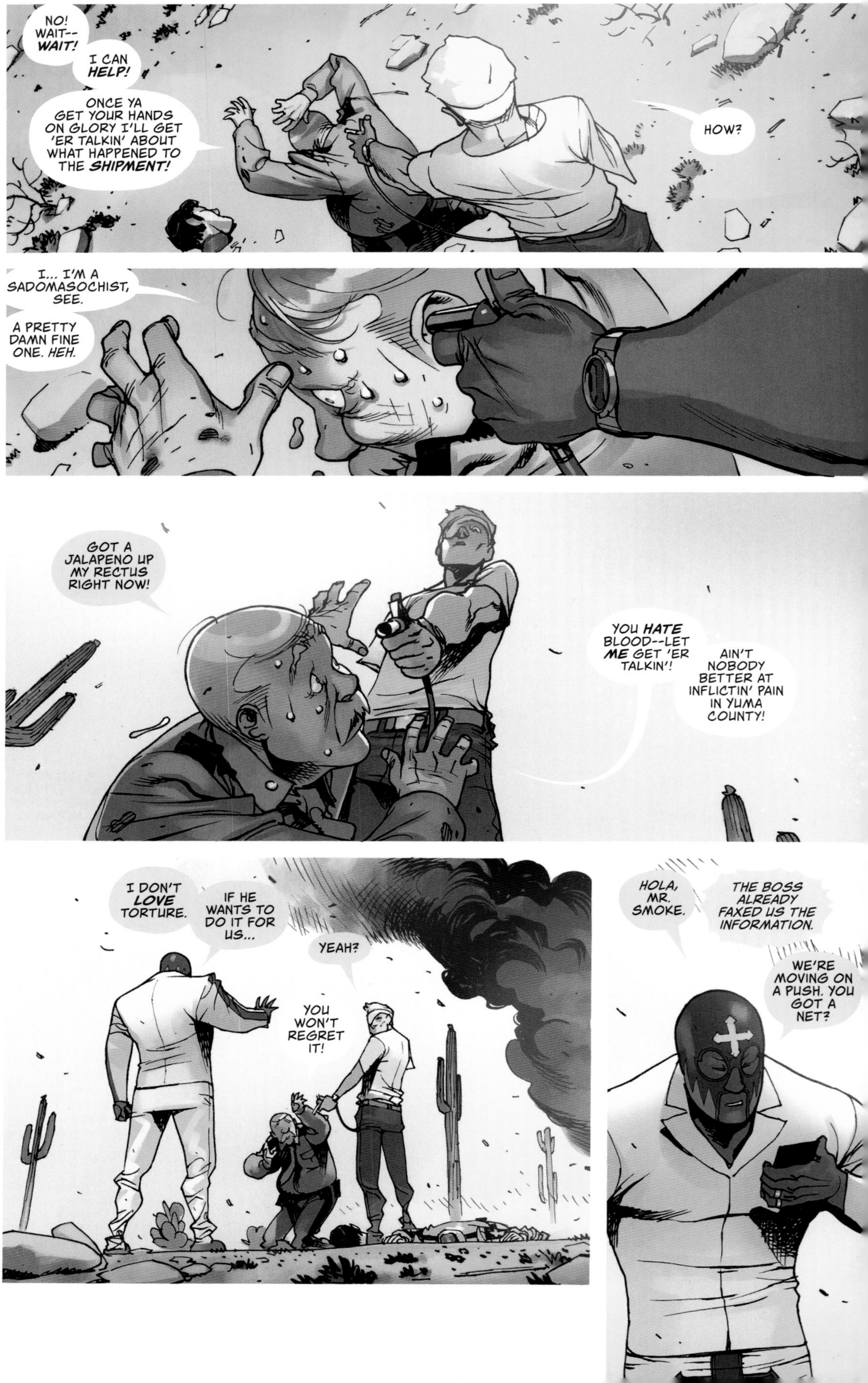
NO! WAIT-- WAIT!
I CAN HELP!
ONCE YA GET YOUR HANDS ON GLORY I'LL GET 'ER TALKIN' ABOUT WHAT HAPPENED TO THE SHIPMENT!
HOW?
I... I'M A SADOMASOCHIST, SEE.
A PRETTY DAMN FINE ONE. HEH.
GOT A JALAPENO UP MY RECTUS RIGHT NOW!
YOU HATE BLOOD--LET ME GET 'ER TALKIN'!
AIN'T NOBODY BETTER AT INFLICTIN' PAIN IN YUMA COUNTY!
I DON'T LOVE TORTURE.
IF HE WANTS TO DO IT FOR US...
YEAH?
YOU WON'T REGRET IT!
HOLA, MR. SMOKE.
THE BOSS ALREADY FAXED US THE INFORMATION.
WE'RE MOVING ON A PUSH. YOU GOT A NET?

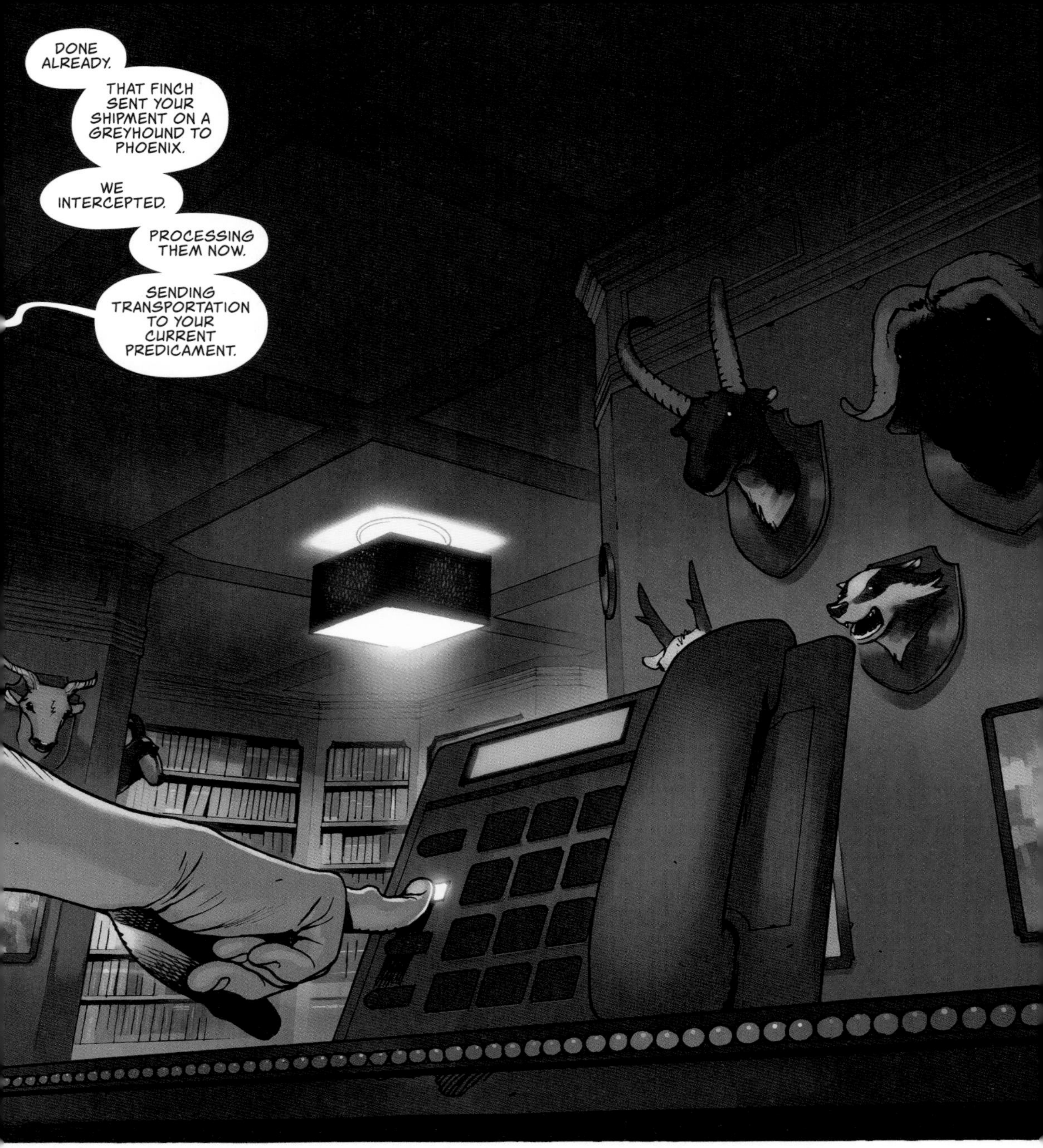
DONE ALREADY.
THAT FINCH SENT YOUR SHIPMENT ON A GREYHOUND TO PHOENIX.
WE INTERCEPTED.
PROCESSING THEM NOW.
SENDING TRANSPORTATION TO YOUR CURRENT PREDICAMENT.

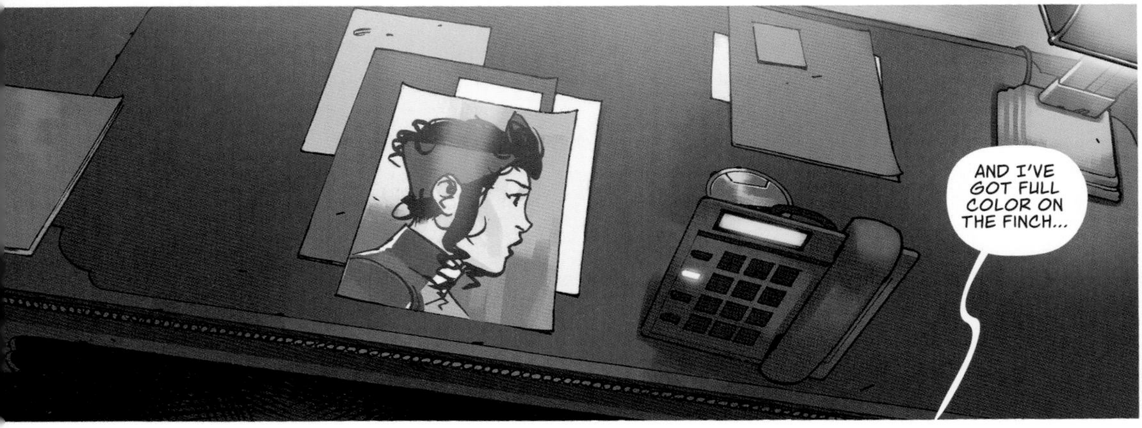
AND I'VE GOT FULL COLOR ON THE FINCH...

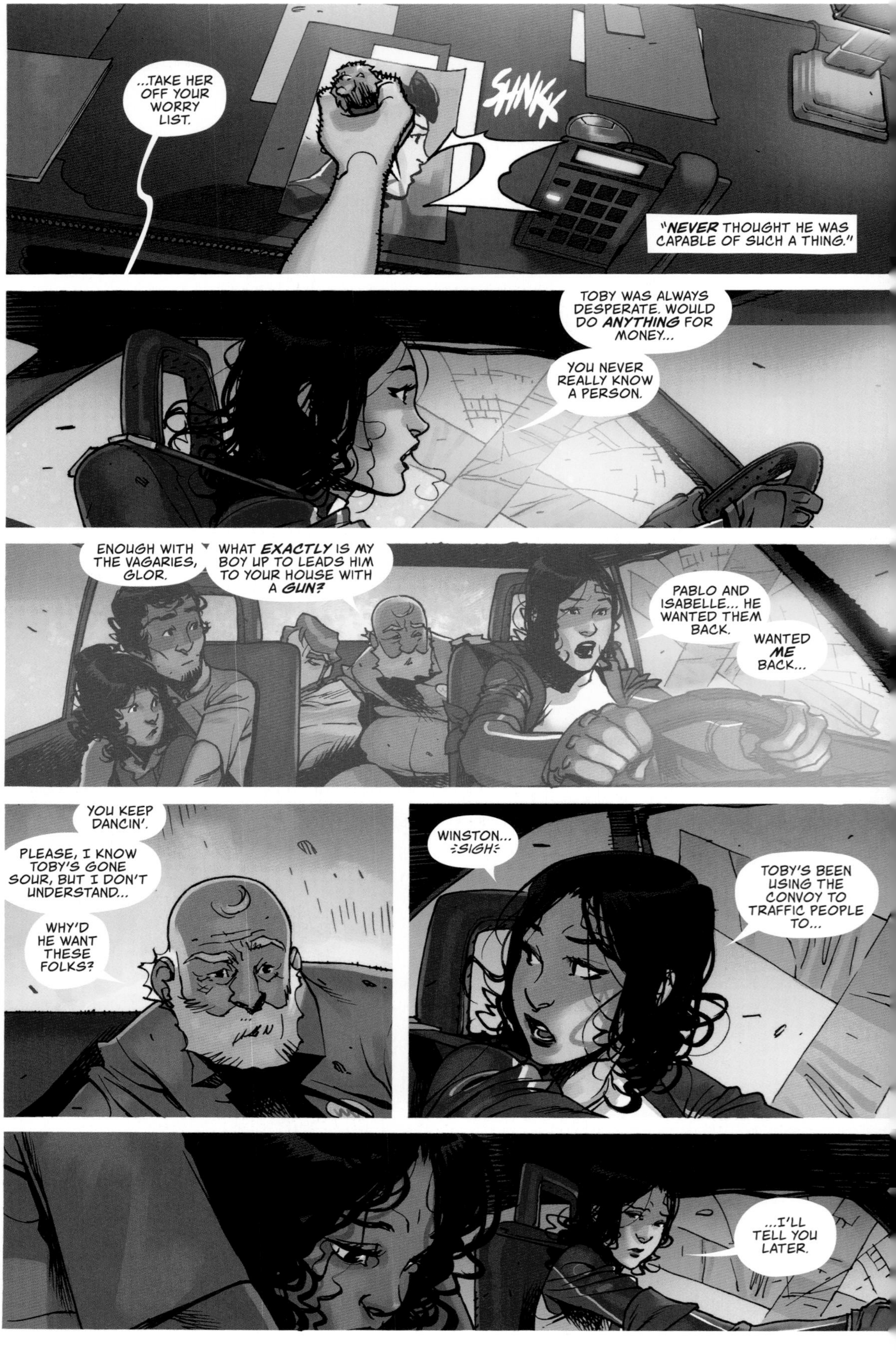
...TAKE HER OFF YOUR WORRY LIST.
SHNKK
"NEVER THOUGHT HE WAS CAPABLE OF SUCH A THING."
TOBY WAS ALWAYS DESPERATE. WOULD DO ANYTHING FOR MONEY...
YOU NEVER REALLY KNOW A PERSON.
ENOUGH WITH THE VAGARIES, GLOR.
WHAT EXACTLY IS MY BOY UP TO LEADS HIM TO YOUR HOUSE WITH A GUN?
PABLO AND ISABELLE... HE WANTED THEM BACK.
WANTED ME BACK...
YOU KEEP DANCIN'.
PLEASE, I KNOW TOBY'S GONE SOUR, BUT I DON'T UNDERSTAND...
WHY'D HE WANT THESE FOLKS?
WINSTON... SIGH
TOBY'S BEEN USING THE CONVOY TO TRAFFIC PEOPLE TO...
...I'LL TELL YOU LATER.

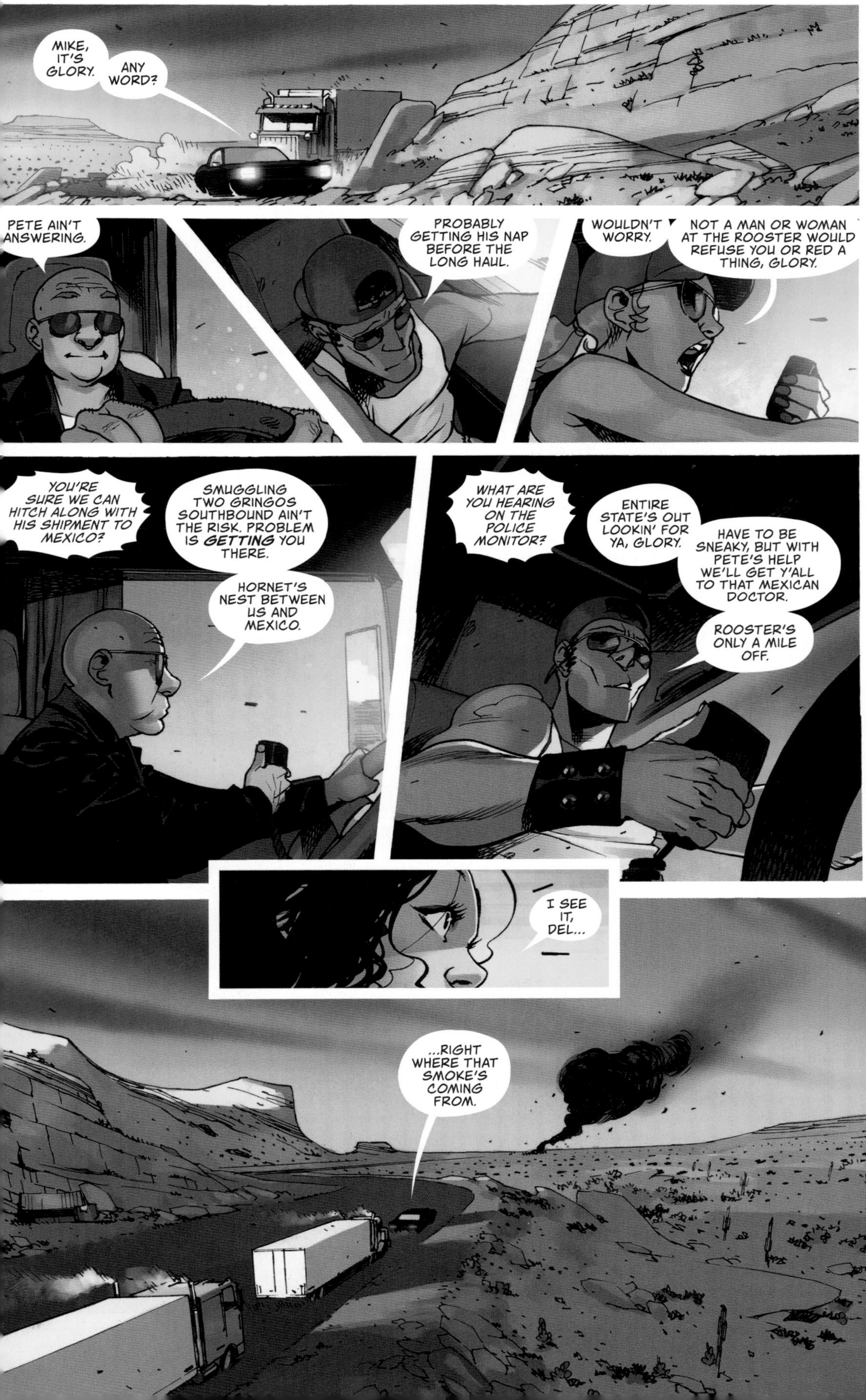
MIKE, IT'S GLORY.
ANY WORD?
PETE AIN'T ANSWERING.
PROBABLY GETTING HIS NAP BEFORE THE LONG HAUL.
WOULDN'T WORRY.
NOT A MAN OR WOMAN AT THE ROOSTER WOULD REFUSE YOU OR RED A THING, GLORY.
YOU'RE SURE WE CAN HITCH ALONG WITH HIS SHIPMENT TO MEXICO?
SMUGGLING TWO GRINGOS SOUTHBOUND AIN'T THE RISK. PROBLEM IS GETTING YOU THERE.
HORNET'S NEST BETWEEN US AND MEXICO.
WHAT ARE YOU HEARING ON THE POLICE MONITOR?
ENTIRE STATE'S OUT LOOKIN' FOR YA, GLORY.
HAVE TO BE SNEAKY, BUT WITH PETE'S HELP WE'LL GET Y'ALL TO THAT MEXICAN DOCTOR.
ROOSTER'S ONLY A MILE OFF.
I SEE IT, DEL...
...RIGHT WHERE THAT SMOKE'S COMING FROM.

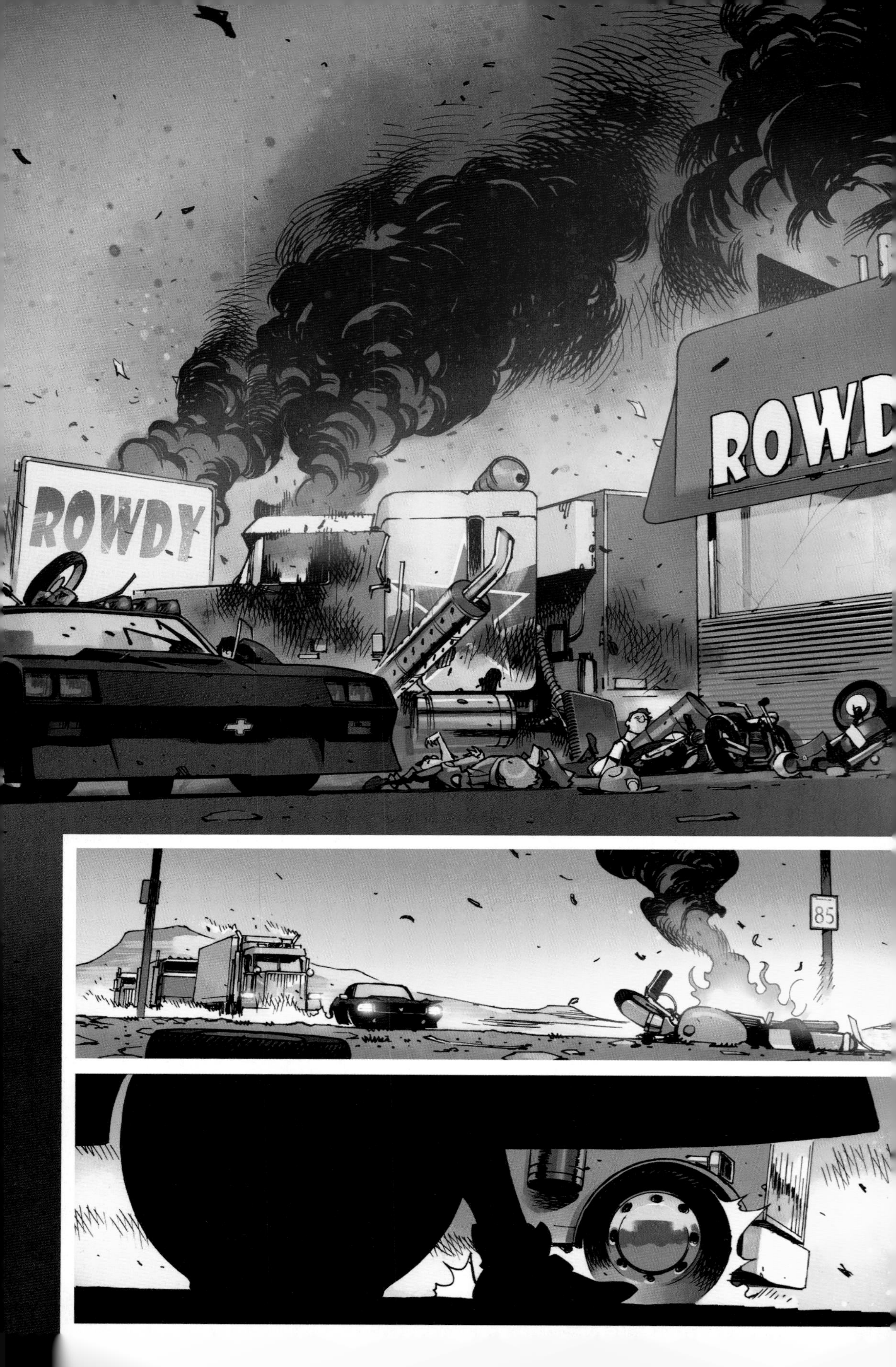
ROWDY
ROWD
85

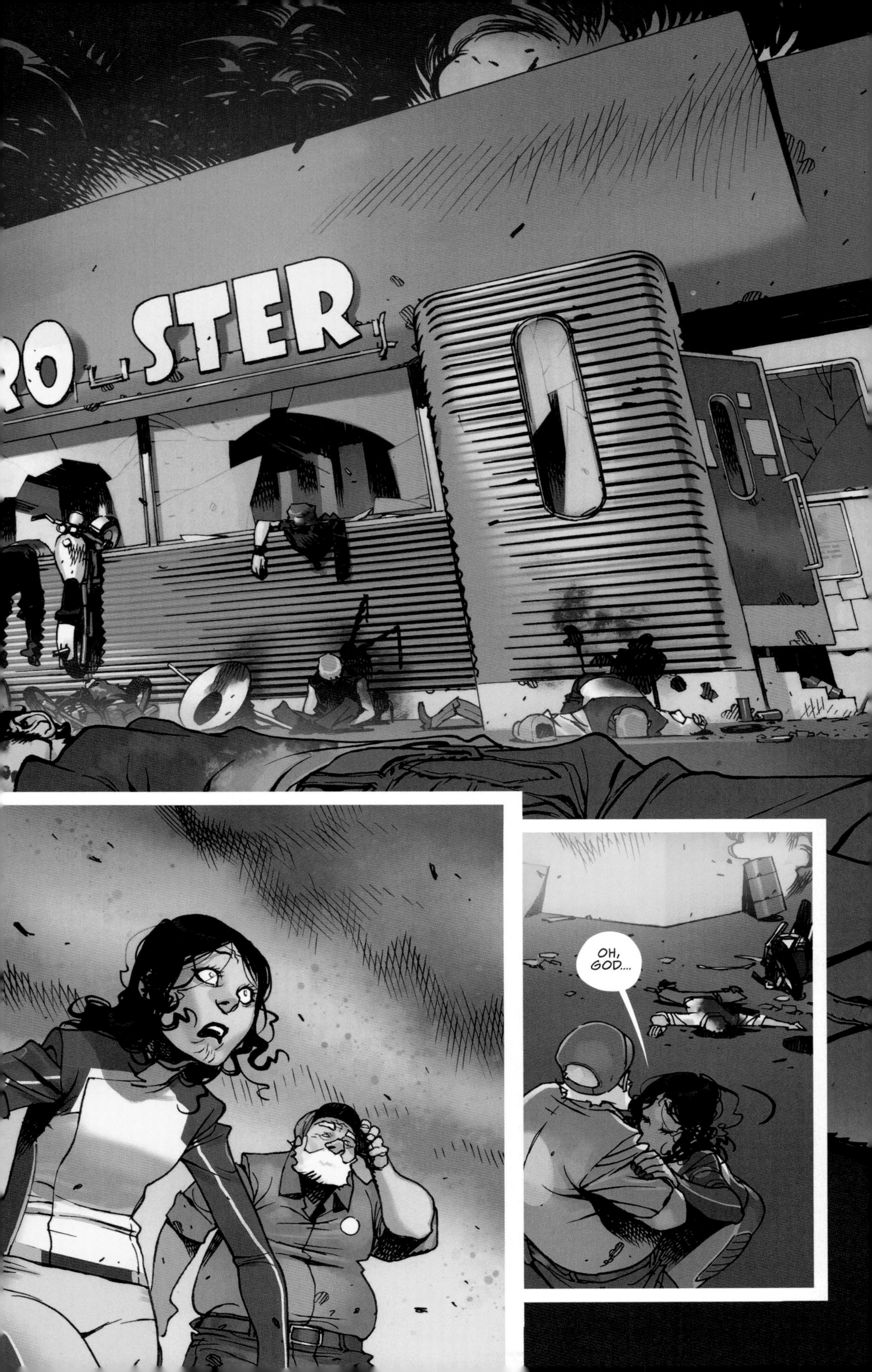
RO STER
OH, GOD....

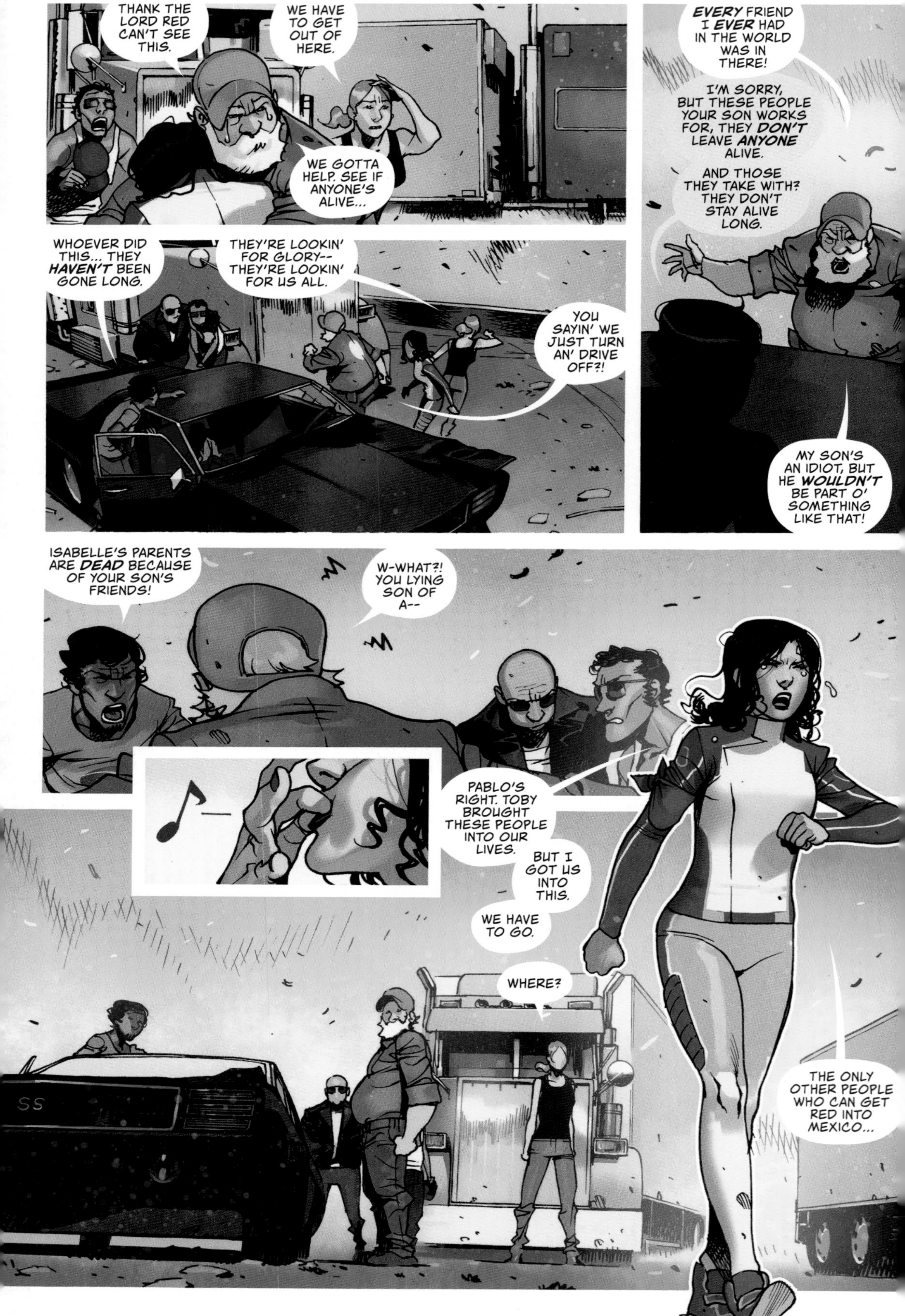
THANK THE LORD RED CAN'T SEE THIS.
WE HAVE TO GET OUT OF HERE.
WE GOTTA HELP. SEE IF ANYONE'S ALIVE...
EVERY FRIEND I EVER HAD IN THE WORLD WAS IN THERE!
I'M SORRY, BUT THESE PEOPLE YOUR SON WORKS FOR, THEY DON'T LEAVE ANYONE ALIVE.
AND THOSE THEY TAKE WITH? THEY DON'T STAY ALIVE LONG.
WHOEVER DID THIS... THEY HAVEN'T BEEN GONE LONG.
THEY'RE LOOKIN' FOR GLORY-- THEY'RE LOOKIN' FOR US ALL.
YOU SAYIN' WE JUST TURN AN' DRIVE OFF?!
MY SON'S AN IDIOT, BUT HE WOULDN'T BE PART O' SOMETHING LIKE THAT!
ISABELLE'S PARENTS ARE DEAD BECAUSE OF YOUR SON'S FRIENDS!
W-WHAT?! YOU LYING SON OF A--
♪—
PABLO'S RIGHT. TOBY BROUGHT THESE PEOPLE INTO OUR LIVES.
BUT I GOT US INTO THIS.
WE HAVE TO GO.
WHERE?
THE ONLY OTHER PEOPLE WHO CAN GET RED INTO MEXICO...

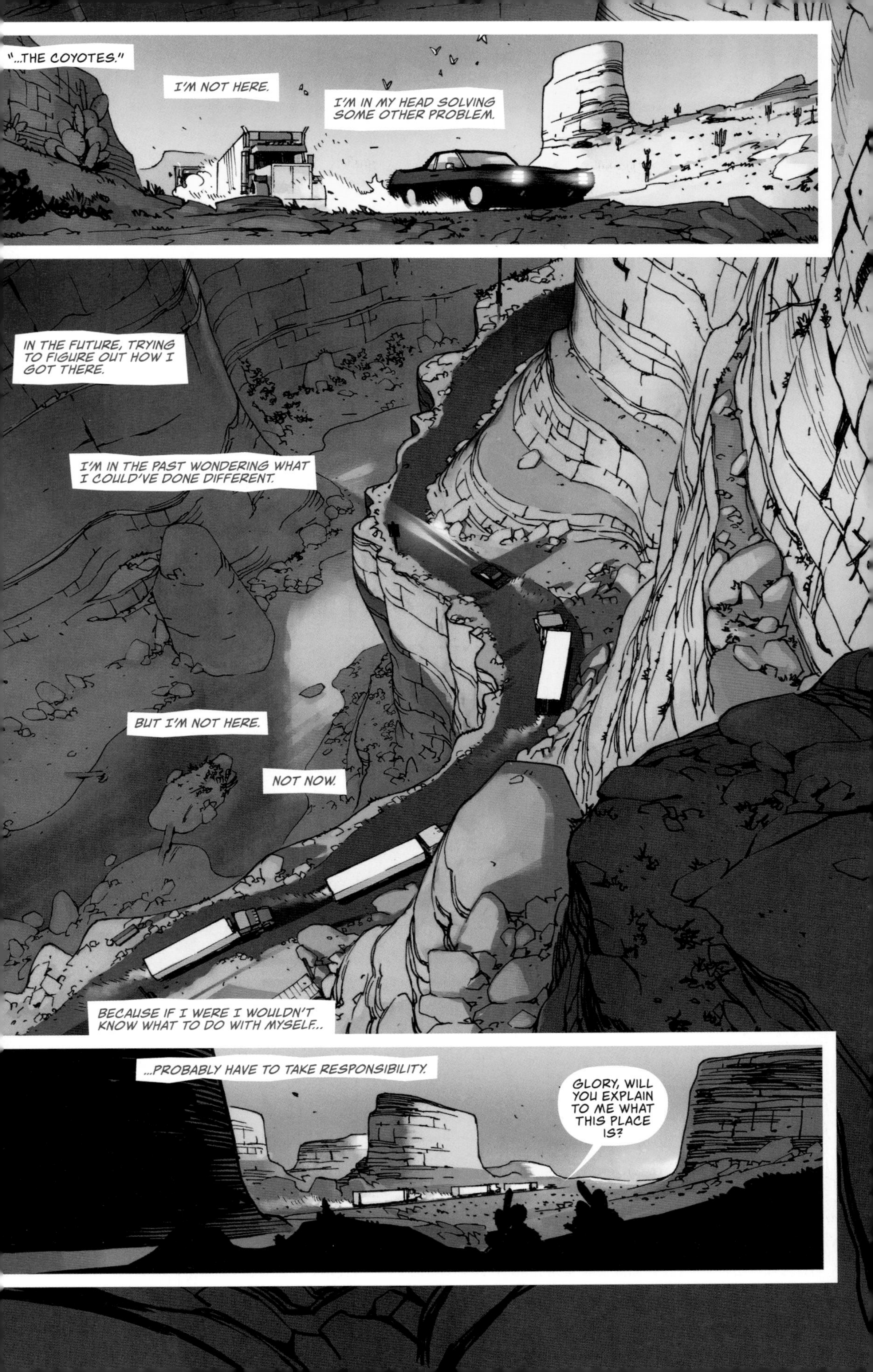

"...THE COYOTES."
I'M NOT HERE.
I'M IN MY HEAD SOLVING SOME OTHER PROBLEM.
IN THE FUTURE, TRYING TO FIGURE OUT HOW I GOT THERE.
I'M IN THE PAST WONDERING WHAT I COULD'VE DONE DIFFERENT.
BUT I'M NOT HERE.
NOT NOW.
BECAUSE IF I WERE I WOULDN'T KNOW WHAT TO DO WITH MYSELF...
...PROBABLY HAVE TO TAKE RESPONSIBILITY.
GLORY, WILL YOU EXPLAIN TO ME WHAT THIS PLACE IS?

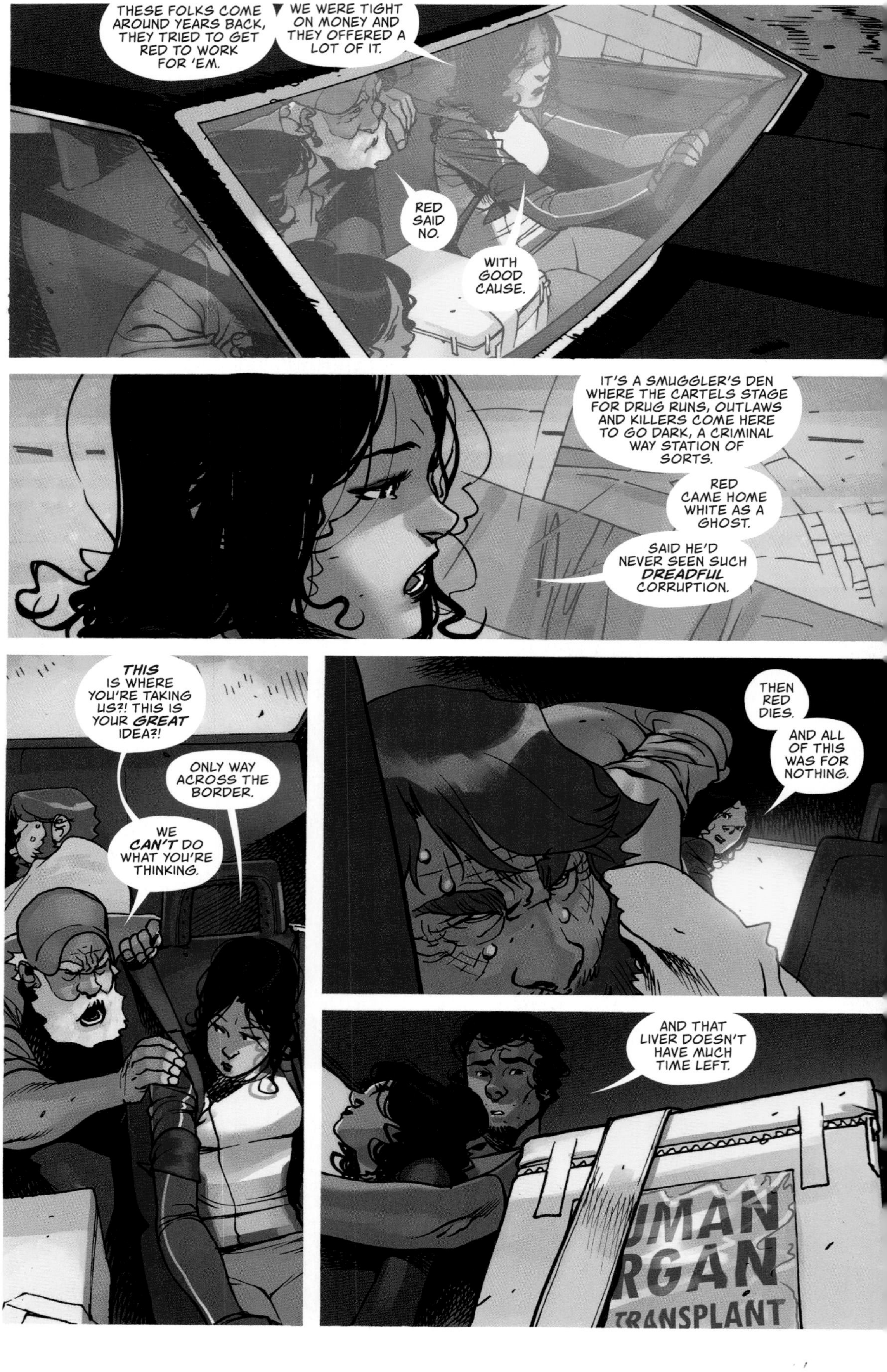
THESE FOLKS COME AROUND YEARS BACK, THEY TRIED TO GET RED TO WORK FOR 'EM.
WE WERE TIGHT ON MONEY AND THEY OFFERED A LOT OF IT.
RED SAID NO.
WITH GOOD CAUSE.
IT'S A SMUGGLER'S DEN WHERE THE CARTELS STAGE FOR DRUG RUNS, OUTLAWS AND KILLERS COME HERE TO GO DARK, A CRIMINAL WAY STATION OF SORTS.
RED CAME HOME WHITE AS A GHOST.
SAID HE'D NEVER SEEN SUCH DREADFUL CORRUPTION.
THIS IS WHERE YOU'RE TAKING US?! THIS IS YOUR GREAT IDEA?!
ONLY WAY ACROSS THE BORDER.
WE CAN'T DO WHAT YOU'RE THINKING.
THEN RED DIES.
AND ALL OF THIS WAS FOR NOTHING.
AND THAT LIVER DOESN'T HAVE MUCH TIME LEFT.
UMAN
RGAN
TRANSPLANT

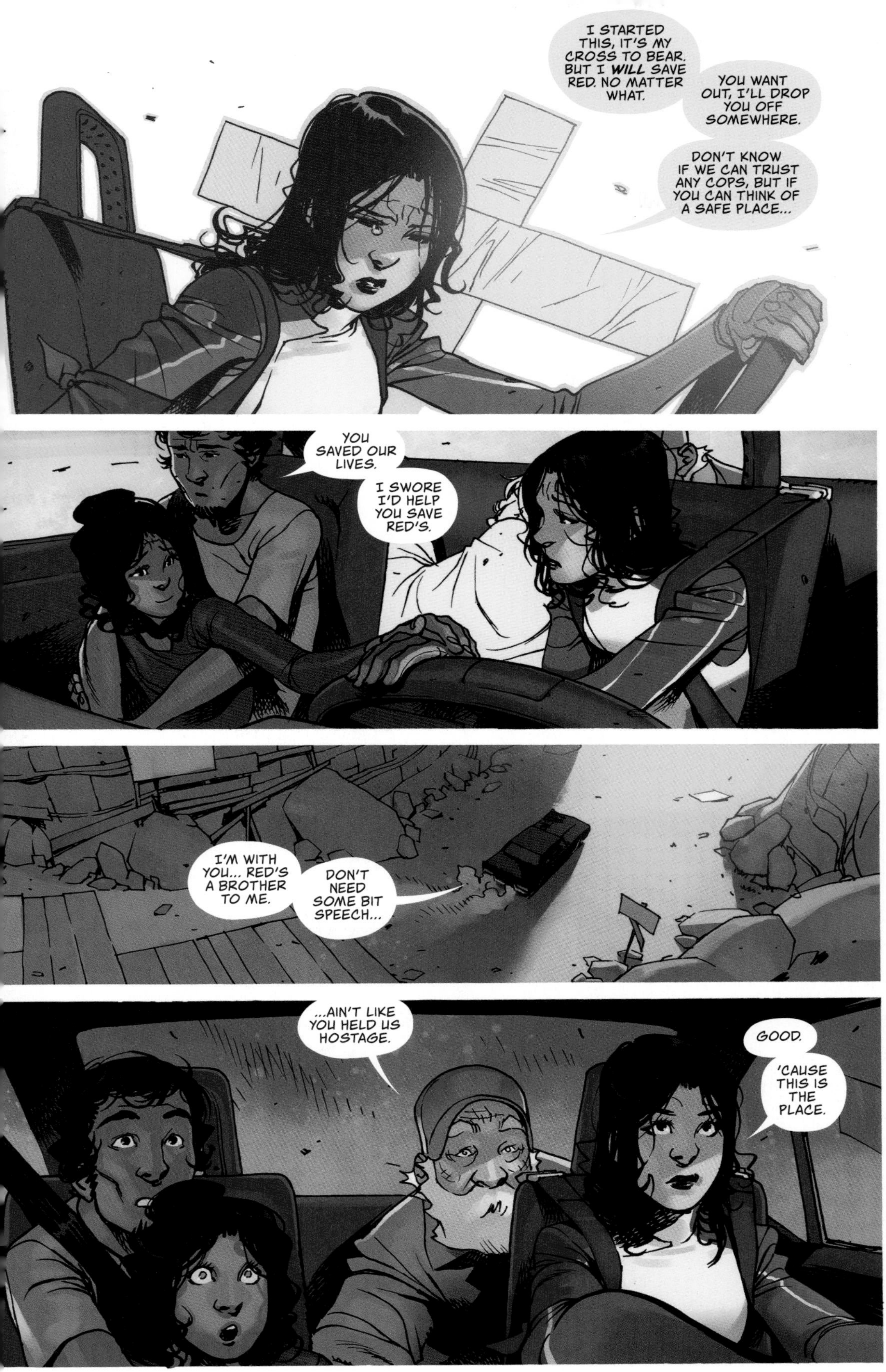
I STARTED THIS, IT'S MY CROSS TO BEAR. BUT I WILL SAVE RED. NO MATTER WHAT.
YOU WANT OUT, I'LL DROP YOU OFF SOMEWHERE.
DON'T KNOW IF WE CAN TRUST ANY COPS, BUT IF YOU CAN THINK OF A SAFE PLACE...
YOU SAVED OUR LIVES.
I SWORE I'D HELP YOU SAVE RED'S.
I'M WITH YOU... RED'S A BROTHER TO ME.
DON'T NEED SOME BIT SPEECH...
...AIN'T LIKE YOU HELD US HOSTAGE.
GOOD.
'CAUSE THIS IS THE PLACE.

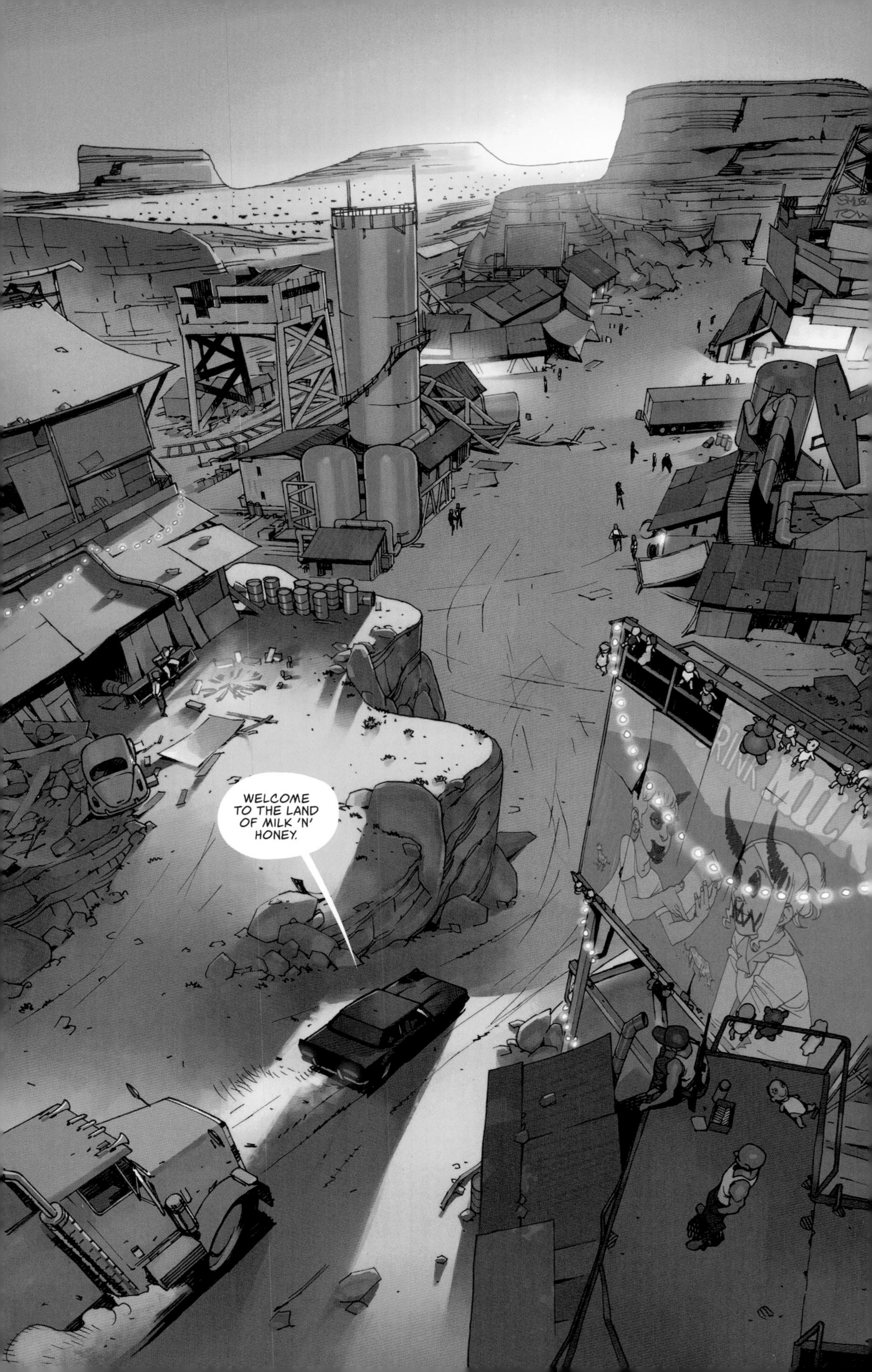
WELCOME TO THE LAND OF MILK 'N' HONEY.

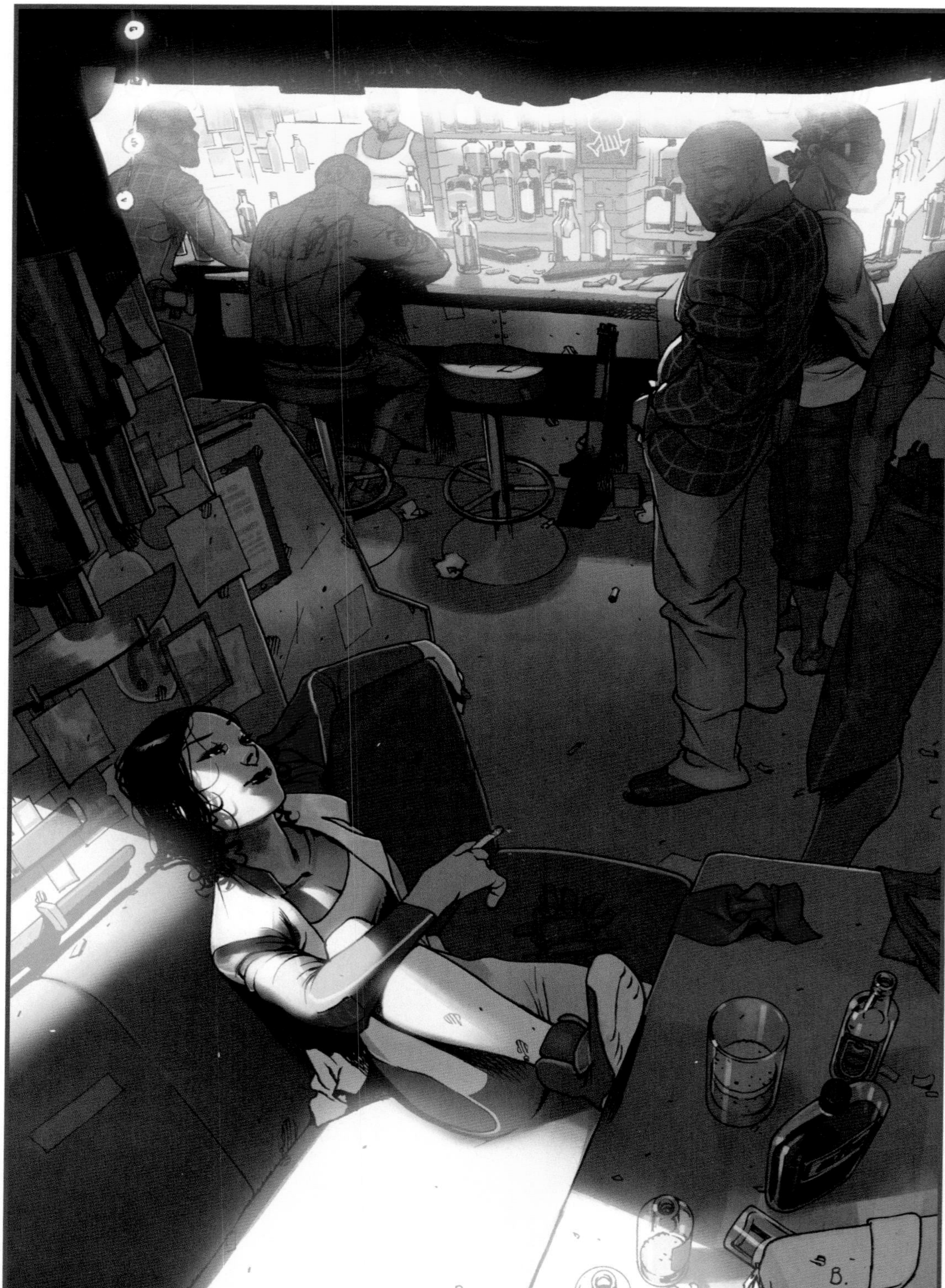

S E V E N

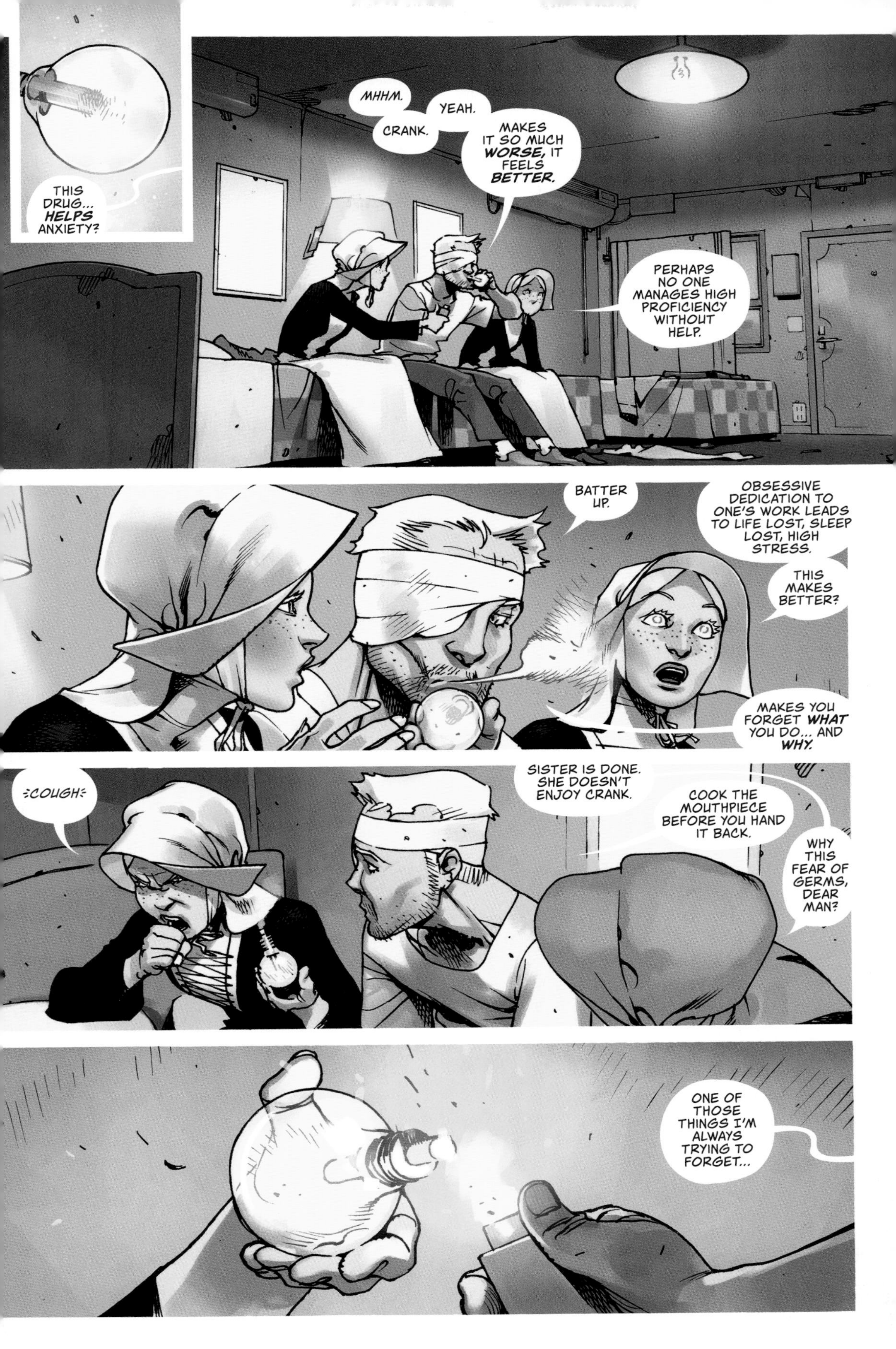
THIS DRUG... HELPS ANXIETY?
MHHM.
CRANK.
YEAH.
MAKES IT SO MUCH WORSE, IT FEELS BETTER.
PERHAPS NO ONE MANAGES HIGH PROFICIENCY WITHOUT HELP.
BATTER UP.
OBSESSIVE DEDICATION TO ONE'S WORK LEADS TO LIFE LOST, SLEEP LOST, HIGH STRESS.
THIS MAKES BETTER?
MAKES YOU FORGET WHAT YOU DO... AND WHY.
COUGH
SISTER IS DONE. SHE DOESN'T ENJOY CRANK.
COOK THE MOUTHPIECE BEFORE YOU HAND IT BACK.
WHY THIS FEAR OF GERMS, DEAR MAN?
ONE OF THOSE THINGS I'M ALWAYS TRYING TO FORGET...

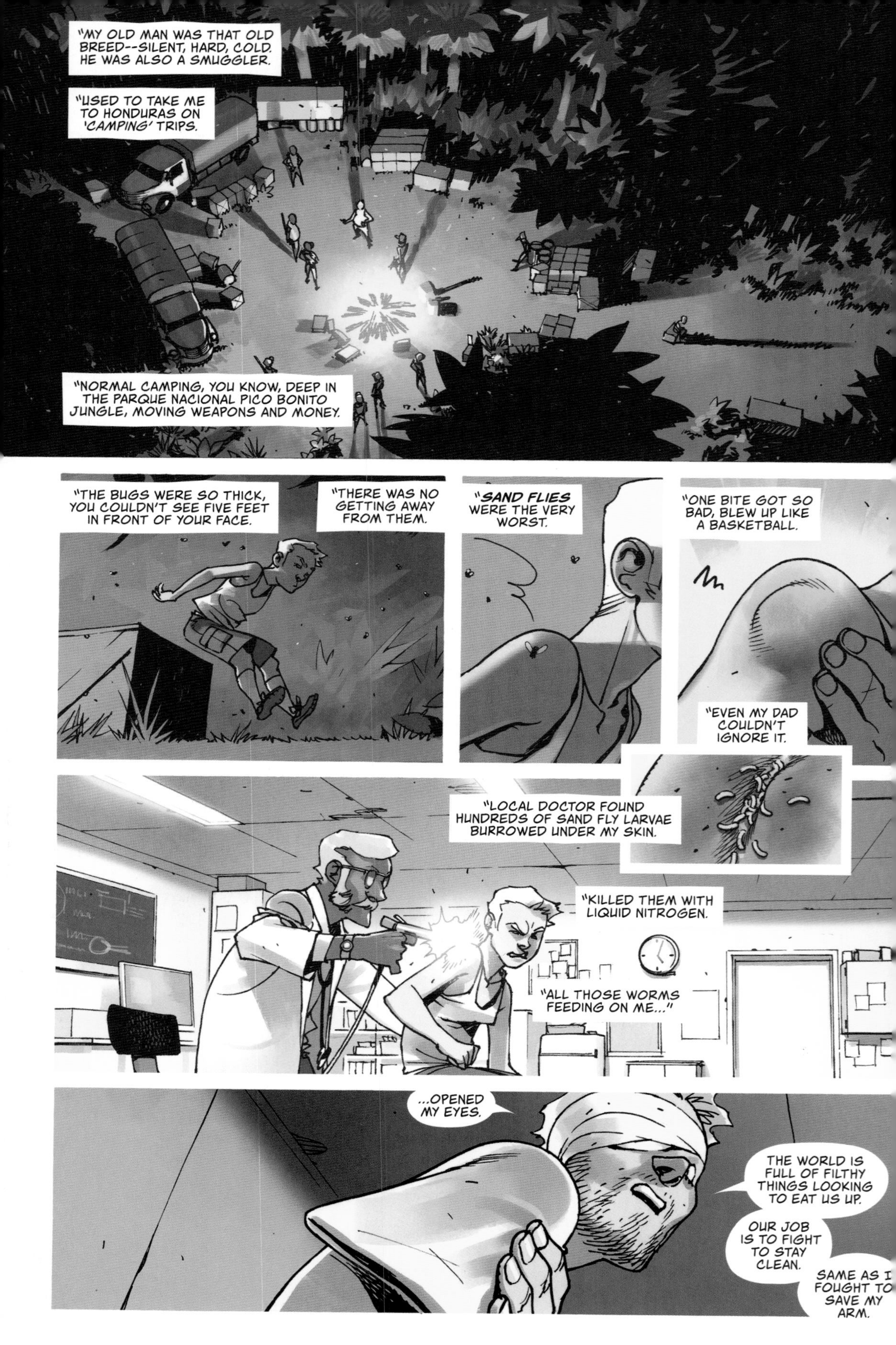

"MY OLD MAN WAS THAT OLD BREED--SILENT, HARD, COLD. HE WAS ALSO A SMUGGLER.
"USED TO TAKE ME TO HONDURAS ON 'CAMPING' TRIPS.
"NORMAL CAMPING, YOU KNOW, DEEP IN THE PARQUE NACIONAL PICO BONITO JUNGLE, MOVING WEAPONS AND MONEY.
"THE BUGS WERE SO THICK, YOU COULDN'T SEE FIVE FEET IN FRONT OF YOUR FACE.
"THERE WAS NO GETTING AWAY FROM THEM.
"SAND FLIES WERE THE VERY WORST.
"ONE BITE GOT SO BAD, BLEW UP LIKE A BASKETBALL.
"EVEN MY DAD COULDN'T IGNORE IT.
"LOCAL DOCTOR FOUND HUNDREDS OF SAND FLY LARVAE BURROWED UNDER MY SKIN.
"KILLED THEM WITH LIQUID NITROGEN.
"ALL THOSE WORMS FEEDING ON ME..."
...OPENED MY EYES.
THE WORLD IS FULL OF FILTHY THINGS LOOKING TO EAT US UP.
OUR JOB IS TO FIGHT TO STAY CLEAN.
SAME AS I FOUGHT TO SAVE MY ARM.

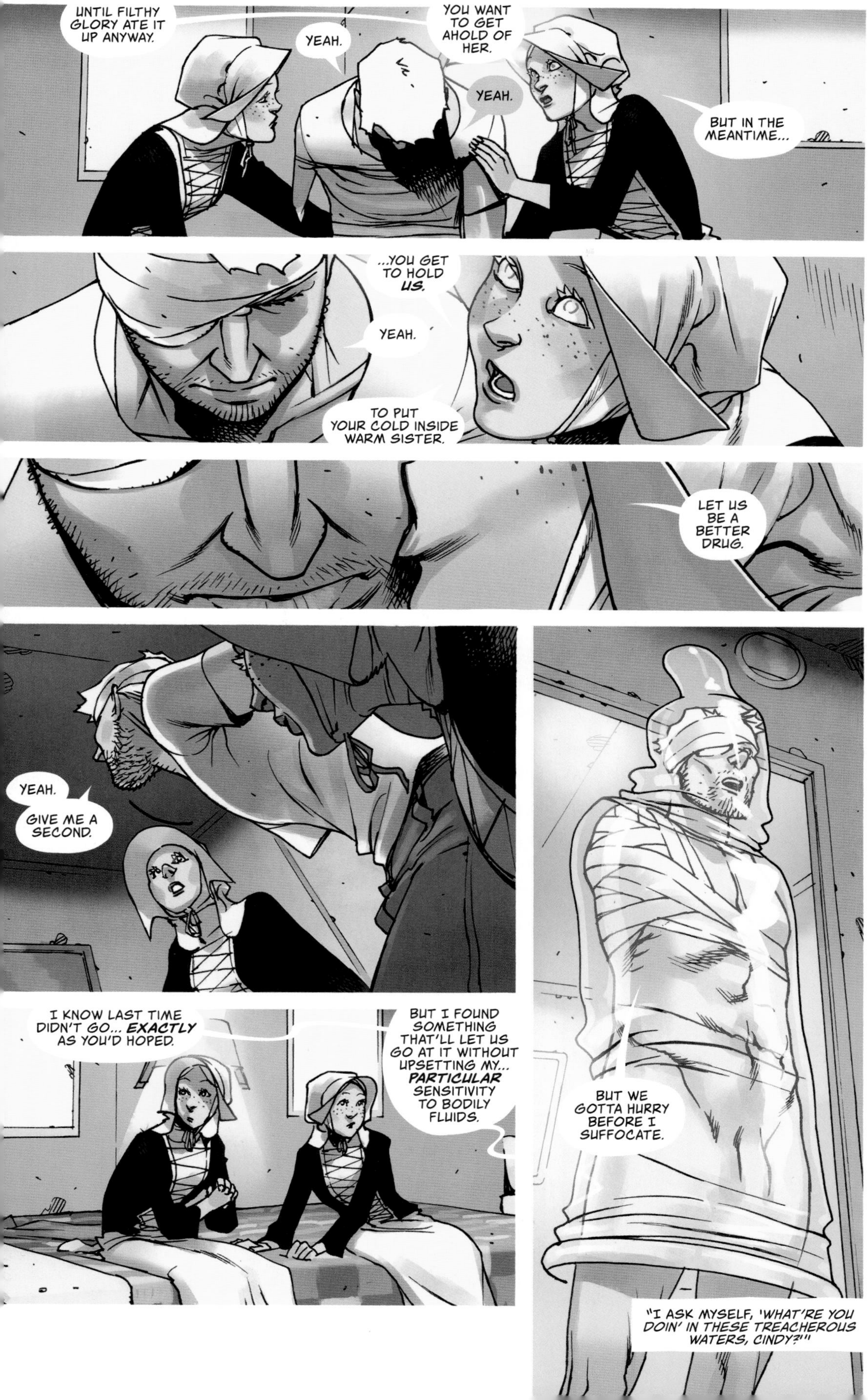
UNTIL FILTHY GLORY ATE IT UP ANYWAY.
YEAH.
YOU WANT TO GET AHOLD OF HER.
YEAH.
BUT IN THE MEANTIME...
...YOU GET TO HOLD *US.*
YEAH.
TO PUT YOUR COLD INSIDE WARM SISTER.
LET US BE A BETTER DRUG.
YEAH.
GIVE ME A SECOND.
I KNOW LAST TIME DIDN'T GO... *EXACTLY* AS YOU'D HOPED.
BUT I FOUND SOMETHING THAT'LL LET US GO AT IT WITHOUT UPSETTING MY... *PARTICULAR* SENSITIVITY TO BODILY FLUIDS.
BUT WE GOTTA HURRY BEFORE I SUFFOCATE.
"I ASK MYSELF, 'WHAT'RE YOU DOIN' IN THESE TREACHEROUS WATERS, CINDY?'"

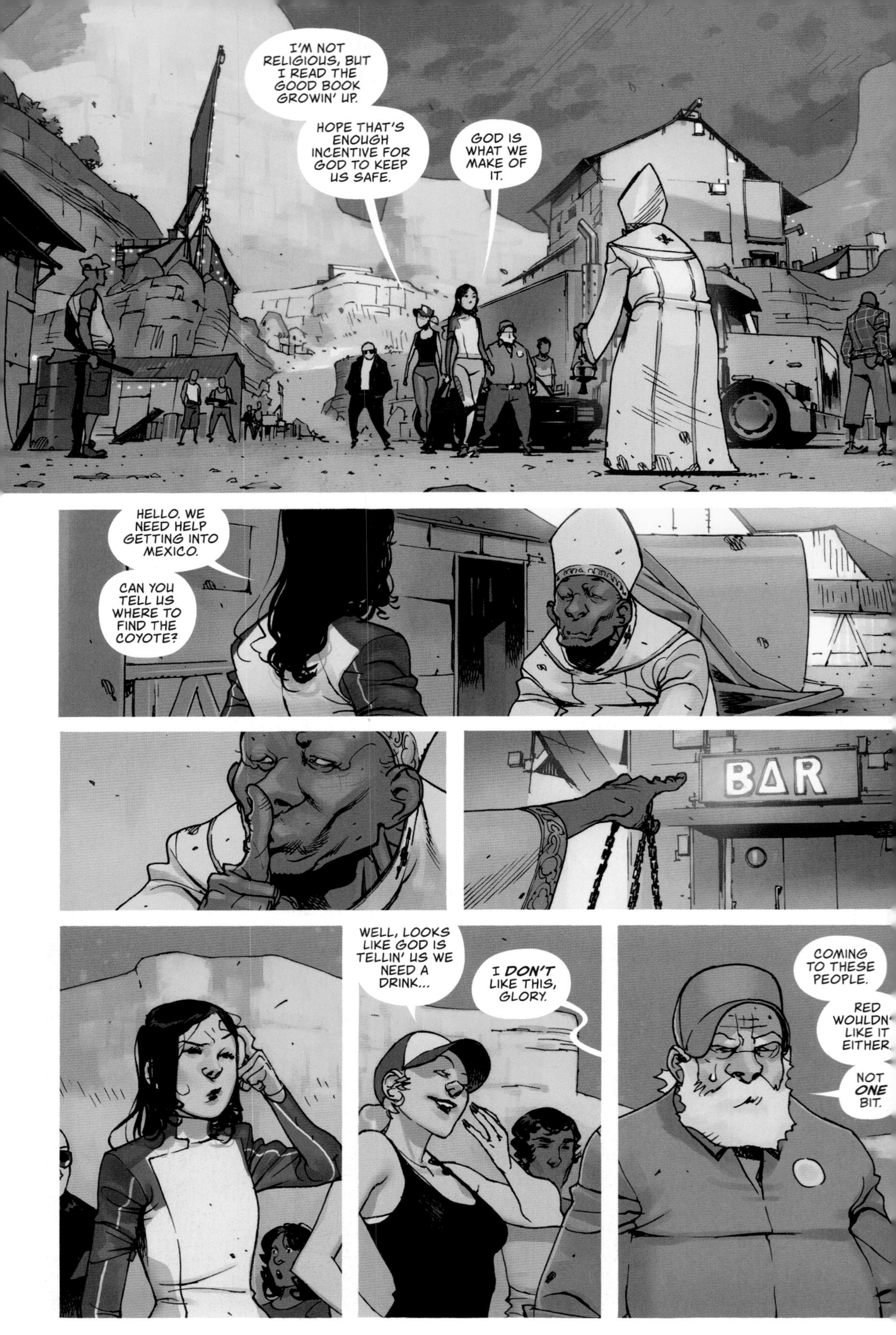
I'M NOT RELIGIOUS, BUT I READ THE GOOD BOOK GROWIN' UP.
HOPE THAT'S ENOUGH INCENTIVE FOR GOD TO KEEP US SAFE.
GOD IS WHAT WE MAKE OF IT.
HELLO. WE NEED HELP GETTING INTO MEXICO.
CAN YOU TELL US WHERE TO FIND THE COYOTE?
BAR
WELL, LOOKS LIKE GOD IS TELLIN' US WE NEED A DRINK...
I *DON'T* LIKE THIS, GLORY.
COMING TO THESE PEOPLE.
RED WOULDN' LIKE IT EITHER.
NOT *ONE* BIT.

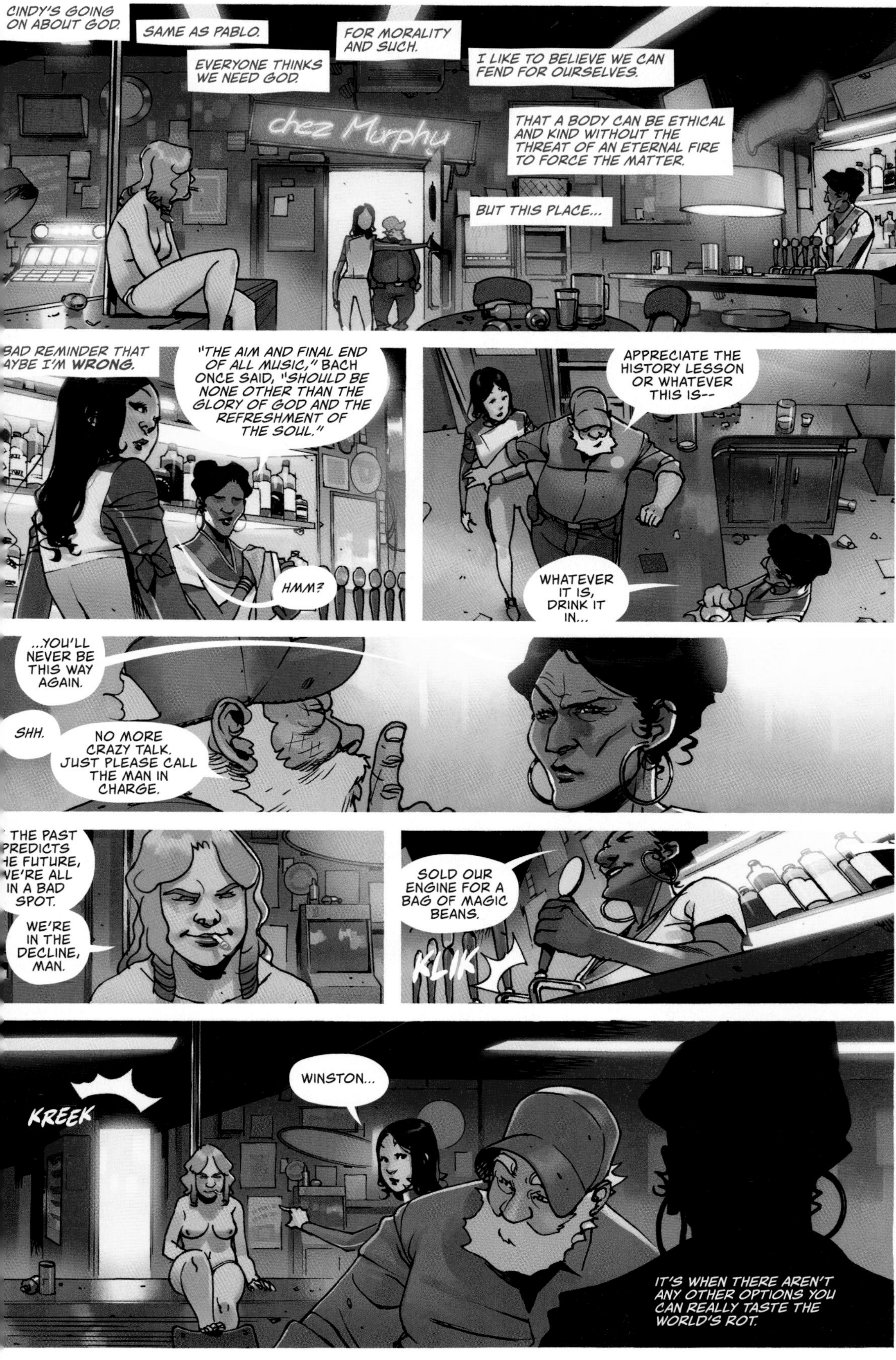
CINDY'S GOING ON ABOUT GOD.
SAME AS PABLO.
EVERYONE THINKS WE NEED GOD.
FOR MORALITY AND SUCH.
I LIKE TO BELIEVE WE CAN FEND FOR OURSELVES.
THAT A BODY CAN BE ETHICAL AND KIND WITHOUT THE THREAT OF AN ETERNAL FIRE TO FORCE THE MATTER.
BUT THIS PLACE...
chez Murphy
BAD REMINDER THAT AYBE I'M WRONG.
"THE AIM AND FINAL END OF ALL MUSIC," BACH ONCE SAID, "SHOULD BE NONE OTHER THAN THE GLORY OF GOD AND THE REFRESHMENT OF THE SOUL."
HMM?
APPRECIATE THE HISTORY LESSON OR WHATEVER THIS IS--
WHATEVER IT IS, DRINK IT IN...
...YOU'LL NEVER BE THIS WAY AGAIN.
SHH.
NO MORE CRAZY TALK. JUST PLEASE CALL THE MAN IN CHARGE.
THE PAST PREDICTS HE FUTURE, VE'RE ALL IN A BAD SPOT.
WE'RE IN THE DECLINE, MAN.
SOLD OUR ENGINE FOR A BAG OF MAGIC BEANS.
KLIK
KREEK
WINSTON...
IT'S WHEN THERE AREN'T ANY OTHER OPTIONS YOU CAN REALLY TASTE THE WORLD'S ROT.

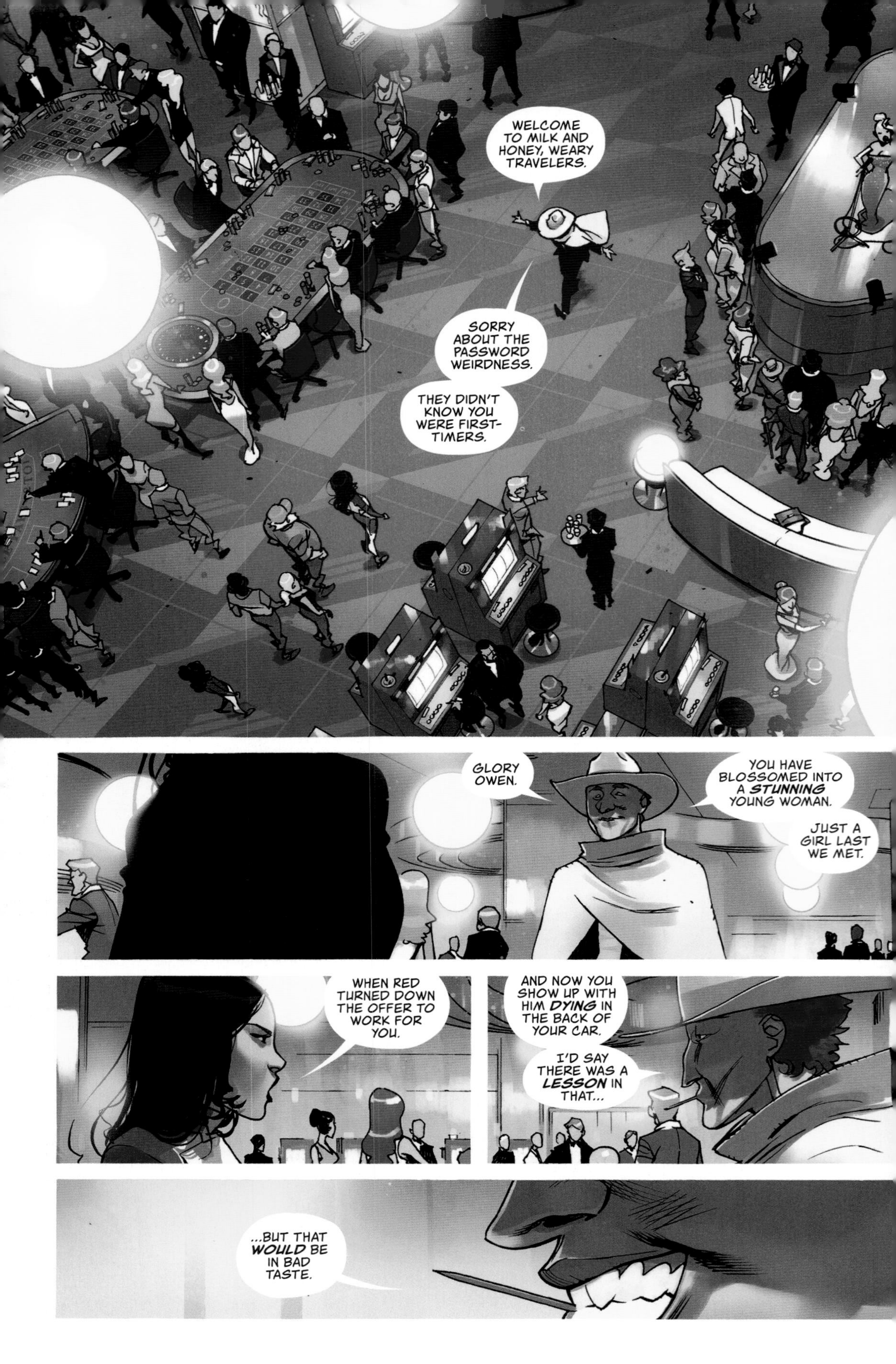
WELCOME TO MILK AND HONEY, WEARY TRAVELERS.
SORRY ABOUT THE PASSWORD WEIRDNESS.
THEY DIDN'T KNOW YOU WERE FIRST-TIMERS.
GLORY OWEN.
YOU HAVE BLOSSOMED INTO A STUNNING YOUNG WOMAN.
JUST A GIRL LAST WE MET.
WHEN RED TURNED DOWN THE OFFER TO WORK FOR YOU.
AND NOW YOU SHOW UP WITH HIM DYING IN THE BACK OF YOUR CAR.
I'D SAY THERE WAS A LESSON IN THAT...
...BUT THAT WOULD BE IN BAD TASTE.

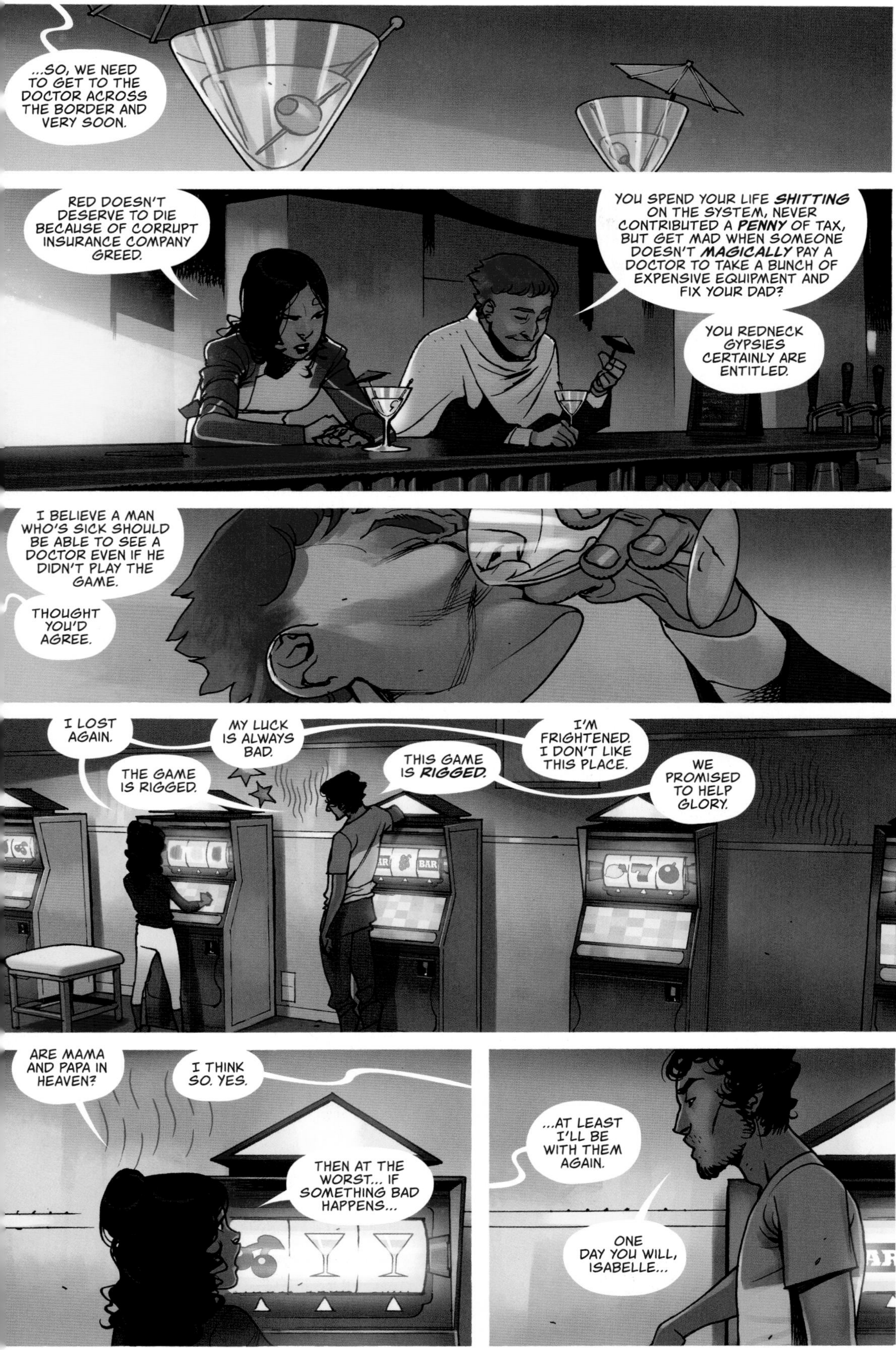
...SO, WE NEED TO GET TO THE DOCTOR ACROSS THE BORDER AND VERY SOON.
RED DOESN'T DESERVE TO DIE BECAUSE OF CORRUPT INSURANCE COMPANY GREED.
YOU SPEND YOUR LIFE **SHITTING** ON THE SYSTEM, NEVER CONTRIBUTED A **PENNY** OF TAX, BUT GET MAD WHEN SOMEONE DOESN'T **MAGICALLY** PAY A DOCTOR TO TAKE A BUNCH OF EXPENSIVE EQUIPMENT AND FIX YOUR DAD?
YOU REDNECK GYPSIES CERTAINLY ARE ENTITLED.
I BELIEVE A MAN WHO'S SICK SHOULD BE ABLE TO SEE A DOCTOR EVEN IF HE DIDN'T PLAY THE GAME.
THOUGHT YOU'D AGREE.
I LOST AGAIN.
MY LUCK IS ALWAYS BAD.
THE GAME IS RIGGED.
THIS GAME IS ***RIGGED.***
I'M FRIGHTENED. I DON'T LIKE THIS PLACE.
WE PROMISED TO HELP GLORY.
ARE MAMA AND PAPA IN HEAVEN?
I THINK SO. YES.
THEN AT THE WORST... IF SOMETHING BAD HAPPENS...
...AT LEAST I'LL BE WITH THEM AGAIN.
ONE DAY YOU WILL, ISABELLE...

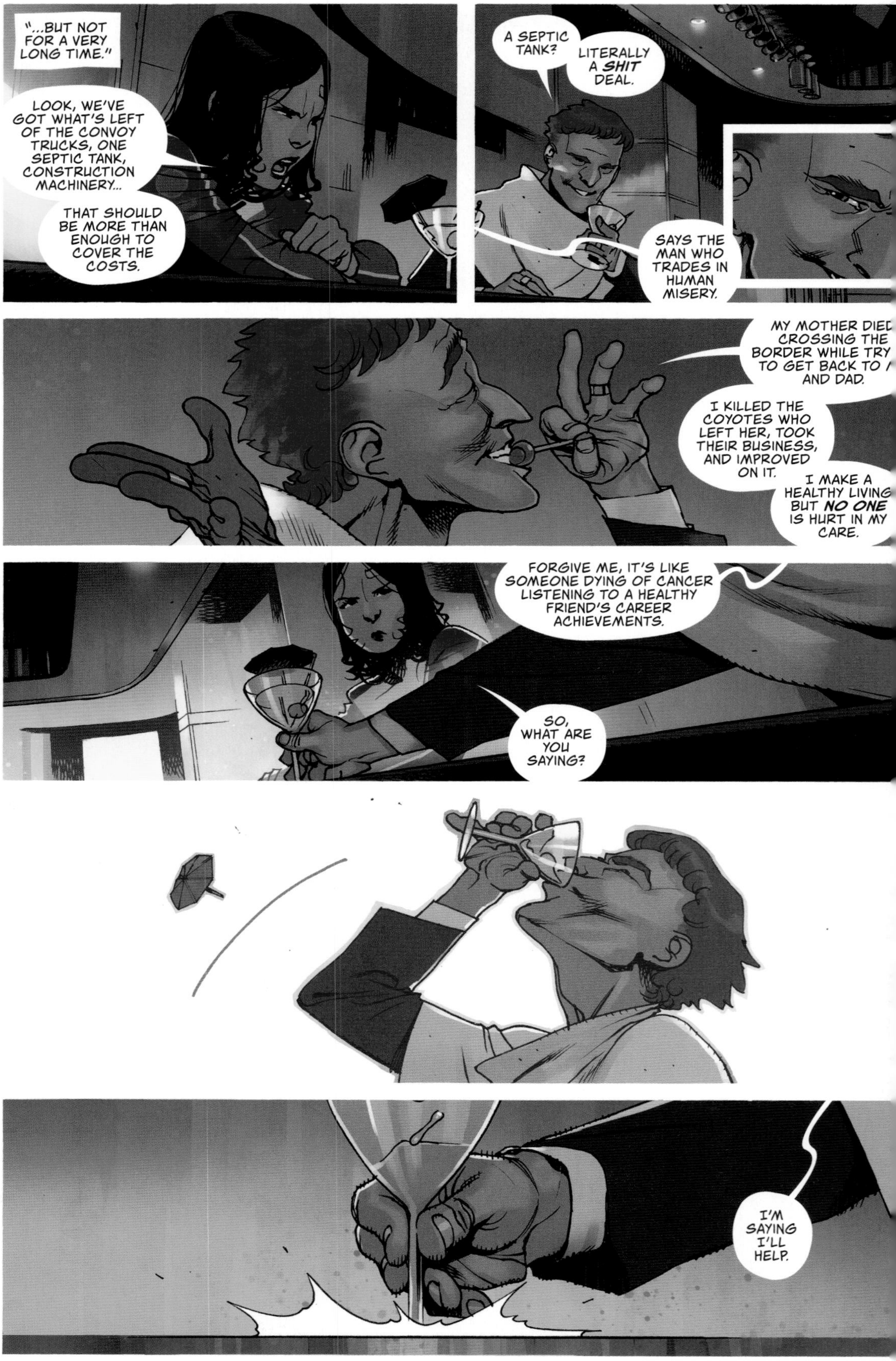
"...BUT NOT FOR A VERY LONG TIME."
LOOK, WE'VE GOT WHAT'S LEFT OF THE CONVOY TRUCKS, ONE SEPTIC TANK, CONSTRUCTION MACHINERY...
THAT SHOULD BE MORE THAN ENOUGH TO COVER THE COSTS.
A SEPTIC TANK?
LITERALLY A SHIT DEAL.
SAYS THE MAN WHO TRADES IN HUMAN MISERY.
MY MOTHER DIED CROSSING THE BORDER WHILE TRY TO GET BACK TO AND DAD.
I KILLED THE COYOTES WHO LEFT HER, TOOK THEIR BUSINESS, AND IMPROVED ON IT.
I MAKE A HEALTHY LIVING BUT NO ONE IS HURT IN MY CARE.
FORGIVE ME, IT'S LIKE SOMEONE DYING OF CANCER LISTENING TO A HEALTHY FRIEND'S CAREER ACHIEVEMENTS.
SO, WHAT ARE YOU SAYING?
I'M SAYING I'LL HELP.

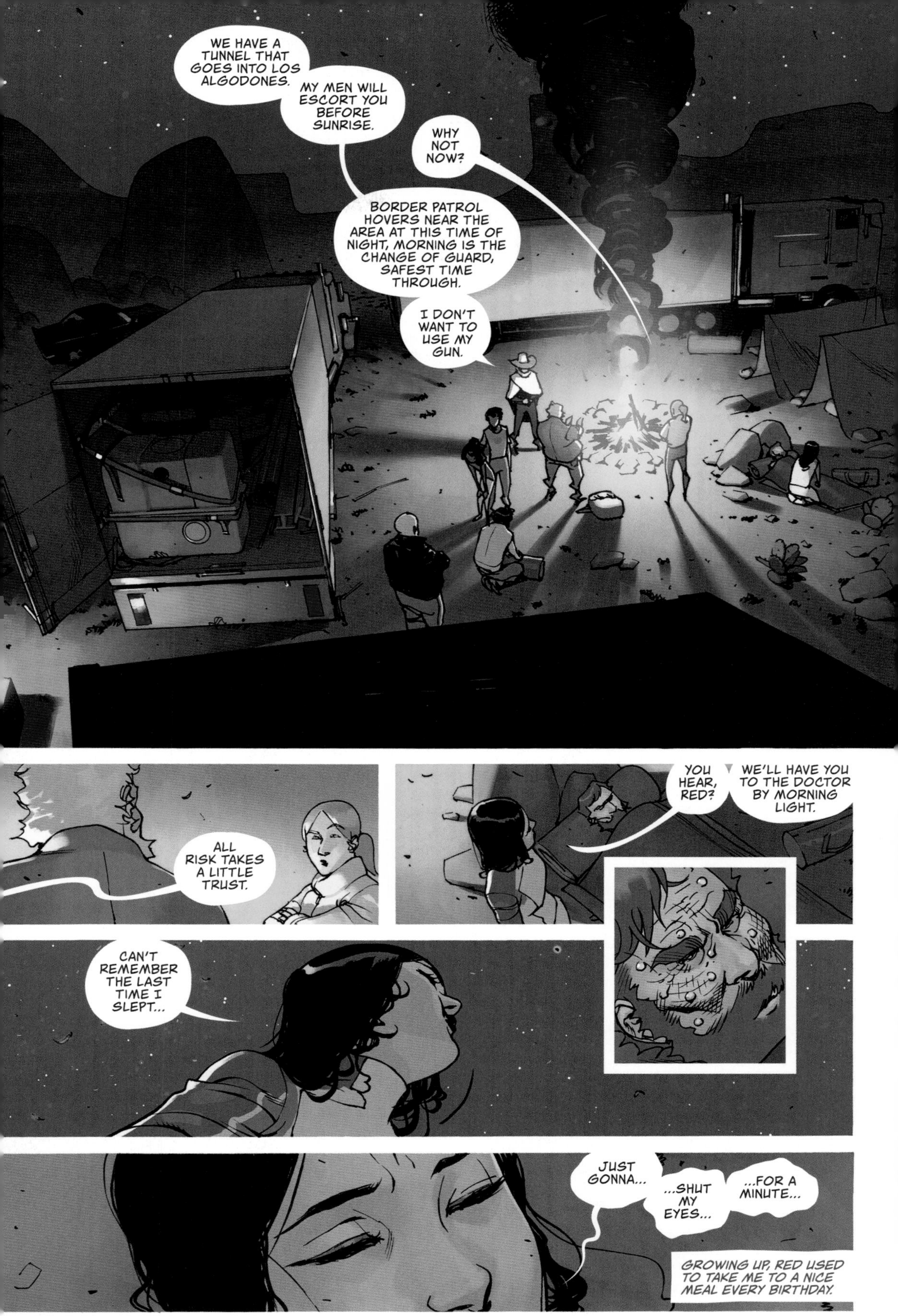
WE HAVE A TUNNEL THAT GOES INTO LOS ALGODONES.
MY MEN WILL ESCORT YOU BEFORE SUNRISE.
WHY NOT NOW?
BORDER PATROL HOVERS NEAR THE AREA AT THIS TIME OF NIGHT, MORNING IS THE CHANGE OF GUARD, SAFEST TIME THROUGH.
I DON'T WANT TO USE MY GUN.
ALL RISK TAKES A LITTLE TRUST.
YOU HEAR, RED?
WE'LL HAVE YOU TO THE DOCTOR BY MORNING LIGHT.
CAN'T REMEMBER THE LAST TIME I SLEPT...
JUST GONNA...
...SHUT MY EYES...
...FOR A MINUTE...
GROWING UP, RED USED TO TAKE ME TO A NICE MEAL EVERY BIRTHDAY.

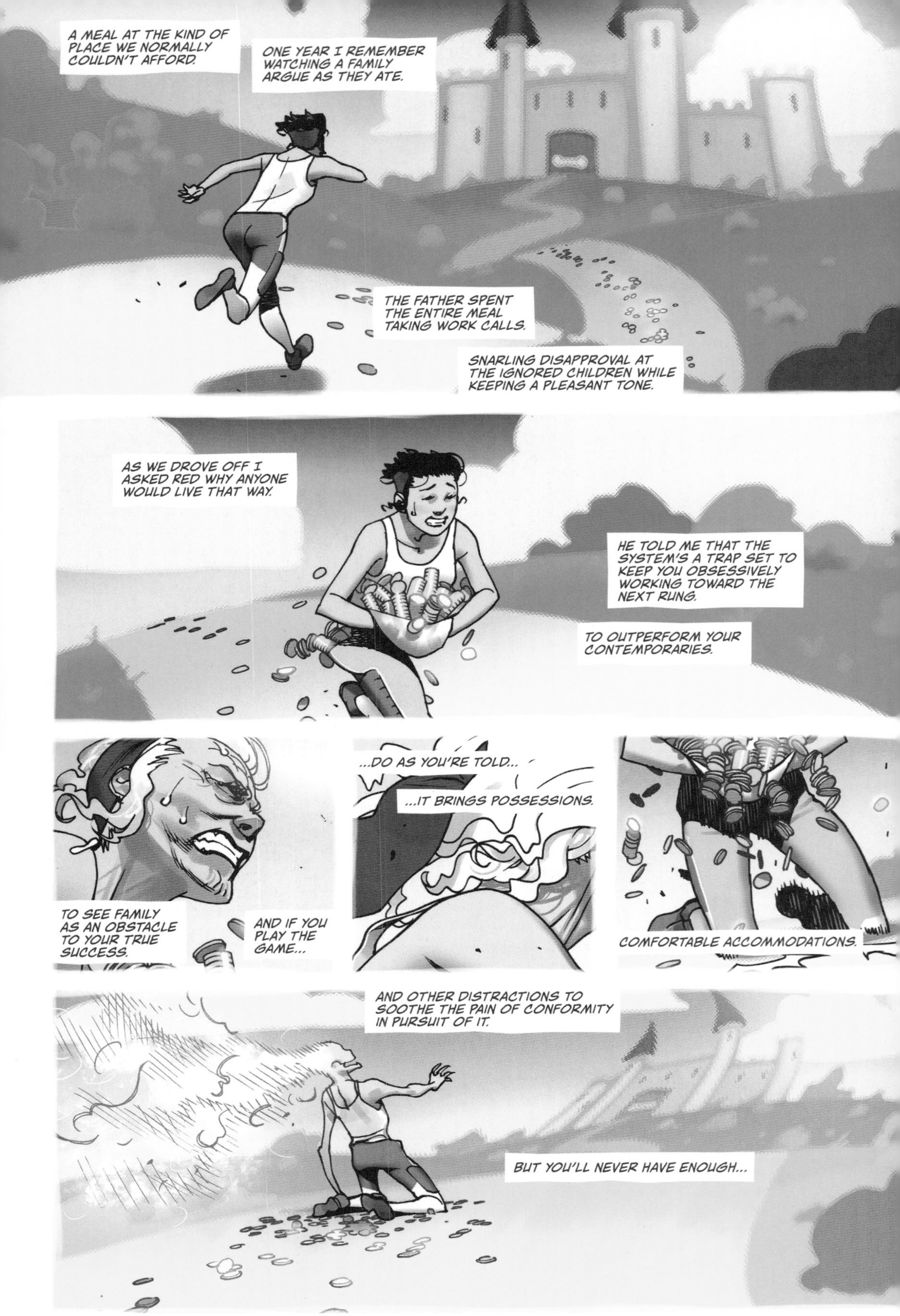
A MEAL AT THE KIND OF PLACE WE NORMALLY COULDN'T AFFORD.
ONE YEAR I REMEMBER WATCHING A FAMILY ARGUE AS THEY ATE.
THE FATHER SPENT THE ENTIRE MEAL TAKING WORK CALLS.
SNARLING DISAPPROVAL AT THE IGNORED CHILDREN WHILE KEEPING A PLEASANT TONE.
AS WE DROVE OFF I ASKED RED WHY ANYONE WOULD LIVE THAT WAY.
HE TOLD ME THAT THE SYSTEM'S A TRAP SET TO KEEP YOU OBSESSIVELY WORKING TOWARD THE NEXT RUNG.
TO OUTPERFORM YOUR CONTEMPORARIES.
TO SEE FAMILY AS AN OBSTACLE TO YOUR TRUE SUCCESS.
AND IF YOU PLAY THE GAME...
...DO AS YOU'RE TOLD...
...IT BRINGS POSSESSIONS.
COMFORTABLE ACCOMMODATIONS.
AND OTHER DISTRACTIONS TO SOOTHE THE PAIN OF CONFORMITY IN PURSUIT OF IT.
BUT YOU'LL NEVER HAVE ENOUGH...

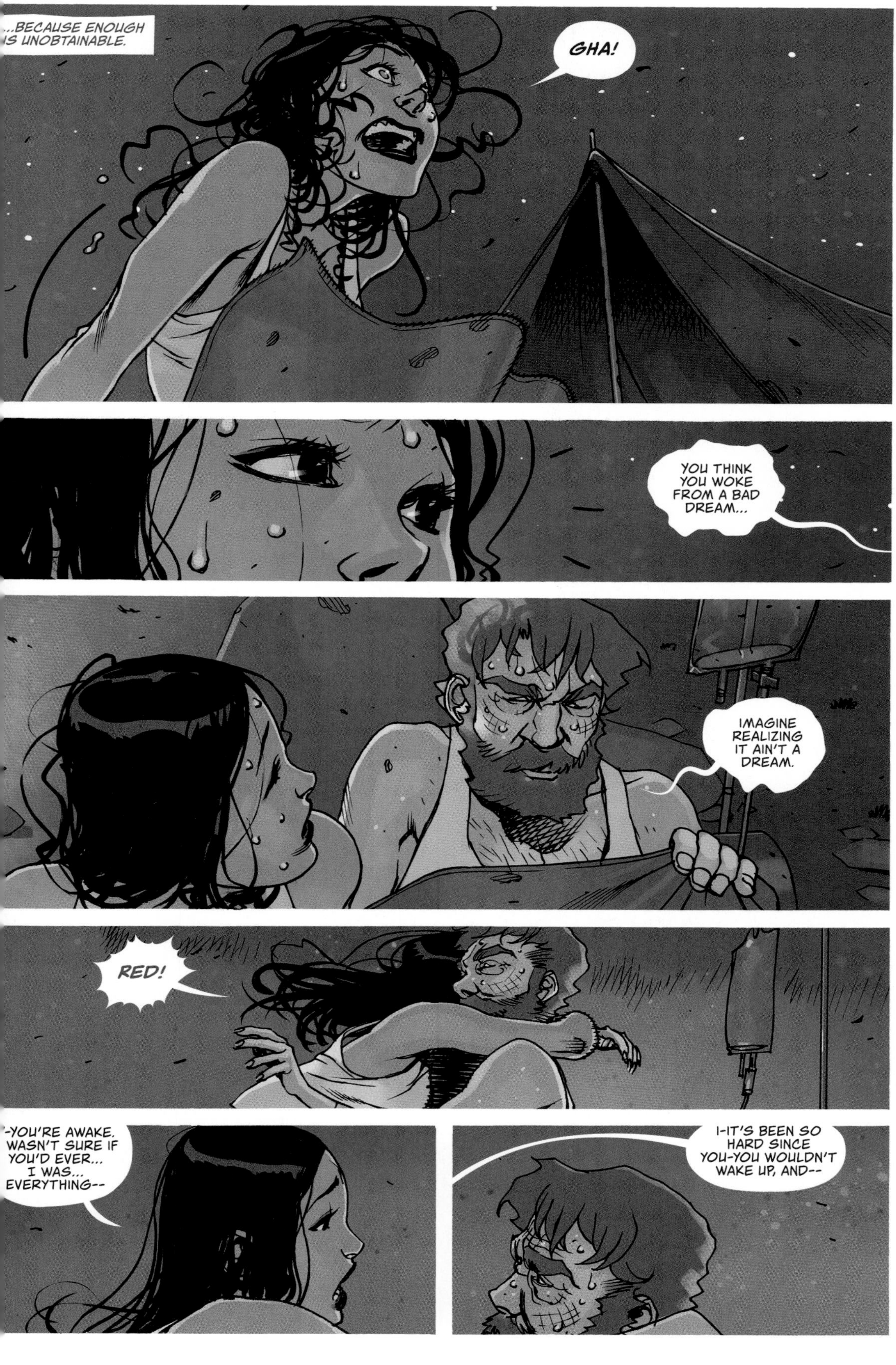

...BECAUSE ENOUGH
IS UNOBTAINABLE.
GHA!
YOU THINK YOU WOKE FROM A BAD DREAM...
IMAGINE REALIZING IT AIN'T A DREAM.
RED!
-YOU'RE AWAKE. WASN'T SURE IF YOU'D EVER... I WAS... EVERYTHING--
I-IT'S BEEN SO HARD SINCE YOU-YOU WOULDN'T WAKE UP, AND--

WHAT IN HELL ARE WE DOING OUT HERE, GLORY?

I FOUND A LIVER FOR YOU.

WINSTON AND CINDY KNOW A DOCTOR ACROSS THE BORDER WHO CAN DO THE TRANSPLANT.

THINK THAT WAS THE LAST OF THE MORPHINE.

GOT ANOTHER BAG OF THE LIGHTER STUFF.

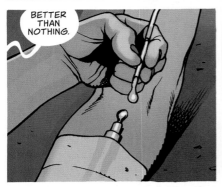

BETTER THAN NOTHING.

I GOT A DIAPER ON. IT'S GODDAMN UNDIGNIFIED.

IT WAS THE BEST I COULD DO. WE HAD TO MOVE YOU AND--

MOVE ME WHY? WHATEVER THE HELL YOU'VE GOTTEN YOURSELF INTO HERE, IT'S FOR NOTHING.

THAT VOICE, THE JERK WHO TELLS YOU NOTHING WILL WORK OUT AND EVERYTHING WILL FALL APART?

IT'S WRONG. I'M NOT LISTENING TO IT. AND IF YOU ARE...

...THEN I'M NOT LISTENING TO YOU.

OVER OCCUPIED WITH OTHER PEOPLE.

YOU GIVE UP YOUR ENTIRE FUTURE TO SAVE AN OLD MAN?

I TAUGHT YOU BETTER.

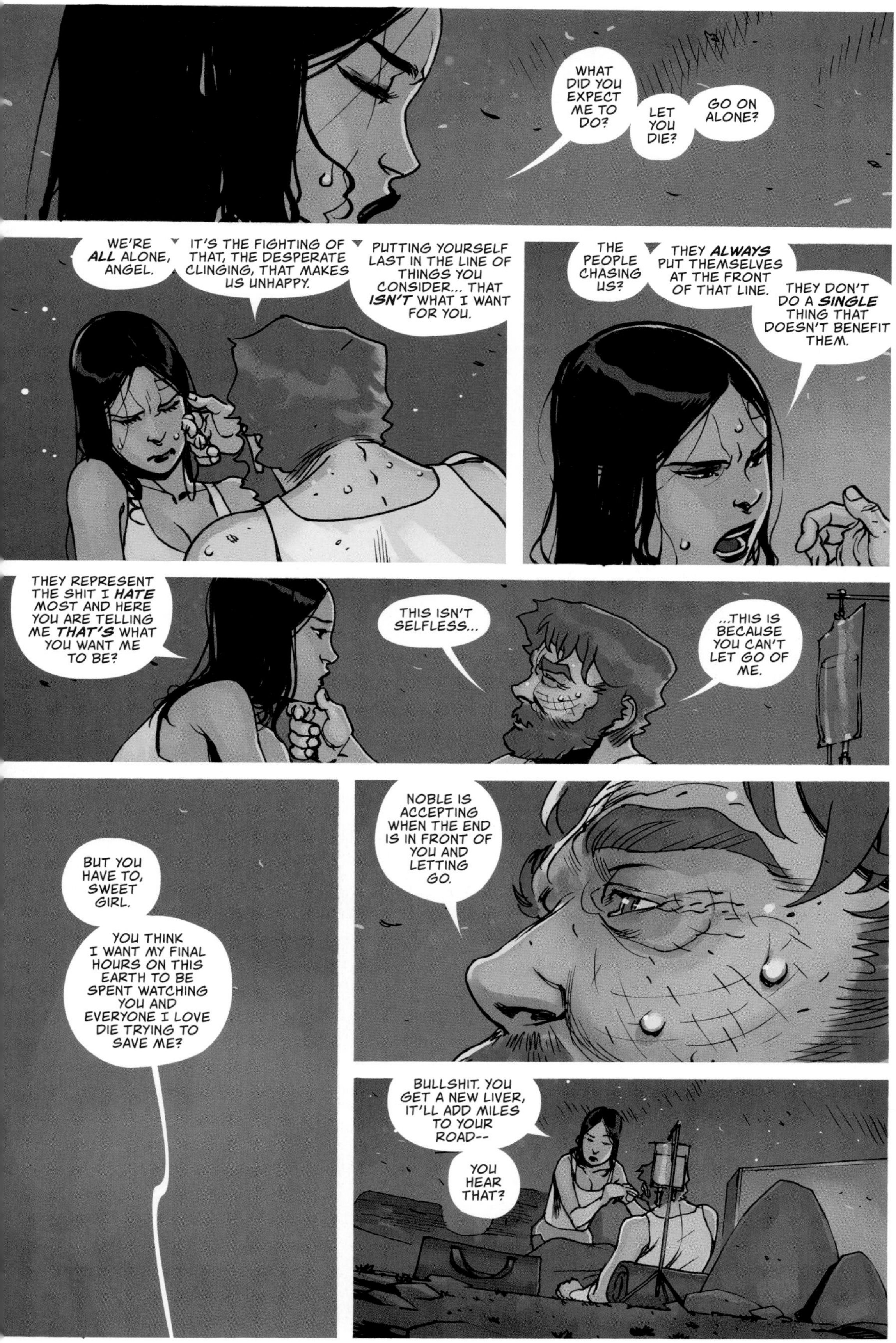

WHAT DID YOU EXPECT ME TO DO?
LET YOU DIE?
GO ON ALONE?
WE'RE **ALL** ALONE, ANGEL.
IT'S THE FIGHTING OF THAT, THE DESPERATE CLINGING, THAT MAKES US UNHAPPY.
PUTTING YOURSELF LAST IN THE LINE OF THINGS YOU CONSIDER... THAT **ISN'T** WHAT I WANT FOR YOU.
THE PEOPLE CHASING US?
THEY **ALWAYS** PUT THEMSELVES AT THE FRONT OF THAT LINE.
THEY DON'T DO A **SINGLE** THING THAT DOESN'T BENEFIT THEM.
THEY REPRESENT THE SHIT I **HATE** MOST AND HERE YOU ARE TELLING ME **THAT'S** WHAT YOU WANT ME TO BE?
THIS ISN'T SELFLESS...
...THIS IS BECAUSE YOU CAN'T LET GO OF ME.
BUT YOU HAVE TO, SWEET GIRL.
YOU THINK I WANT MY FINAL HOURS ON THIS EARTH TO BE SPENT WATCHING YOU AND EVERYONE I LOVE DIE TRYING TO SAVE ME?
NOBLE IS ACCEPTING WHEN THE END IS IN FRONT OF YOU AND LETTING GO.
BULLSHIT. YOU GET A NEW LIVER, IT'LL ADD MILES TO YOUR ROAD--
YOU HEAR THAT?

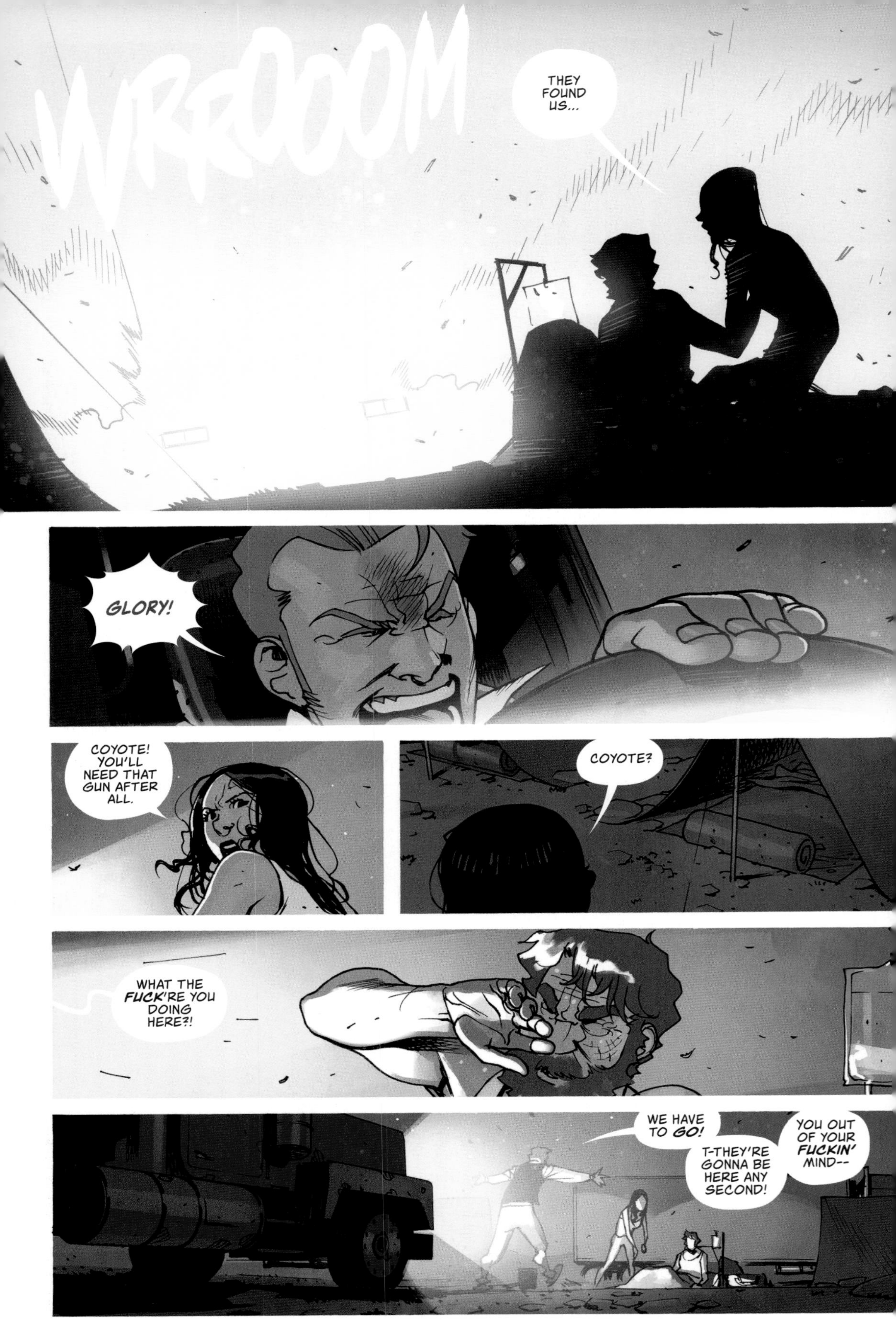
WRROOOM
THEY FOUND US...
GLORY!
COYOTE! YOU'LL NEED THAT GUN AFTER ALL.
COYOTE?
WHAT THE FUCK'RE YOU DOING HERE?!
WE HAVE TO GO!
T-THEY'RE GONNA BE HERE ANY SECOND!
YOU OUT OF YOUR FUCKIN' MIND--

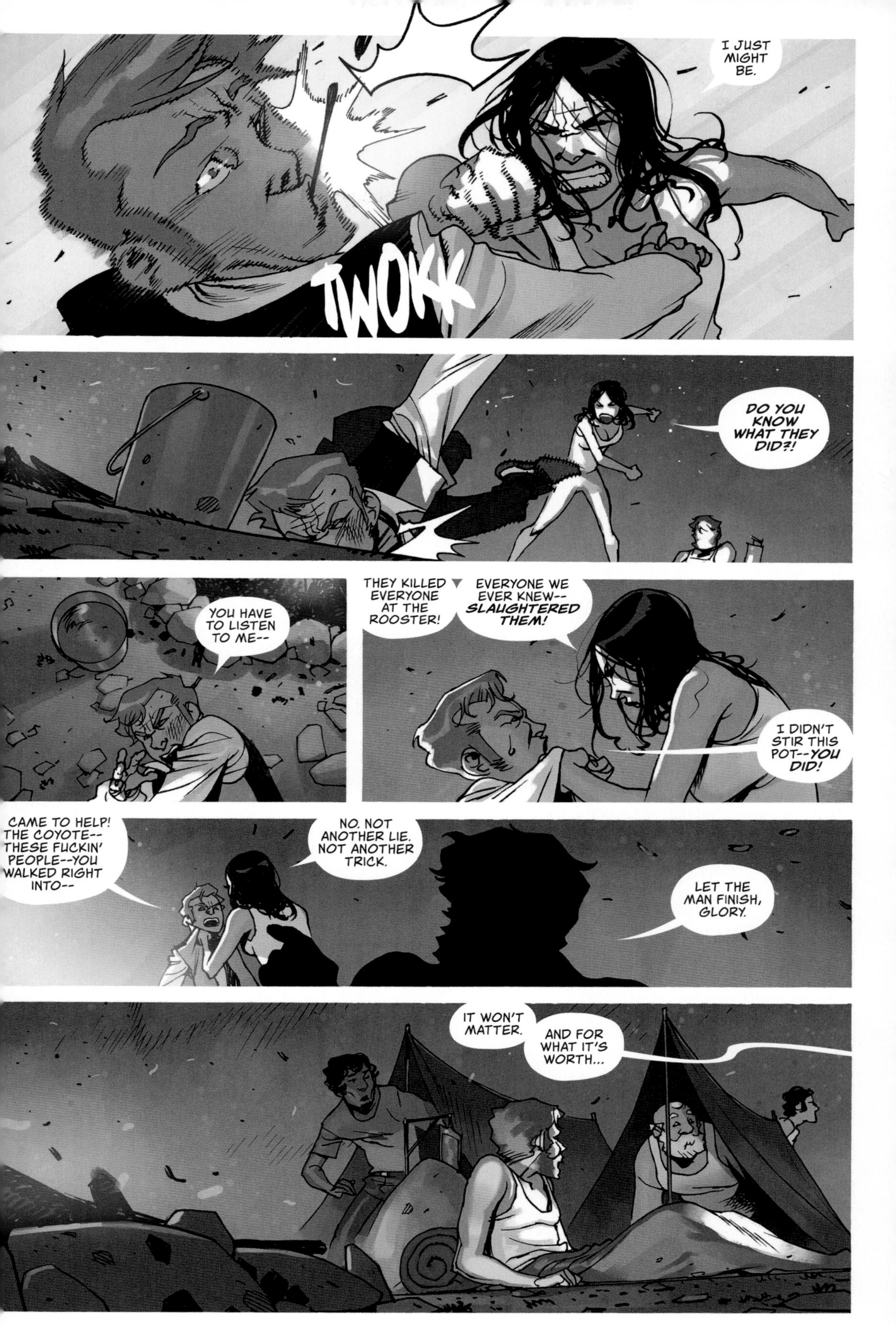
I JUST MIGHT BE.
TWOKK
DO YOU KNOW WHAT THEY DID?!
YOU HAVE TO LISTEN TO ME--
THEY KILLED EVERYONE AT THE ROOSTER!
EVERYONE WE EVER KNEW-- SLAUGHTERED THEM!
I DIDN'T STIR THIS POT--YOU DID!
CAME TO HELP! THE COYOTE-- THESE FUCKIN' PEOPLE--YOU WALKED RIGHT INTO--
NO. NOT ANOTHER LIE. NOT ANOTHER TRICK.
LET THE MAN FINISH, GLORY.
IT WON'T MATTER.
AND FOR WHAT IT'S WORTH...

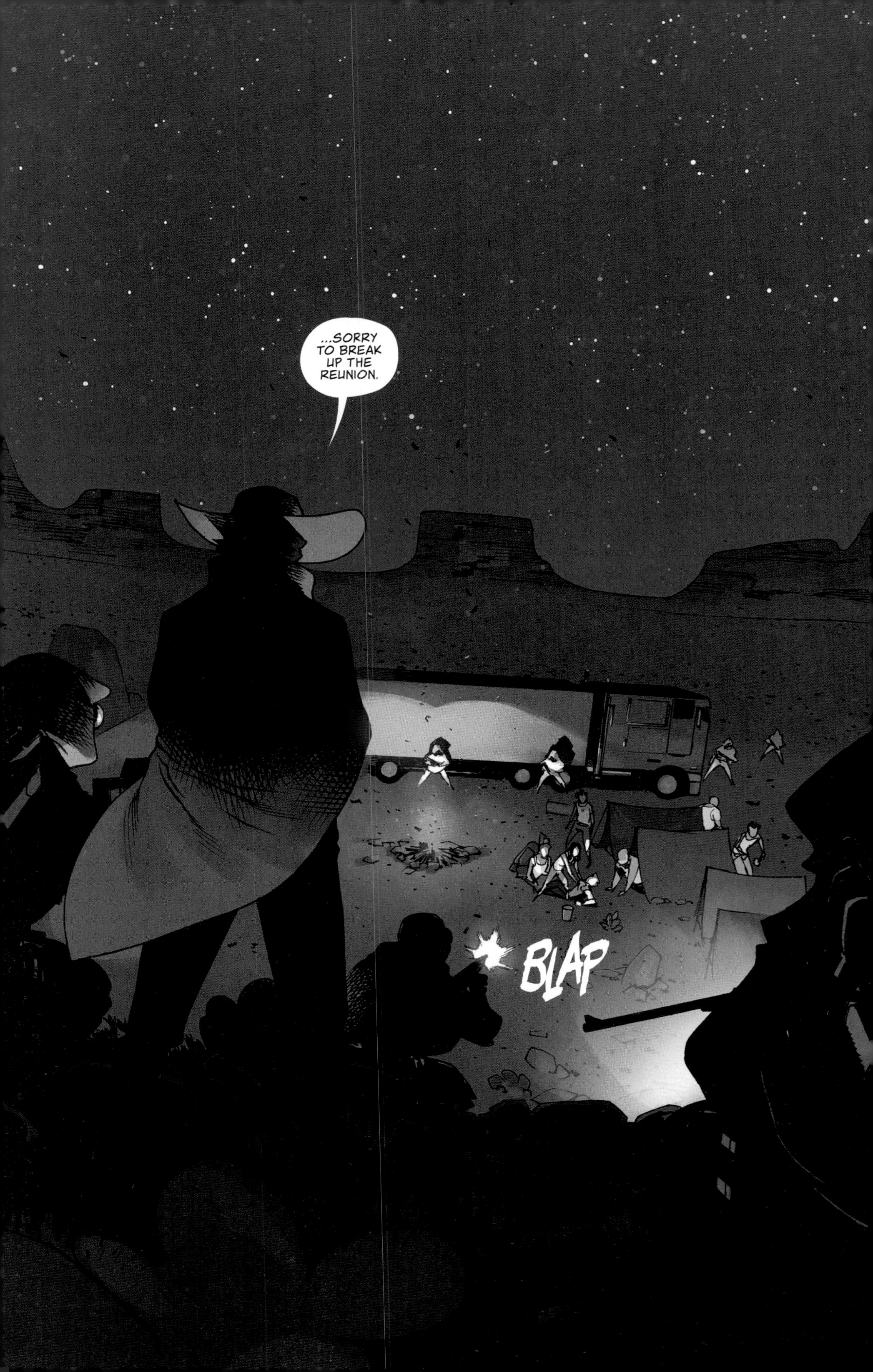
...SORRY TO BREAK UP THE REUNION.
BLAP

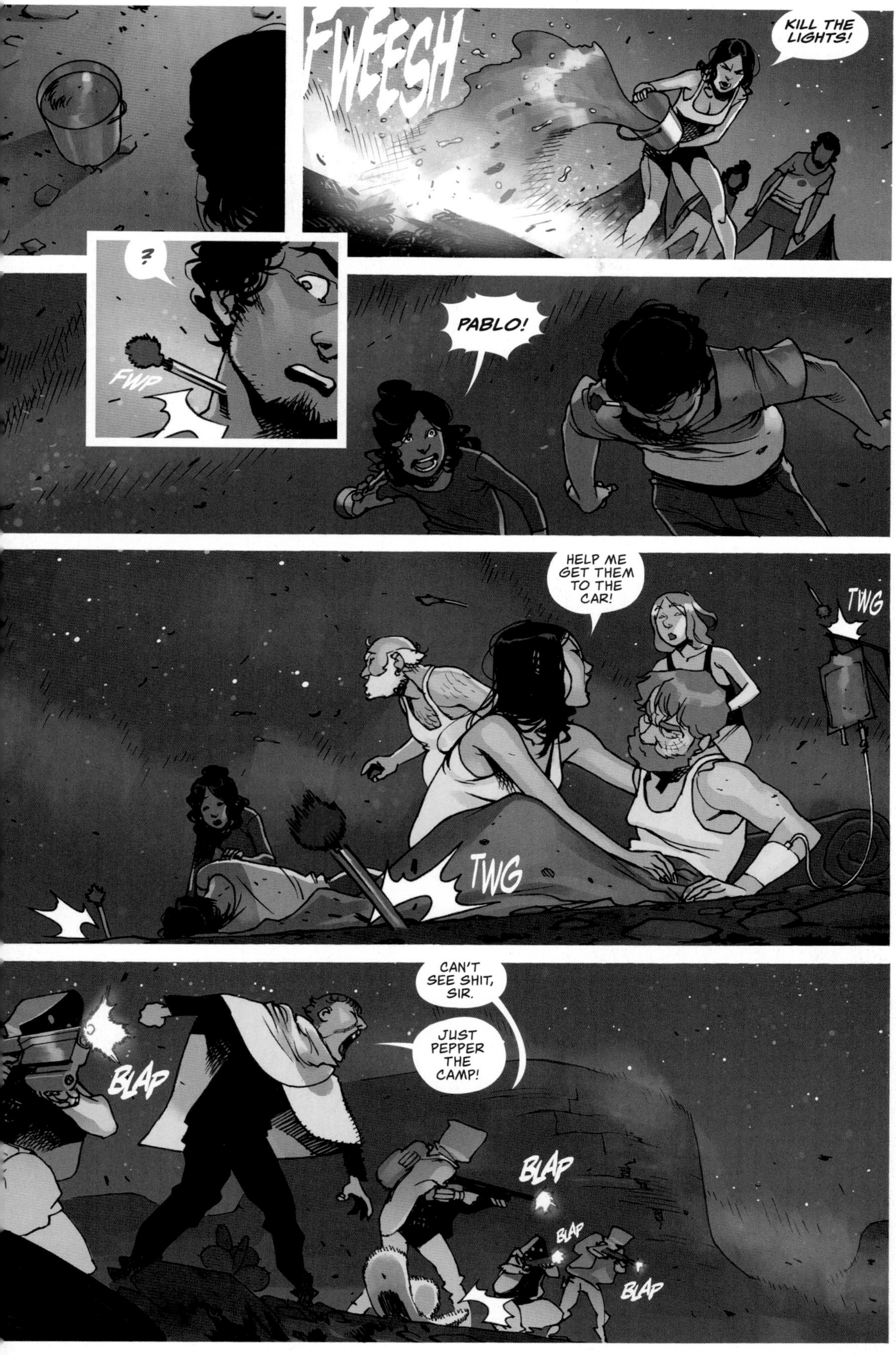
FWEESH
KILL THE LIGHTS!
?
FWP
PABLO!
HELP ME GET THEM TO THE CAR!
TWG
TWG
CAN'T SEE SHIT, SIR.
JUST PEPPER THE CAMP!
BLAP
BLAP
BLAP
BLAP

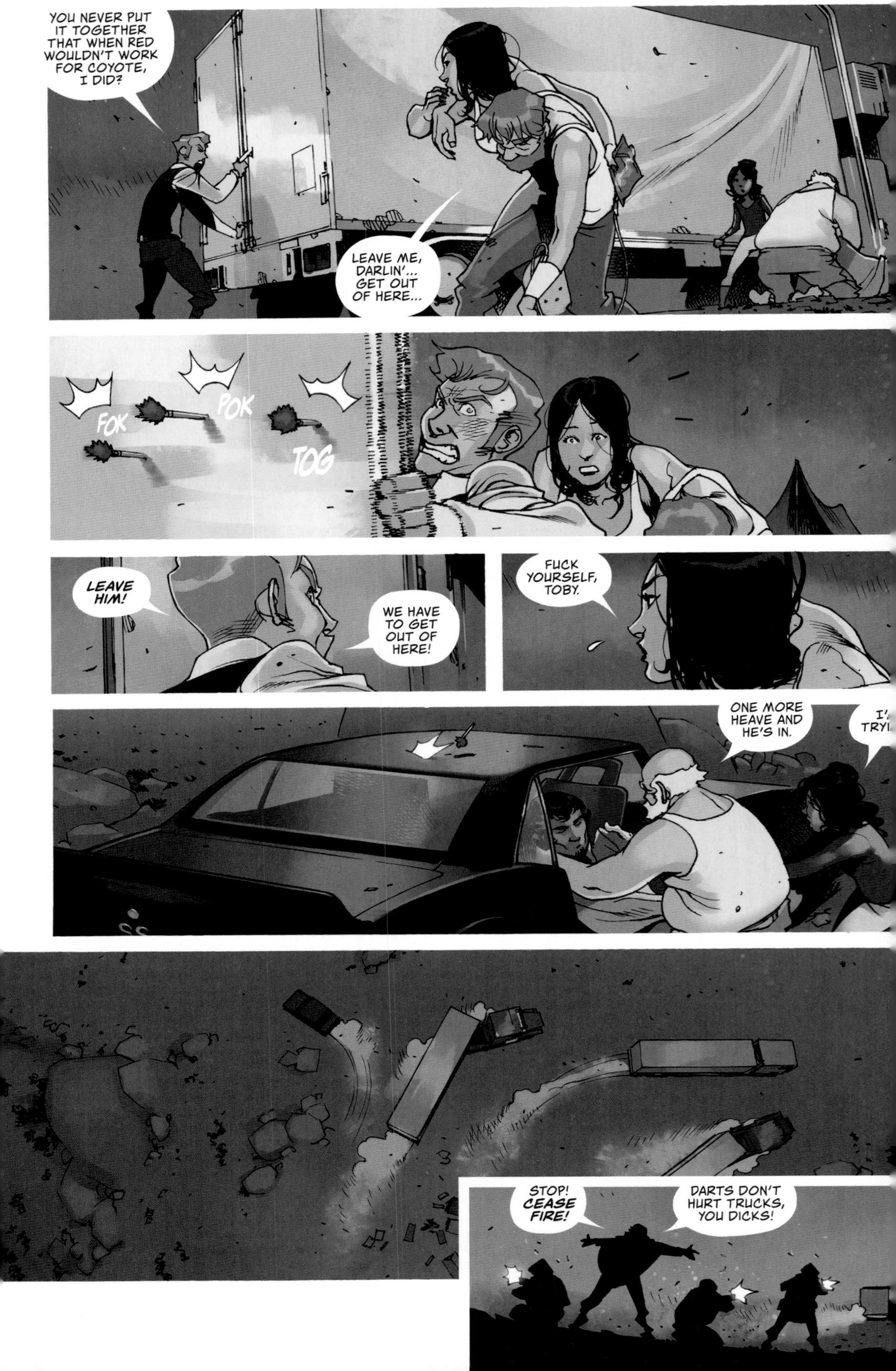

YOU NEVER PUT IT TOGETHER THAT WHEN RED WOULDN'T WORK FOR COYOTE, I DID?
LEAVE ME, DARLIN'... GET OUT OF HERE...
FOK
POK
TOG
LEAVE HIM!
WE HAVE TO GET OUT OF HERE!
FUCK YOURSELF, TOBY.
ONE MORE HEAVE AND HE'S IN.
STOP! CEASE FIRE!
DARTS DON'T HURT TRUCKS, YOU DICKS!

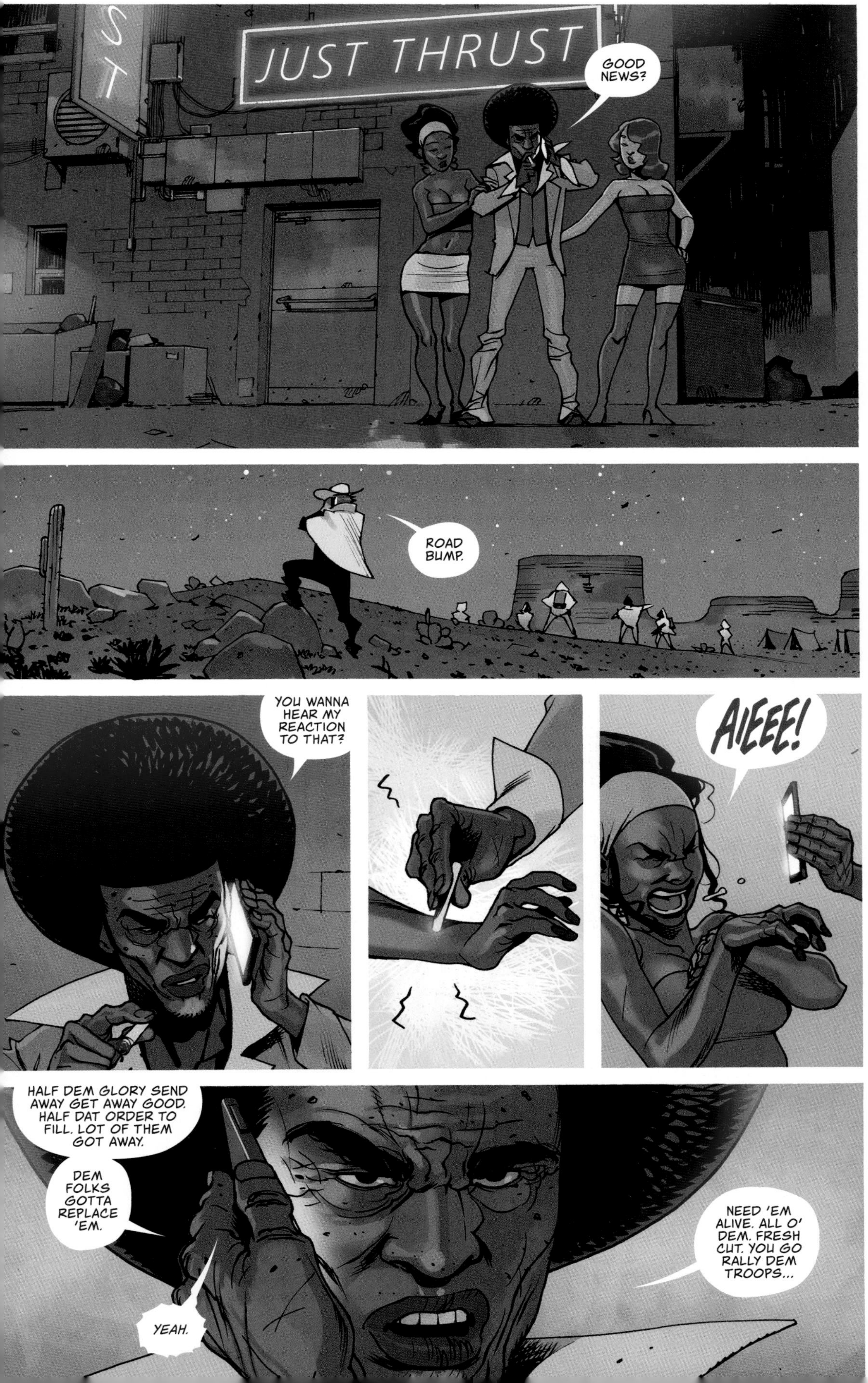
JUST THRUST
GOOD NEWS?
ROAD BUMP.
YOU WANNA HEAR MY REACTION TO THAT?
AIEEE!
HALF DEM GLORY SEND AWAY GET AWAY GOOD. HALF DAT ORDER TO FILL. LOT OF THEM GOT AWAY.
DEM FOLKS GOTTA REPLACE 'EM.
YEAH.
NEED 'EM ALIVE. ALL O' DEM. FRESH CUT. YOU GO RALLY DEM TROOPS...

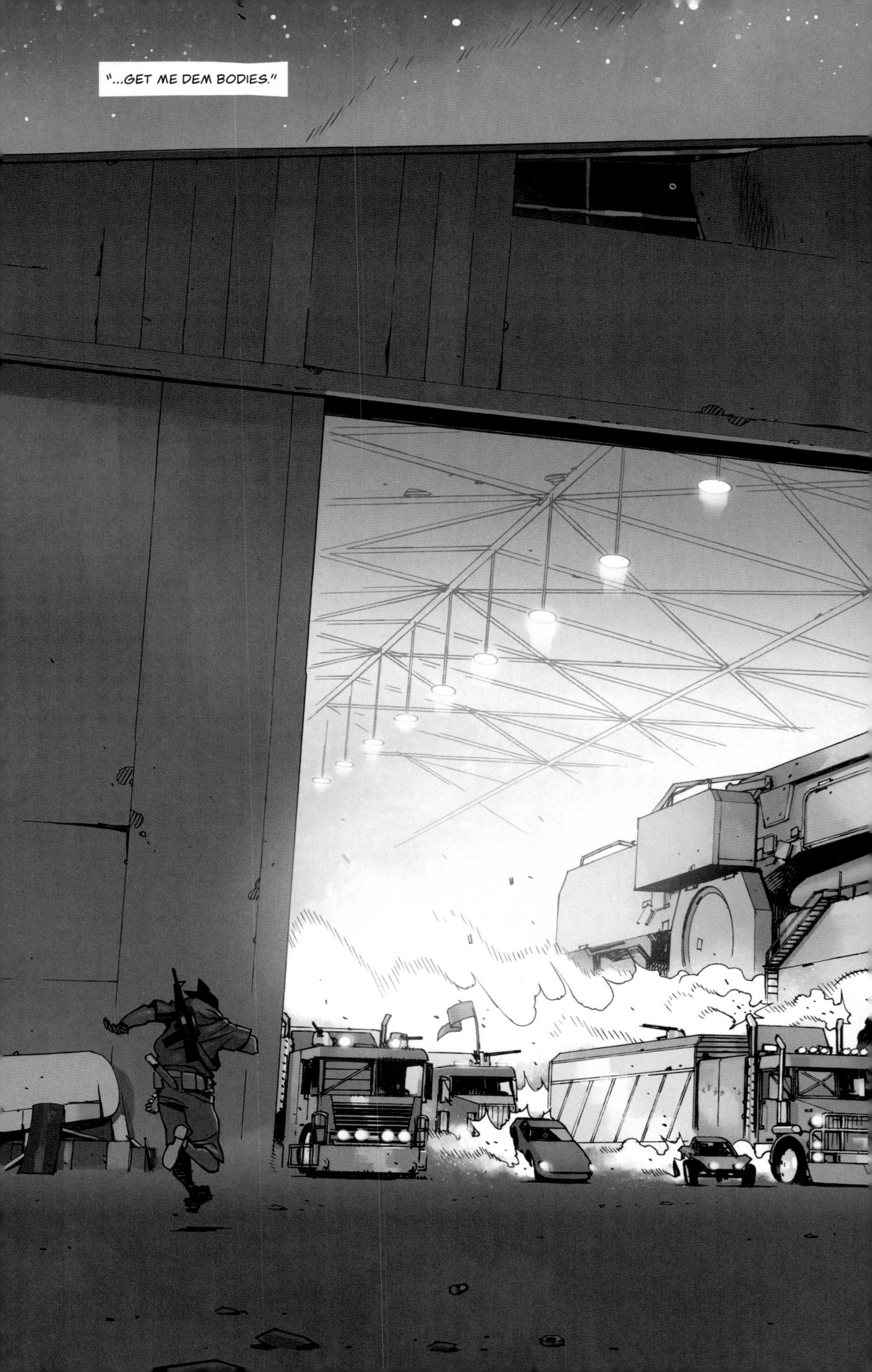
"...GET ME DEM BODIES."

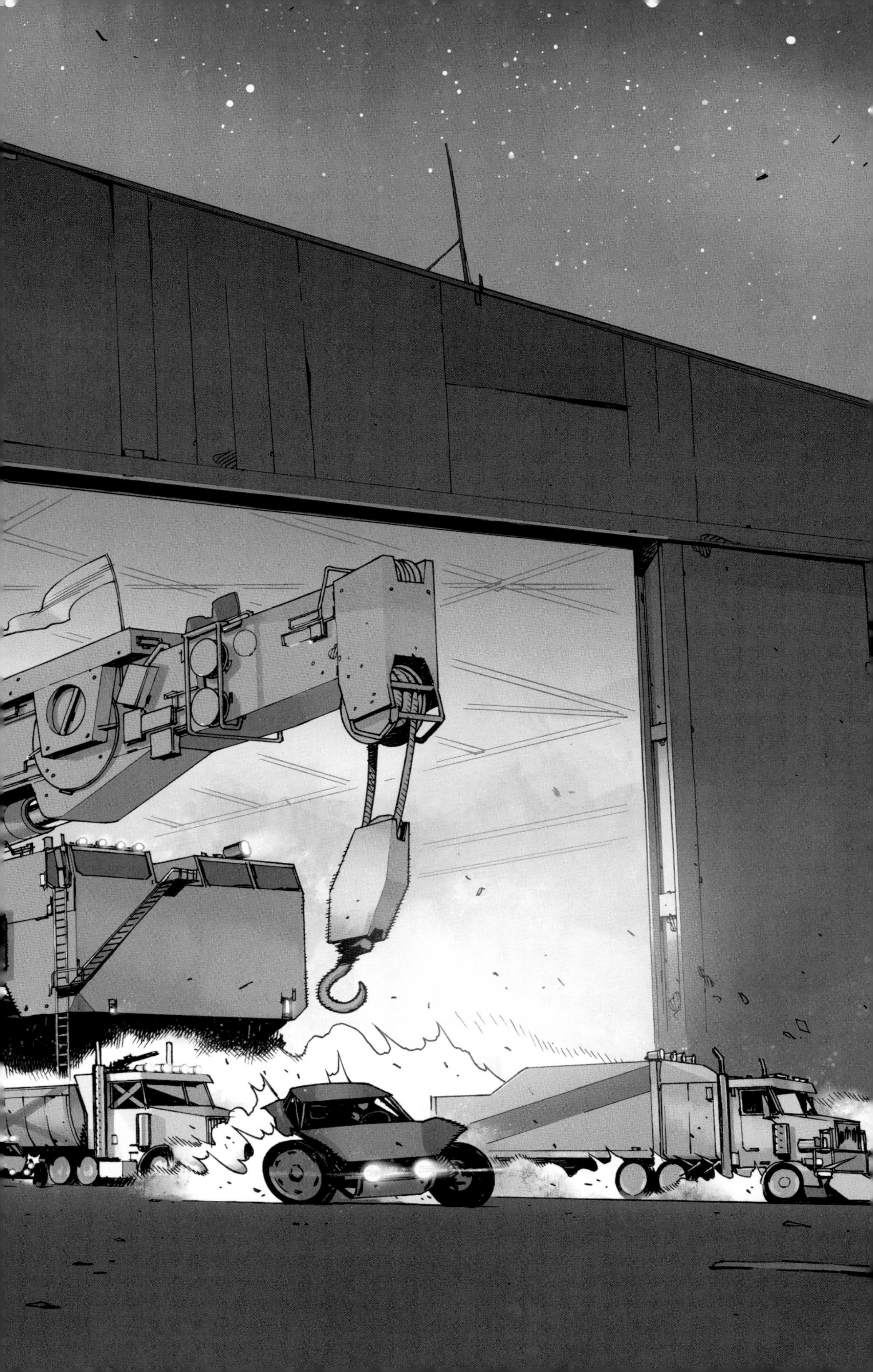

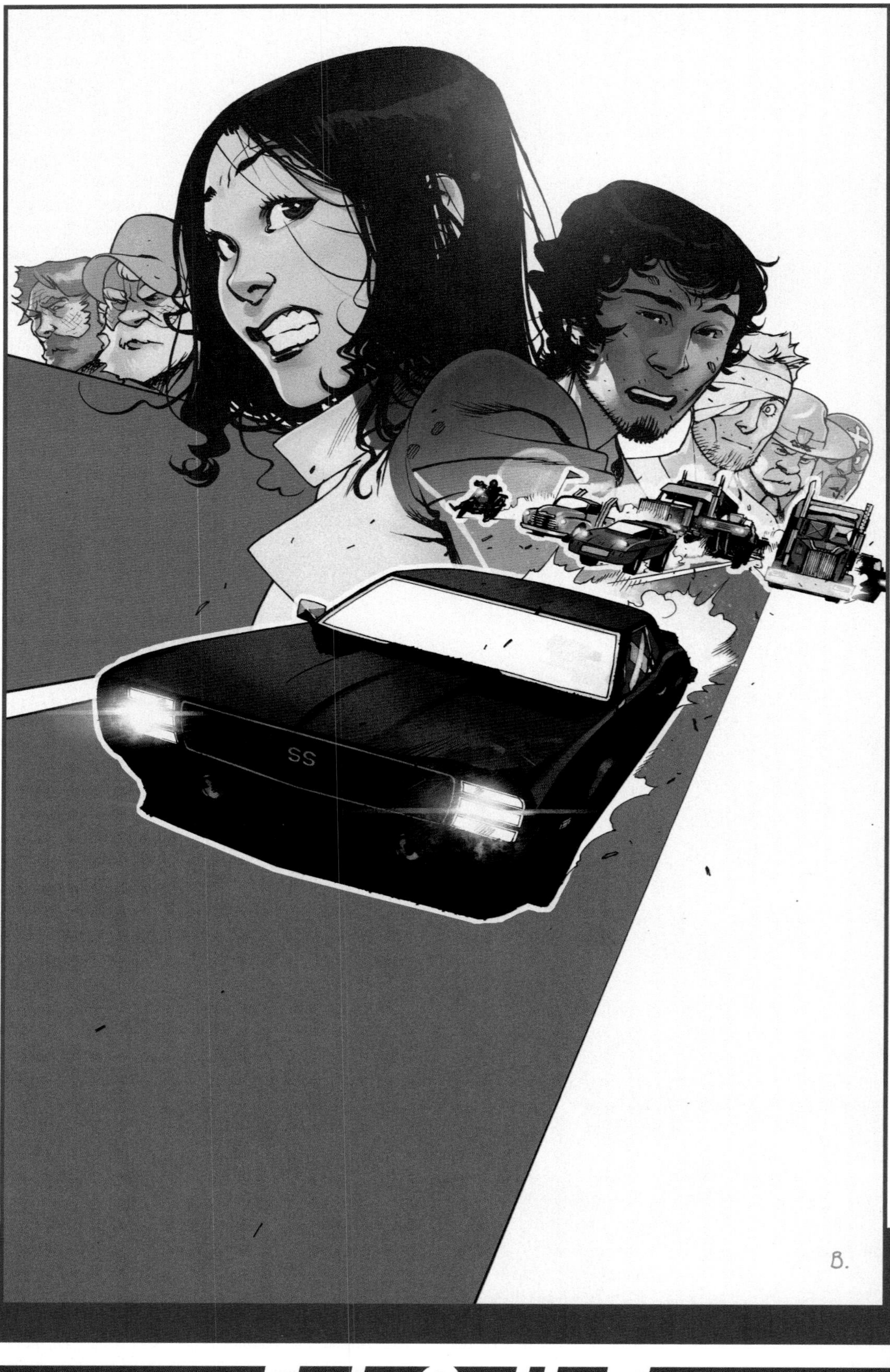
SS
B.

EIGHT

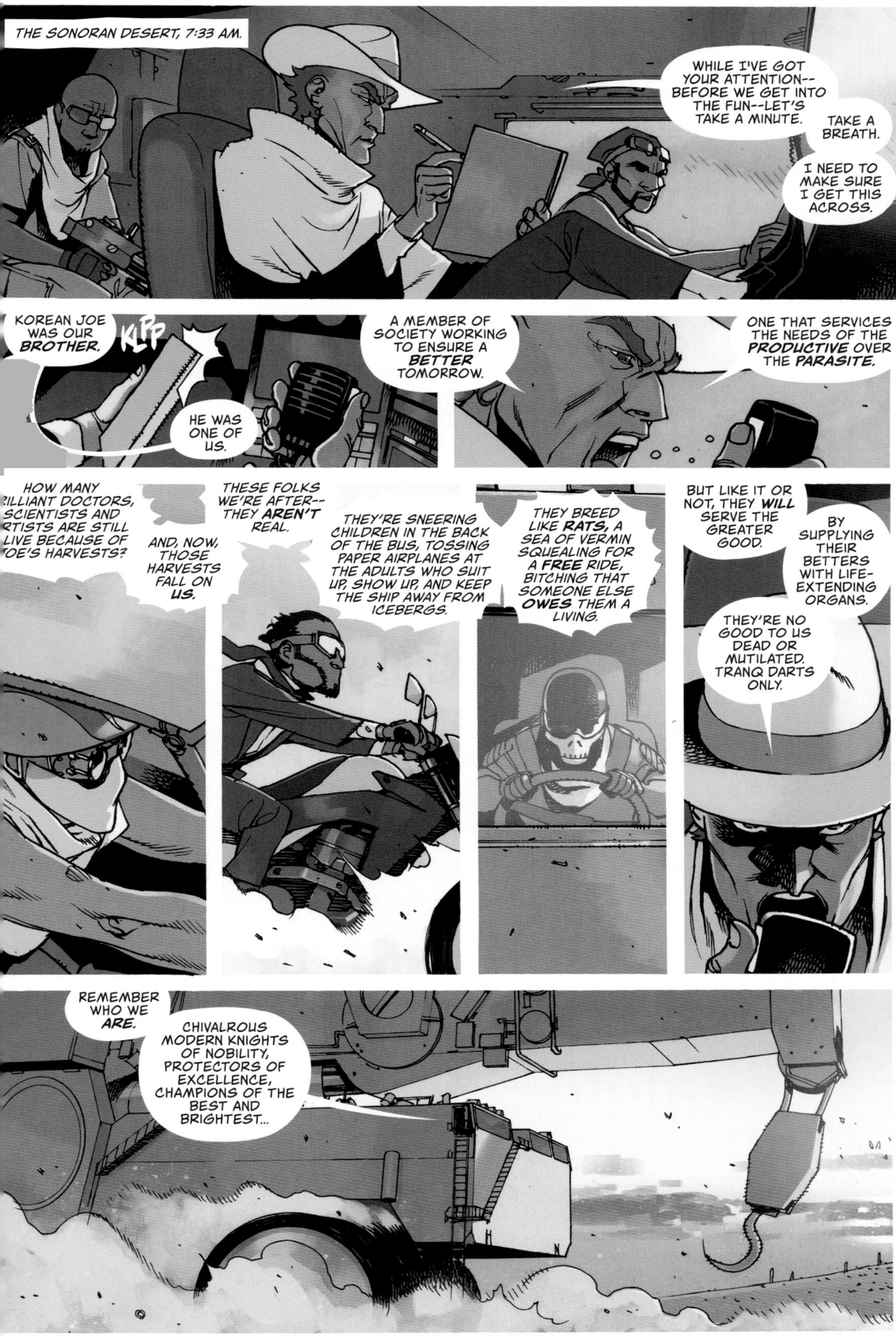
THE SONORAN DESERT, 7:33 AM.
WHILE I'VE GOT YOUR ATTENTION-- BEFORE WE GET INTO THE FUN--LET'S TAKE A MINUTE.
TAKE A BREATH.
I NEED TO MAKE SURE I GET THIS ACROSS.
KOREAN JOE WAS OUR BROTHER.
KLPP
HE WAS ONE OF US.
A MEMBER OF SOCIETY WORKING TO ENSURE A BETTER TOMORROW.
ONE THAT SERVICES THE NEEDS OF THE PRODUCTIVE OVER THE PARASITE.
HOW MANY RILLIANT DOCTORS, SCIENTISTS AND RTISTS ARE STILL LIVE BECAUSE OF OE'S HARVESTS?
AND, NOW, THOSE HARVESTS FALL ON US.
THESE FOLKS WE'RE AFTER-- THEY AREN'T REAL.
THEY'RE SNEERING CHILDREN IN THE BACK OF THE BUS, TOSSING PAPER AIRPLANES AT THE ADULTS WHO SUIT UP, SHOW UP, AND KEEP THE SHIP AWAY FROM ICEBERGS.
THEY BREED LIKE RATS, A SEA OF VERMIN SQUEALING FOR A FREE RIDE, BITCHING THAT SOMEONE ELSE OWES THEM A LIVING.
BUT LIKE IT OR NOT, THEY WILL SERVE THE GREATER GOOD.
BY SUPPLYING THEIR BETTERS WITH LIFE-EXTENDING ORGANS.
THEY'RE NO GOOD TO US DEAD OR MUTILATED. TRANQ DARTS ONLY.
REMEMBER WHO WE ARE.
CHIVALROUS MODERN KNIGHTS OF NOBILITY, PROTECTORS OF EXCELLENCE, CHAMPIONS OF THE BEST AND BRIGHTEST...

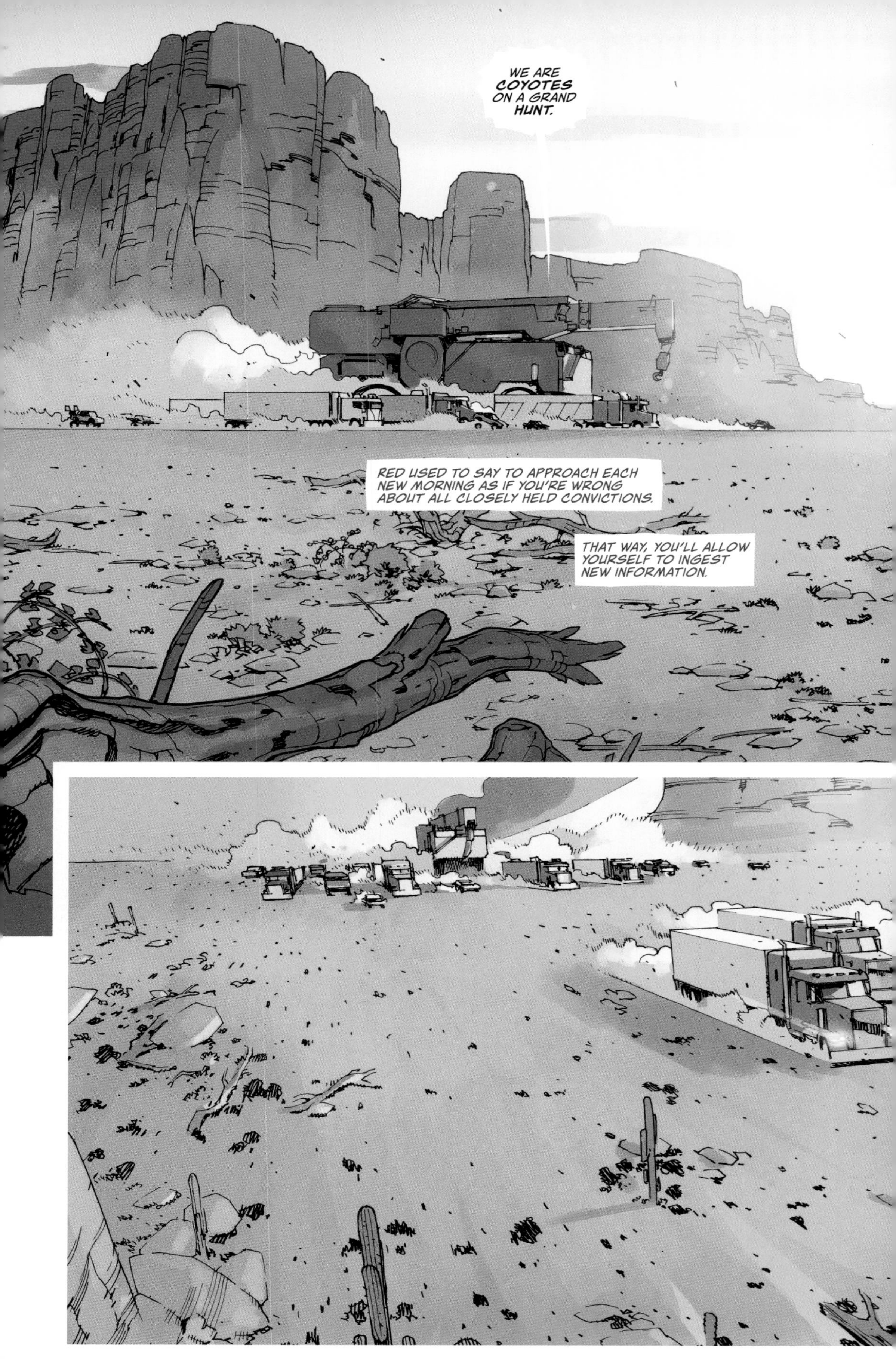
WE ARE COYOTES ON A GRAND HUNT.
RED USED TO SAY TO APPROACH EACH NEW MORNING AS IF YOU'RE WRONG ABOUT ALL CLOSELY HELD CONVICTIONS.
THAT WAY, YOU'LL ALLOW YOURSELF TO INGEST NEW INFORMATION.

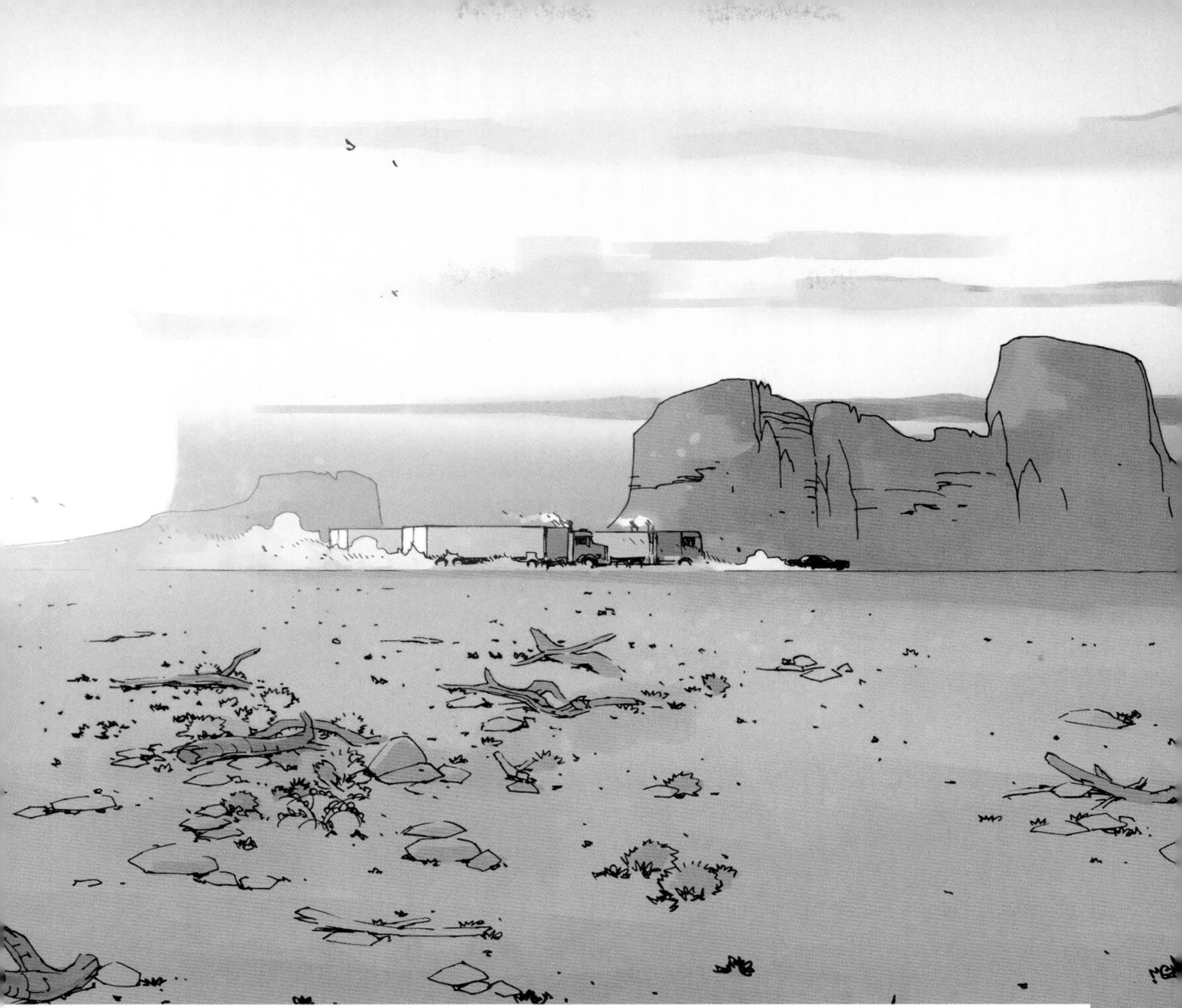

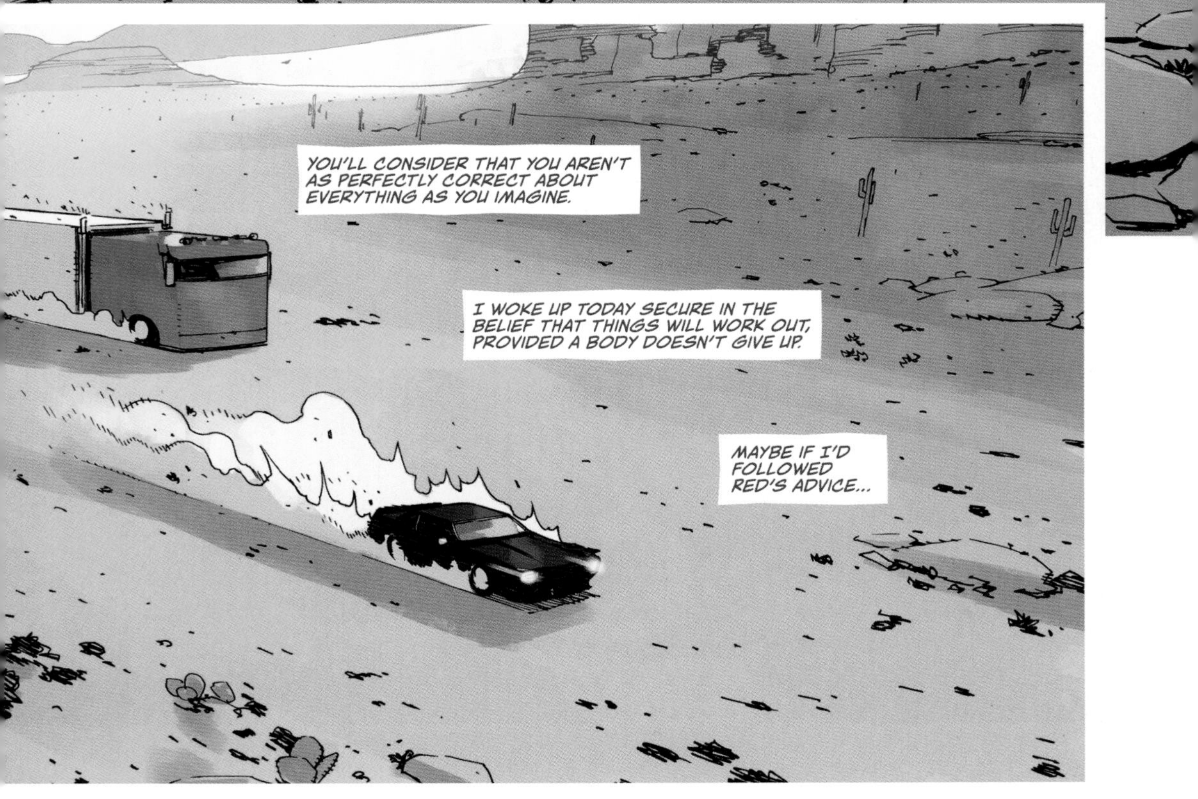
YOU'LL CONSIDER THAT YOU AREN'T AS PERFECTLY CORRECT ABOUT EVERYTHING AS YOU IMAGINE.
I WOKE UP TODAY SECURE IN THE BELIEF THAT THINGS WILL WORK OUT, PROVIDED A BODY DOESN'T GIVE UP.
MAYBE IF I'D FOLLOWED RED'S ADVICE...

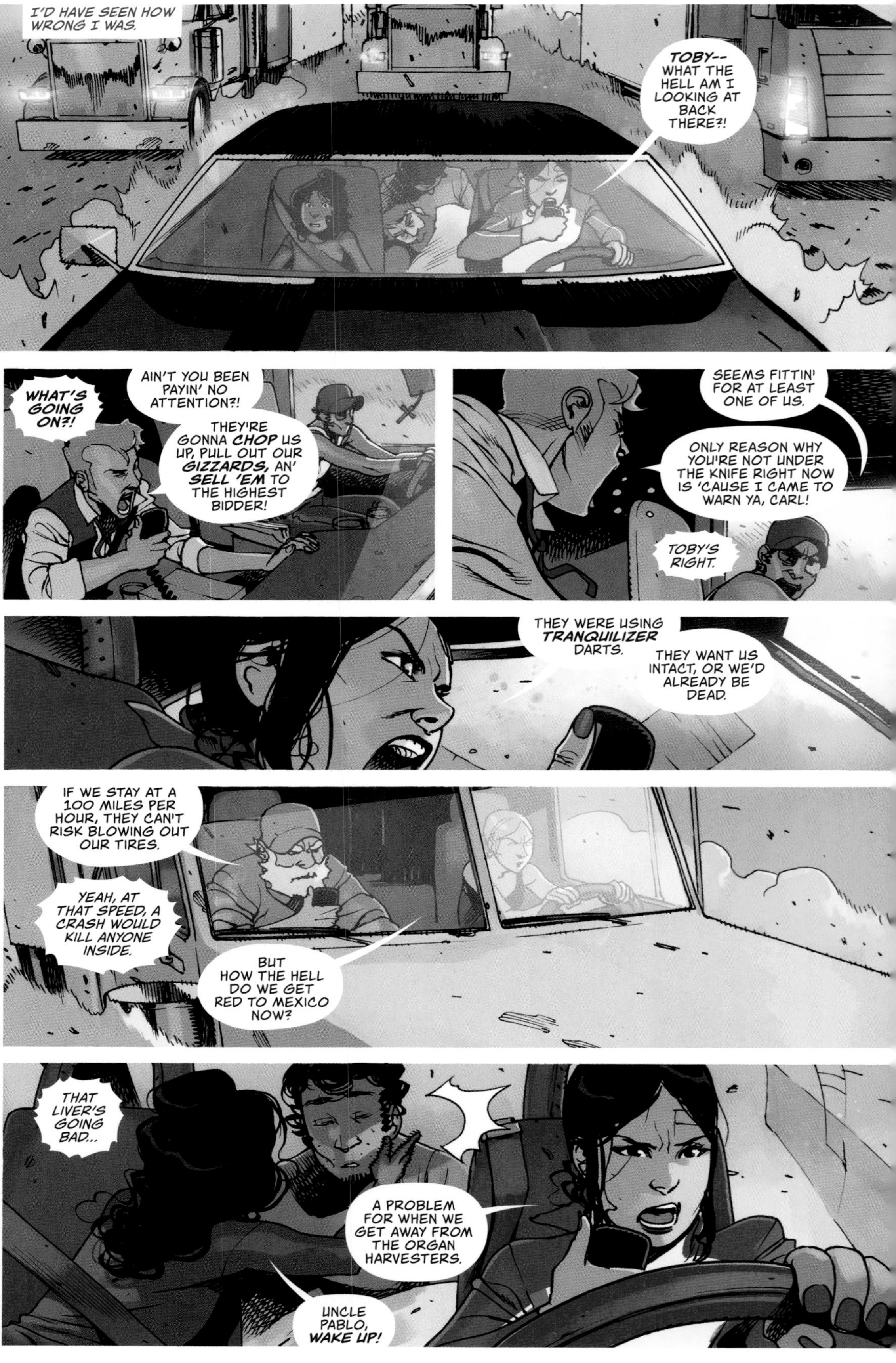
I'D HAVE SEEN HOW WRONG I WAS.
TOBY-- WHAT THE HELL AM I LOOKING AT BACK THERE?!
WHAT'S GOING ON?!
AIN'T YOU BEEN PAYIN' NO ATTENTION?!
THEY'RE GONNA CHOP US UP, PULL OUT OUR GIZZARDS, AN' SELL 'EM TO THE HIGHEST BIDDER!
SEEMS FITTIN' FOR AT LEAST ONE OF US.
ONLY REASON WHY YOU'RE NOT UNDER THE KNIFE RIGHT NOW IS 'CAUSE I CAME TO WARN YA, CARL!
TOBY'S RIGHT.
THEY WERE USING TRANQUILIZER DARTS.
THEY WANT US INTACT, OR WE'D ALREADY BE DEAD.
IF WE STAY AT A 100 MILES PER HOUR, THEY CAN'T RISK BLOWING OUT OUR TIRES.
YEAH, AT THAT SPEED, A CRASH WOULD KILL ANYONE INSIDE.
BUT HOW THE HELL DO WE GET RED TO MEXICO NOW?
THAT LIVER'S GOING BAD...
A PROBLEM FOR WHEN WE GET AWAY FROM THE ORGAN HARVESTERS.
UNCLE PABLO, WAKE UP!

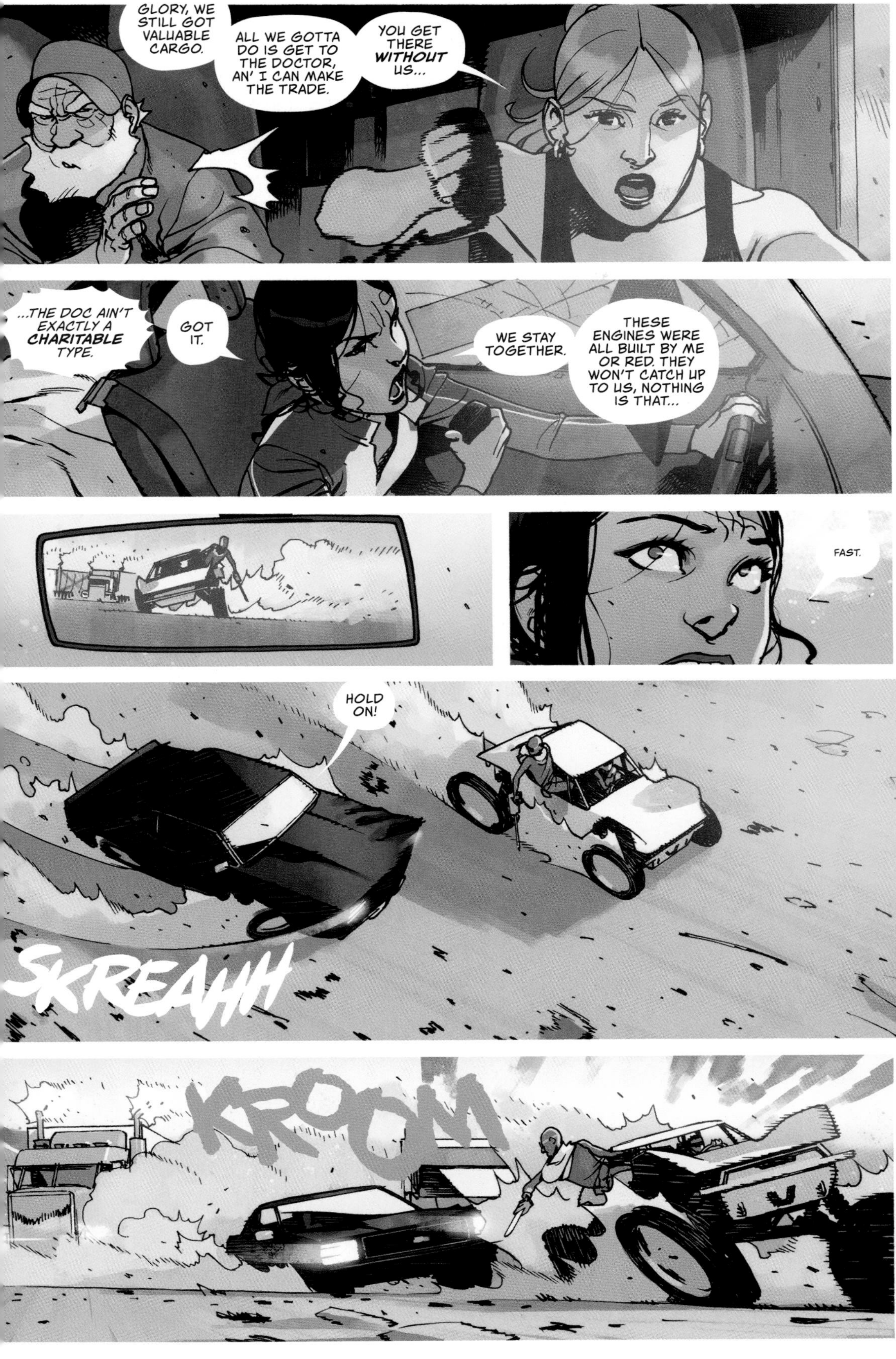
GLORY, WE STILL GOT VALUABLE CARGO.
ALL WE GOTTA DO IS GET TO THE DOCTOR, AN' I CAN MAKE THE TRADE.
YOU GET THERE WITHOUT US...
...THE DOC AIN'T EXACTLY A CHARITABLE TYPE.
GOT IT.
WE STAY TOGETHER.
THESE ENGINES WERE ALL BUILT BY ME OR RED. THEY WON'T CATCH UP TO US, NOTHING IS THAT...
FAST.
HOLD ON!
SKREAHH
KROOM

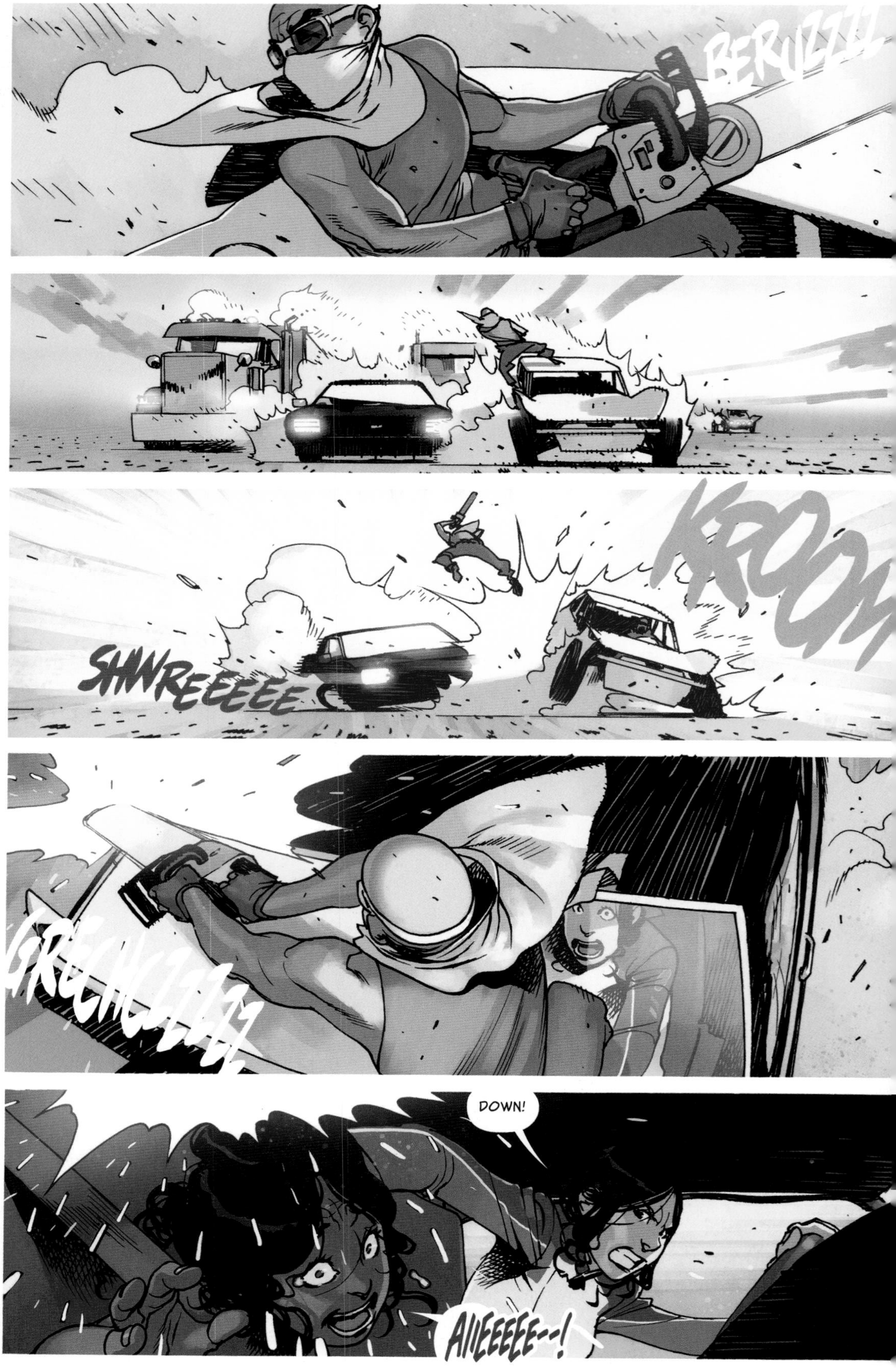
BERUZZZZ
KROOM
SHWREEEEE
GRECHZZZZ
DOWN!
AIIEEEEE--!

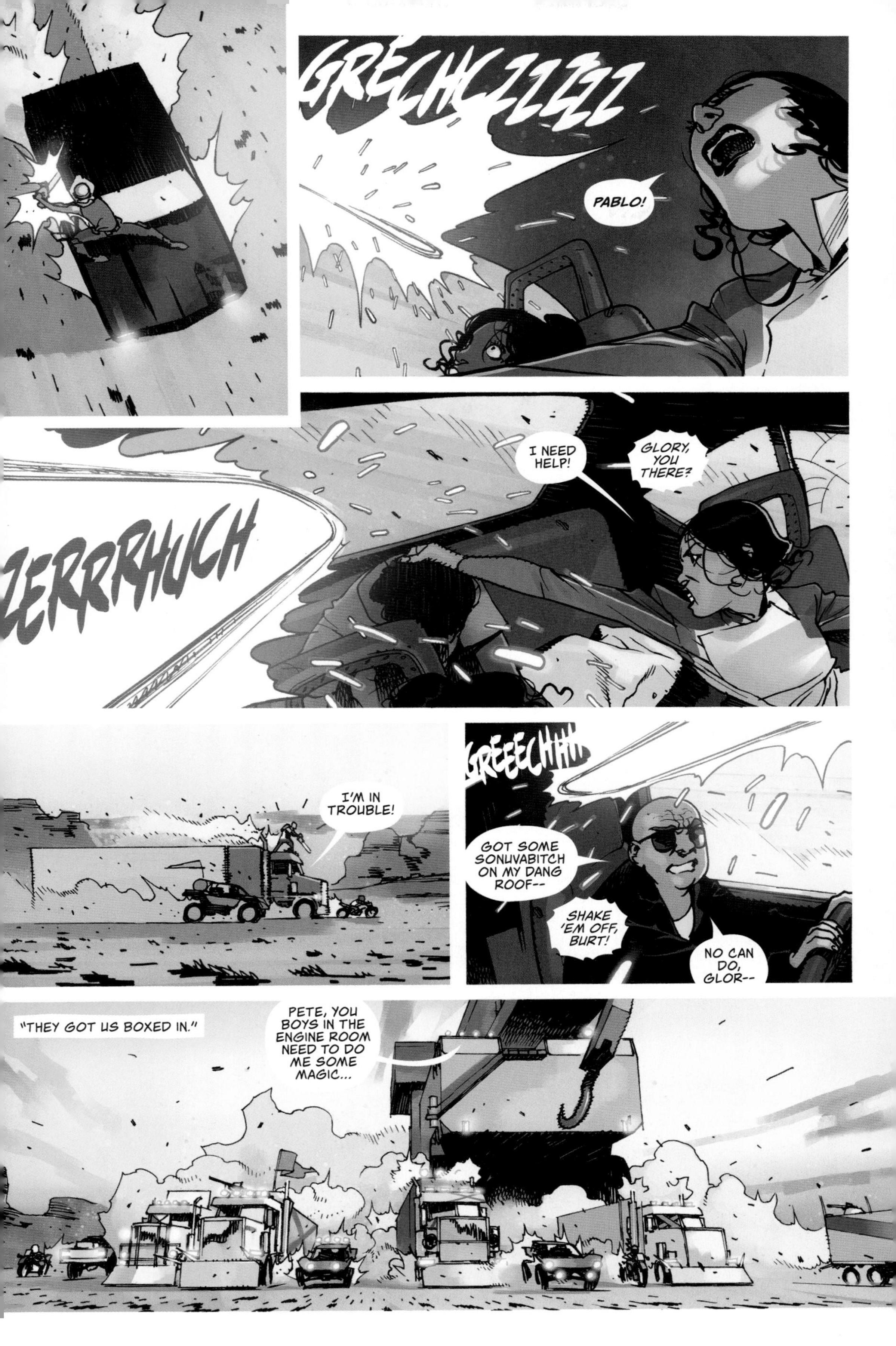
GRECHCZZZZZ
PABLO!
ZERRRHUCH
I NEED HELP!
GLORY, YOU THERE?
I'M IN TROUBLE!
GREEECHHH
GOT SOME SONUVABITCH ON MY DANG ROOF--
SHAKE 'EM OFF, BURT!
NO CAN DO, GLOR--
"THEY GOT US BOXED IN."
PETE, YOU BOYS IN THE ENGINE ROOM NEED TO DO ME SOME MAGIC...

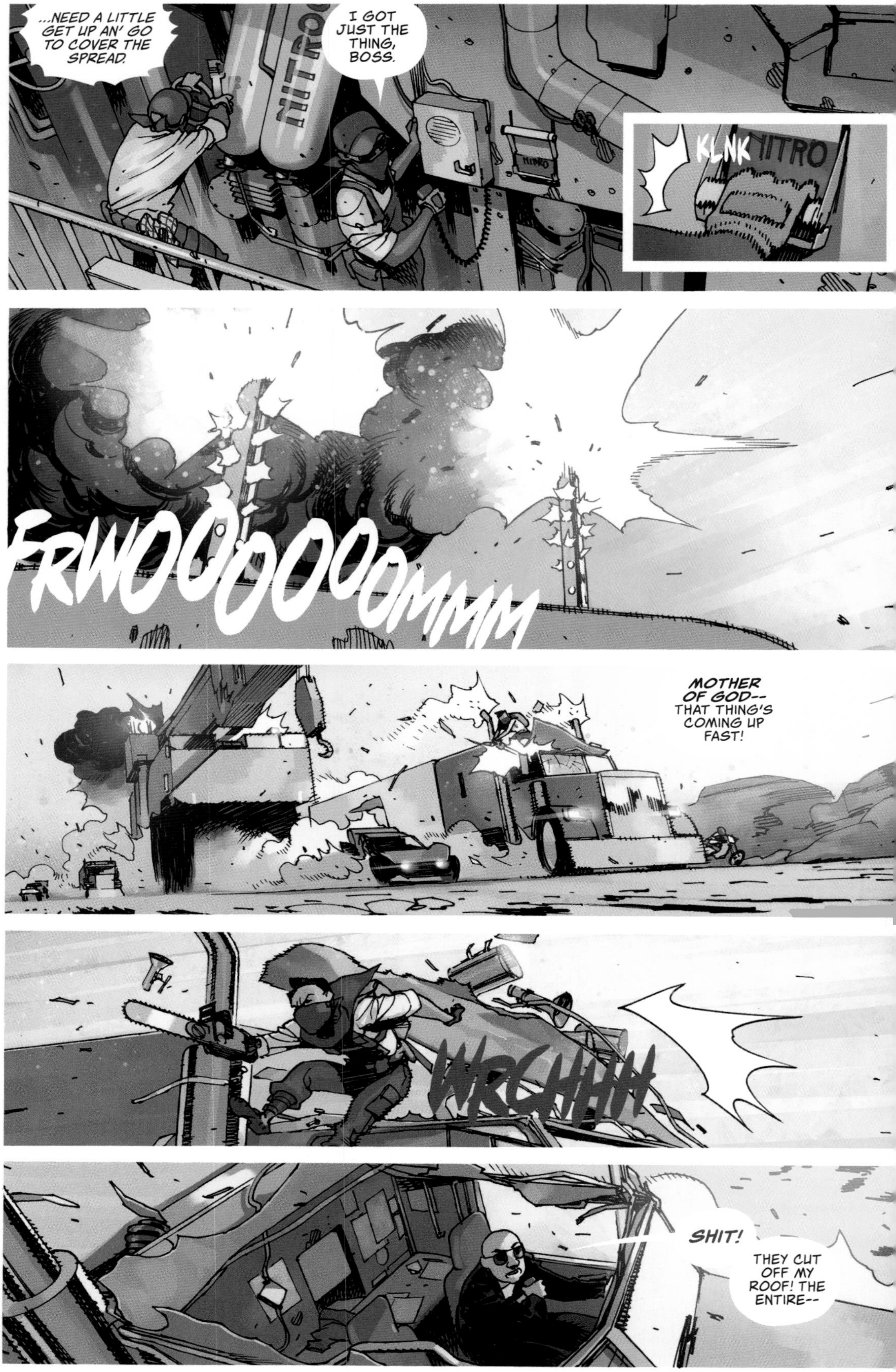
...NEED A LITTLE GET UP AN' GO TO COVER THE SPREAD.
I GOT JUST THE THING, BOSS.
NITRO
KLNK
NITRO
FRWOOOOOOOMMM
MOTHER OF GOD-- THAT THING'S COMING UP FAST!
WRCHHH
SHIT!
THEY CUT OFF MY ROOF! THE ENTIRE--

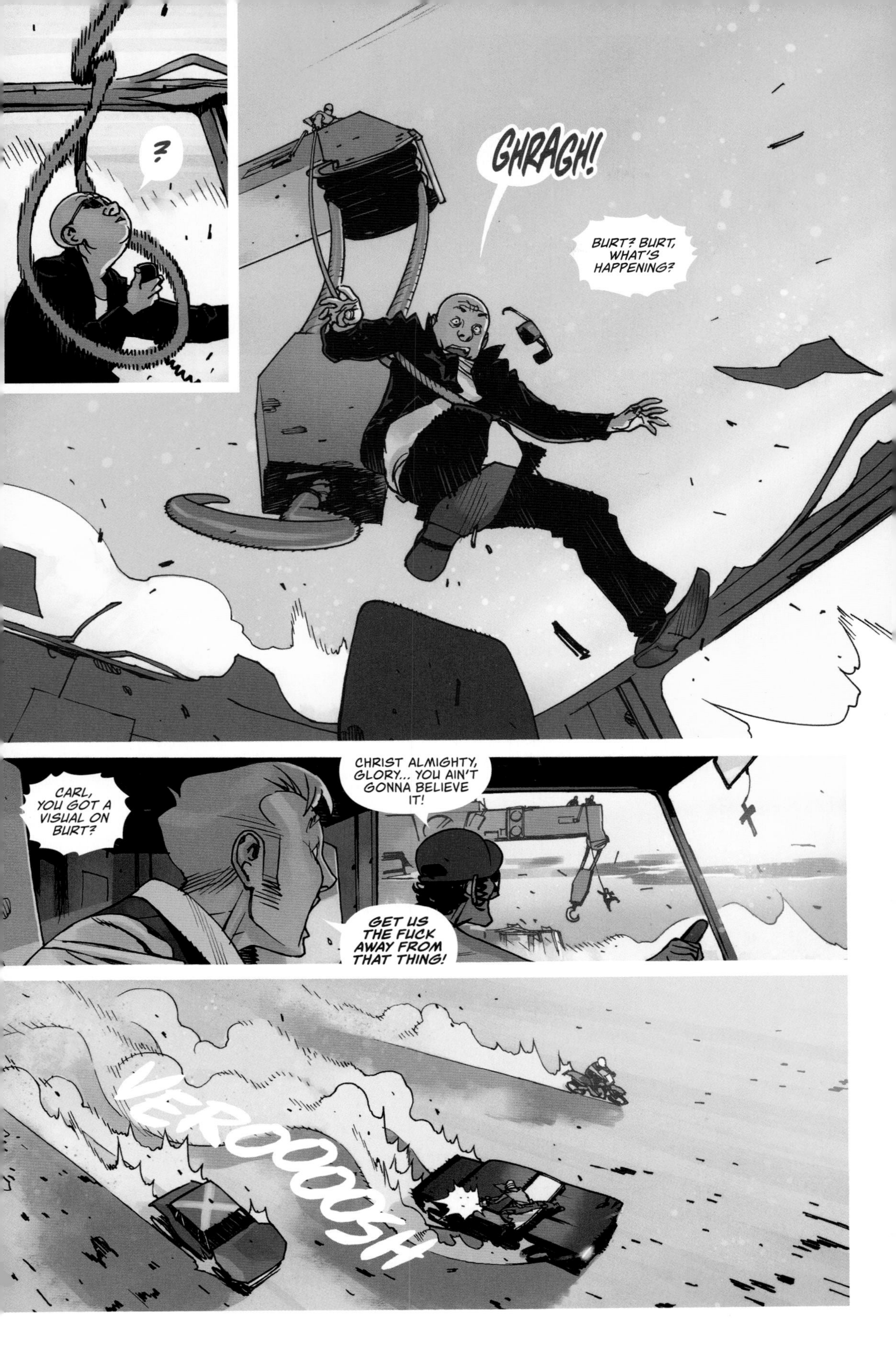
?
GHRAGH!
BURT? BURT, WHAT'S HAPPENING?
CARL, YOU GOT A VISUAL ON BURT?
CHRIST ALMIGHTY, GLORY... YOU AIN'T GONNA BELIEVE IT!
GET US THE FUCK AWAY FROM THAT THING!
VEROOOOSH

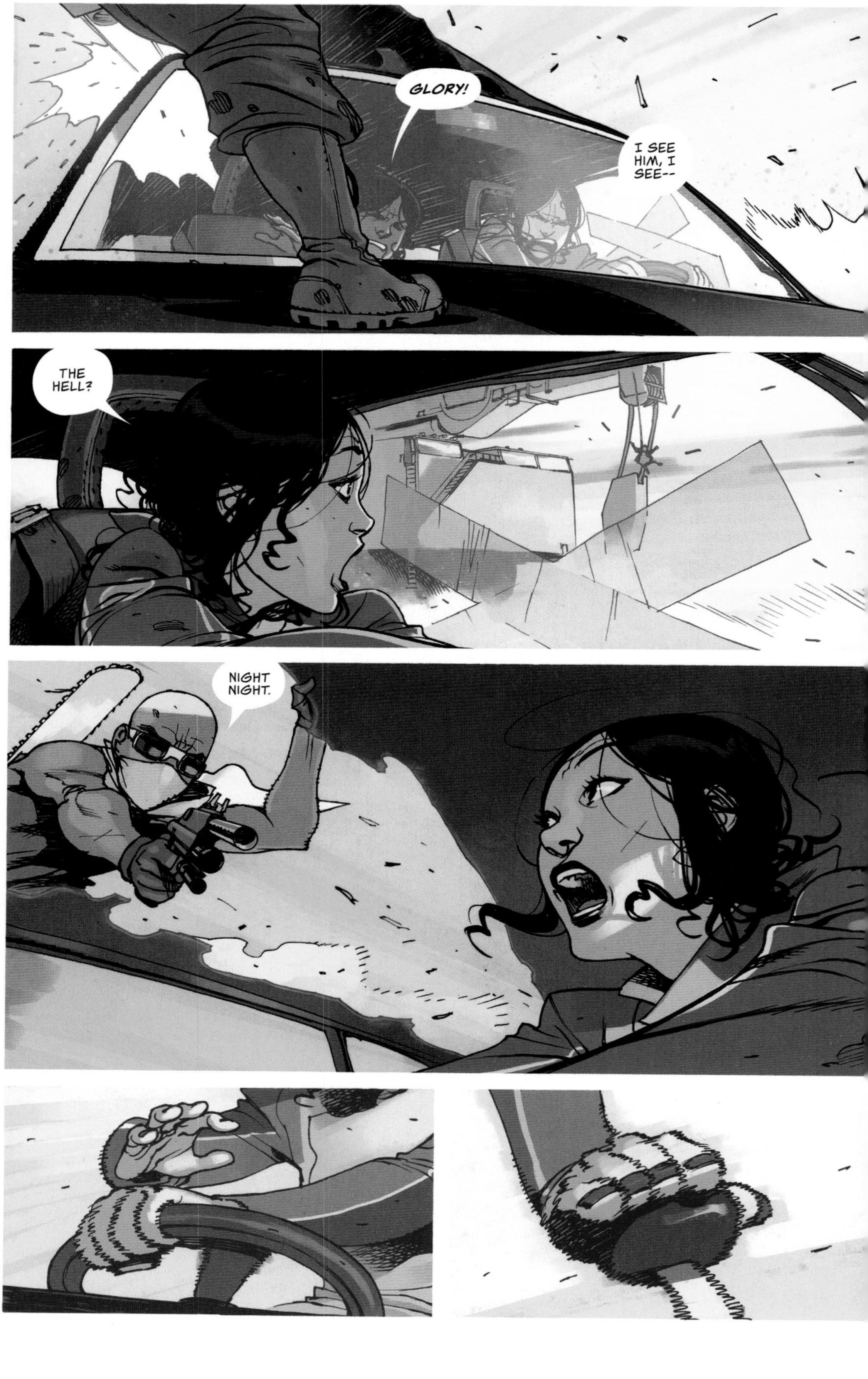
GLORY!
I SEE HIM, I SEE--
THE HELL?
NIGHT NIGHT.

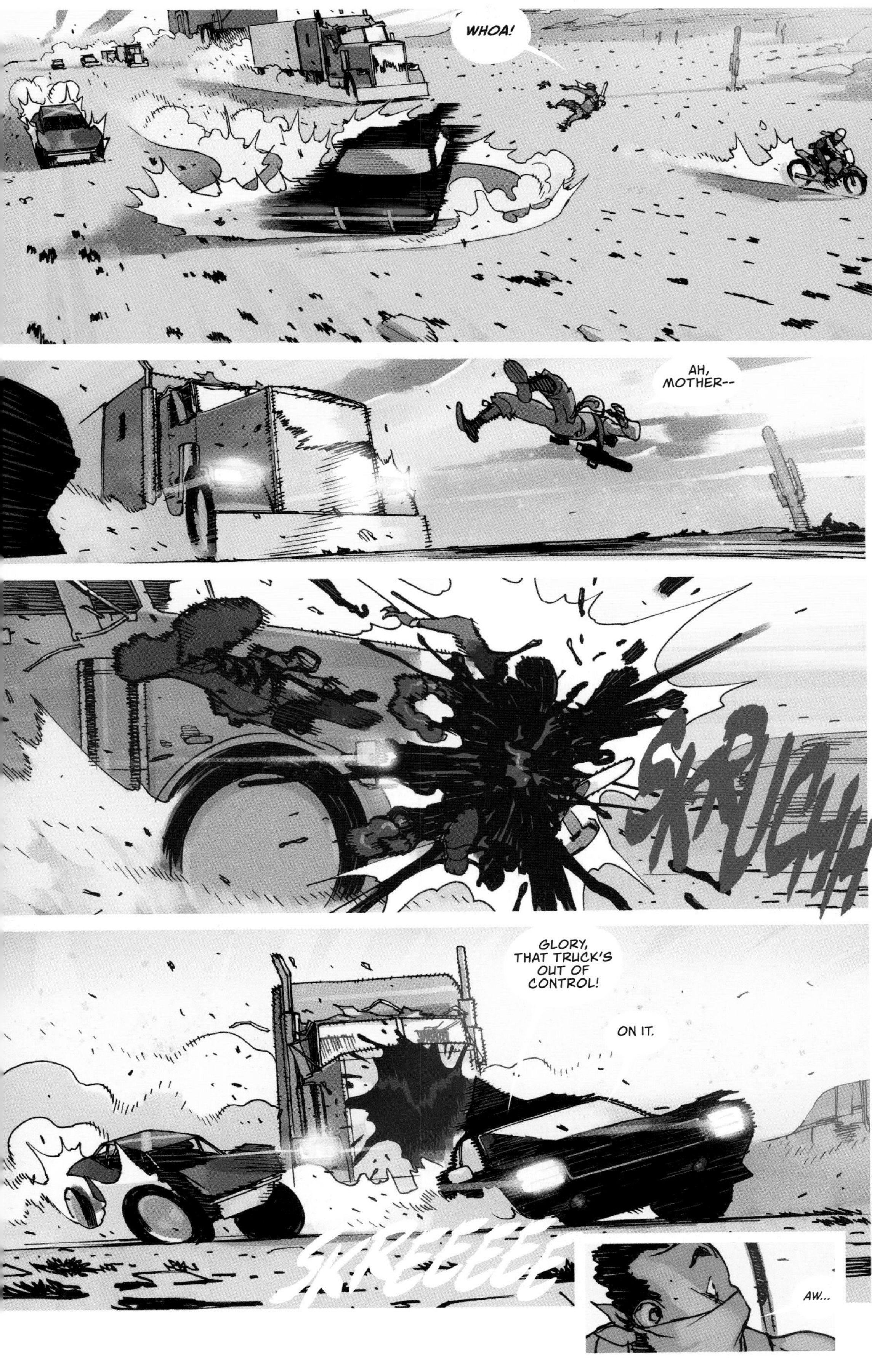
WHOA!
AH, MOTHER--
SKRUNCHH
GLORY, THAT TRUCK'S OUT OF CONTROL!
ON IT.
SKREEEEEE
AW...

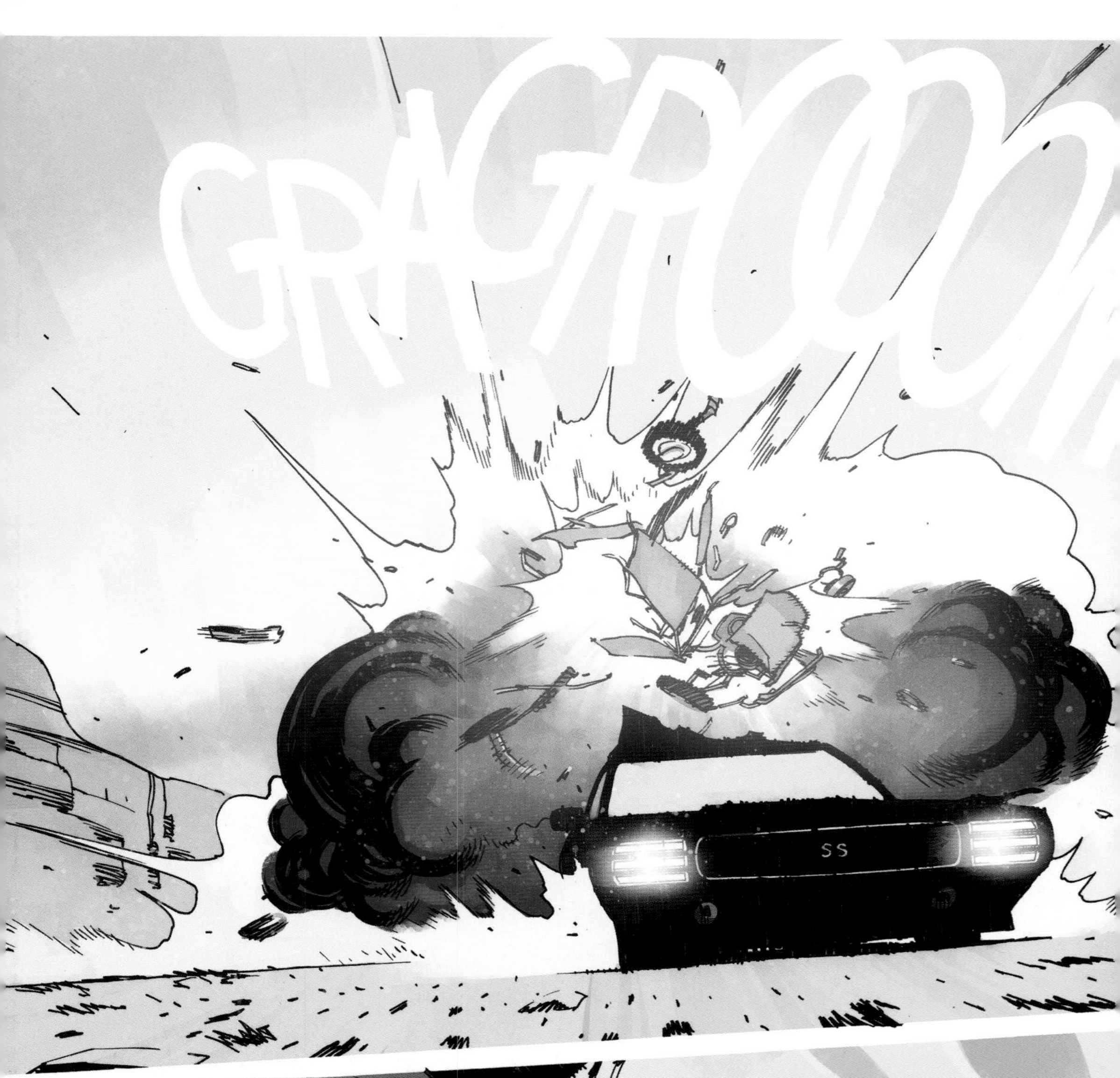
GRAGROOOM

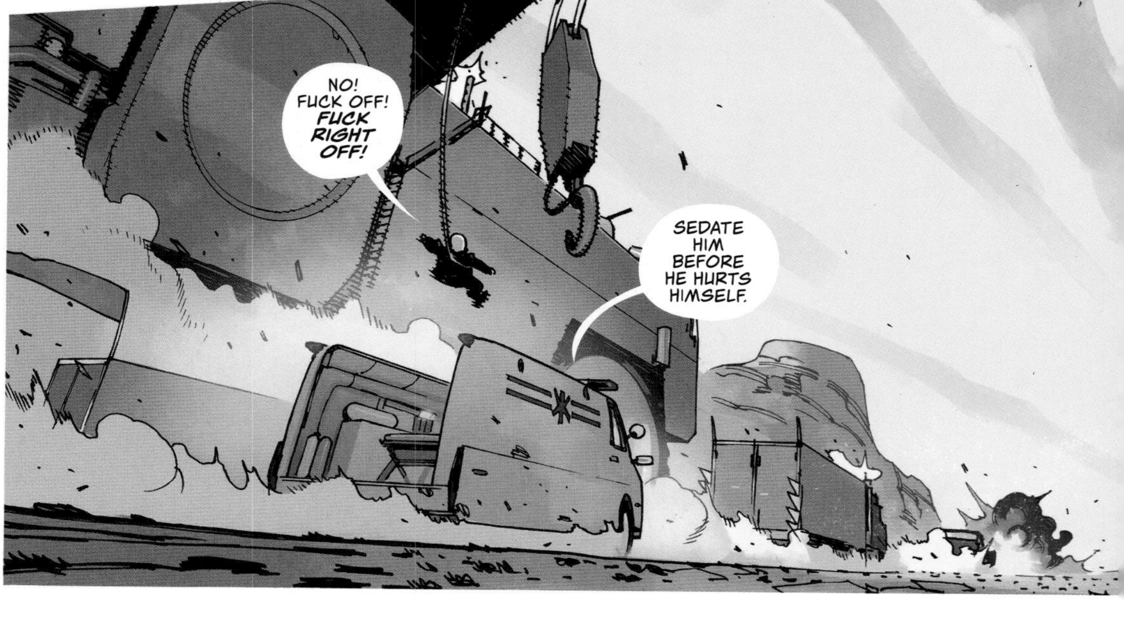
NO! FUCK OFF! FUCK RIGHT OFF!
SEDATE HIM BEFORE HE HURTS HIMSELF.

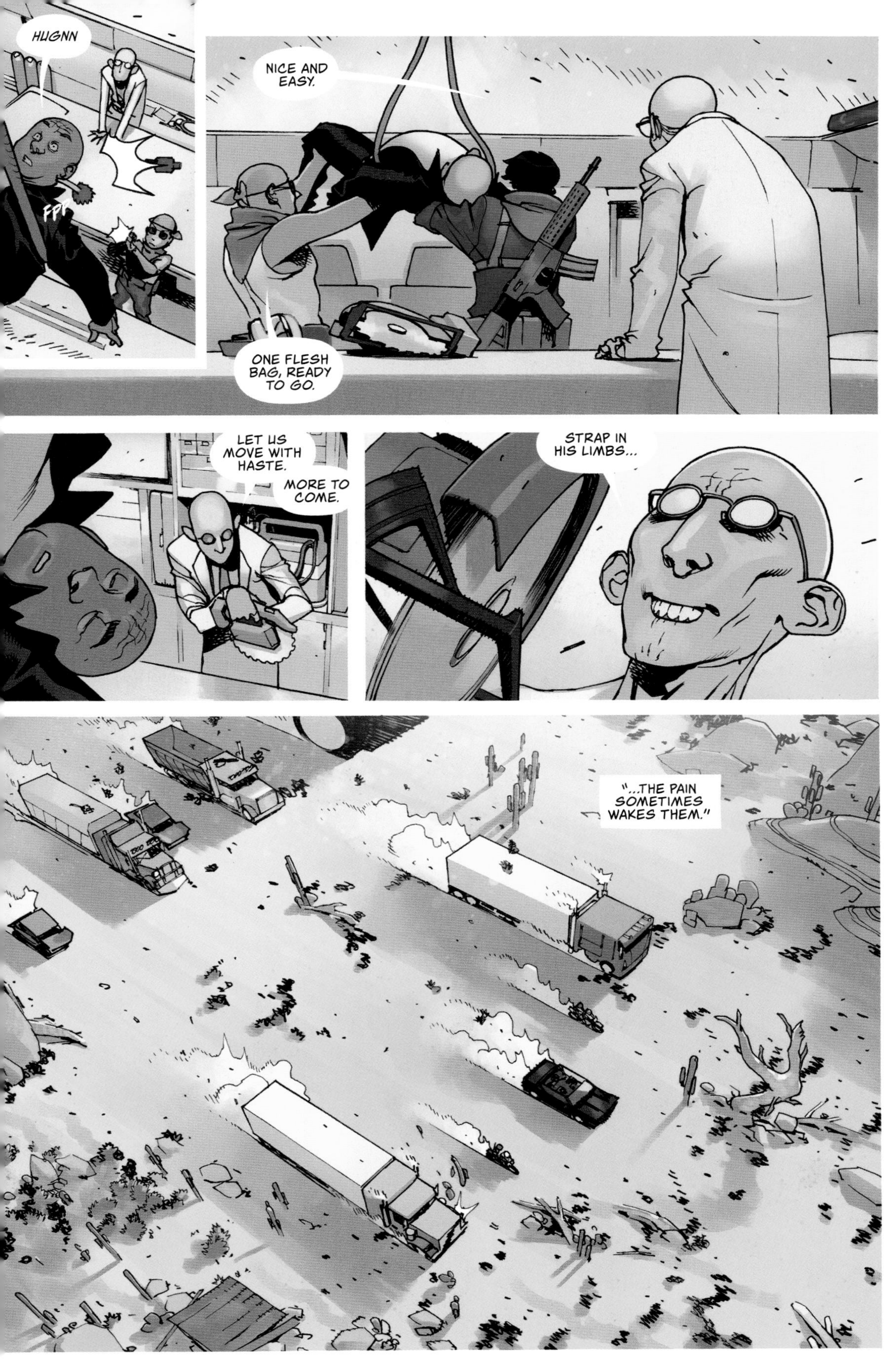
HUGNN
FPP
NICE AND EASY.
ONE FLESH BAG, READY TO GO.
LET US MOVE WITH HASTE.
MORE TO COME.
STRAP IN HIS LIMBS...
"...THE PAIN SOMETIMES WAKES THEM."

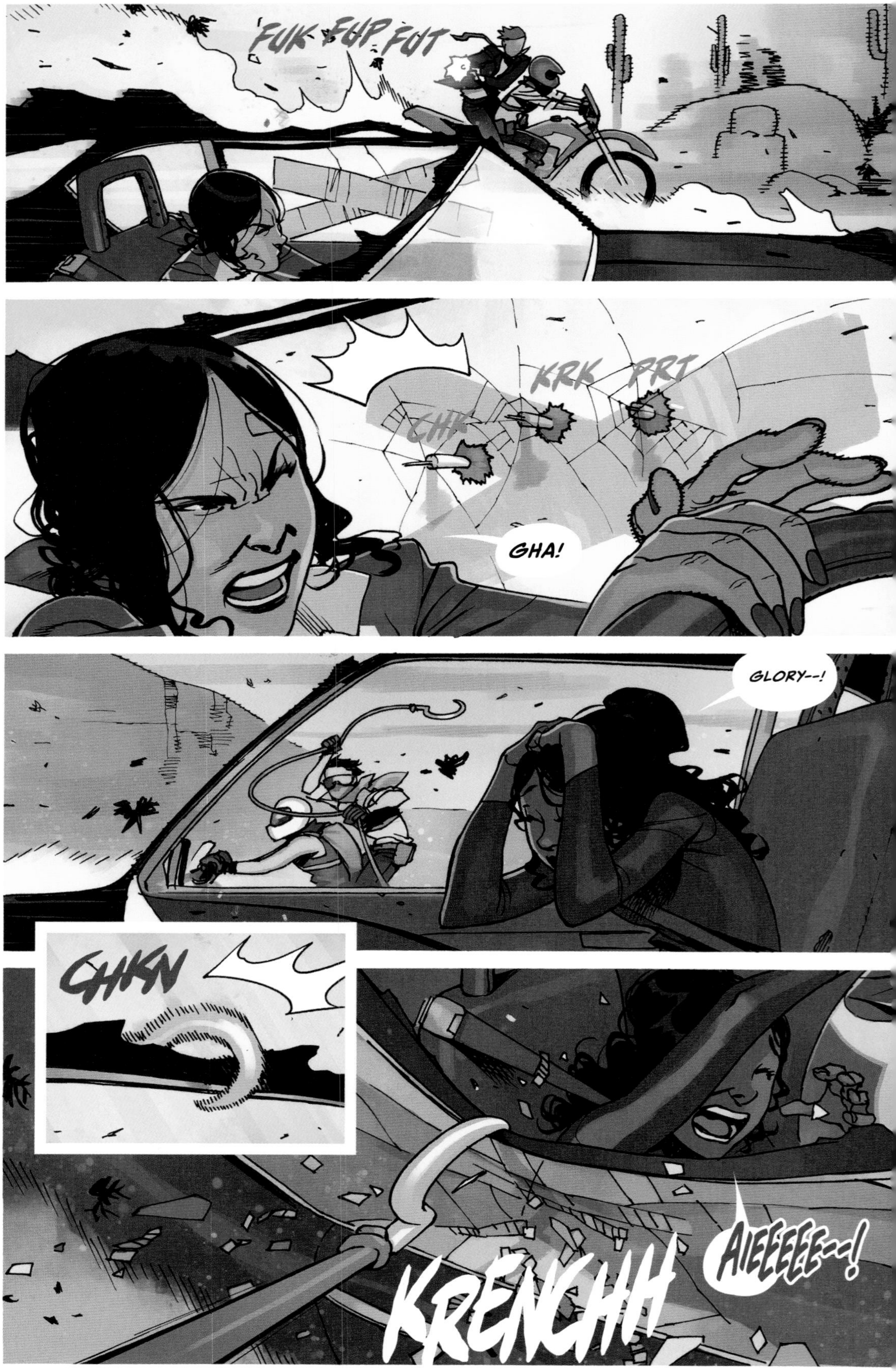
FUK FUP FUT
KRK
PRT
CHK
GHA!
GLORY--!
CHKN
KRENCHH
AIEEEEE--!

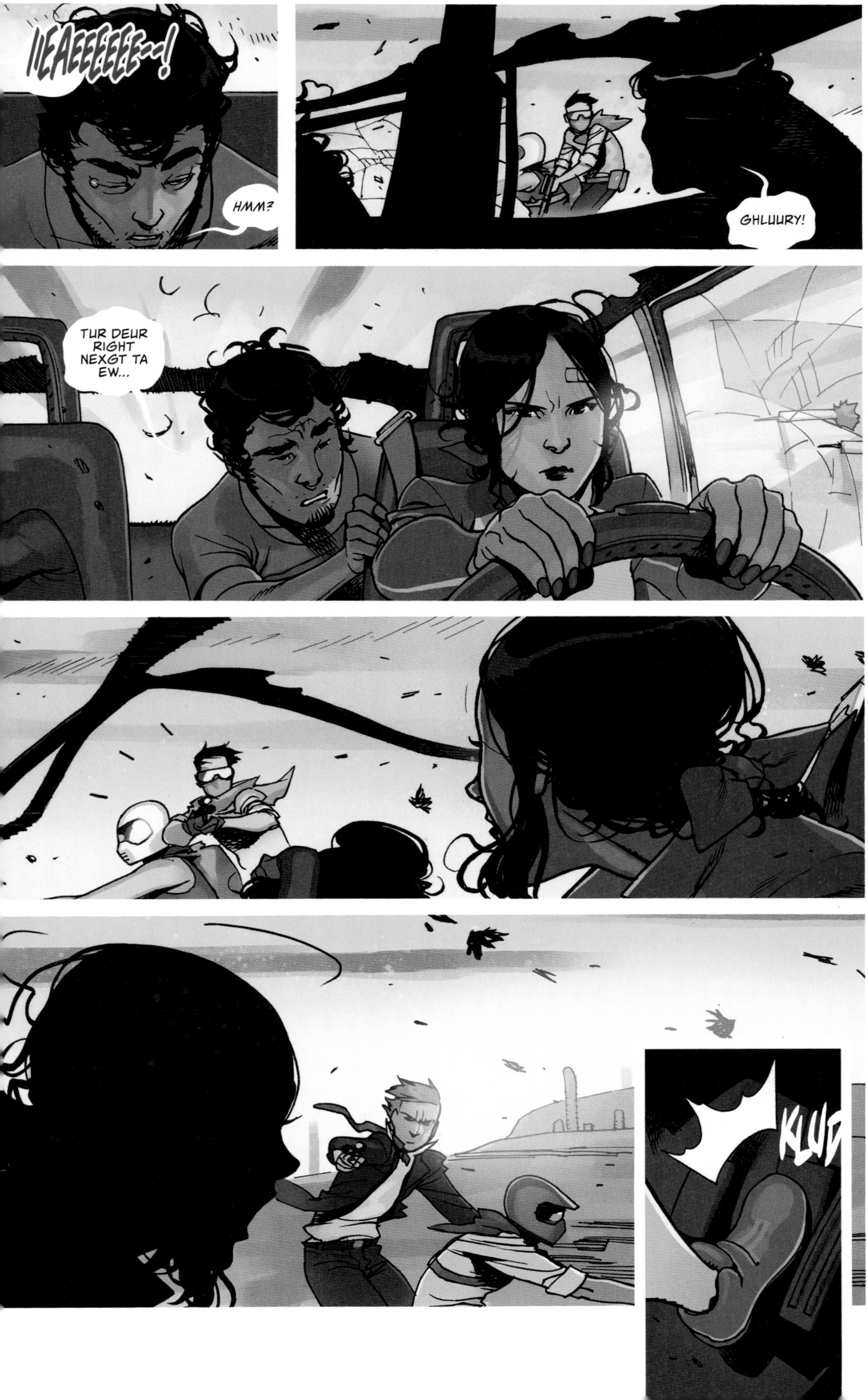

IIEAEEEEEE--!
HMM?
GHLUURY!
TUR DEUR RIGHT NEXGT TA EW...
KLUD

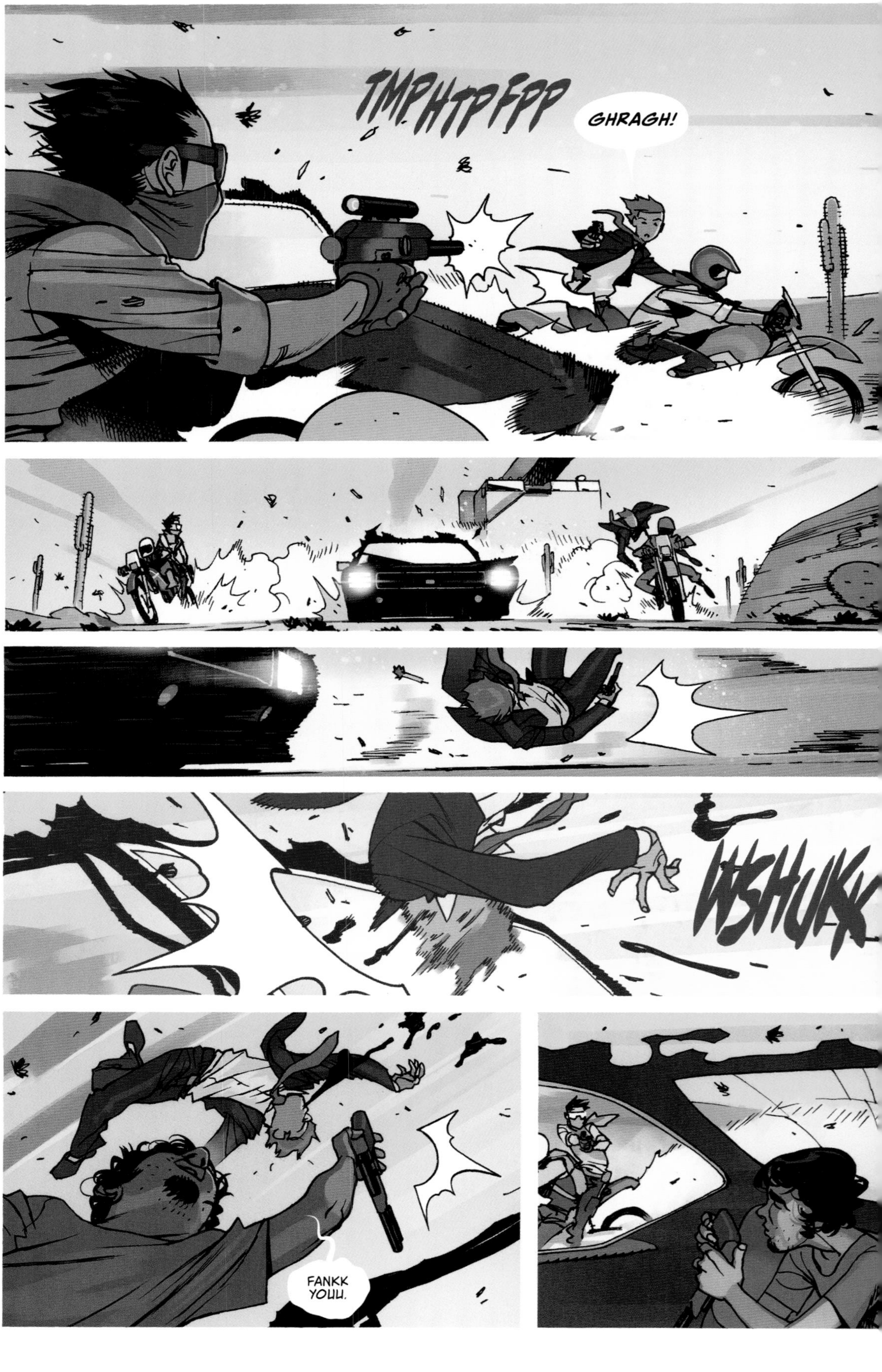
TMPHTPFPP
GHRAGH!
WSHUKK
FANKK YOUU.

ROOM

LAST OF THE CYCLISTS FAR AS I CAN SEE.

SOME JUGS OF WATER DOWN THERE, CLEAN THE DAMN WINDSHIELD!

STAY AWAY FROM THAT CRANE! YOU HEAR?

THEY GRABBED BURT WITH IT!

WELL, WITH THAT BIT OF NEWS, AT LEAST ON THE BRIGHT SIDE...

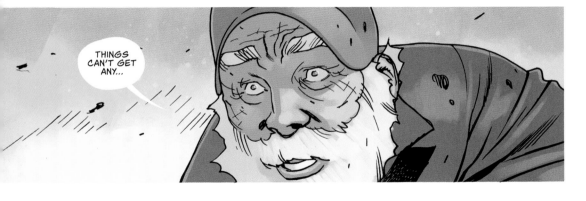

THINGS CAN'T GET ANY...

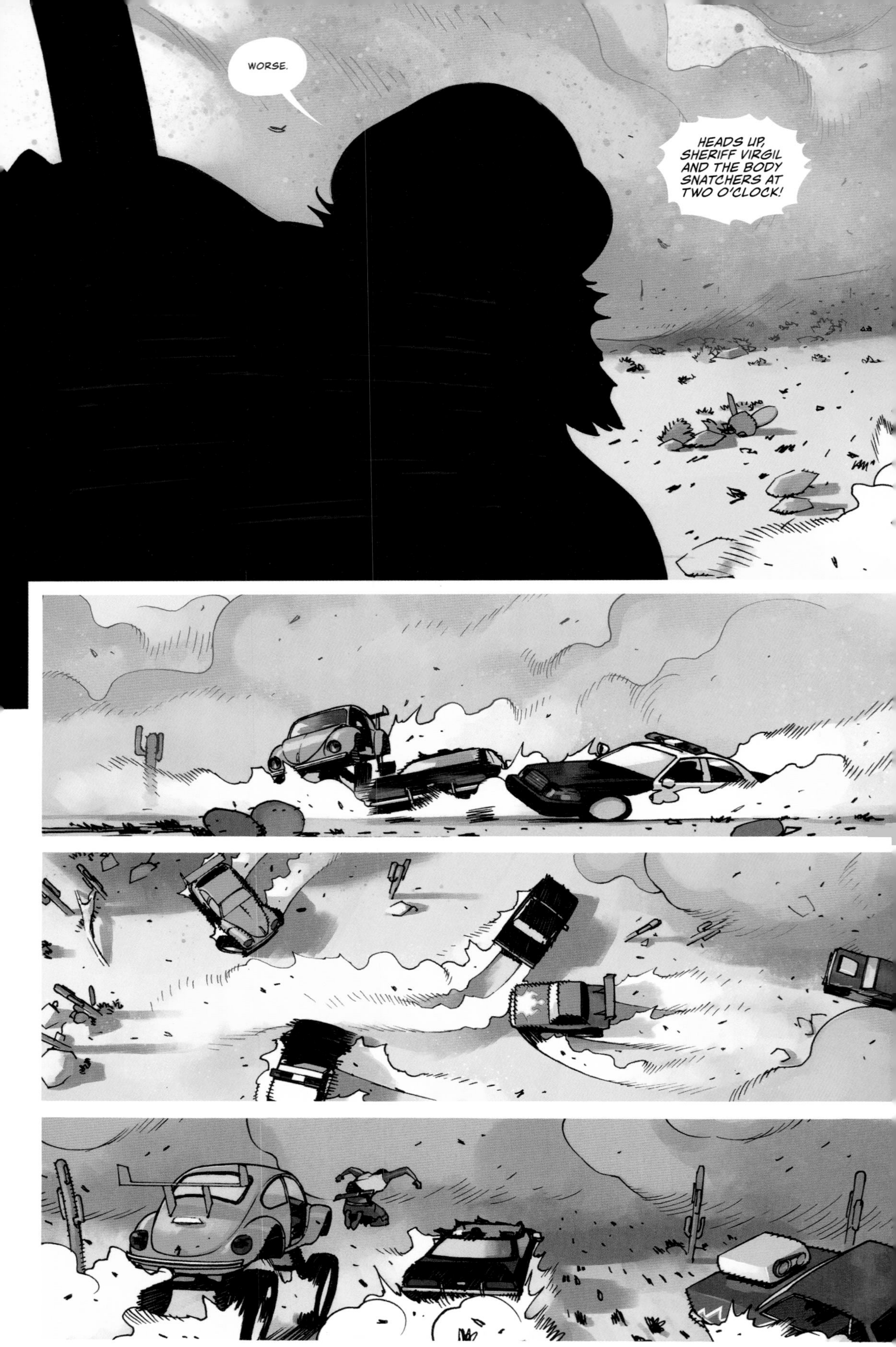
WORSE.
HEADS UP, SHERIFF VIRGIL AND THE BODY SNATCHERS AT TWO O'CLOCK!

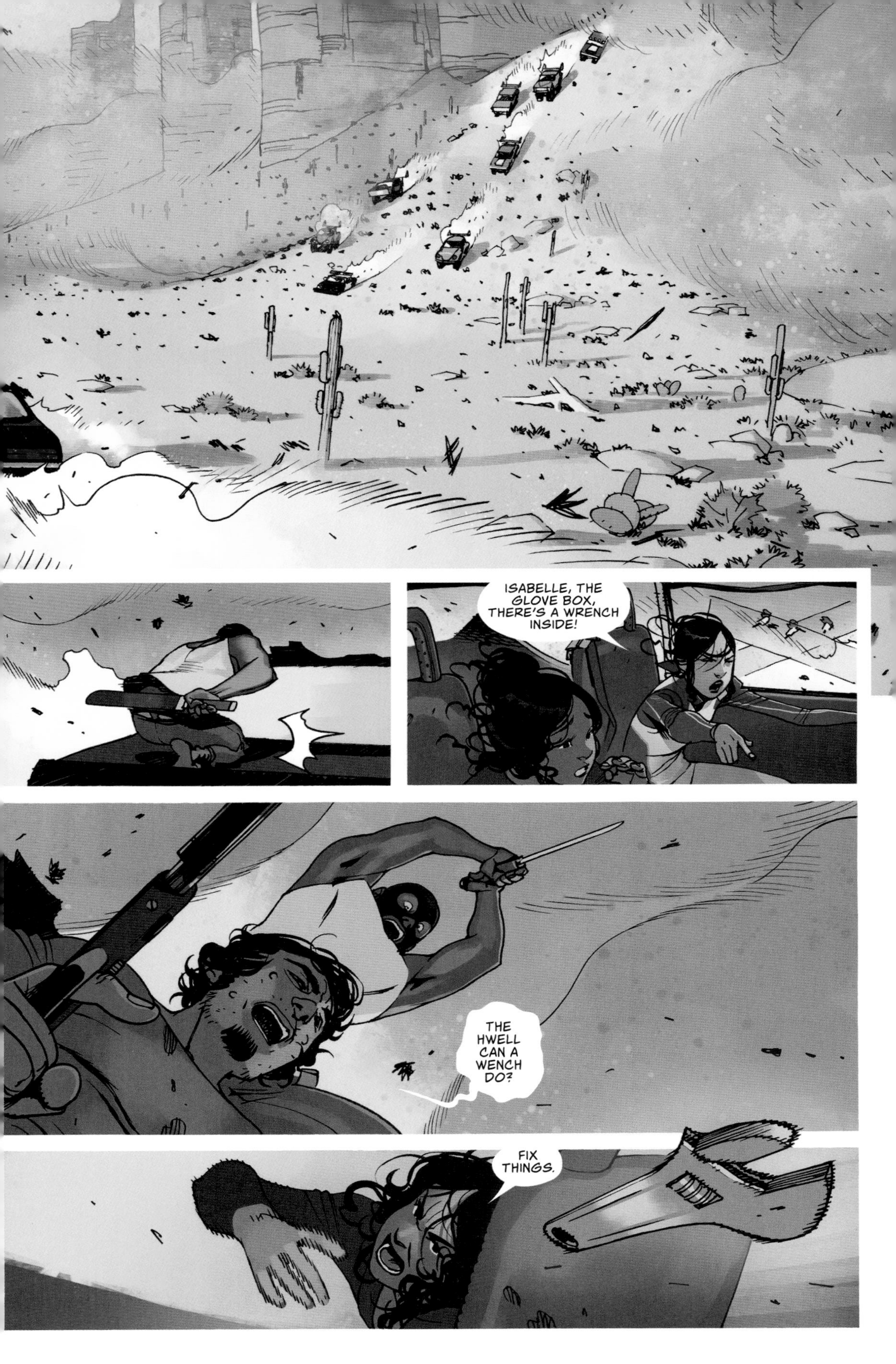
ISABELLE, THE GLOVE BOX, THERE'S A WRENCH INSIDE!
THE HWELL CAN A WENCH DO?
FIX THINGS.

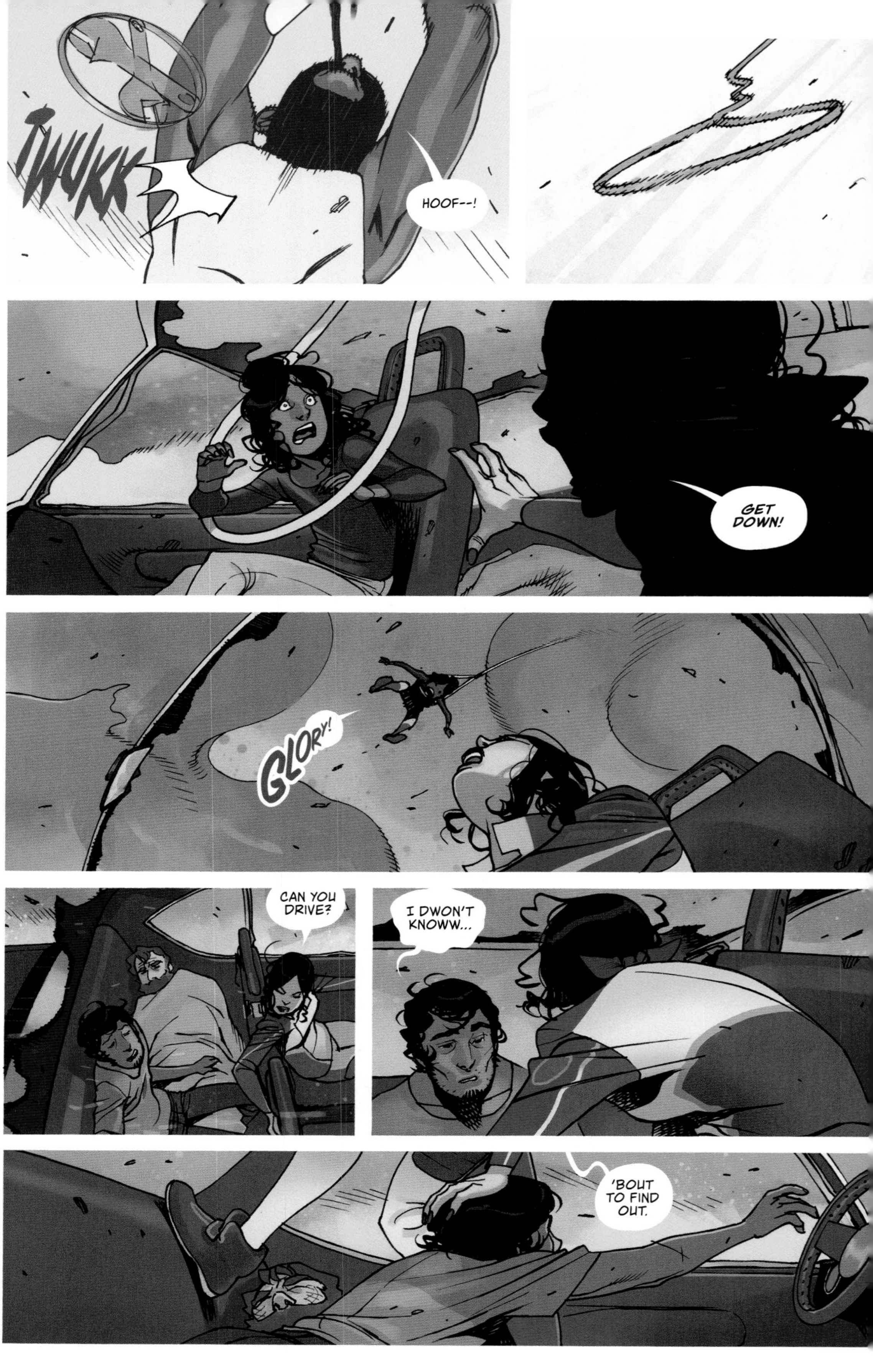
TWUKK
HOOF--!
GET DOWN!
GLORY!
CAN YOU DRIVE?
I DWON'T KNOWW...
'BOUT TO FIND OUT.

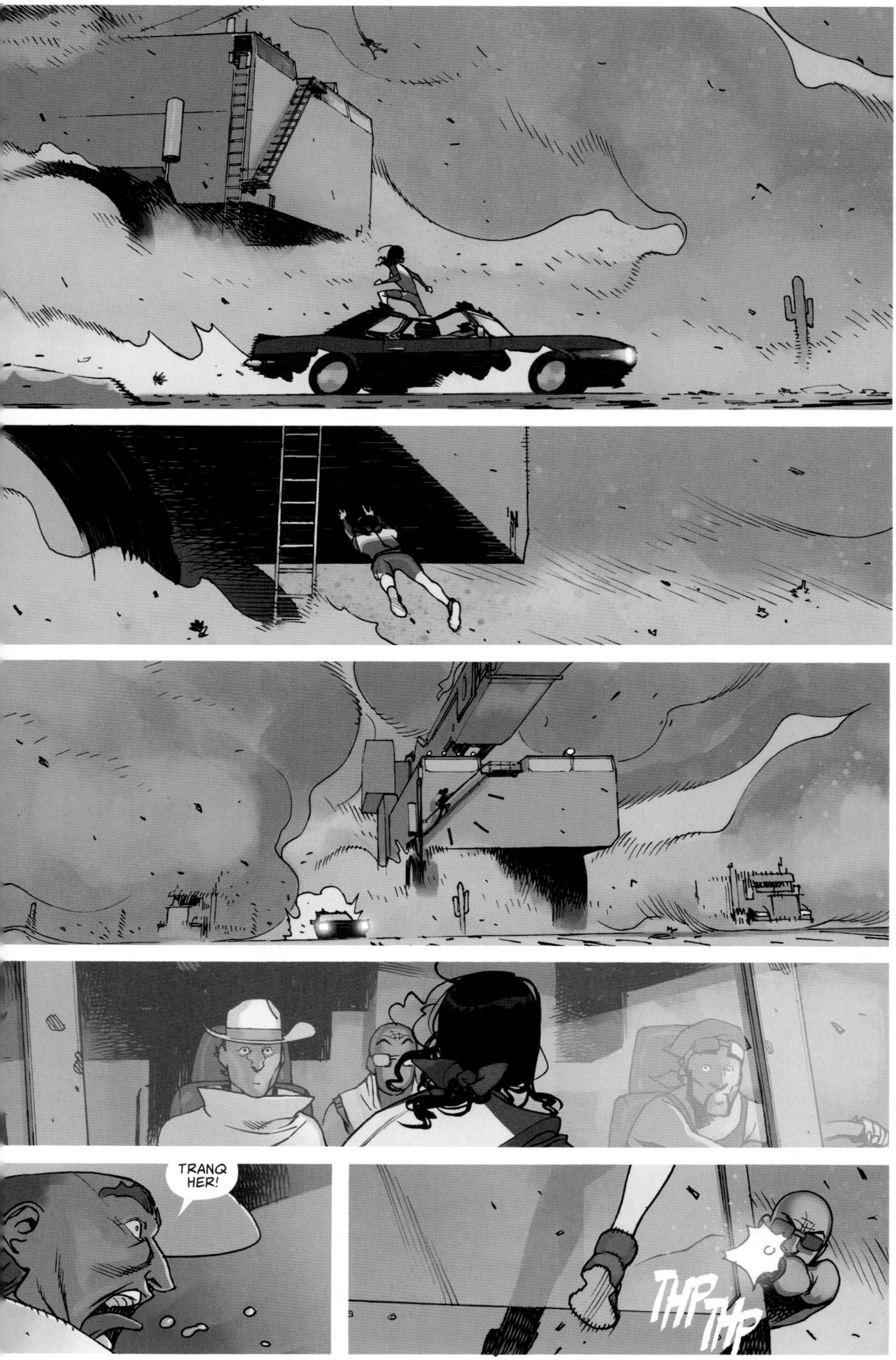
TRANQ HER!
THP THP

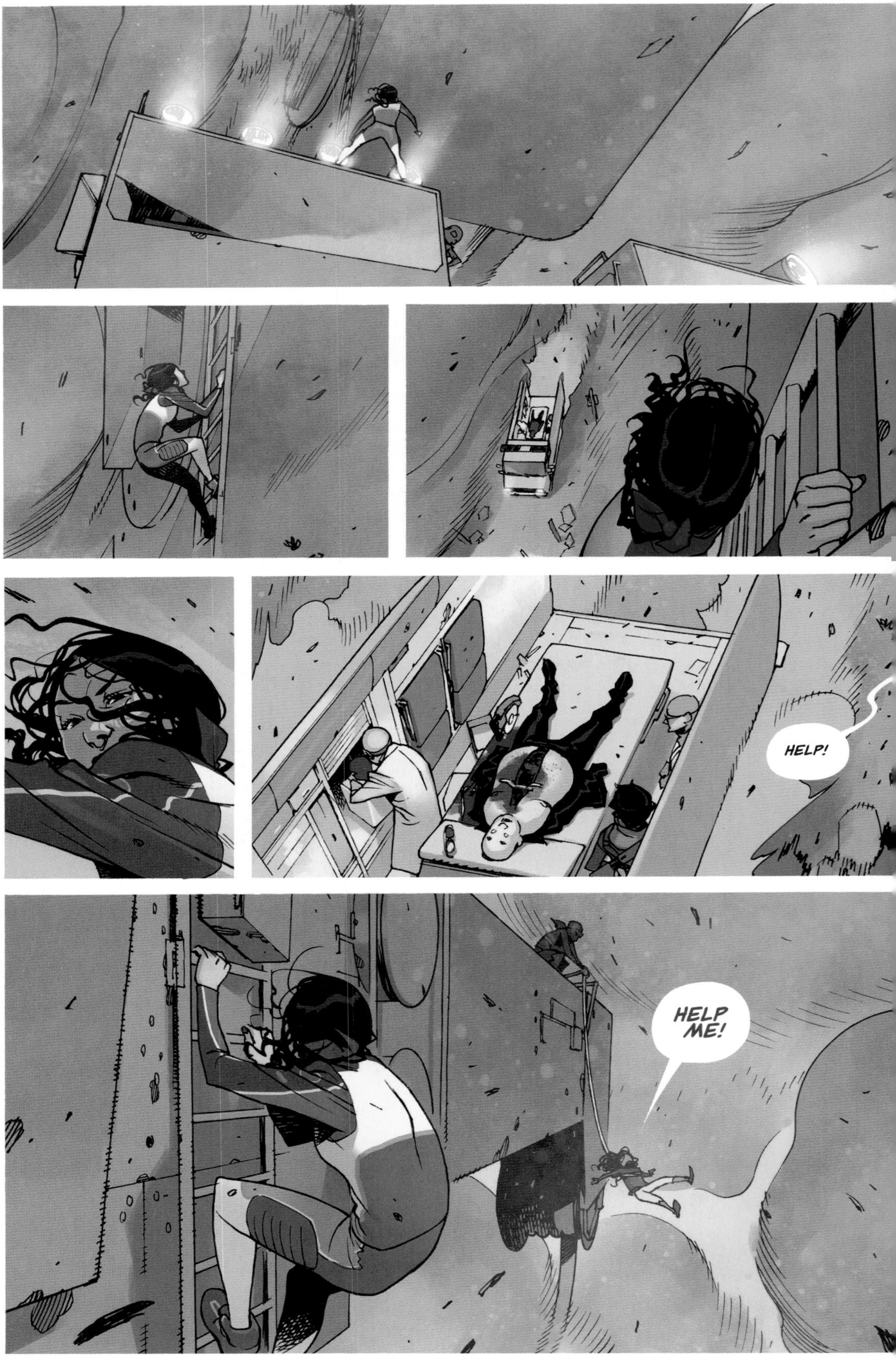
HELP!
HELP ME!

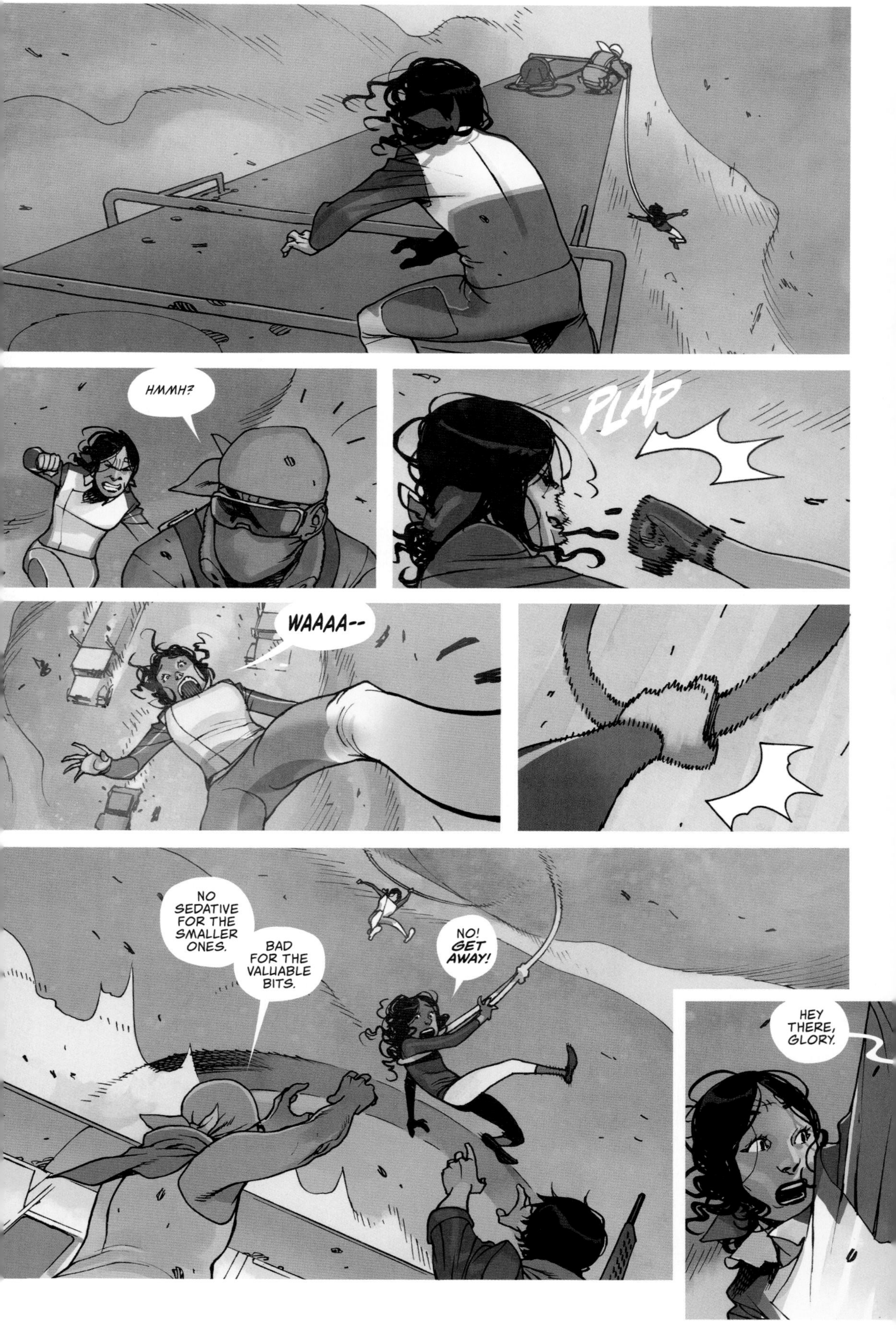
HMMH?
PLAP
WAAAA--
NO SEDATIVE FOR THE SMALLER ONES.
BAD FOR THE VALUABLE BITS.
NO! GET AWAY!
HEY THERE, GLORY.

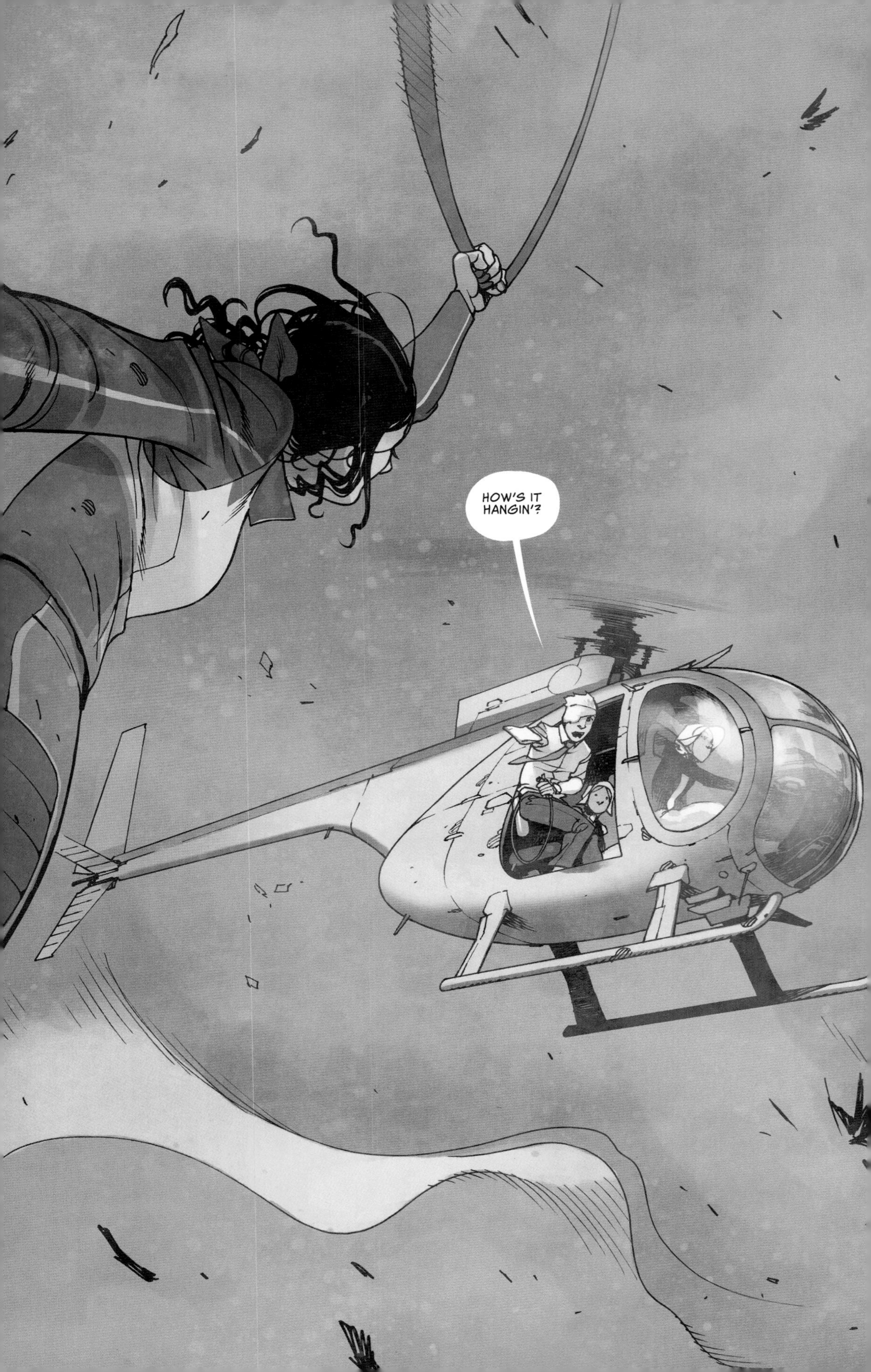
HOW'S IT HANGIN'?

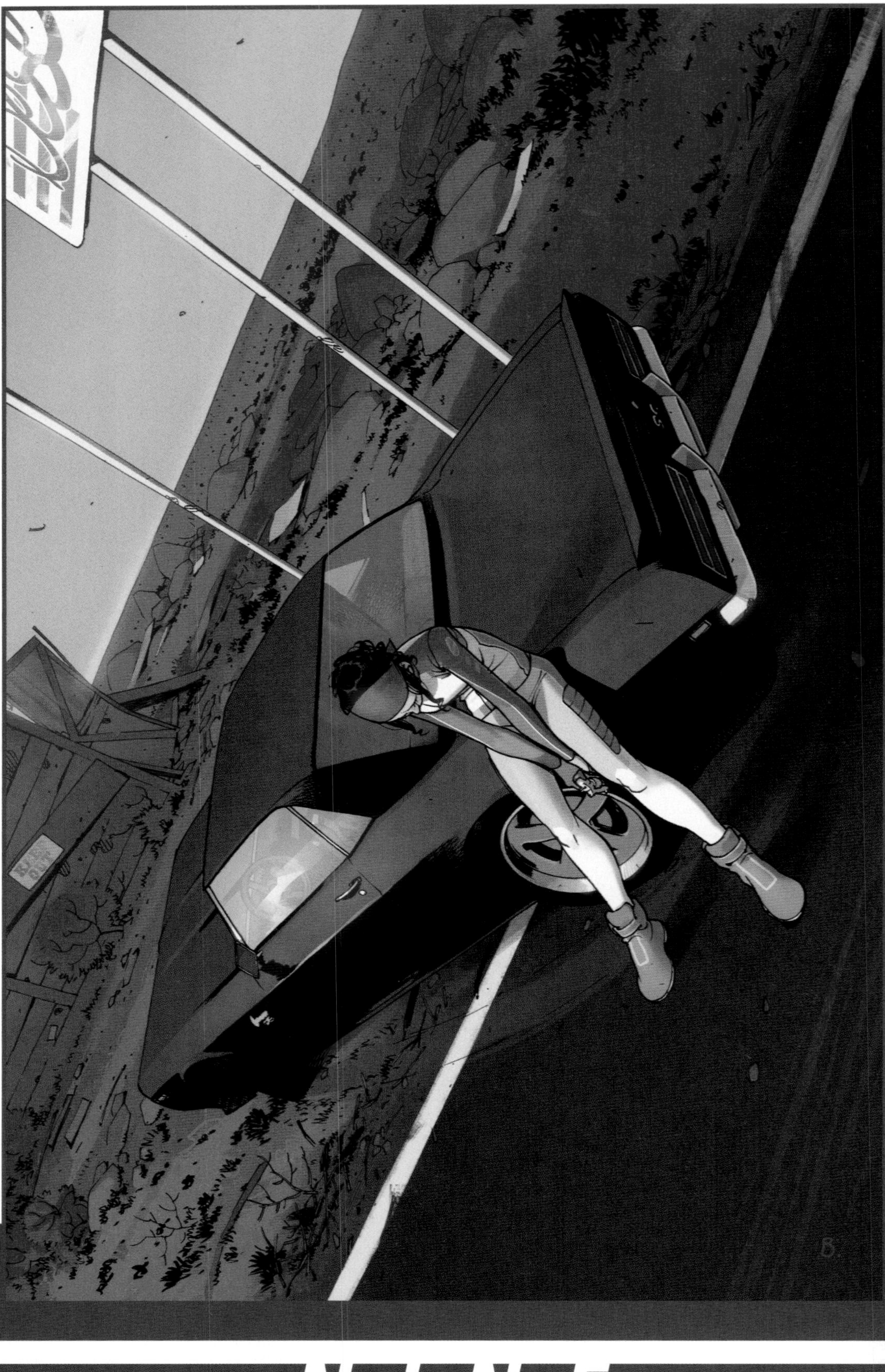

NINE

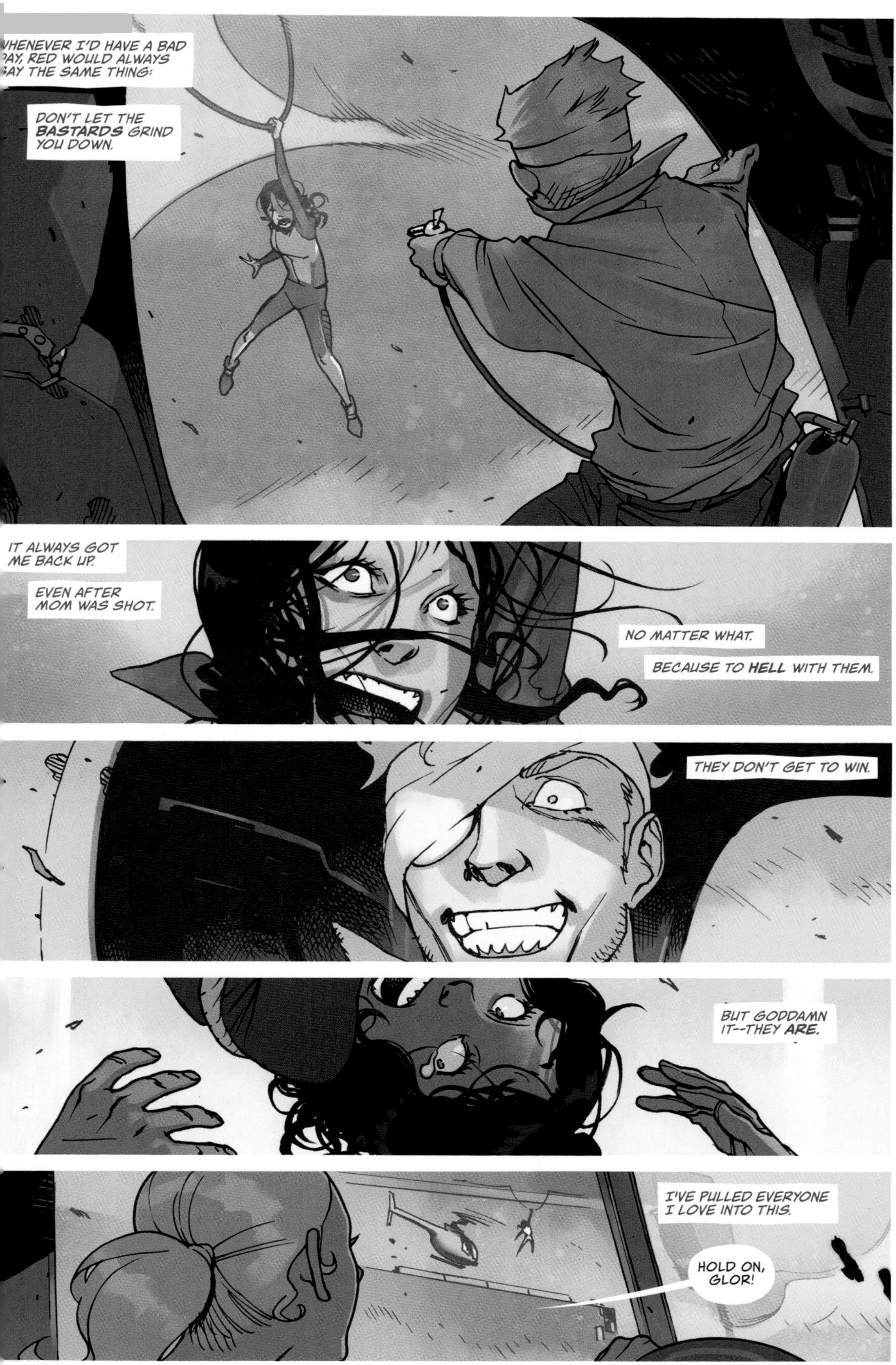
WHENEVER I'D HAVE A BAD DAY, RED WOULD ALWAYS SAY THE SAME THING:
DON'T LET THE BASTARDS GRIND YOU DOWN.
IT ALWAYS GOT ME BACK UP.
EVEN AFTER MOM WAS SHOT.
NO MATTER WHAT.
BECAUSE TO HELL WITH THEM.
THEY DON'T GET TO WIN.
BUT GODDAMN IT--THEY ARE.
I'VE PULLED EVERYONE I LOVE INTO THIS.
HOLD ON, GLOR!

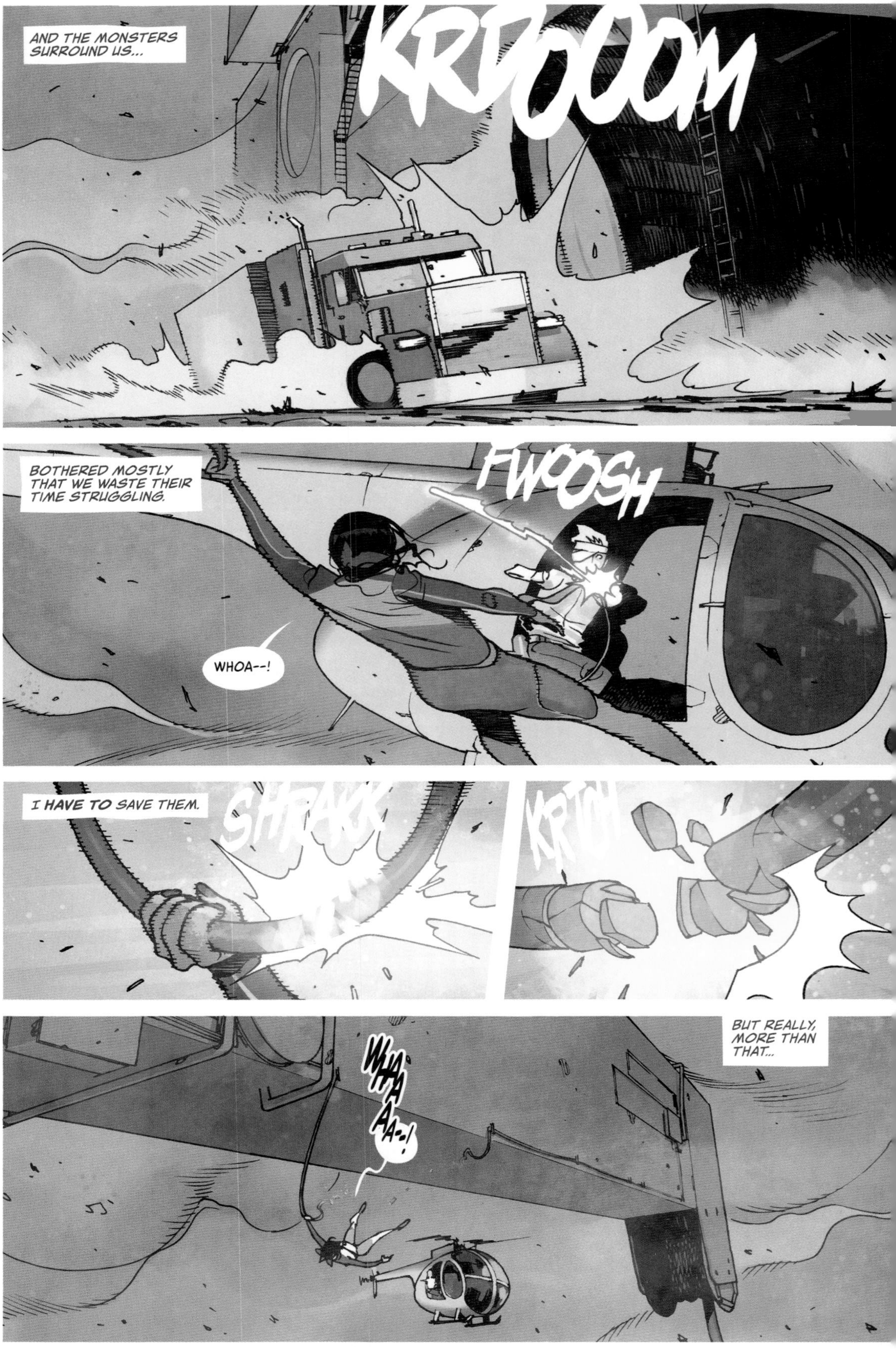
AND THE MONSTERS SURROUND US...
KRDOOOM
BOTHERED MOSTLY THAT WE WASTE THEIR TIME STRUGGLING.
FWOOSH
WHOA--!
I HAVE TO SAVE THEM.
SHRAKK
KRTCH
BUT REALLY, MORE THAN THAT...
WHAAAA--!

HAVE TO PROVE THE BASTARDS **WRONG**.

OOF--!

AHHH!

WHAT THE--

SHARK!

TWAMP

IT'S ALL FUEL IF YOU KNOW HOW TO USE IT.

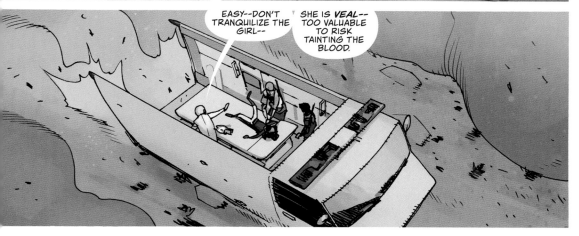

EASY--DON'T TRANQUILIZE THE GIRL--

SHE IS **VEAL**-- TOO VALUABLE TO RISK TAINTING THE BLOOD.

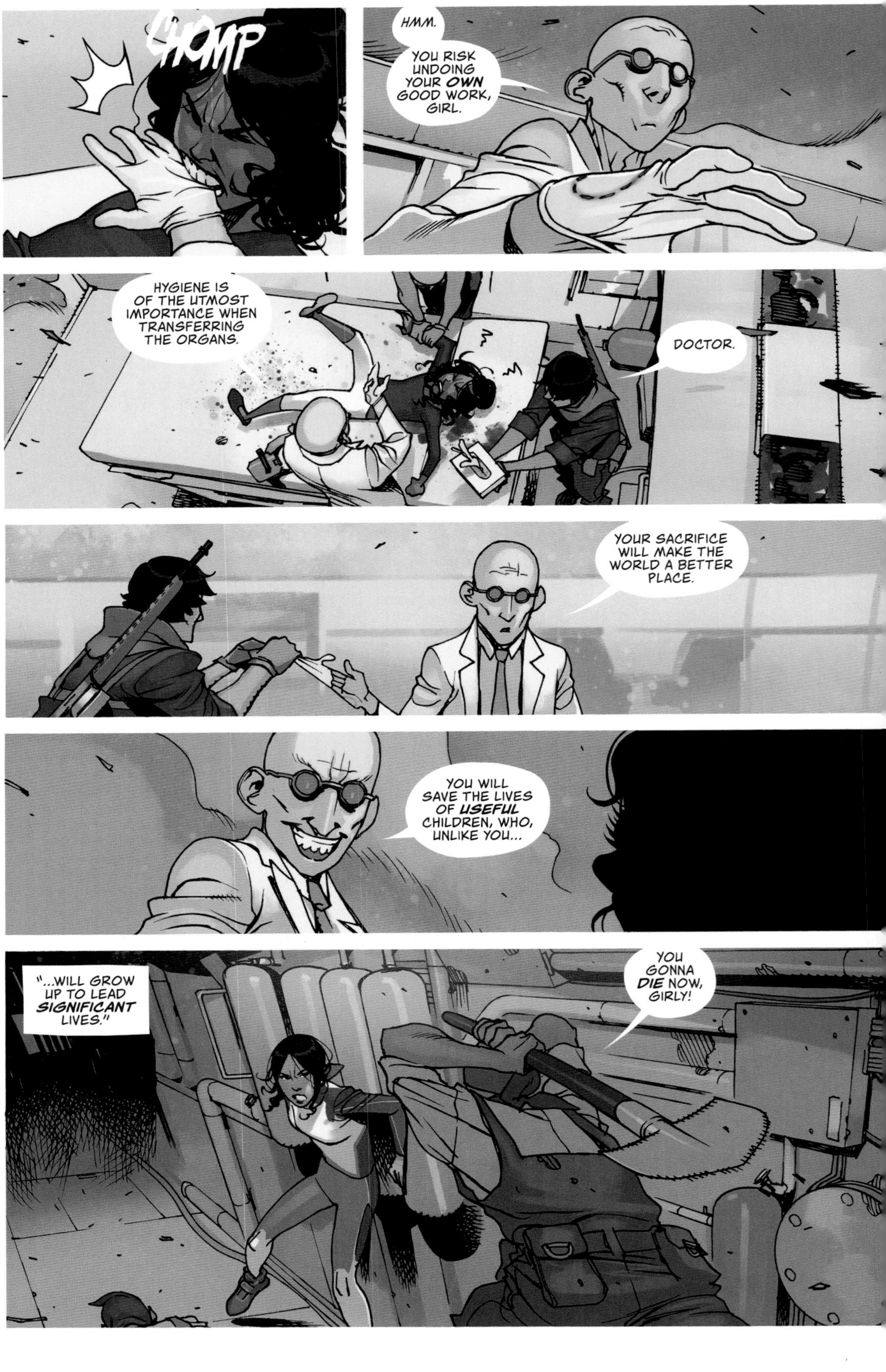
CHOMP
HMM.
YOU RISK UNDOING YOUR OWN GOOD WORK, GIRL.
HYGIENE IS OF THE UTMOST IMPORTANCE WHEN TRANSFERRING THE ORGANS.
DOCTOR.
YOUR SACRIFICE WILL MAKE THE WORLD A BETTER PLACE.
YOU WILL SAVE THE LIVES OF USEFUL CHILDREN, WHO, UNLIKE YOU...
"...WILL GROW UP TO LEAD SIGNIFICANT LIVES."
YOU GONNA DIE NOW, GIRLY!

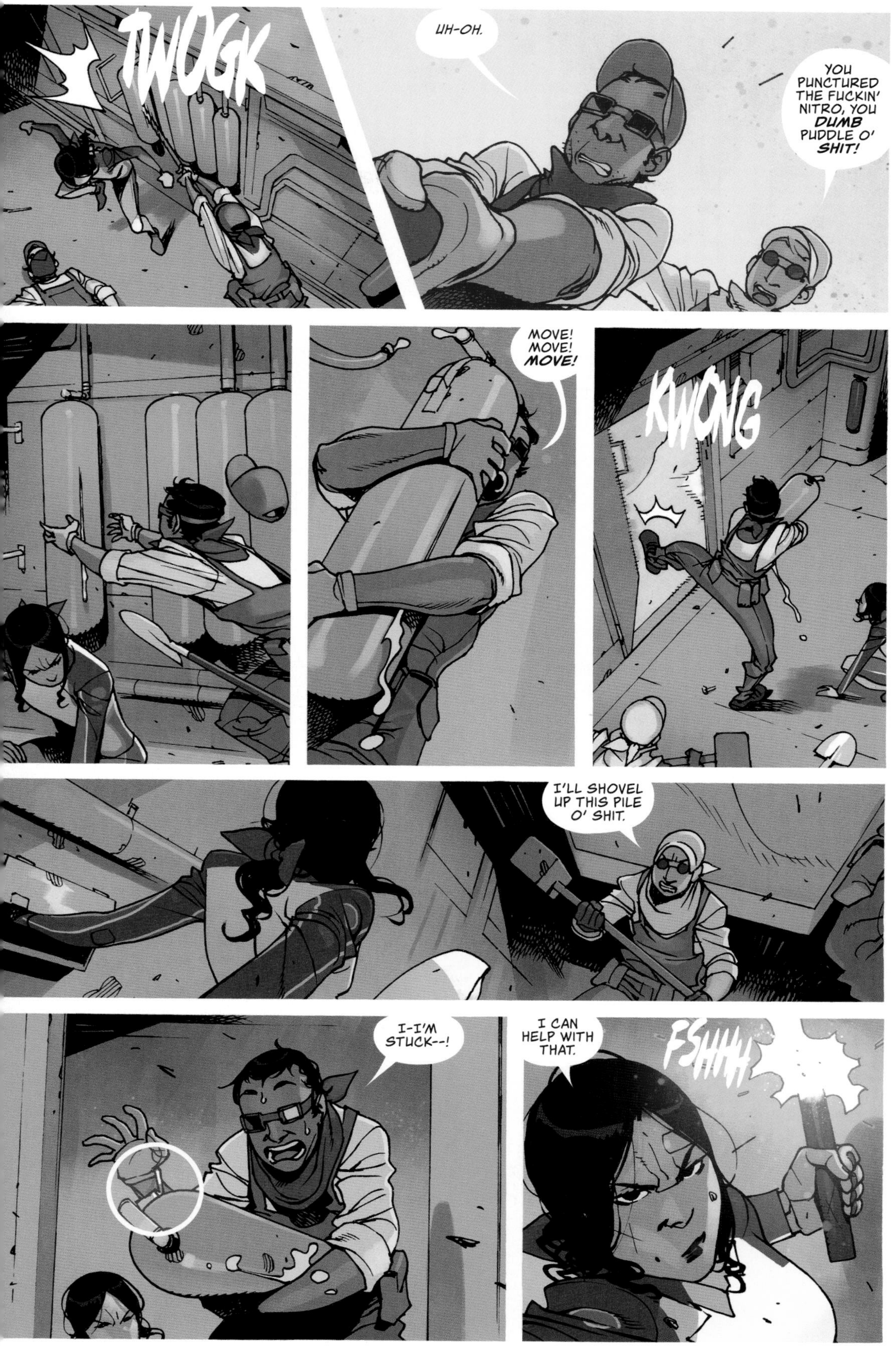
TWOGK
UH-OH.
YOU PUNCTURED THE FUCKIN' NITRO, YOU DUMB PUDDLE O' SHIT!
MOVE! MOVE! MOVE!
KWONG
I'LL SHOVEL UP THIS PILE O' SHIT.
I-I'M STUCK--!
I CAN HELP WITH THAT.
FSHHH

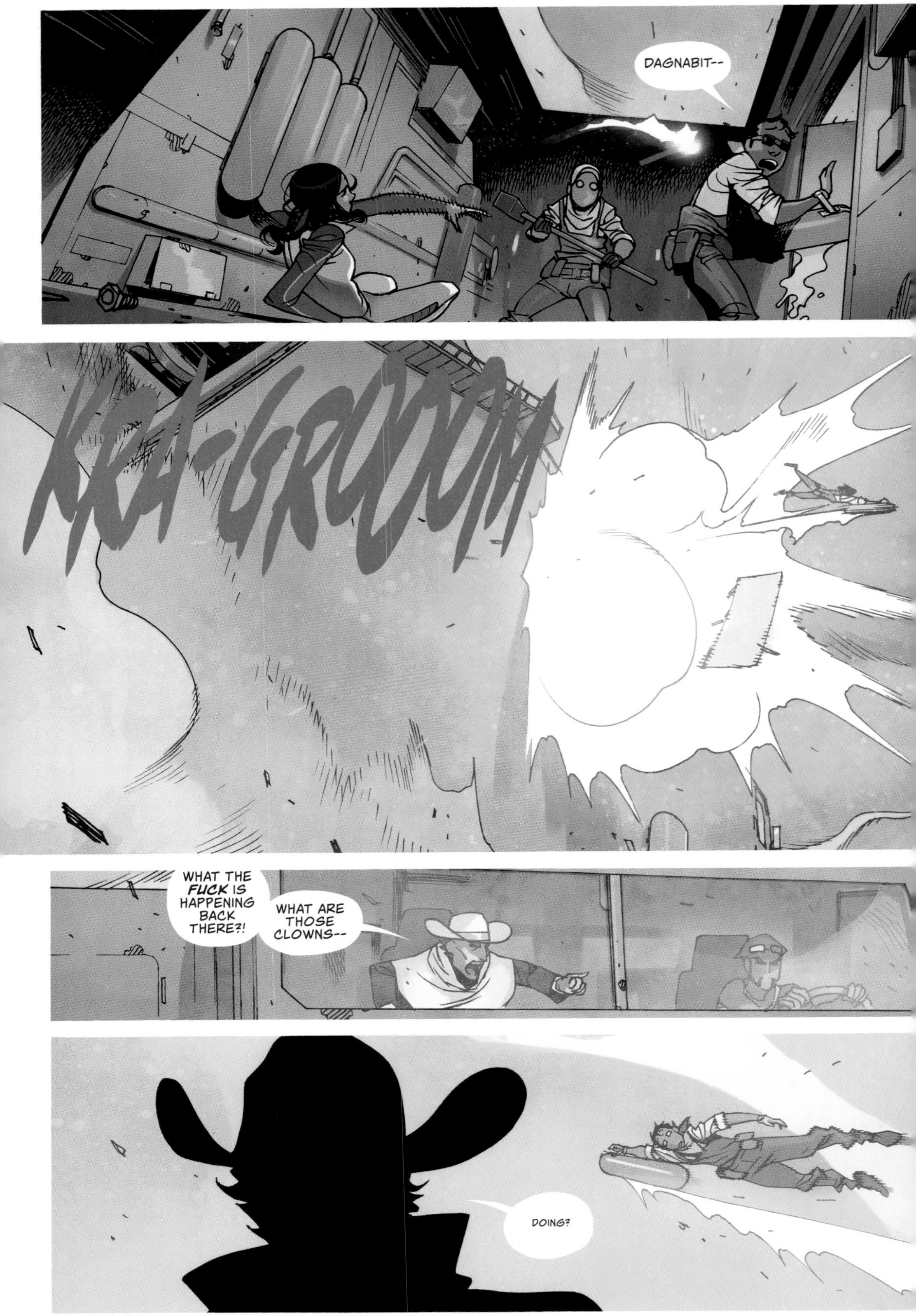
DAGNABIT--
KRA-GROOOM
WHAT THE FUCK IS HAPPENING BACK THERE?!
WHAT ARE THOSE CLOWNS--
DOING?

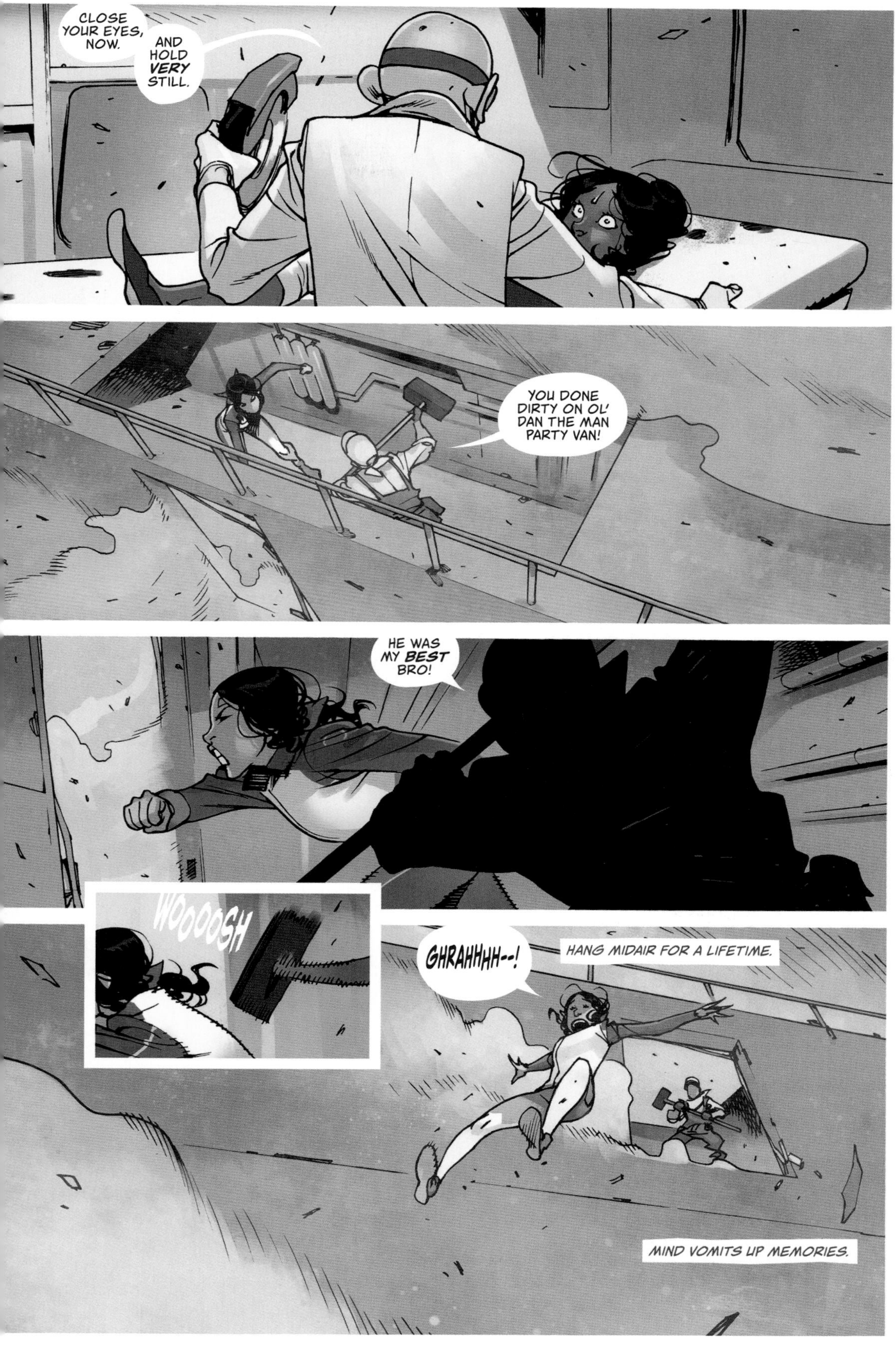
CLOSE YOUR EYES, NOW.
AND HOLD VERY STILL.
YOU DONE DIRTY ON OL' DAN THE MAN PARTY VAN!
HE WAS MY BEST BRO!
WOOOOSH
GHRAHHHH--!
HANG MIDAIR FOR A LIFETIME.
MIND VOMITS UP MEMORIES.

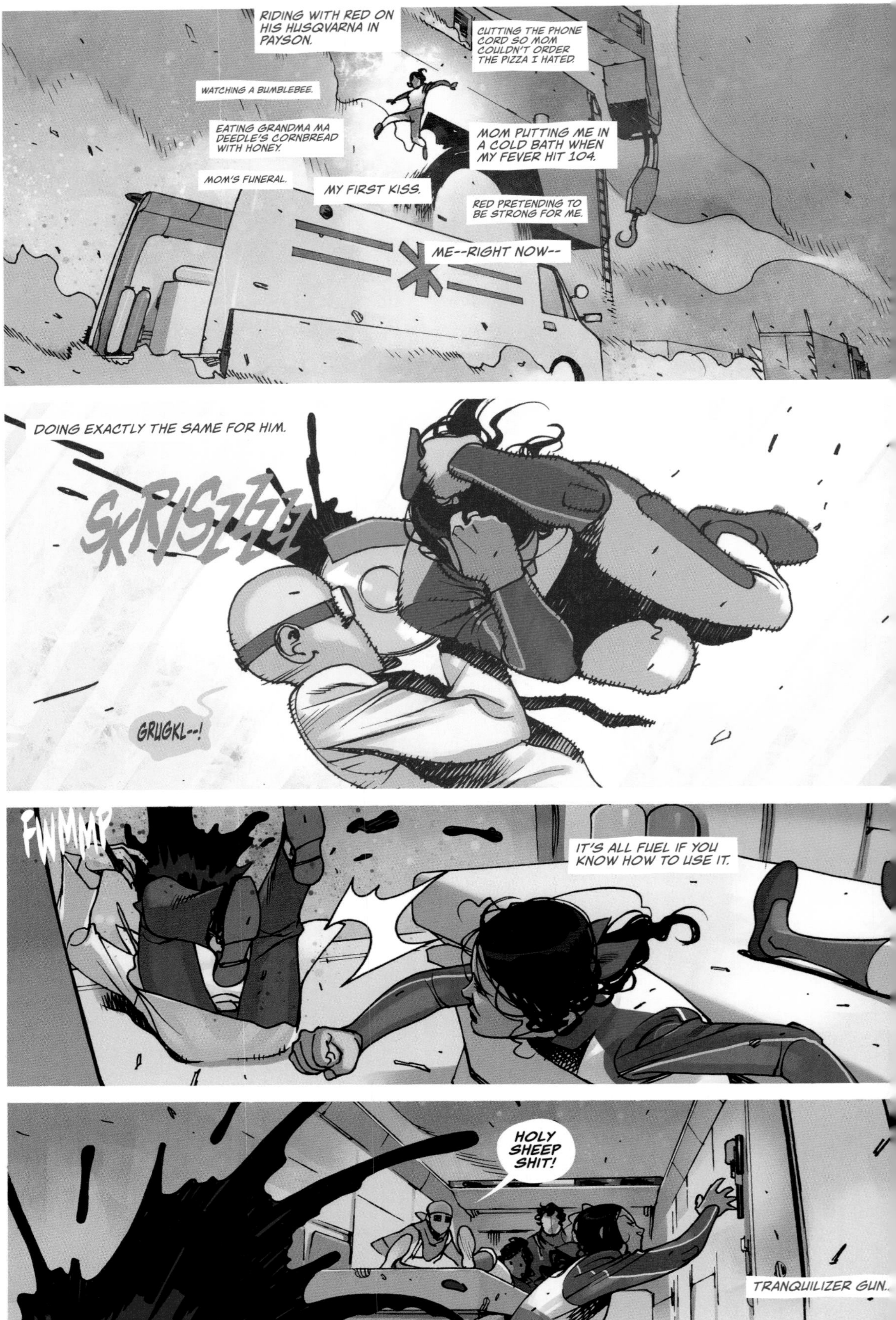
RIDING WITH RED ON HIS HUSQVARNA IN PAYSON.
CUTTING THE PHONE CORD SO MOM COULDN'T ORDER THE PIZZA I HATED.
WATCHING A BUMBLEBEE.
EATING GRANDMA MA DEEDLE'S CORNBREAD WITH HONEY.
MOM PUTTING ME IN A COLD BATH WHEN MY FEVER HIT 104.
MOM'S FUNERAL.
MY FIRST KISS.
RED PRETENDING TO BE STRONG FOR ME.
ME--RIGHT NOW--
DOING EXACTLY THE SAME FOR HIM.
SKRISZZZZ
GRUGKL--!
FWMMP
IT'S ALL FUEL IF YOU KNOW HOW TO USE IT.
HOLY SHEEP SHIT!
TRANQUILIZER GUN.

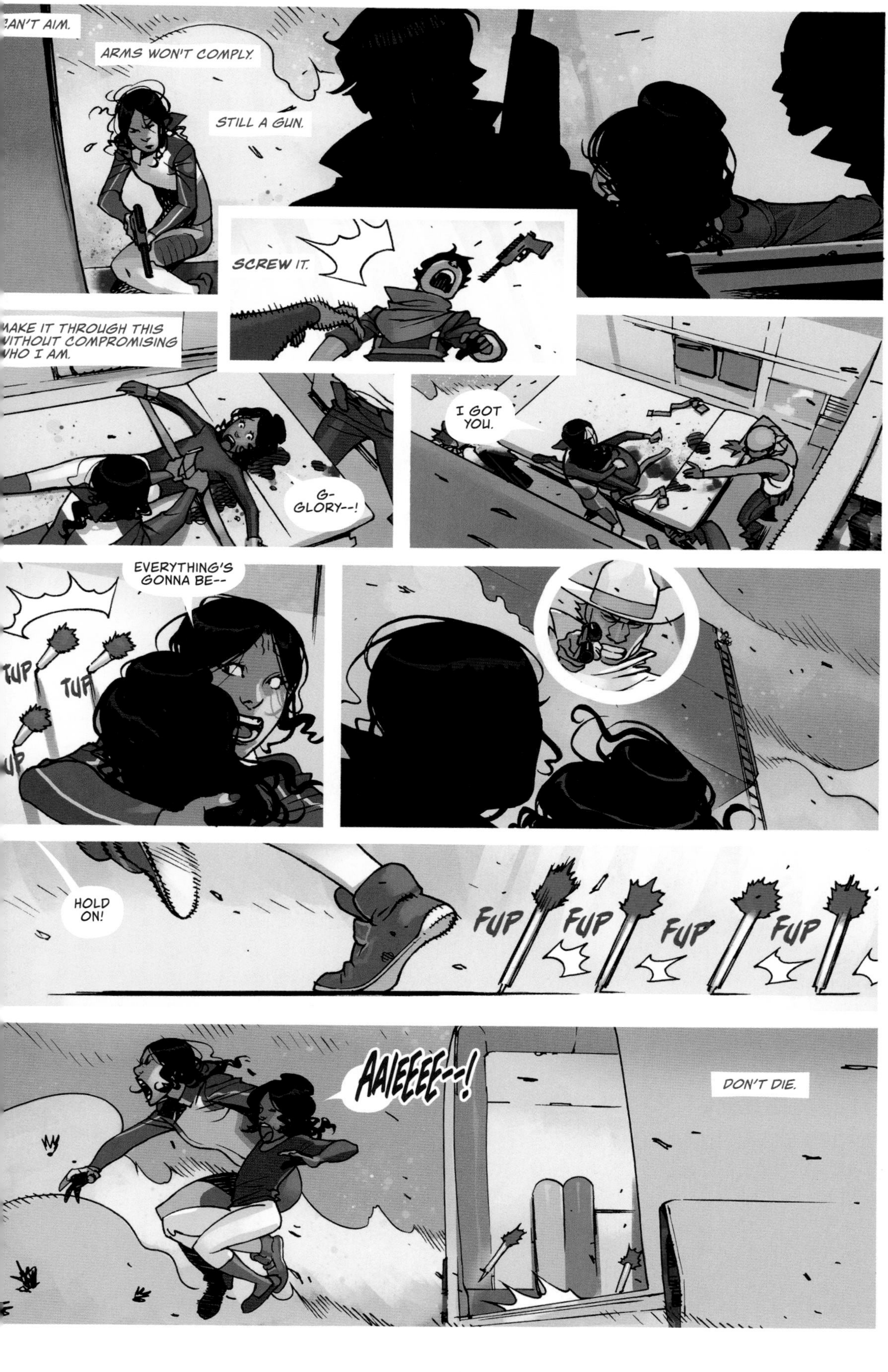

CAN'T AIM.
ARMS WON'T COMPLY.
STILL A GUN.
SCREW IT.
MAKE IT THROUGH THIS WITHOUT COMPROMISING WHO I AM.
G- GLORY--!
I GOT YOU.
EVERYTHING'S GONNA BE--
TUP
TUP
HOLD ON!
FUP
FUP
FUP
FUP
AAIEEEE--!
DON'T DIE.

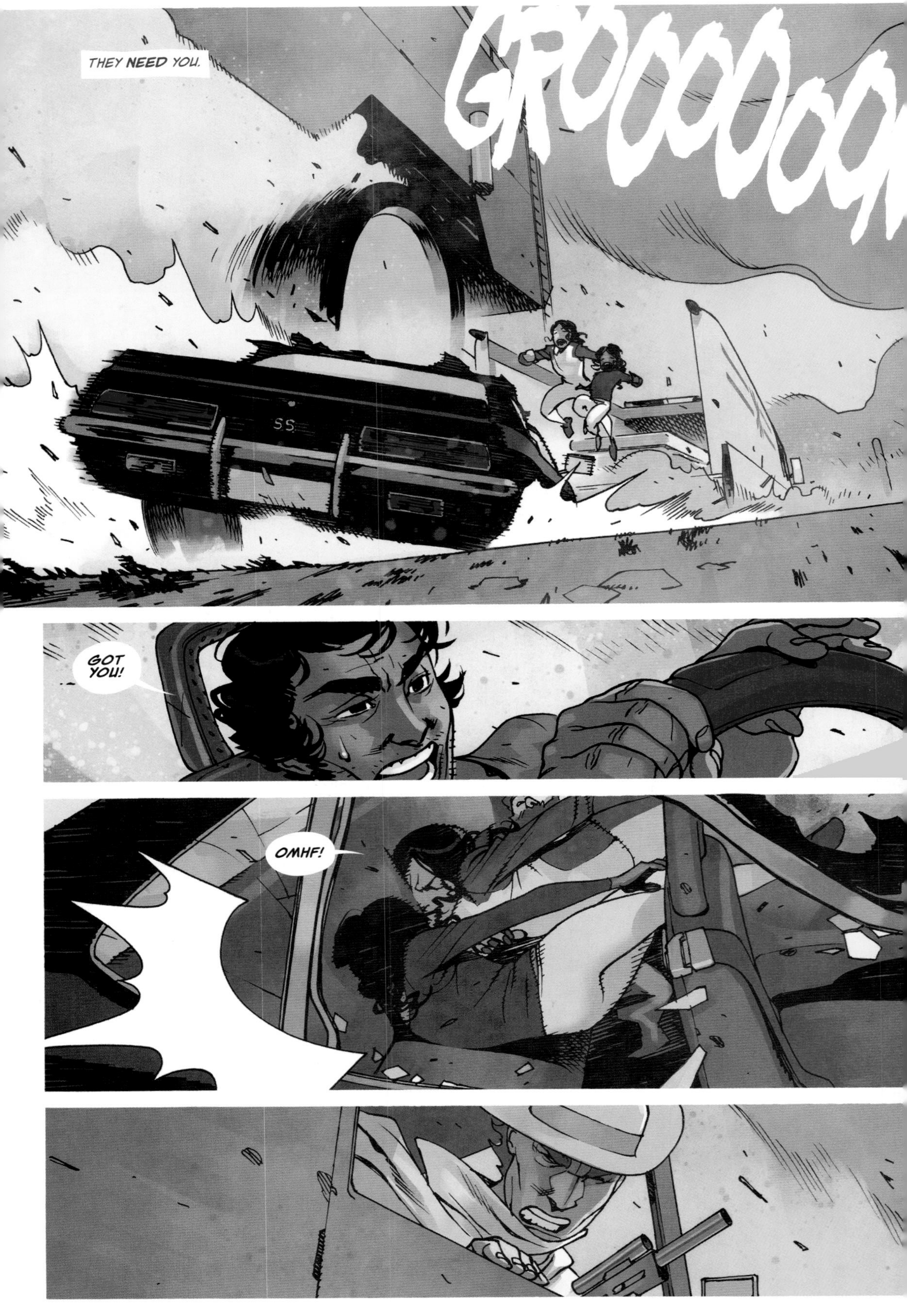
THEY NEED YOU.
GROOOOOOM
S.S.
GOT YOU!
OMHF!

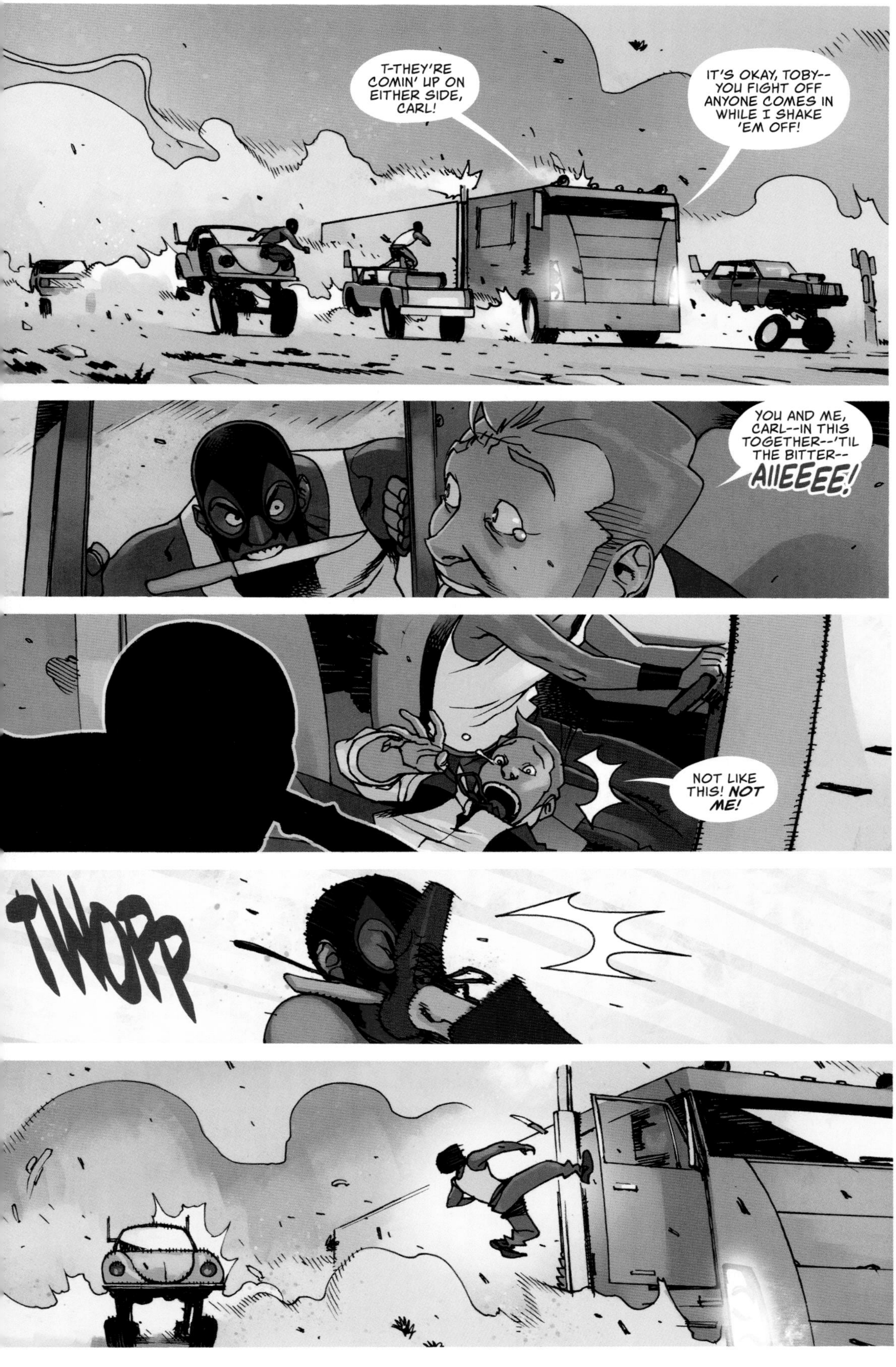
T-THEY'RE COMIN' UP ON EITHER SIDE, CARL!
IT'S OKAY, TOBY-- YOU FIGHT OFF ANYONE COMES IN WHILE I SHAKE 'EM OFF!
YOU AND ME, CARL--IN THIS TOGETHER--'TIL THE BITTER-- AIIEEEE!
NOT LIKE THIS! NOT ME!
TWORP

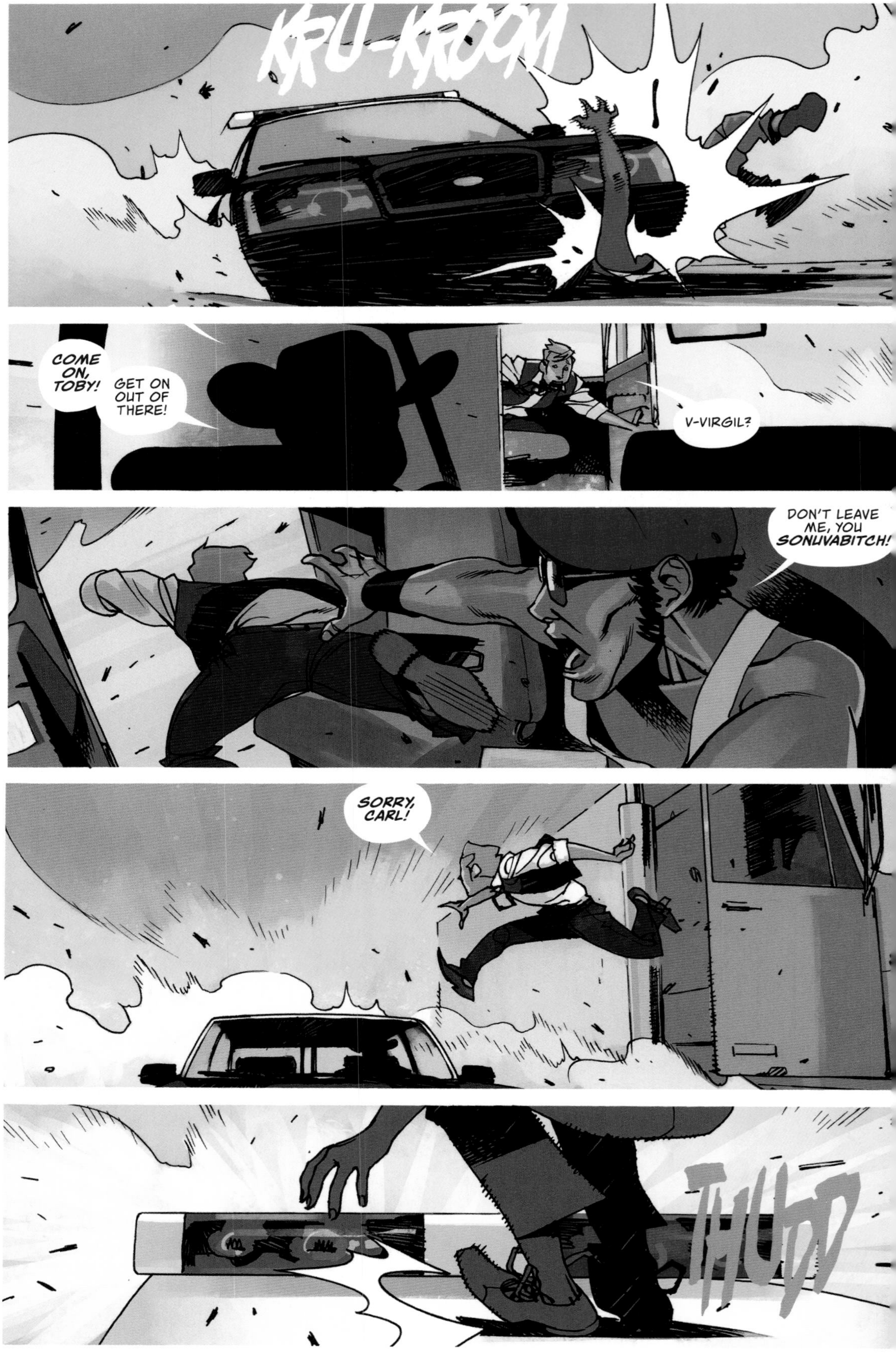
KRU-KROOM
COME ON, TOBY!
GET ON OUT OF THERE!
V-VIRGIL?
DON'T LEAVE ME, YOU SONUVABITCH!
SORRY, CARL!
THUDD

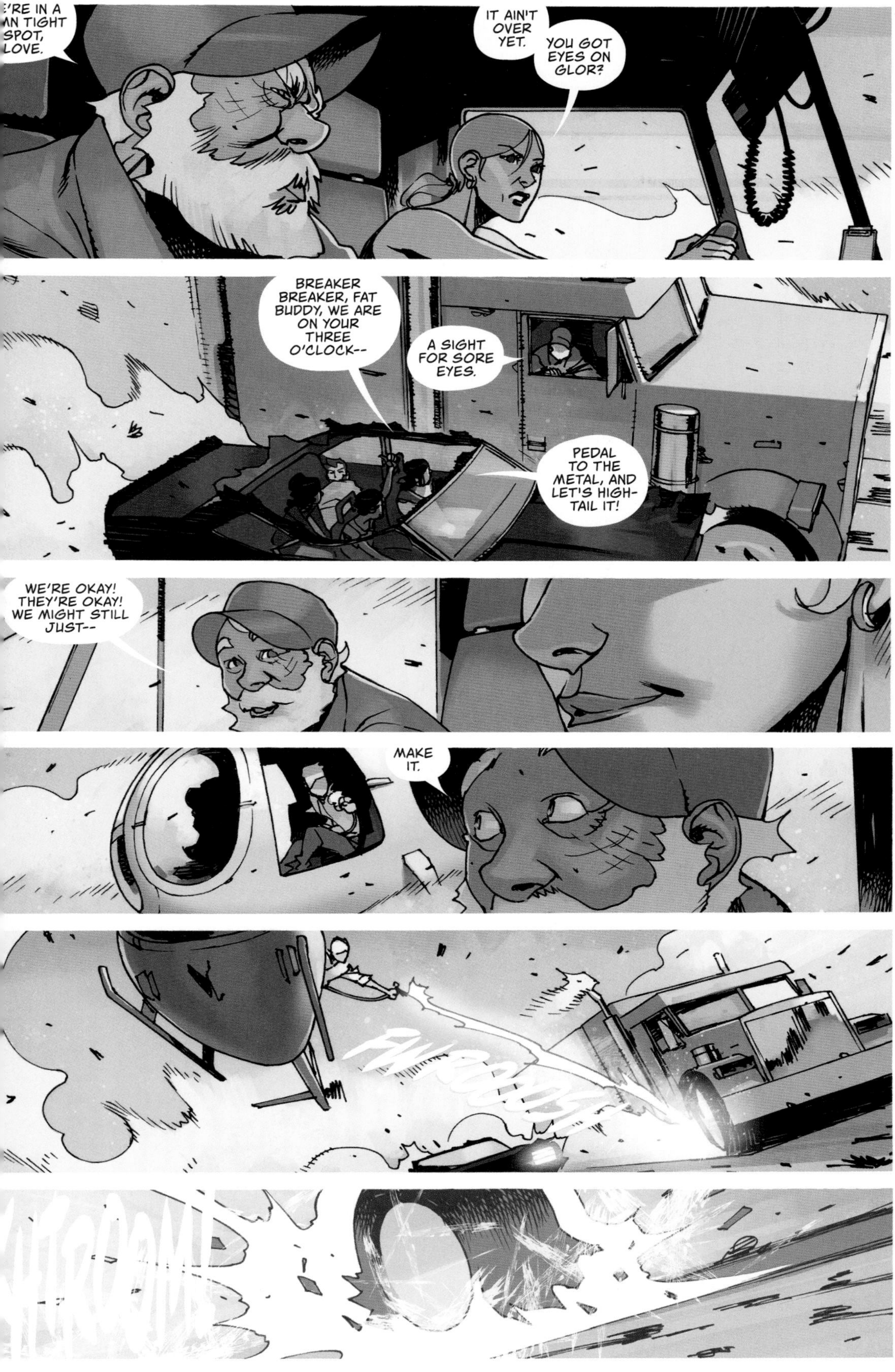
'RE IN A
AN TIGHT
SPOT,
LOVE.
IT AIN'T OVER YET.
YOU GOT EYES ON GLOR?
BREAKER BREAKER, FAT BUDDY, WE ARE ON YOUR THREE O'CLOCK--
A SIGHT FOR SORE EYES.
PEDAL TO THE METAL, AND LET'S HIGH-TAIL IT!
WE'RE OKAY! THEY'RE OKAY! WE MIGHT STILL JUST--
MAKE IT.

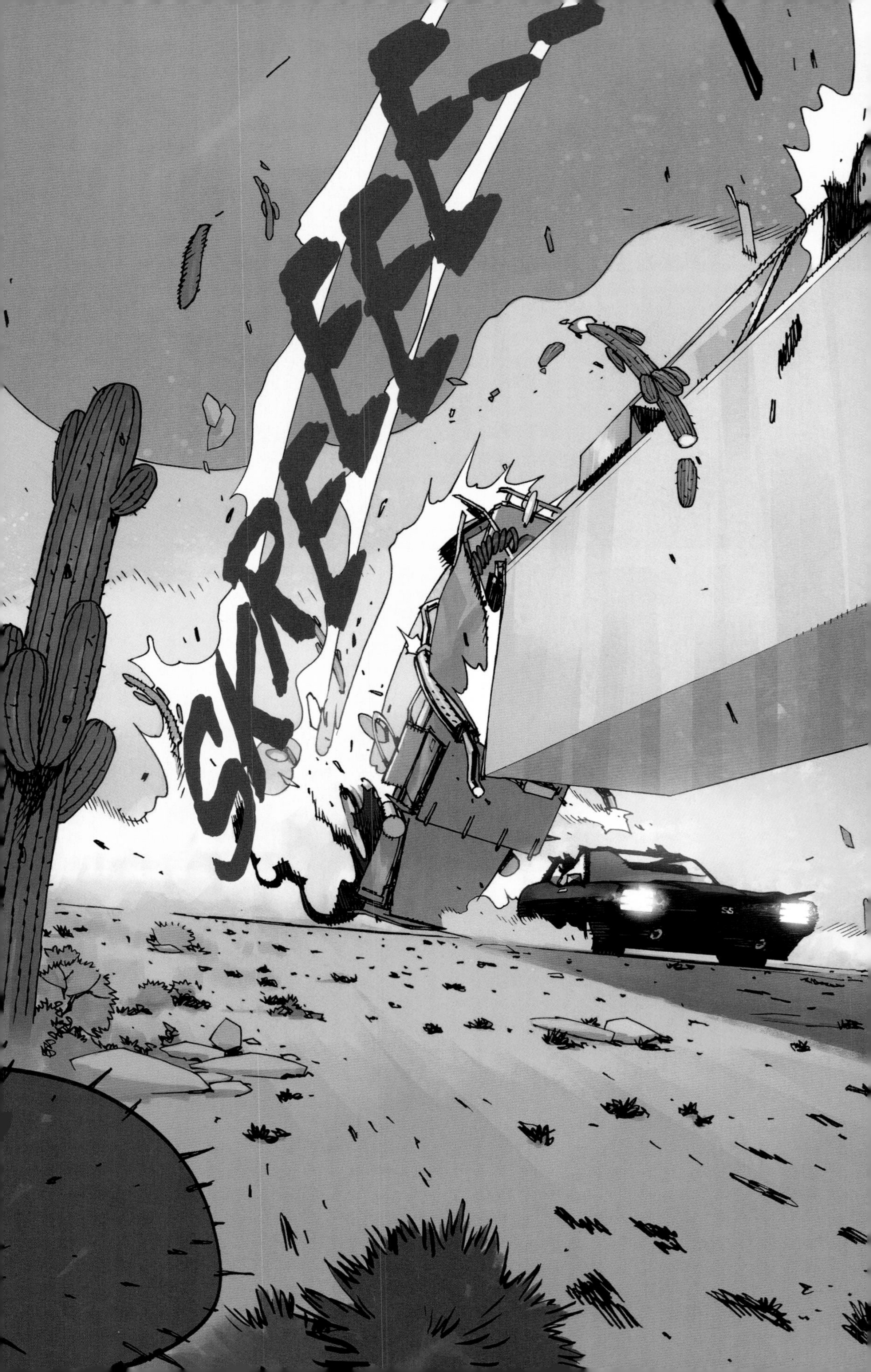
SKREEE—

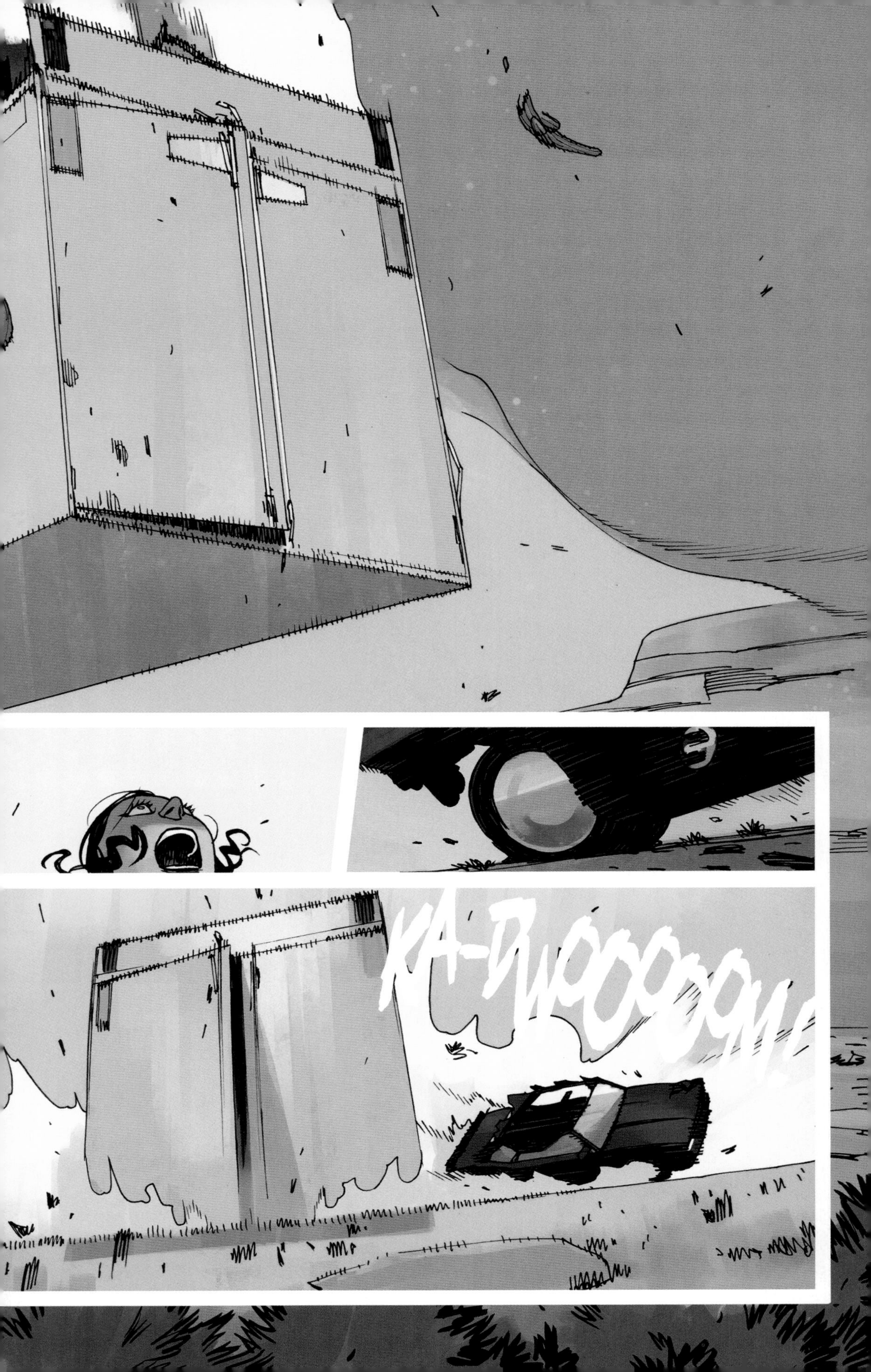
KA-DWOOOOOM

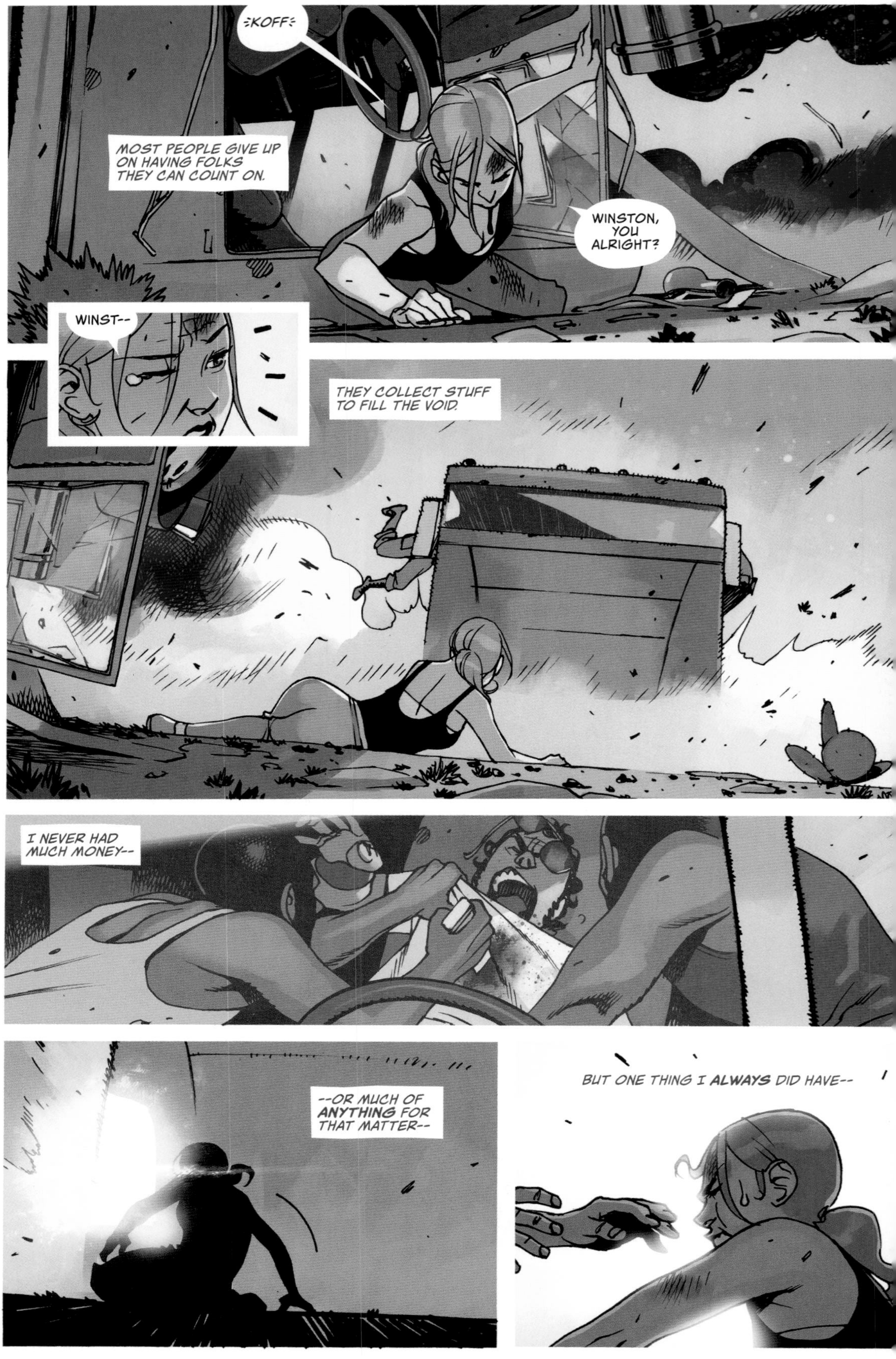

KOFF
MOST PEOPLE GIVE UP ON HAVING FOLKS THEY CAN COUNT ON.
WINSTON, YOU ALRIGHT?
WINST--
THEY COLLECT STUFF TO FILL THE VOID.
I NEVER HAD MUCH MONEY--
--OR MUCH OF ANYTHING FOR THAT MATTER--
BUT ONE THING I ALWAYS DID HAVE--

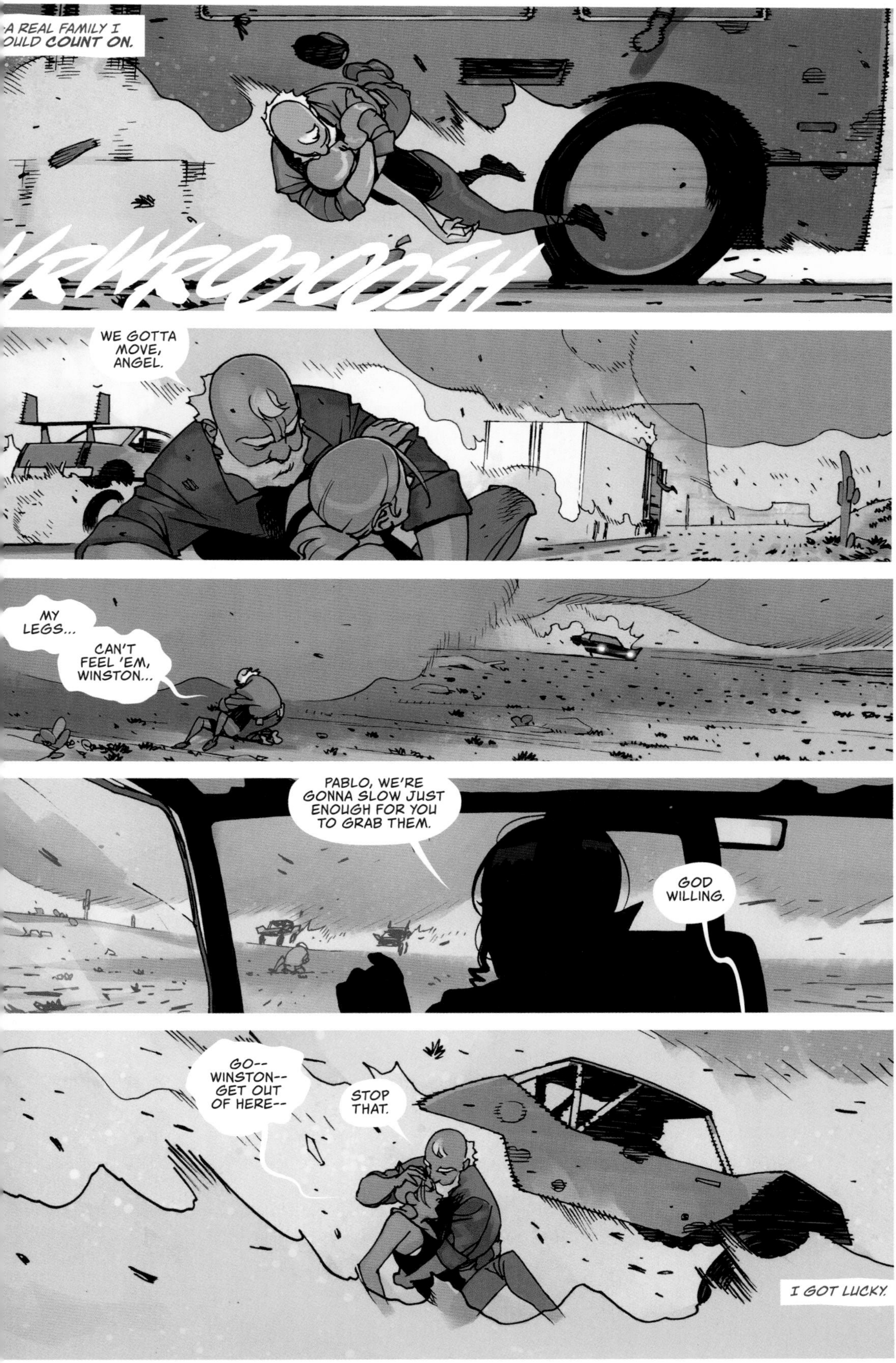
A REAL FAMILY I
OULD COUNT ON.
RWRRROOOSH
WE GOTTA MOVE, ANGEL.
MY LEGS...
CAN'T FEEL 'EM, WINSTON...
PABLO, WE'RE GONNA SLOW JUST ENOUGH FOR YOU TO GRAB THEM.
GOD WILLING.
GO-- WINSTON-- GET OUT OF HERE--
STOP THAT.
I GOT LUCKY.

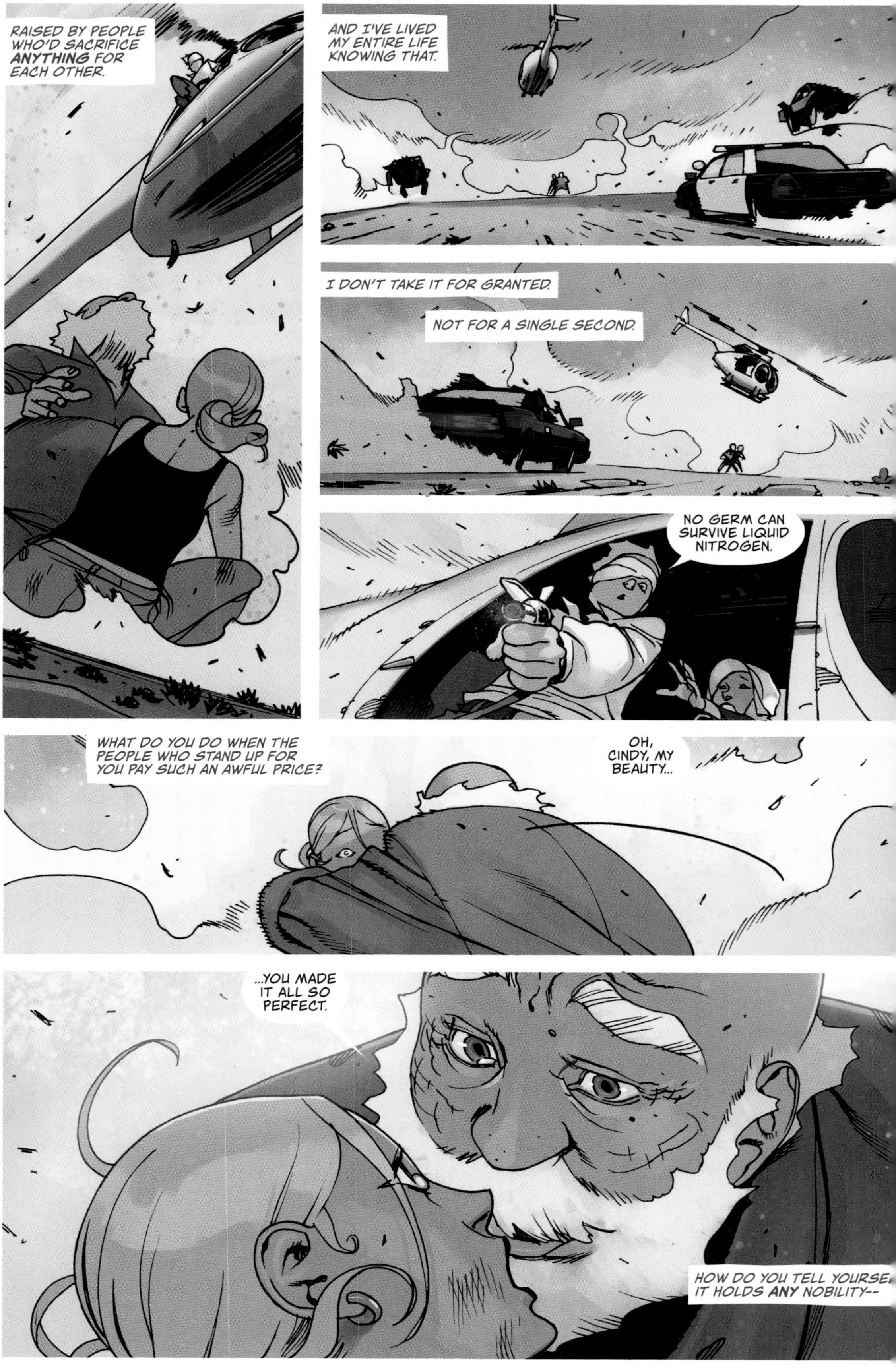
RAISED BY PEOPLE WHO'D SACRIFICE **ANYTHING** FOR EACH OTHER.
AND I'VE LIVED MY ENTIRE LIFE KNOWING THAT.
I DON'T TAKE IT FOR GRANTED.
NOT FOR A SINGLE SECOND.
NO GERM CAN SURVIVE LIQUID NITROGEN.
WHAT DO YOU DO WHEN THE PEOPLE WHO STAND UP FOR YOU PAY SUCH AN AWFUL PRICE?
OH, CINDY, MY BEAUTY...
...YOU MADE IT ALL SO PERFECT.
HOW DO YOU TELL YOURSE
IT HOLDS **ANY** NOBILITY--

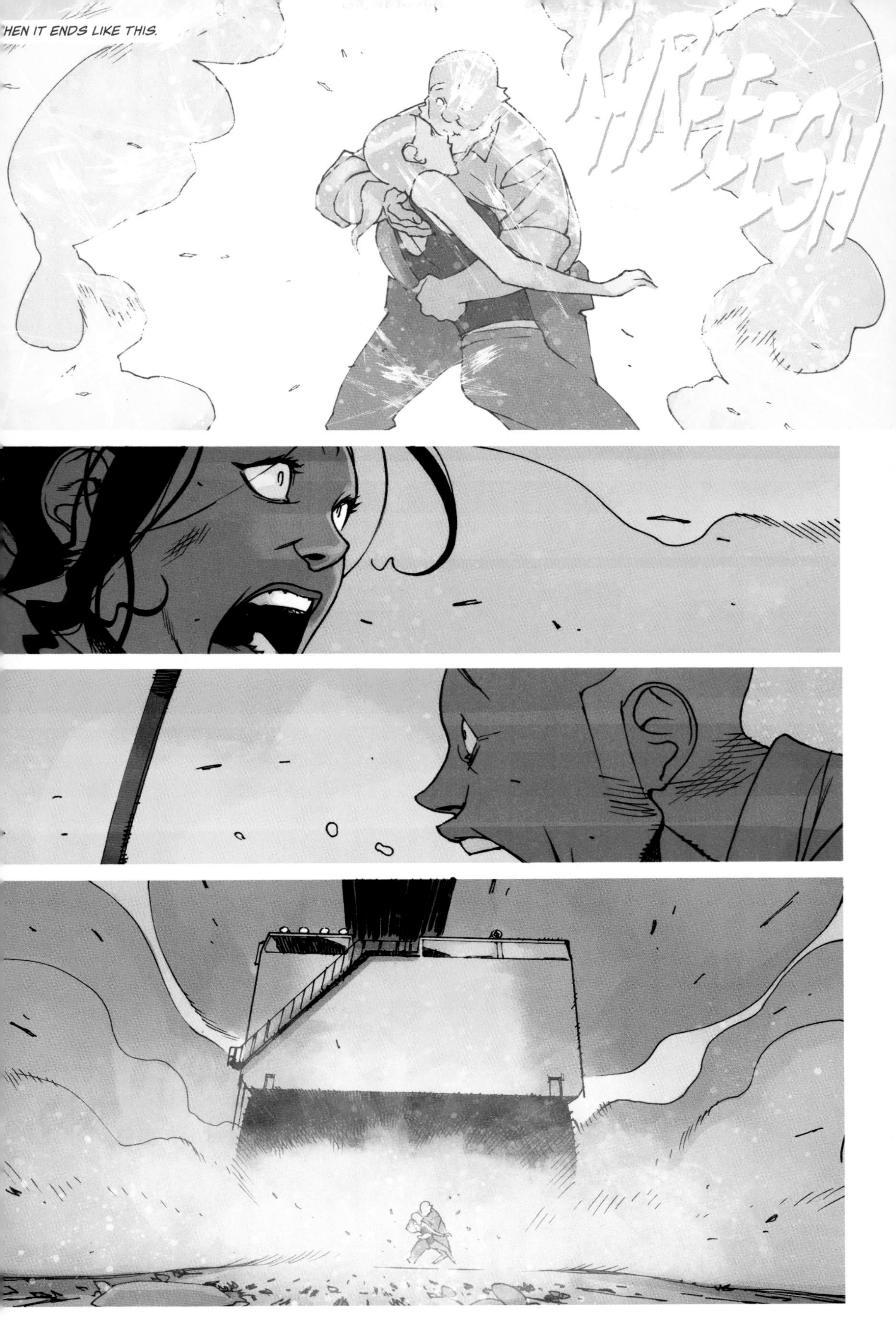
HEN IT ENDS LIKE THIS.
KHREEESH

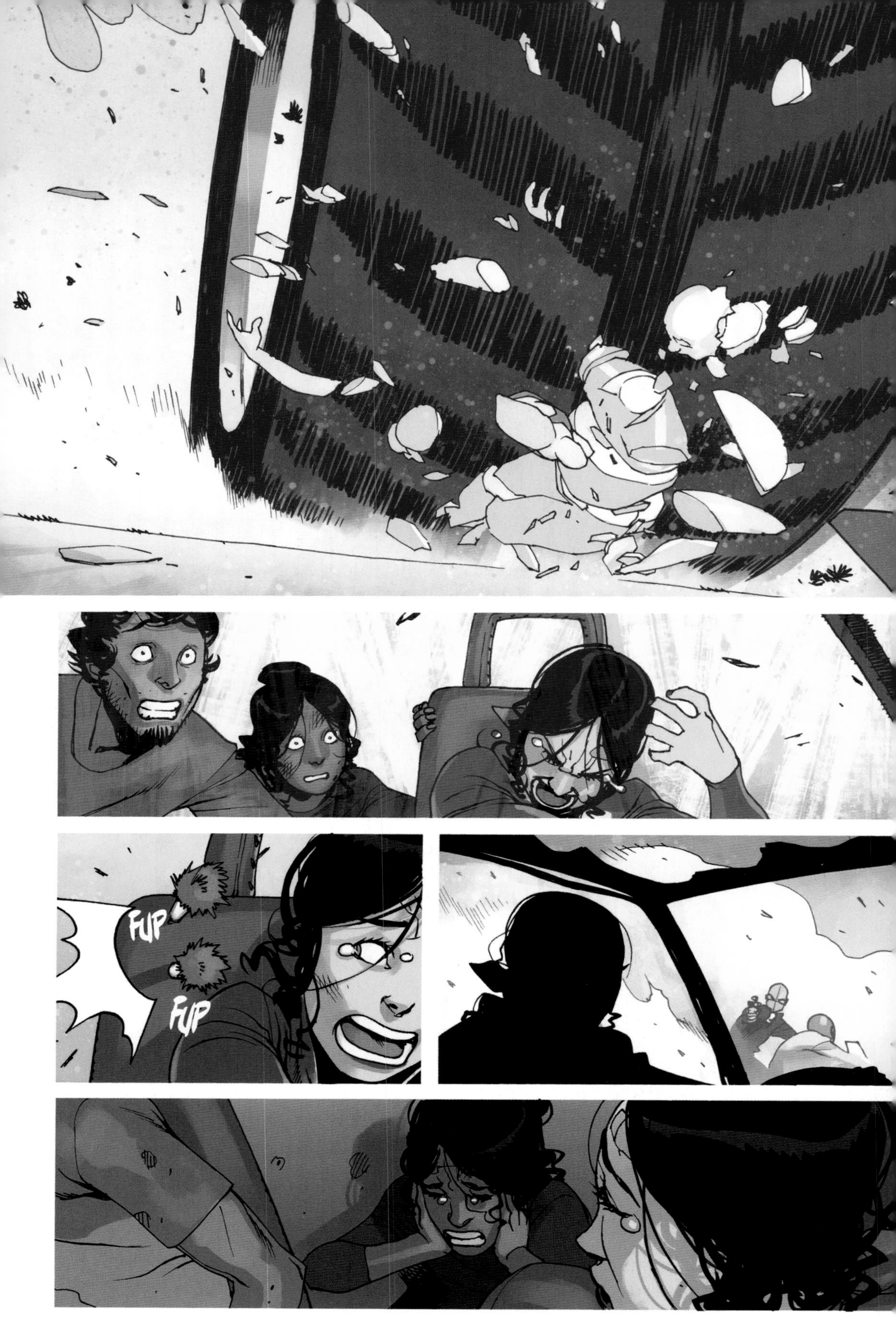
FUP
FUP

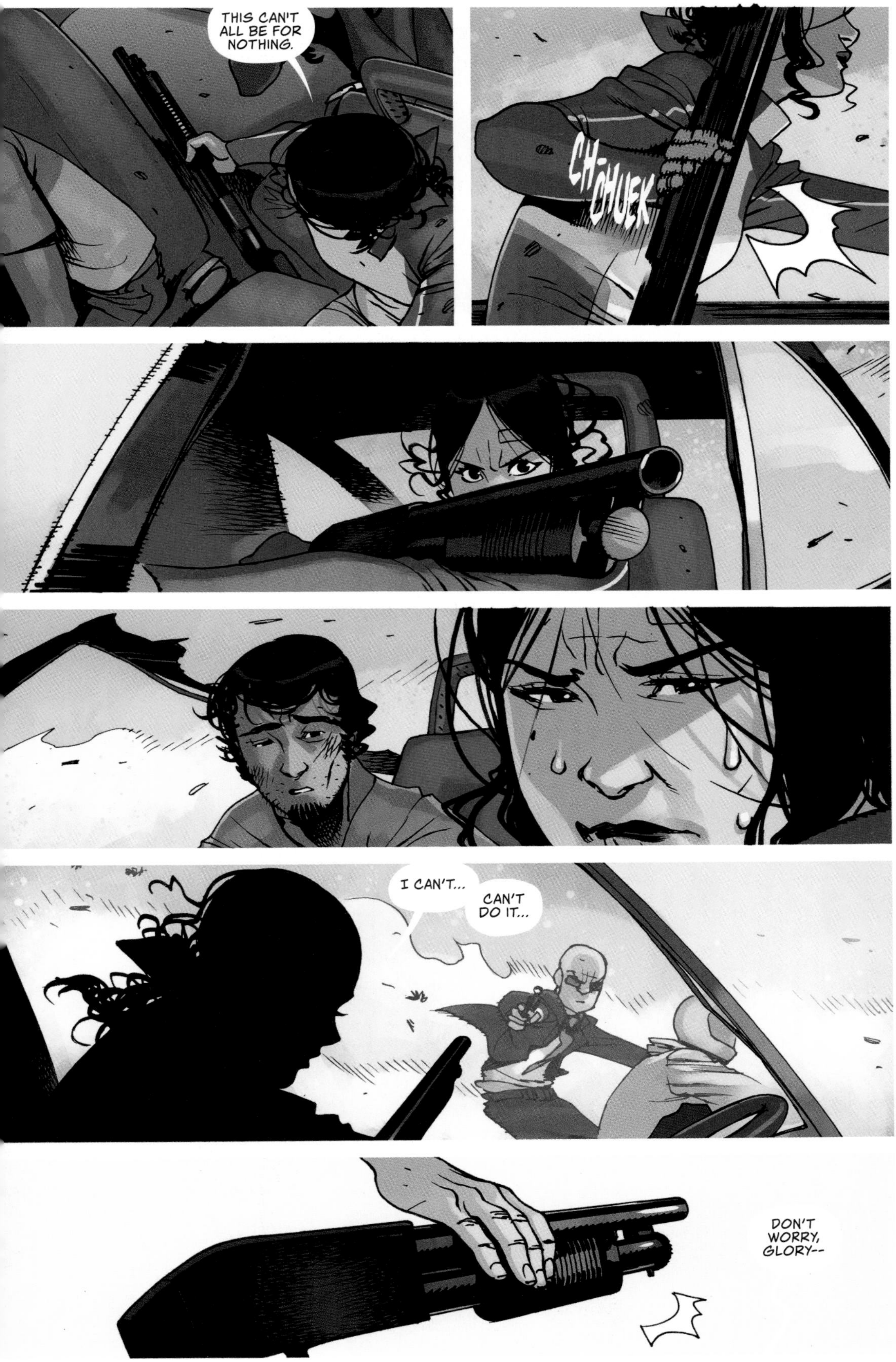
THIS CAN'T ALL BE FOR NOTHING.
CH-CHUEK
I CAN'T...
CAN'T DO IT...
DON'T WORRY, GLORY--

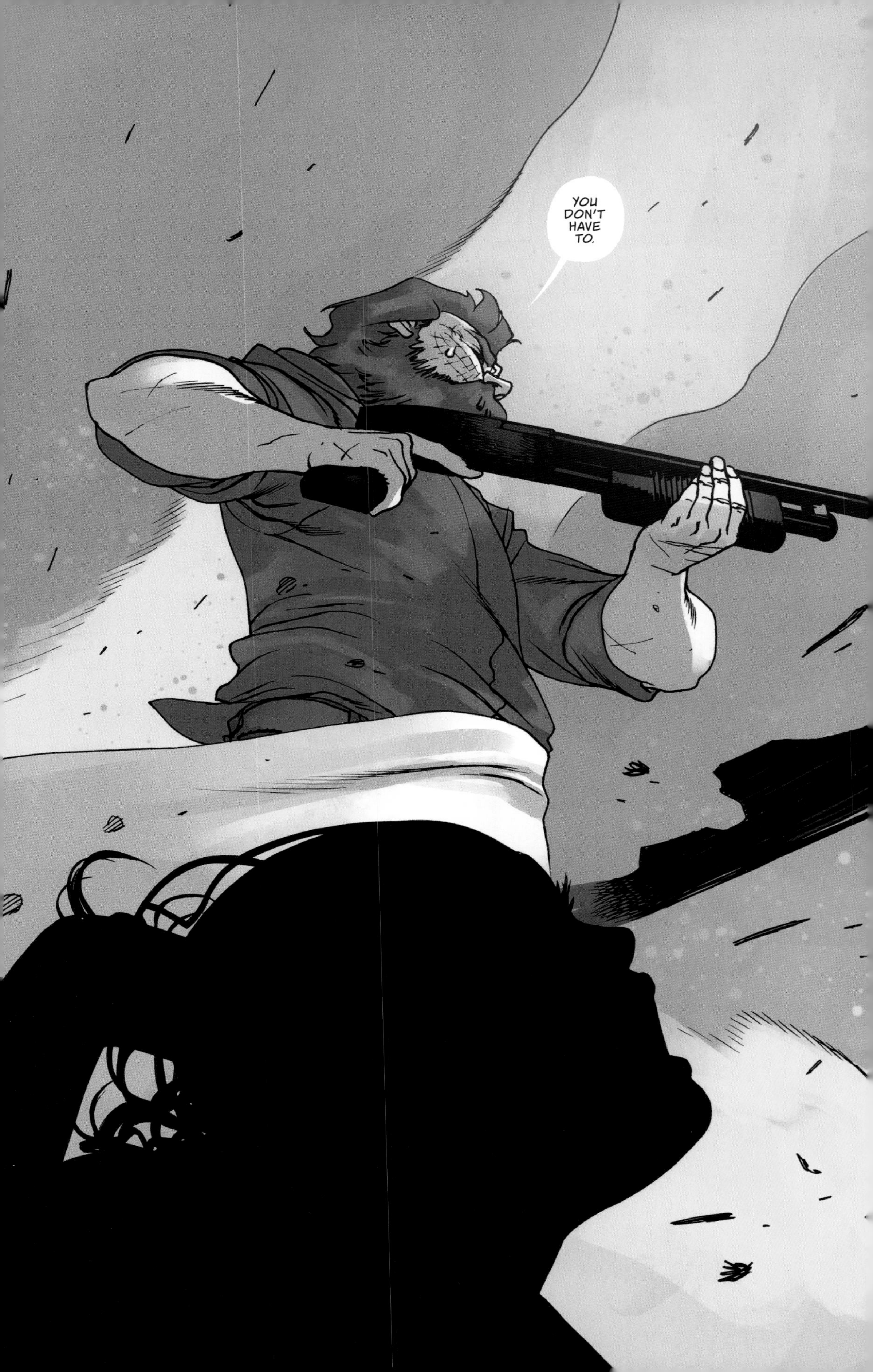
YOU DON'T HAVE TO.

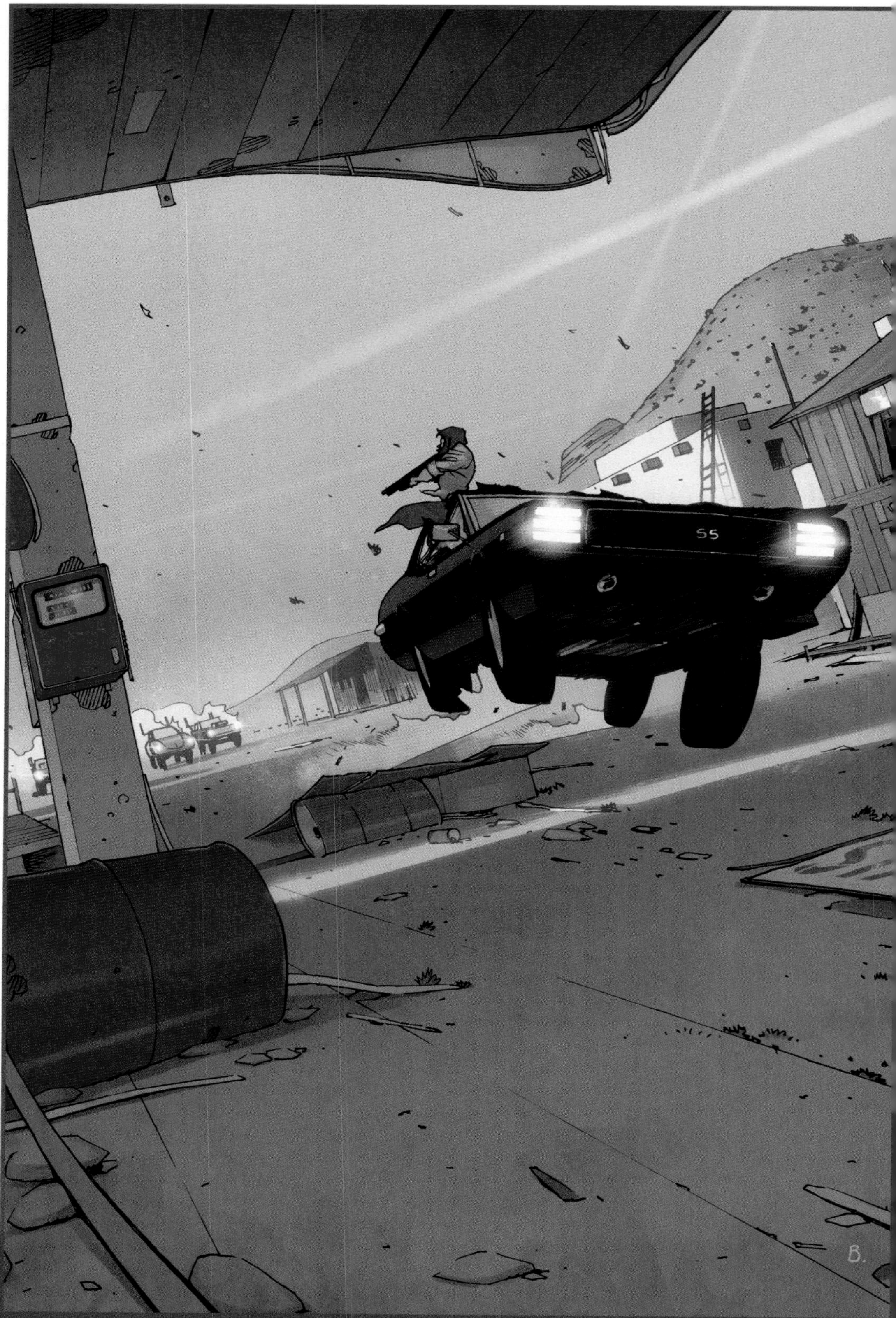
SS
B.

TEN

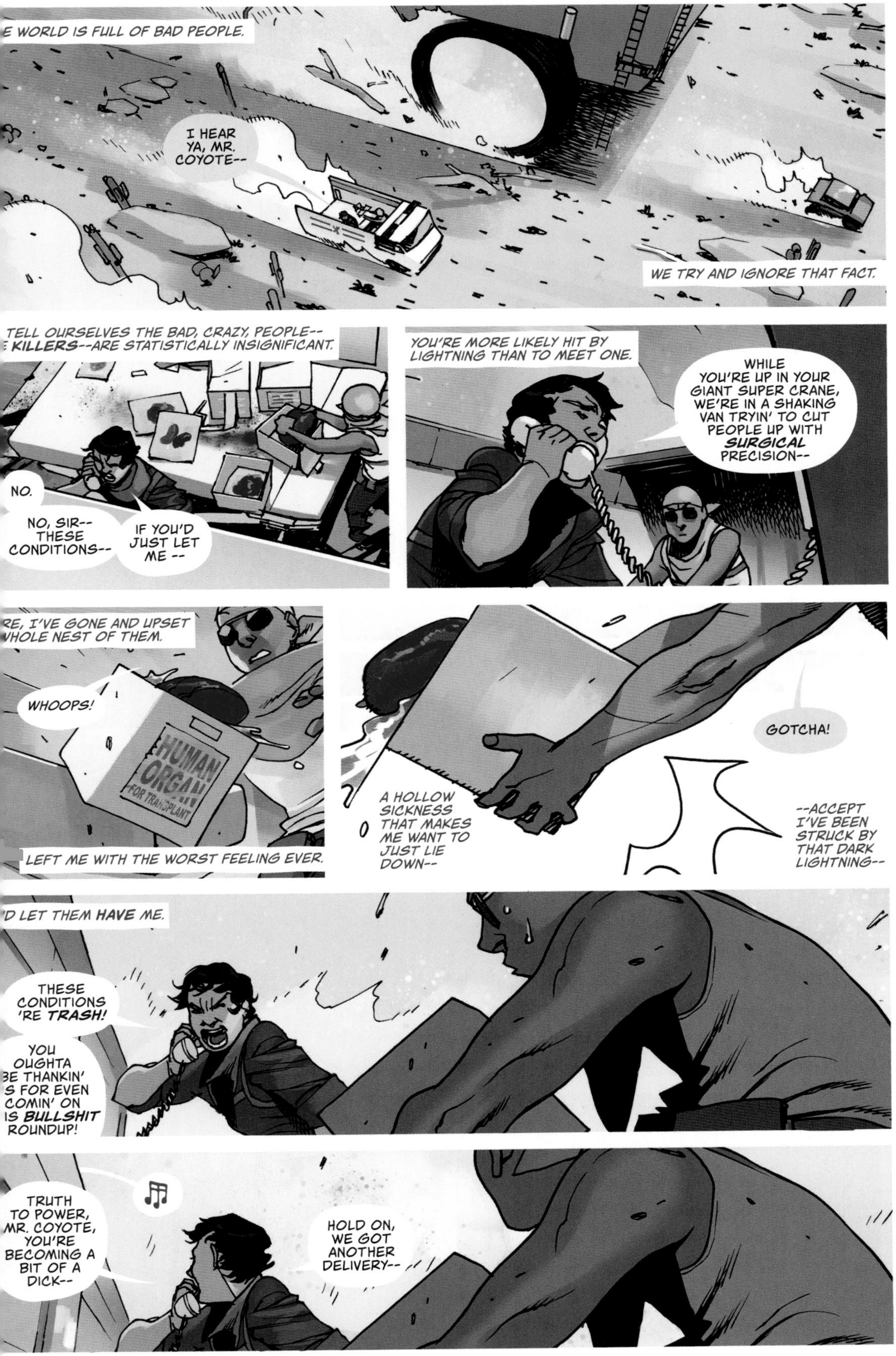
E WORLD IS FULL OF BAD PEOPLE.
I HEAR YA, MR. COYOTE--
WE TRY AND IGNORE THAT FACT.
TELL OURSELVES THE BAD, CRAZY, PEOPLE--
E KILLERS--ARE STATISTICALLY INSIGNIFICANT.
NO.
NO, SIR-- THESE CONDITIONS--
IF YOU'D JUST LET ME --
YOU'RE MORE LIKELY HIT BY LIGHTNING THAN TO MEET ONE.
WHILE YOU'RE UP IN YOUR GIANT SUPER CRANE, WE'RE IN A SHAKING VAN TRYIN' TO CUT PEOPLE UP WITH SURGICAL PRECISION--
RE, I'VE GONE AND UPSET WHOLE NEST OF THEM.
WHOOPS!
HUMAN ORGAN FOR TRANSPLANT
LEFT ME WITH THE WORST FEELING EVER.
GOTCHA!
A HOLLOW SICKNESS THAT MAKES ME WANT TO JUST LIE DOWN--
--ACCEPT I'VE BEEN STRUCK BY THAT DARK LIGHTNING--
'D LET THEM HAVE ME.
THESE CONDITIONS 'RE TRASH!
YOU OUGHTA BE THANKIN' S FOR EVEN COMIN' ON IS BULLSHIT ROUNDUP!
TRUTH TO POWER, MR. COYOTE, YOU'RE BECOMING A BIT OF A DICK--
HOLD ON, WE GOT ANOTHER DELIVERY--

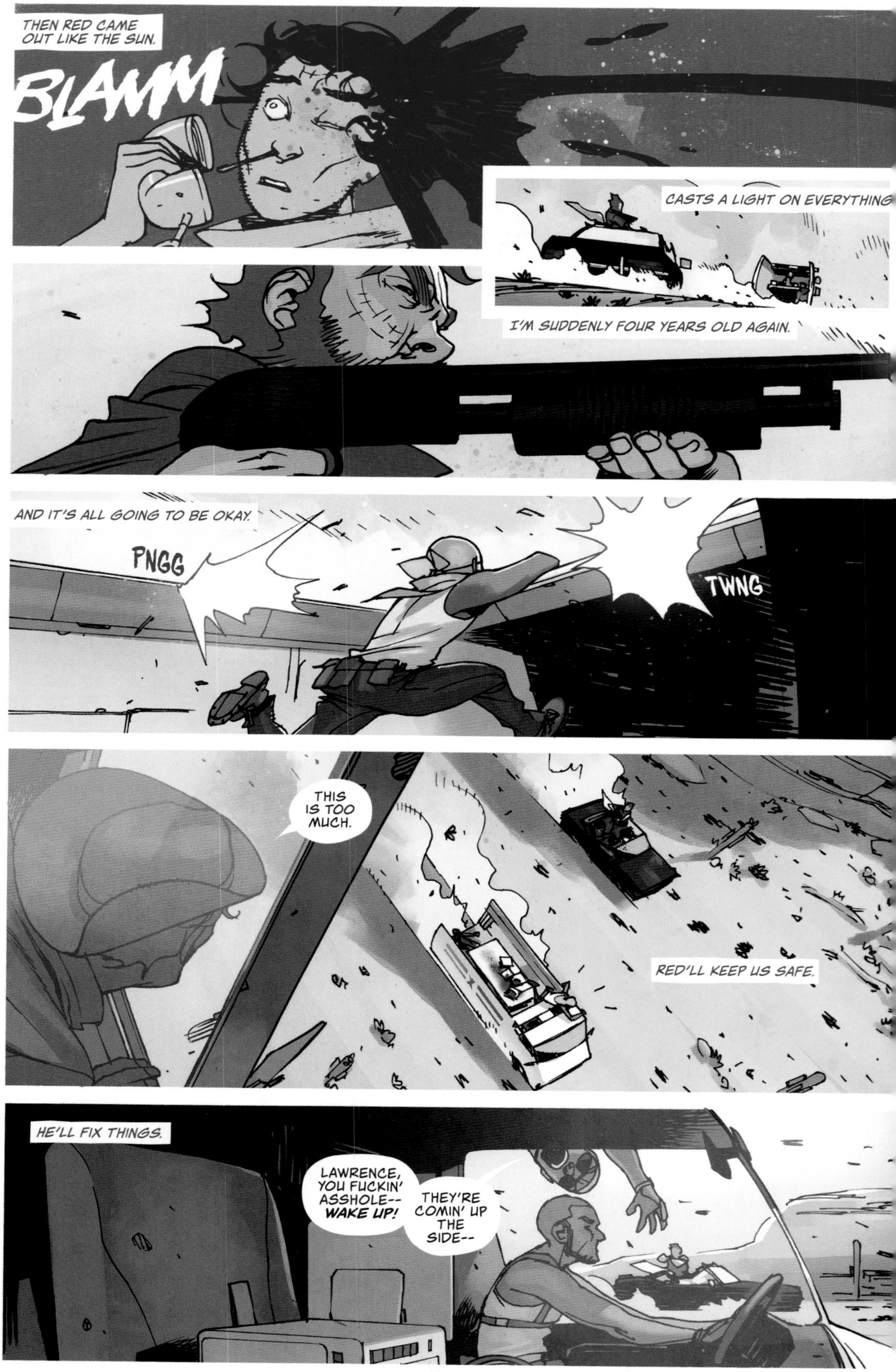

THEN RED CAME OUT LIKE THE SUN.
BLAMM
CASTS A LIGHT ON EVERYTHING
I'M SUDDENLY FOUR YEARS OLD AGAIN.
AND IT'S ALL GOING TO BE OKAY.
PNGG
TWNG
THIS IS TOO MUCH.
RED'LL KEEP US SAFE.
HE'LL FIX THINGS.
LAWRENCE, YOU FUCKIN' ASSHOLE-- WAKE UP!
THEY'RE COMIN' UP THE SIDE--

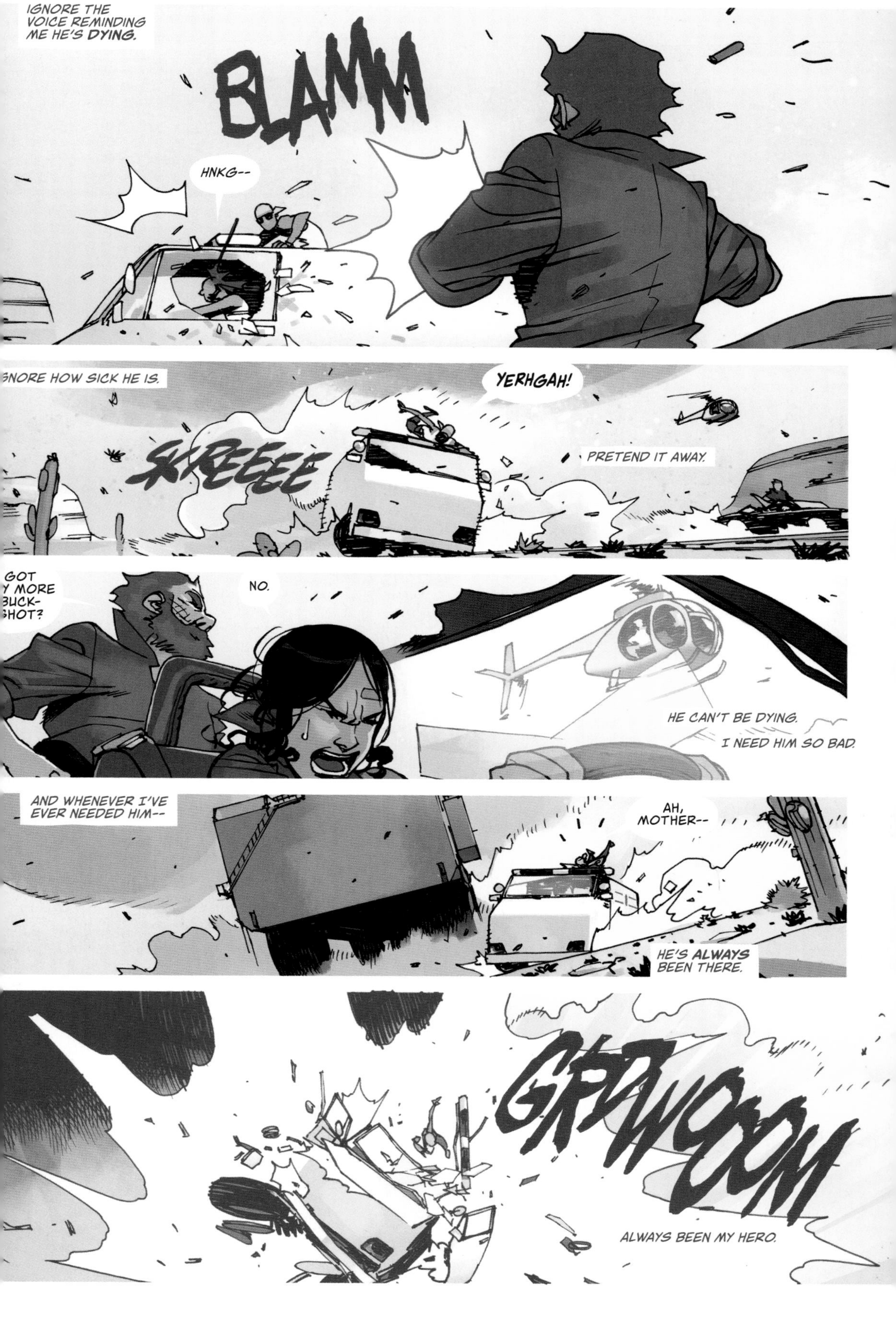
IGNORE THE VOICE REMINDING ME HE'S DYING.
BLAMM
HNKG--
IGNORE HOW SICK HE IS.
YERHGAH!
SKREEEEE
PRETEND IT AWAY.
GOT
Y MORE
BUCK-
SHOT?
NO.
HE CAN'T BE DYING.
I NEED HIM SO BAD.
AND WHENEVER I'VE EVER NEEDED HIM--
AH, MOTHER--
HE'S ALWAYS BEEN THERE.
GRDWOOOM
ALWAYS BEEN MY HERO.

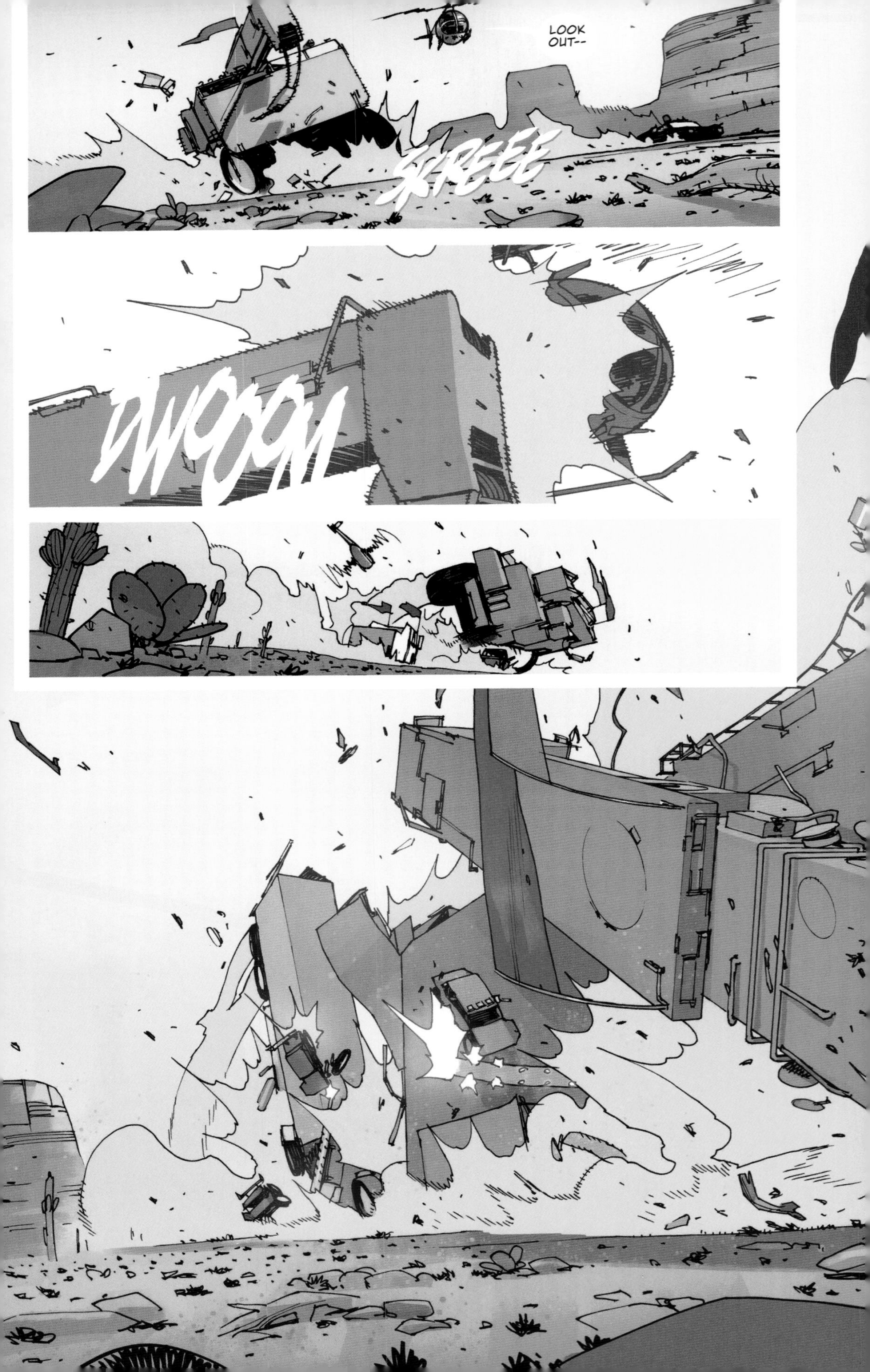
LOOK OUT--
SKREEE
DWOOM

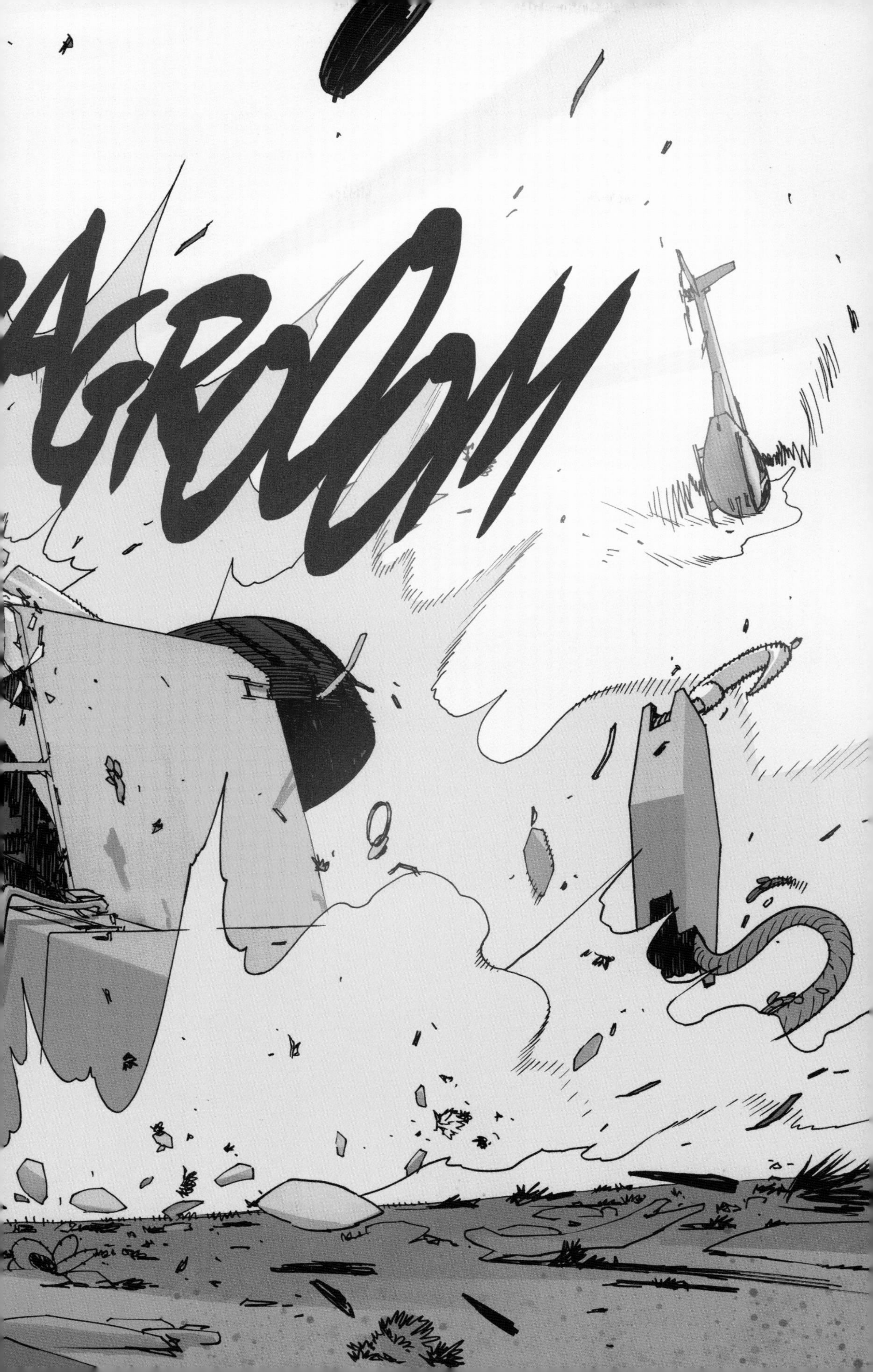
AGROOM

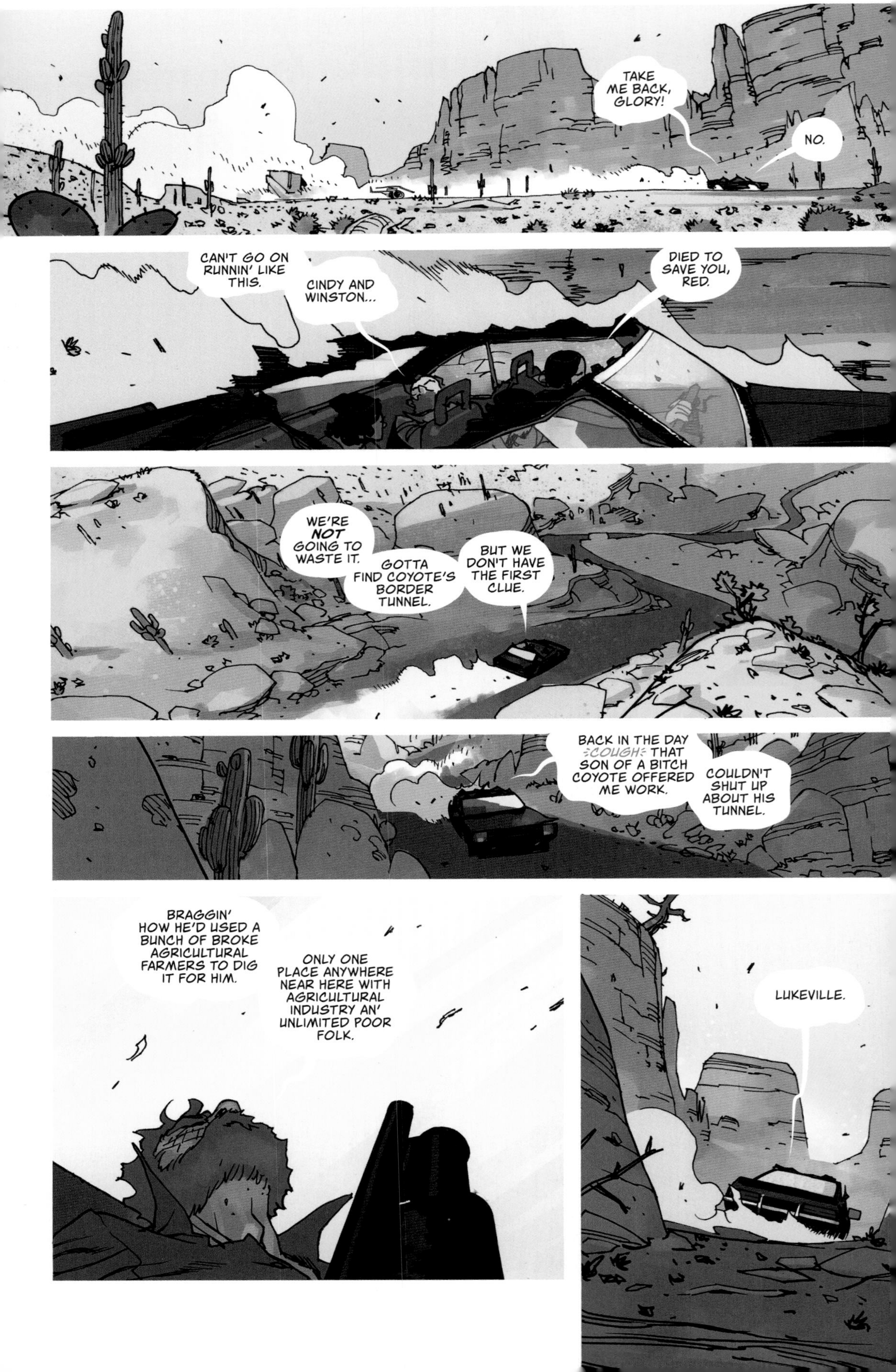
TAKE ME BACK, GLORY!
NO.
CAN'T GO ON RUNNIN' LIKE THIS.
CINDY AND WINSTON...
DIED TO SAVE YOU, RED.
WE'RE **NOT** GOING TO WASTE IT.
GOTTA FIND COYOTE'S BORDER TUNNEL.
BUT WE DON'T HAVE THE FIRST CLUE.
BACK IN THE DAY *COUGH* THAT SON OF A BITCH COYOTE OFFERED ME WORK.
COULDN'T SHUT UP ABOUT HIS TUNNEL.
BRAGGIN' HOW HE'D USED A BUNCH OF BROKE AGRICULTURAL FARMERS TO DIG IT FOR HIM.
ONLY ONE PLACE ANYWHERE NEAR HERE WITH AGRICULTURAL INDUSTRY AN' UNLIMITED POOR FOLK.
LUKEVILLE.

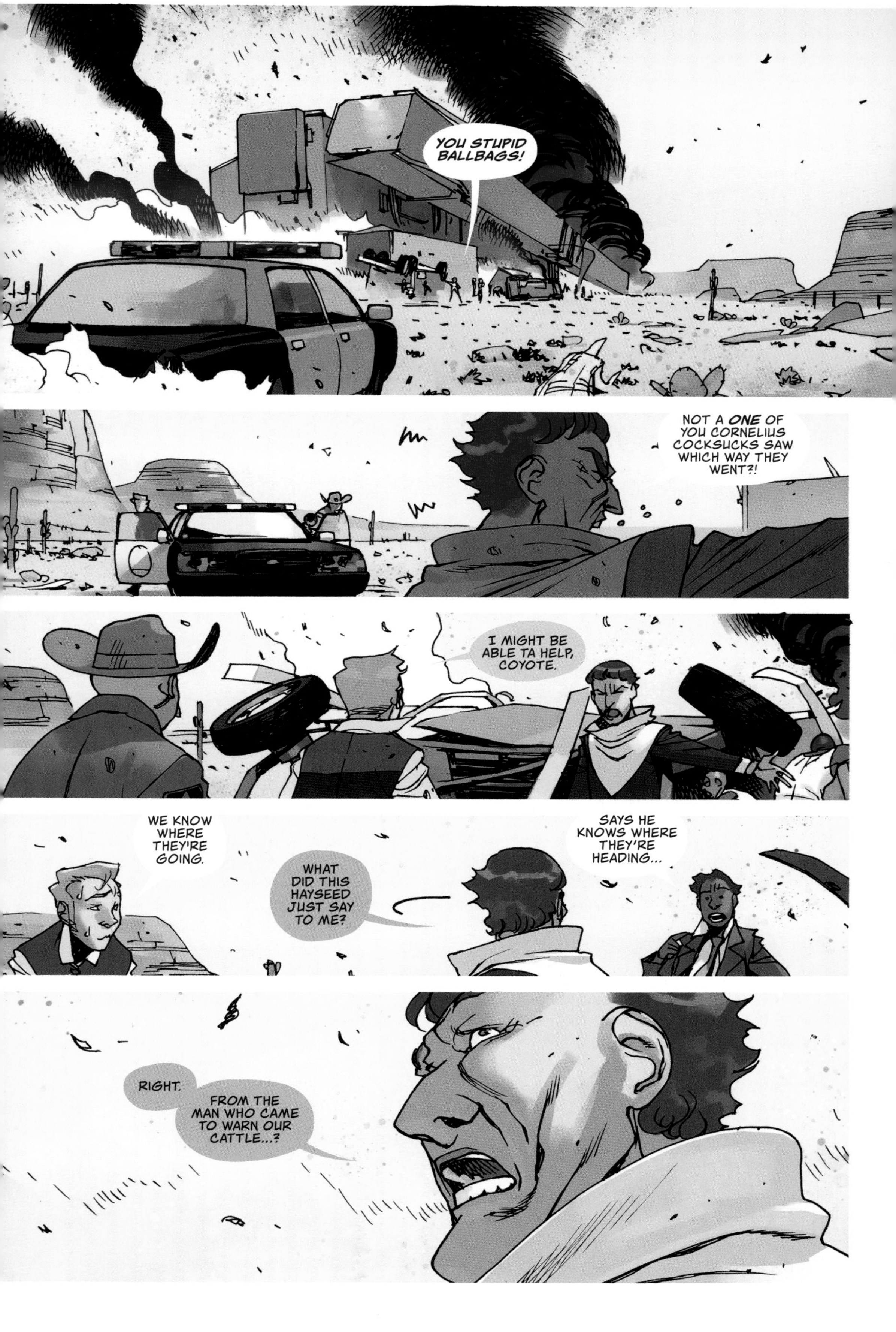
YOU STUPID BALLBAGS!
NOT A ONE OF YOU CORNELIUS COCKSUCKS SAW WHICH WAY THEY WENT?!
I MIGHT BE ABLE TA HELP, COYOTE.
WE KNOW WHERE THEY'RE GOING.
WHAT DID THIS HAYSEED JUST SAY TO ME?
SAYS HE KNOWS WHERE THEY'RE HEADING...
RIGHT.
FROM THE MAN WHO CAME TO WARN OUR CATTLE...?

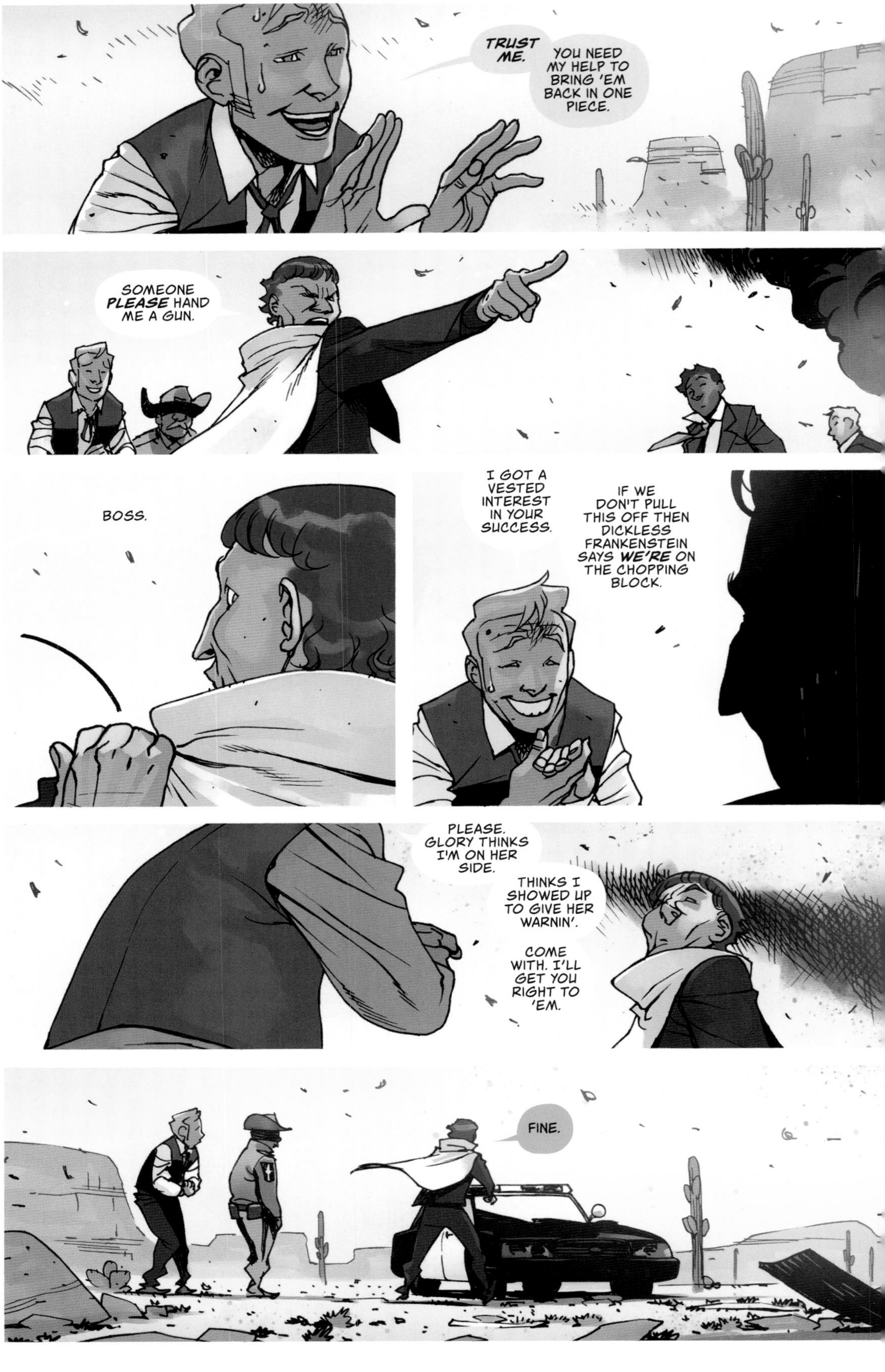
TRUST ME.
YOU NEED MY HELP TO BRING 'EM BACK IN ONE PIECE.
SOMEONE PLEASE HAND ME A GUN.
BOSS.
I GOT A VESTED INTEREST IN YOUR SUCCESS.
IF WE DON'T PULL THIS OFF THEN DICKLESS FRANKENSTEIN SAYS WE'RE ON THE CHOPPING BLOCK.
PLEASE. GLORY THINKS I'M ON HER SIDE.
THINKS I SHOWED UP TO GIVE HER WARNIN'.
COME WITH. I'LL GET YOU RIGHT TO 'EM.
FINE.

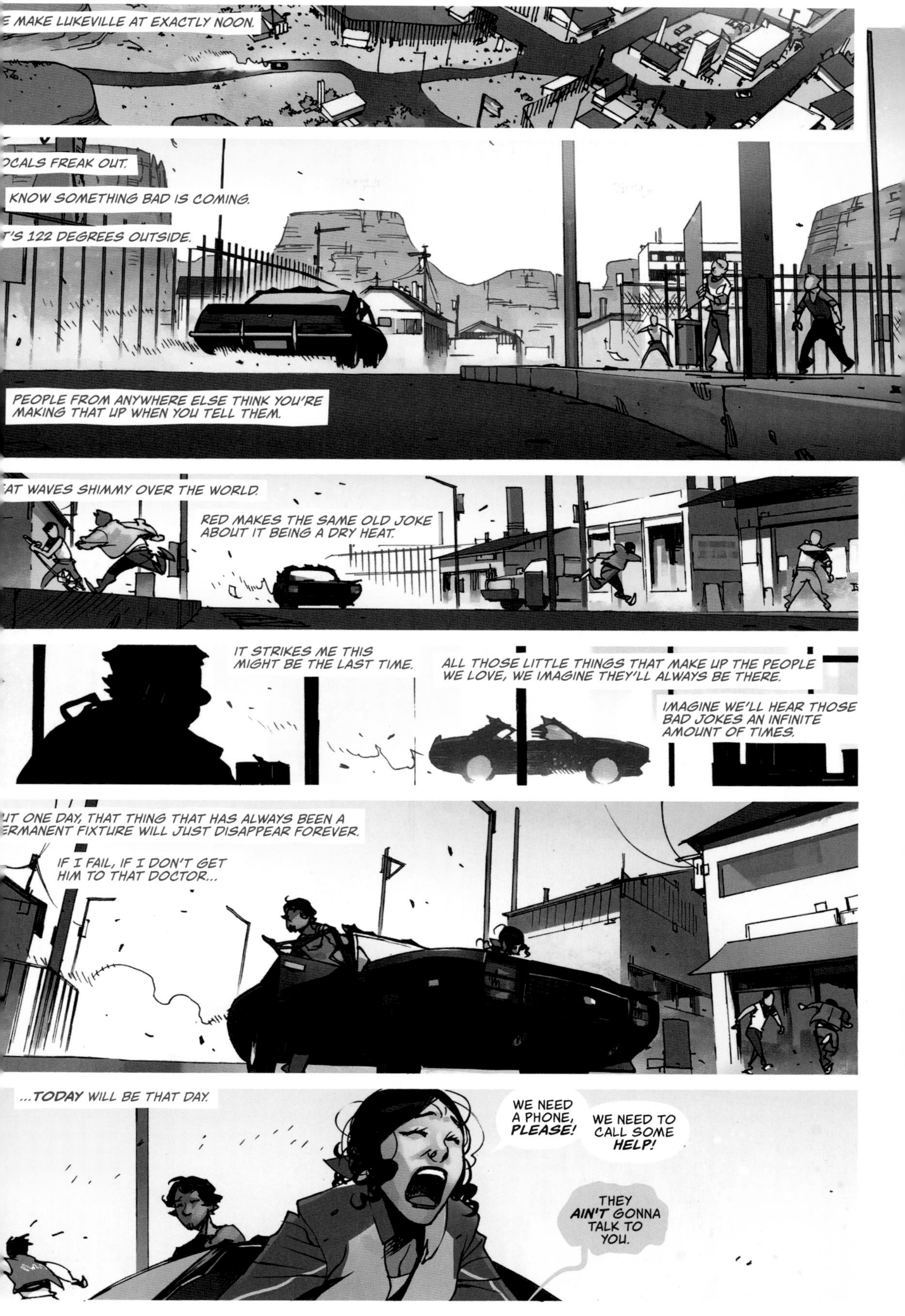

E MAKE LUKEVILLE AT EXACTLY NOON.
OCALS FREAK OUT.
KNOW SOMETHING BAD IS COMING.
T'S 122 DEGREES OUTSIDE.
PEOPLE FROM ANYWHERE ELSE THINK YOU'RE MAKING THAT UP WHEN YOU TELL THEM.
AT WAVES SHIMMY OVER THE WORLD.
RED MAKES THE SAME OLD JOKE ABOUT IT BEING A DRY HEAT.
IT STRIKES ME THIS MIGHT BE THE LAST TIME.
ALL THOSE LITTLE THINGS THAT MAKE UP THE PEOPLE WE LOVE, WE IMAGINE THEY'LL ALWAYS BE THERE.
IMAGINE WE'LL HEAR THOSE BAD JOKES AN INFINITE AMOUNT OF TIMES.
UT ONE DAY, THAT THING THAT HAS ALWAYS BEEN A ERMANENT FIXTURE WILL JUST DISAPPEAR FOREVER.
IF I FAIL, IF I DON'T GET HIM TO THAT DOCTOR...
...TODAY WILL BE THAT DAY.
WE NEED A PHONE, PLEASE!
WE NEED TO CALL SOME HELP!
THEY AIN'T GONNA TALK TO YOU.

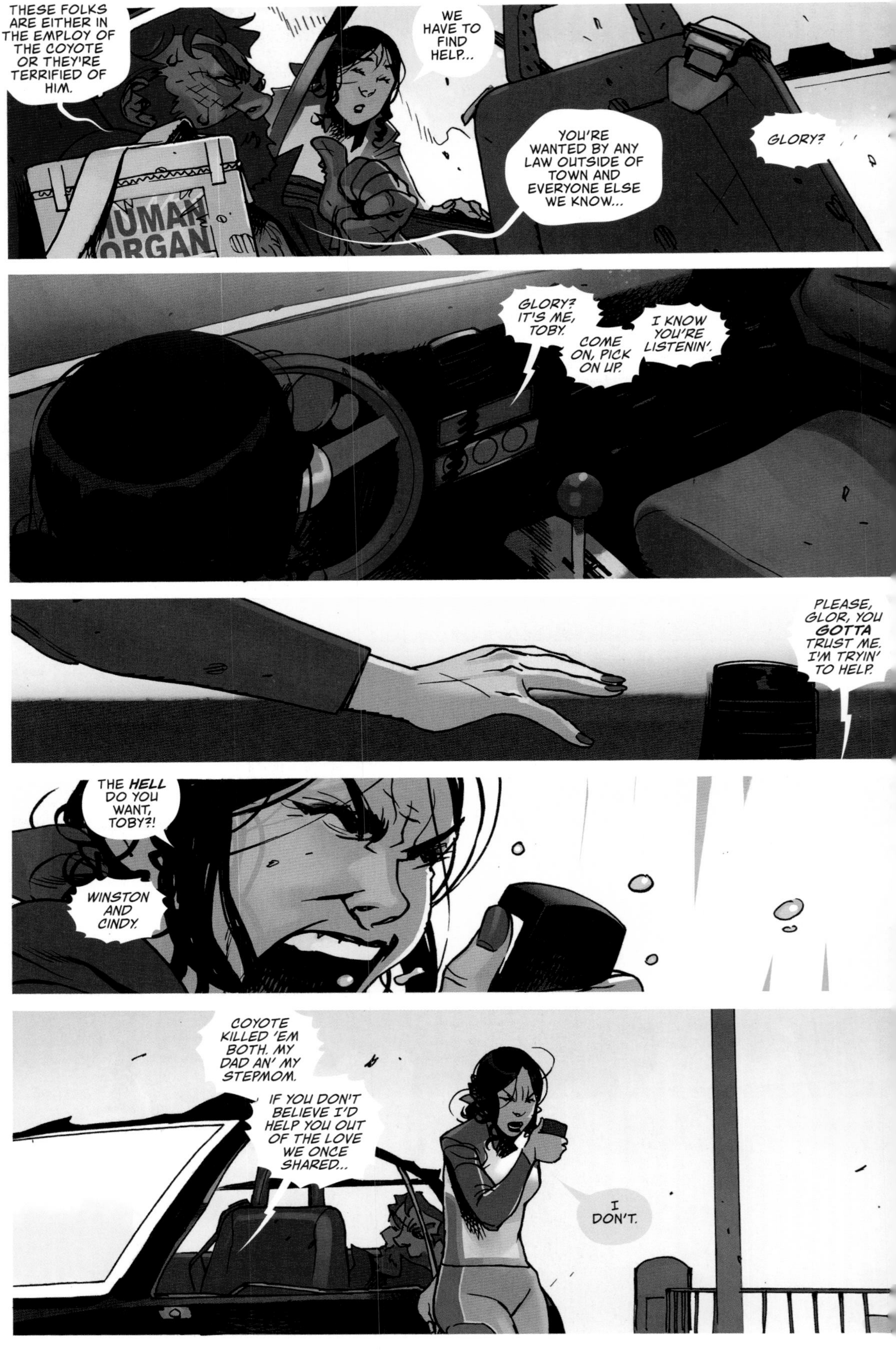
THESE FOLKS ARE EITHER IN THE EMPLOY OF THE COYOTE OR THEY'RE TERRIFIED OF HIM.
HUMAN ORGAN
WE HAVE TO FIND HELP...
YOU'RE WANTED BY ANY LAW OUTSIDE OF TOWN AND EVERYONE ELSE WE KNOW...
GLORY?
GLORY? IT'S ME, TOBY.
COME ON, PICK ON UP.
I KNOW YOU'RE LISTENIN'.
PLEASE, GLOR, YOU **GOTTA** TRUST ME. I'M TRYIN' TO HELP.
THE **HELL** DO YOU WANT, TOBY?!
WINSTON AND CINDY.
COYOTE KILLED 'EM BOTH. MY DAD AN' MY STEPMOM.
IF YOU DON'T BELIEVE I'D HELP YOU OUT OF THE LOVE WE ONCE SHARED...
I DON'T.

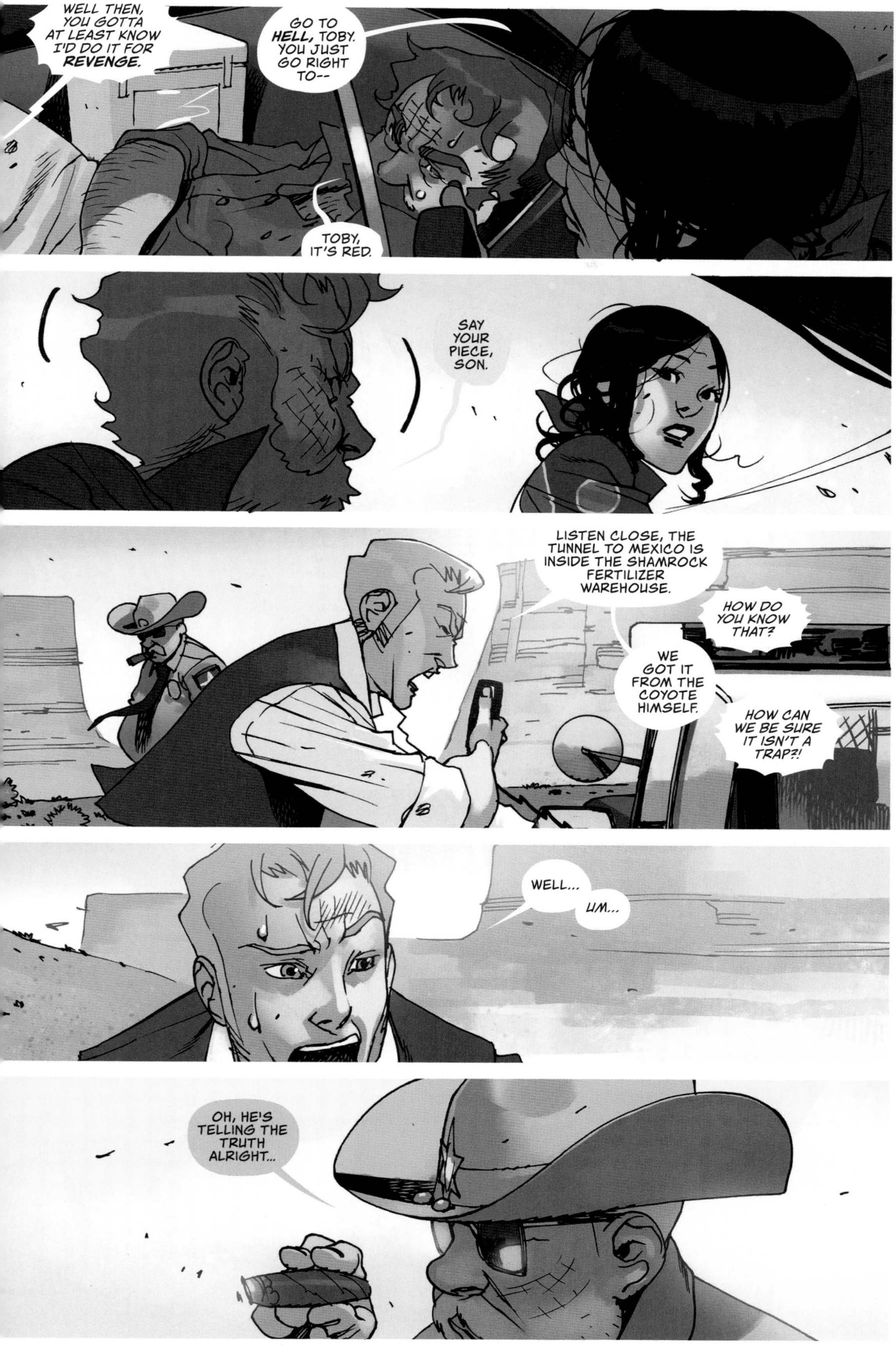
WELL THEN, YOU GOTTA AT LEAST KNOW I'D DO IT FOR **REVENGE.**
GO TO **HELL,** TOBY. YOU JUST GO RIGHT TO--
TOBY, IT'S RED.
SAY YOUR PIECE, SON.
LISTEN CLOSE, THE TUNNEL TO MEXICO IS INSIDE THE SHAMROCK FERTILIZER WAREHOUSE.
HOW DO YOU KNOW THAT?
WE GOT IT FROM THE COYOTE HIMSELF.
HOW CAN WE BE SURE IT ISN'T A TRAP?!
WELL...
UM...
OH, HE'S TELLING THE TRUTH ALRIGHT...

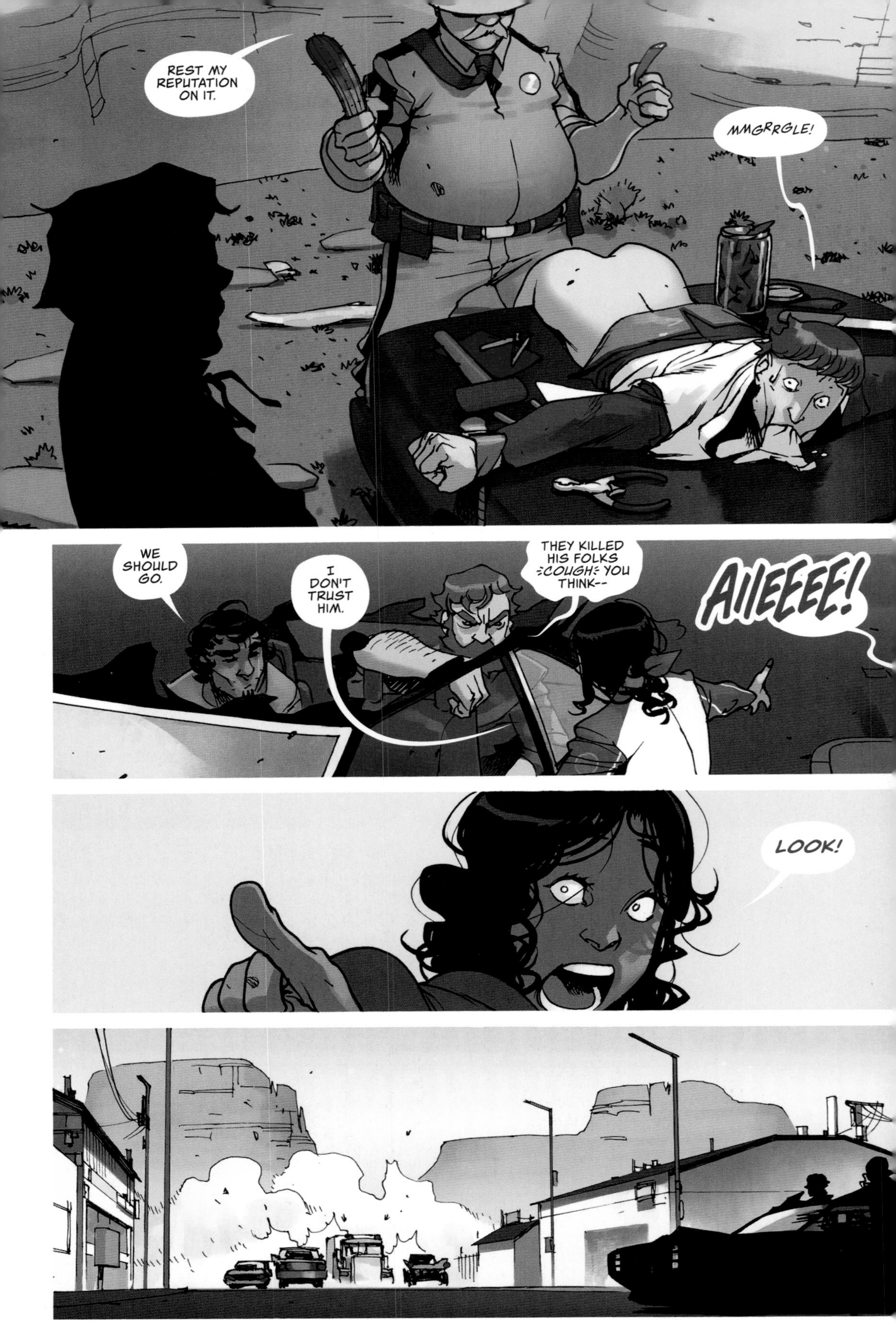
REST MY REPUTATION ON IT.
MMGRRGLE!
WE SHOULD GO.
I DON'T TRUST HIM.
THEY KILLED HIS FOLKS =COUGH= YOU THINK--
AIIEEEE!
LOOK!

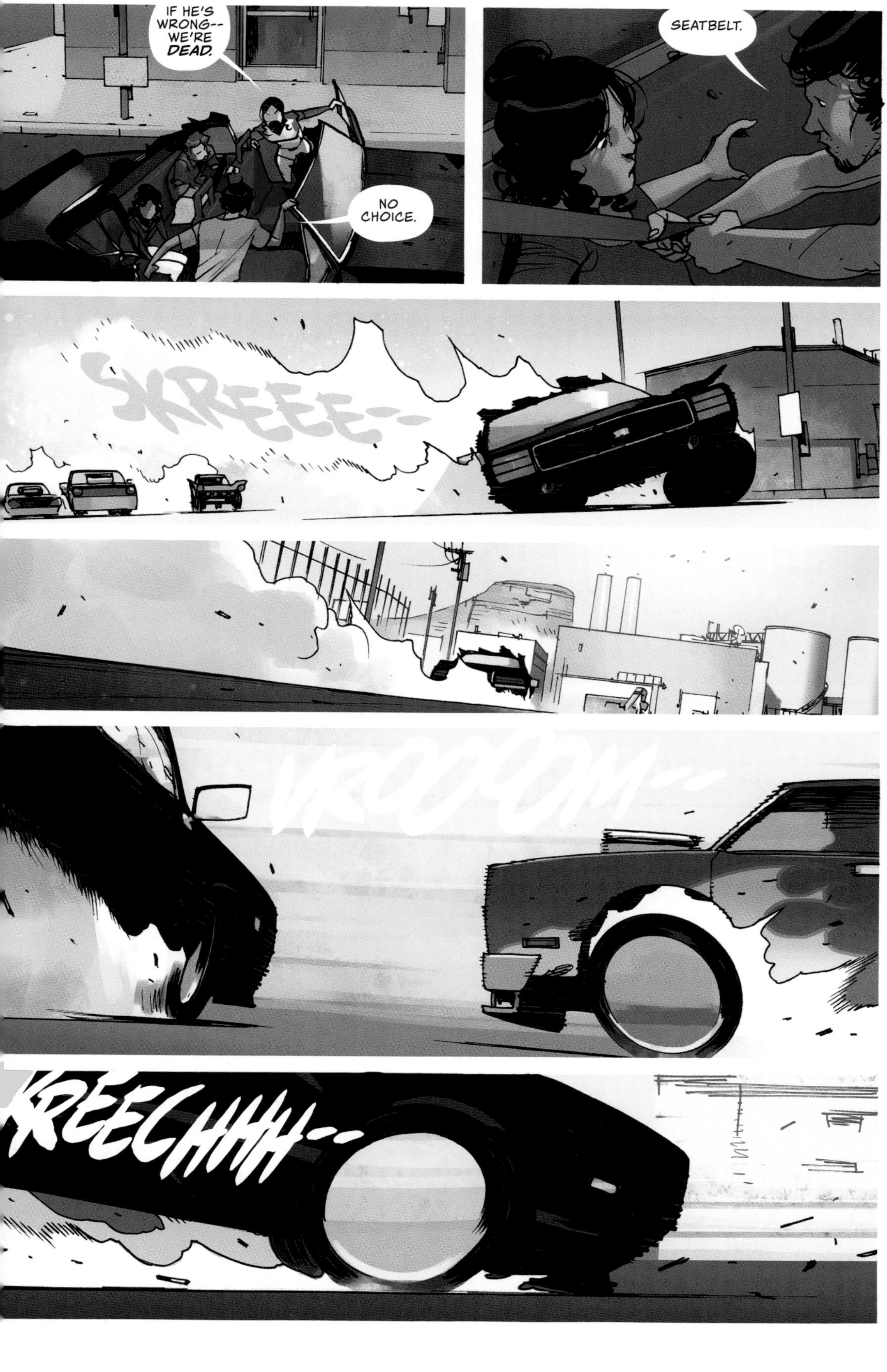
IF HE'S WRONG-- WE'RE DEAD.
NO CHOICE.
SEATBELT.
SKREEEE--
VROOOM--
KREECHHH--

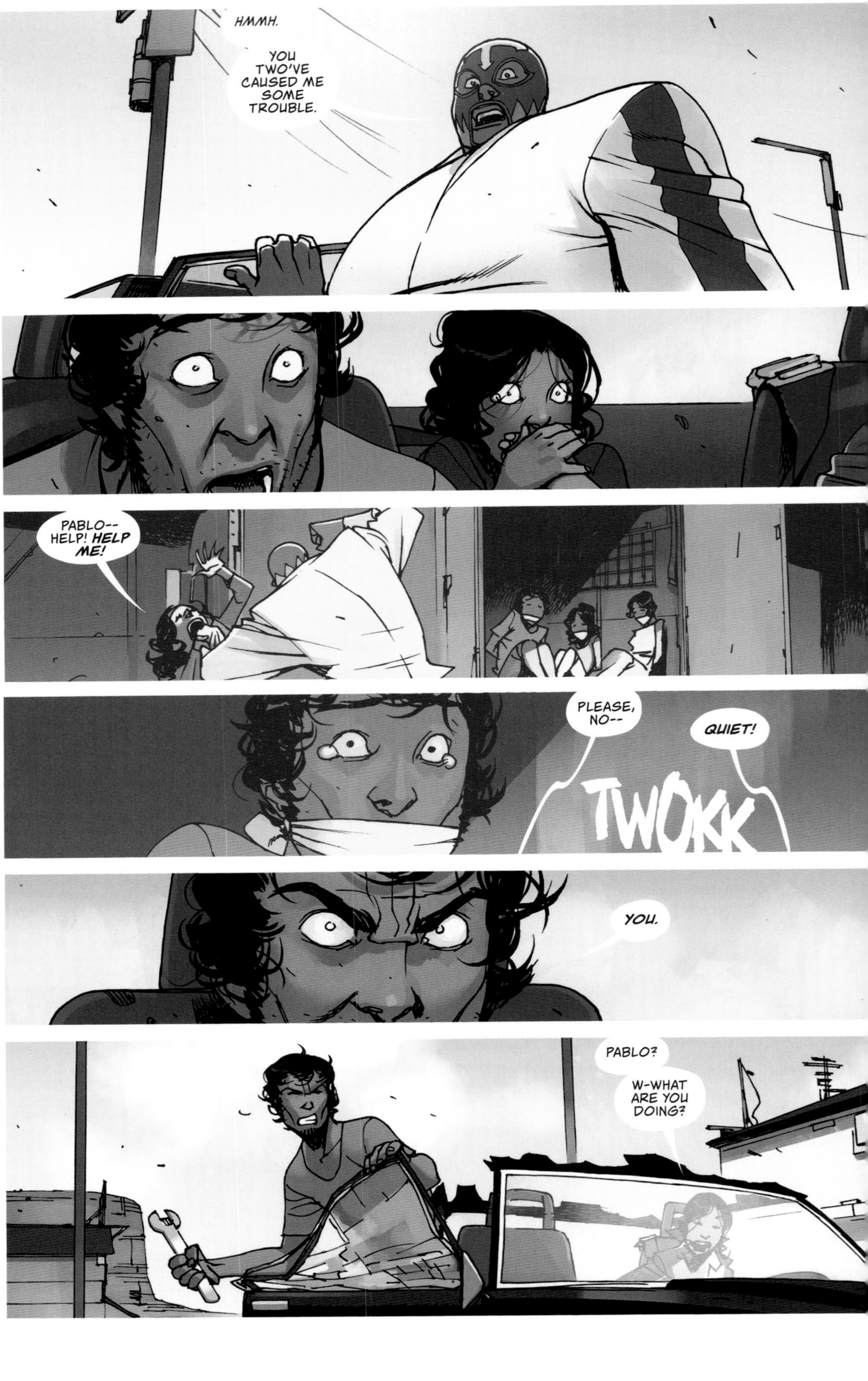
HMMH.
YOU TWO'VE CAUSED ME SOME TROUBLE.
PABLO-- HELP! HELP ME!
PLEASE, NO--
QUIET!
TWOKK
YOU.
PABLO?
W-WHAT ARE YOU DOING?

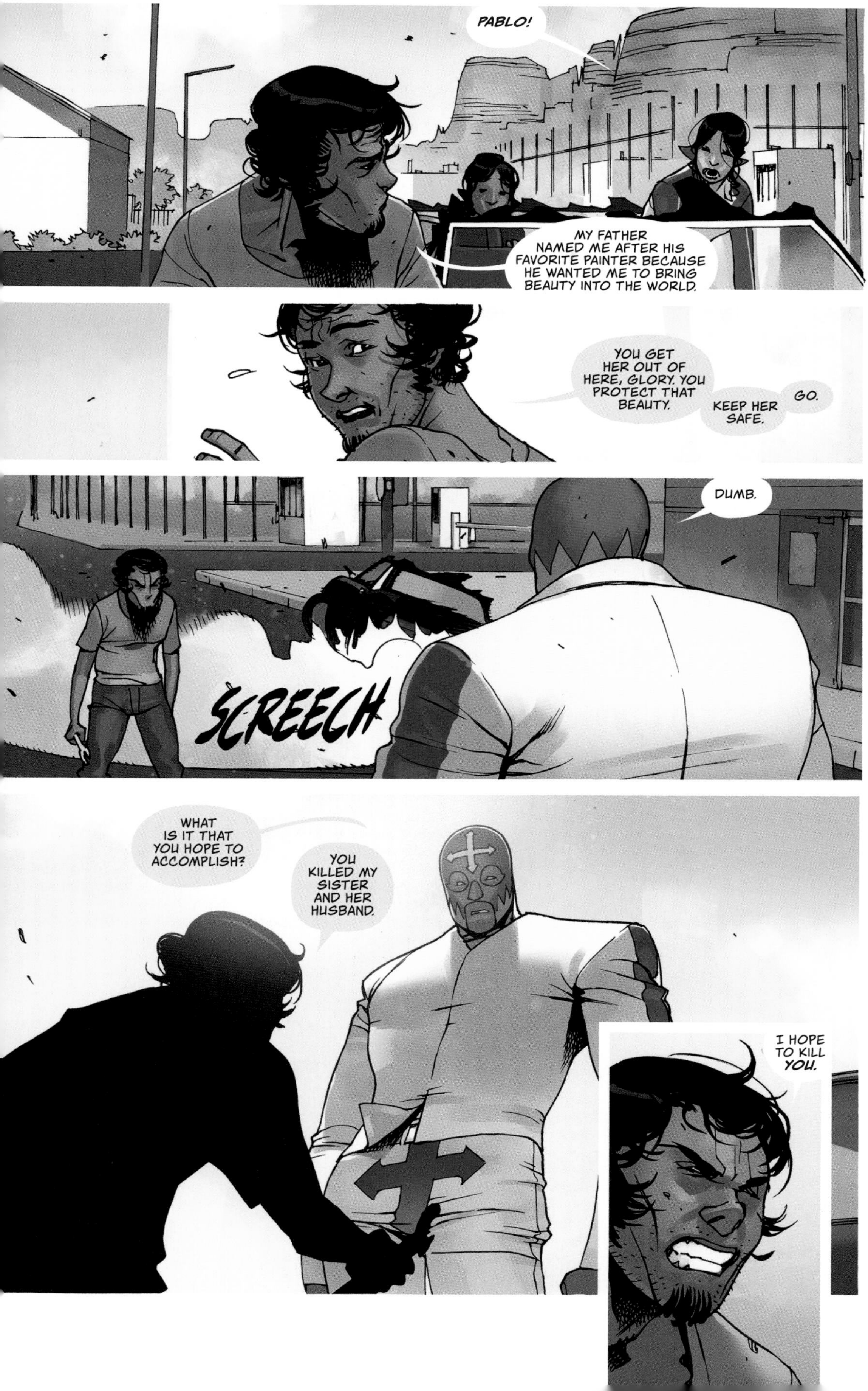
PABLO!
MY FATHER NAMED ME AFTER HIS FAVORITE PAINTER BECAUSE HE WANTED ME TO BRING BEAUTY INTO THE WORLD.
YOU GET HER OUT OF HERE, GLORY. YOU PROTECT THAT BEAUTY.
KEEP HER SAFE.
GO.
DUMB.
SCREECH
WHAT IS IT THAT YOU HOPE TO ACCOMPLISH?
YOU KILLED MY SISTER AND HER HUSBAND.
I HOPE TO KILL YOU.

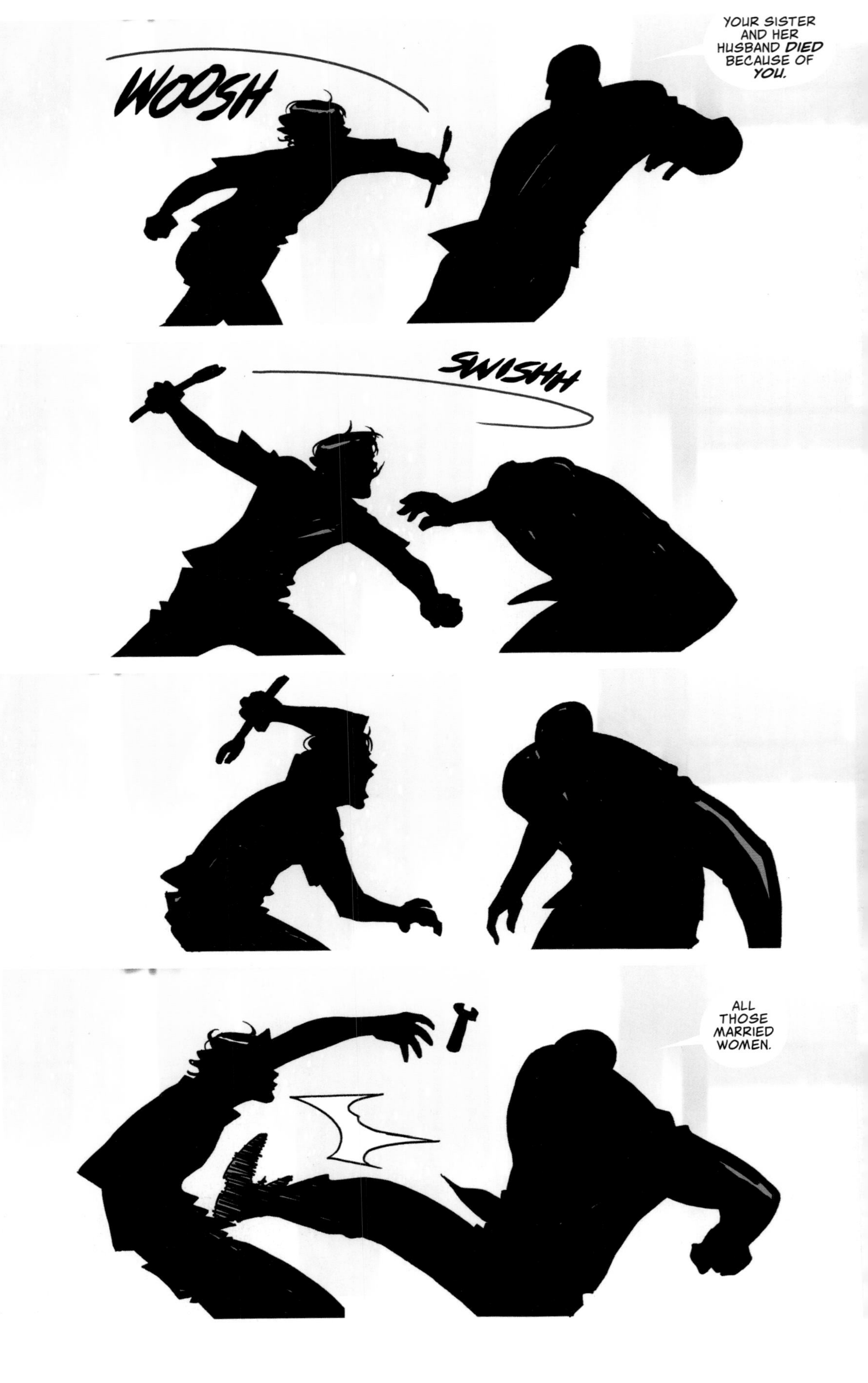
YOUR SISTER AND HER HUSBAND DIED BECAUSE OF YOU.
WOOSH
SWISHH
ALL THOSE MARRIED WOMEN.

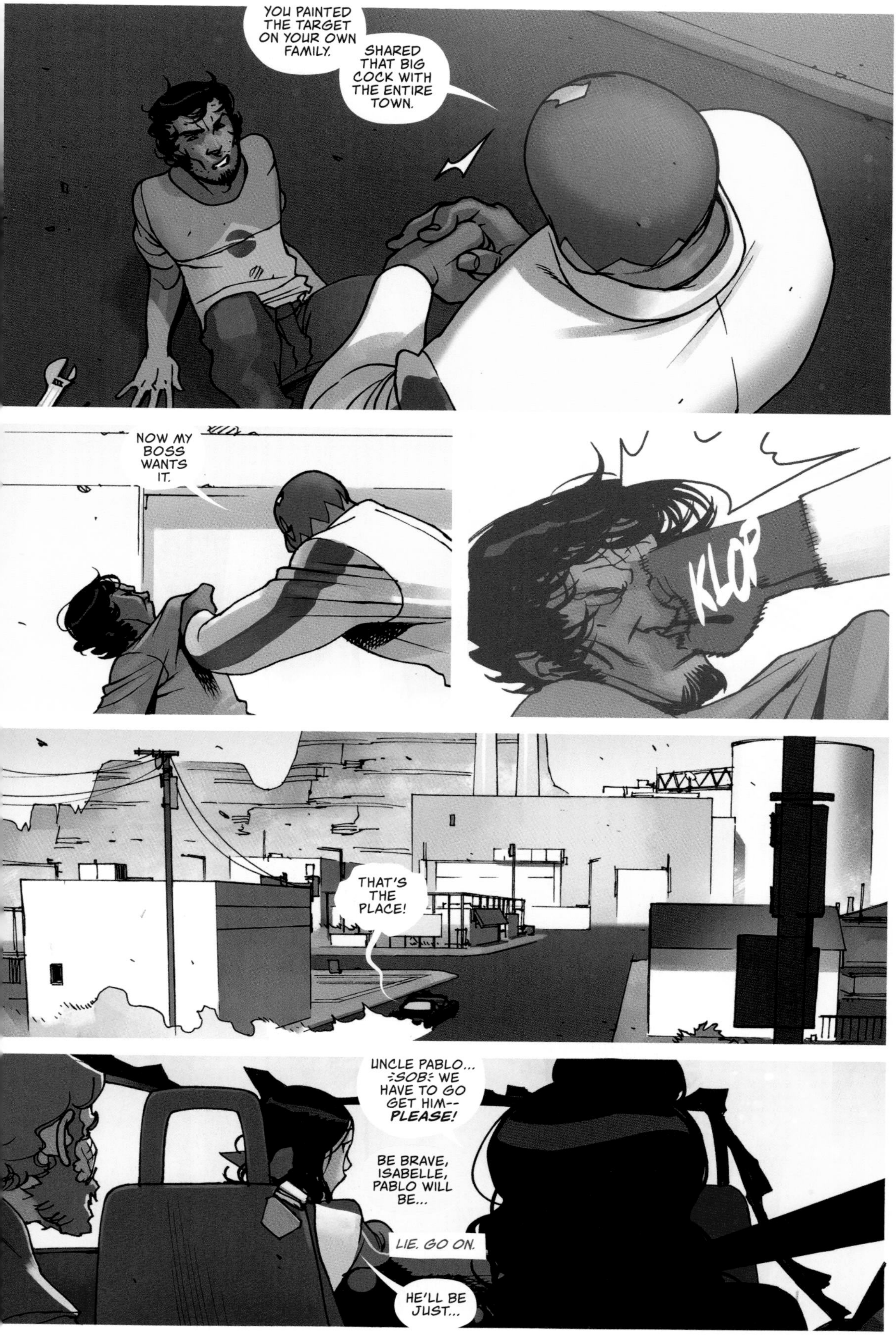
YOU PAINTED THE TARGET ON YOUR OWN FAMILY.
SHARED THAT BIG COCK WITH THE ENTIRE TOWN.
NOW MY BOSS WANTS IT.
KLOP
THAT'S THE PLACE!
UNCLE PABLO... ⁑SOB⁑ WE HAVE TO GO GET HIM--**PLEASE!**
BE BRAVE, ISABELLE, PABLO WILL BE...
LIE. GO ON.
HE'LL BE JUST...

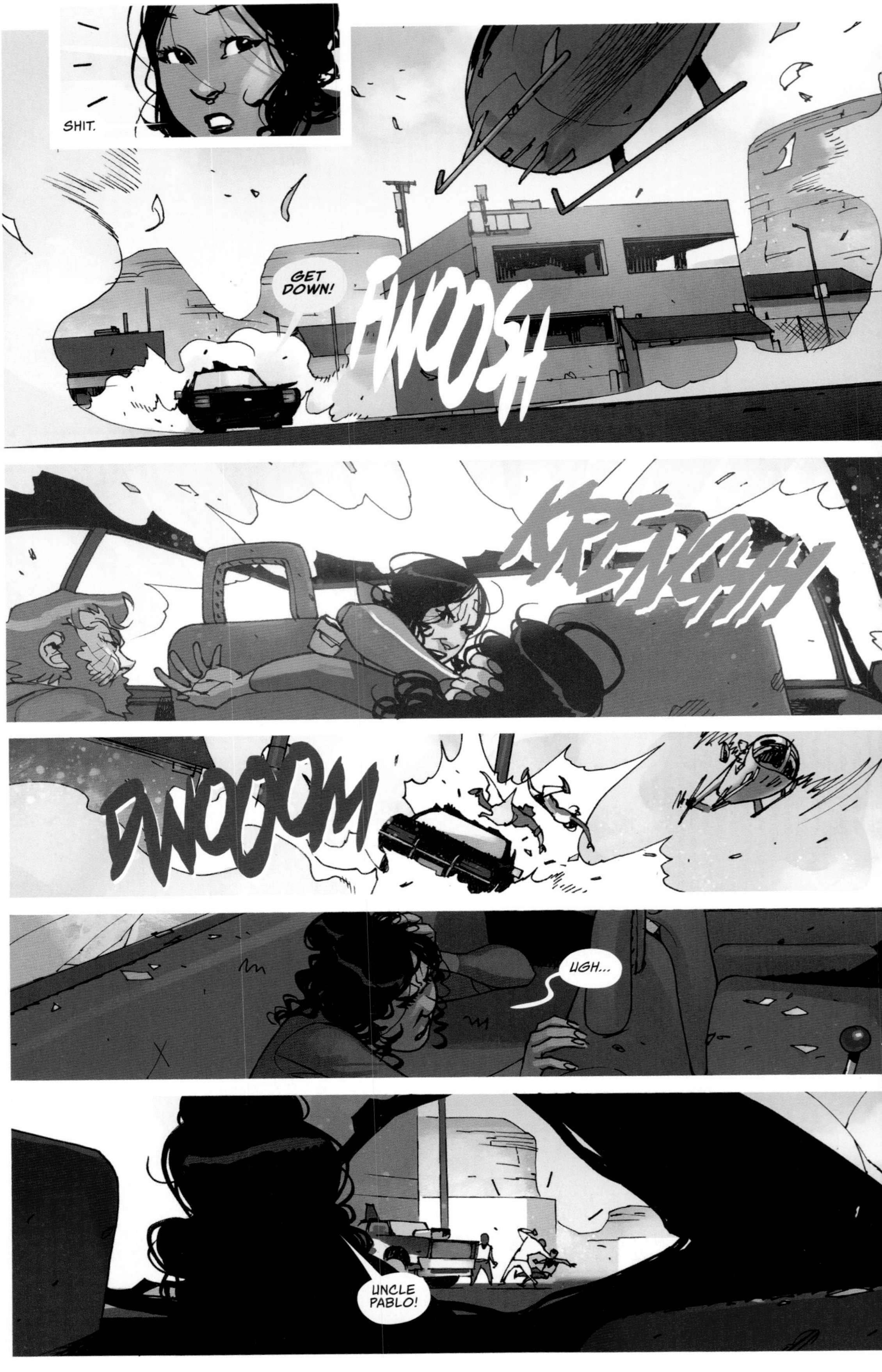
SHIT.
GET DOWN!
FWOOSH
KRENCHH
DWOOOM
UGH...
UNCLE PABLO!

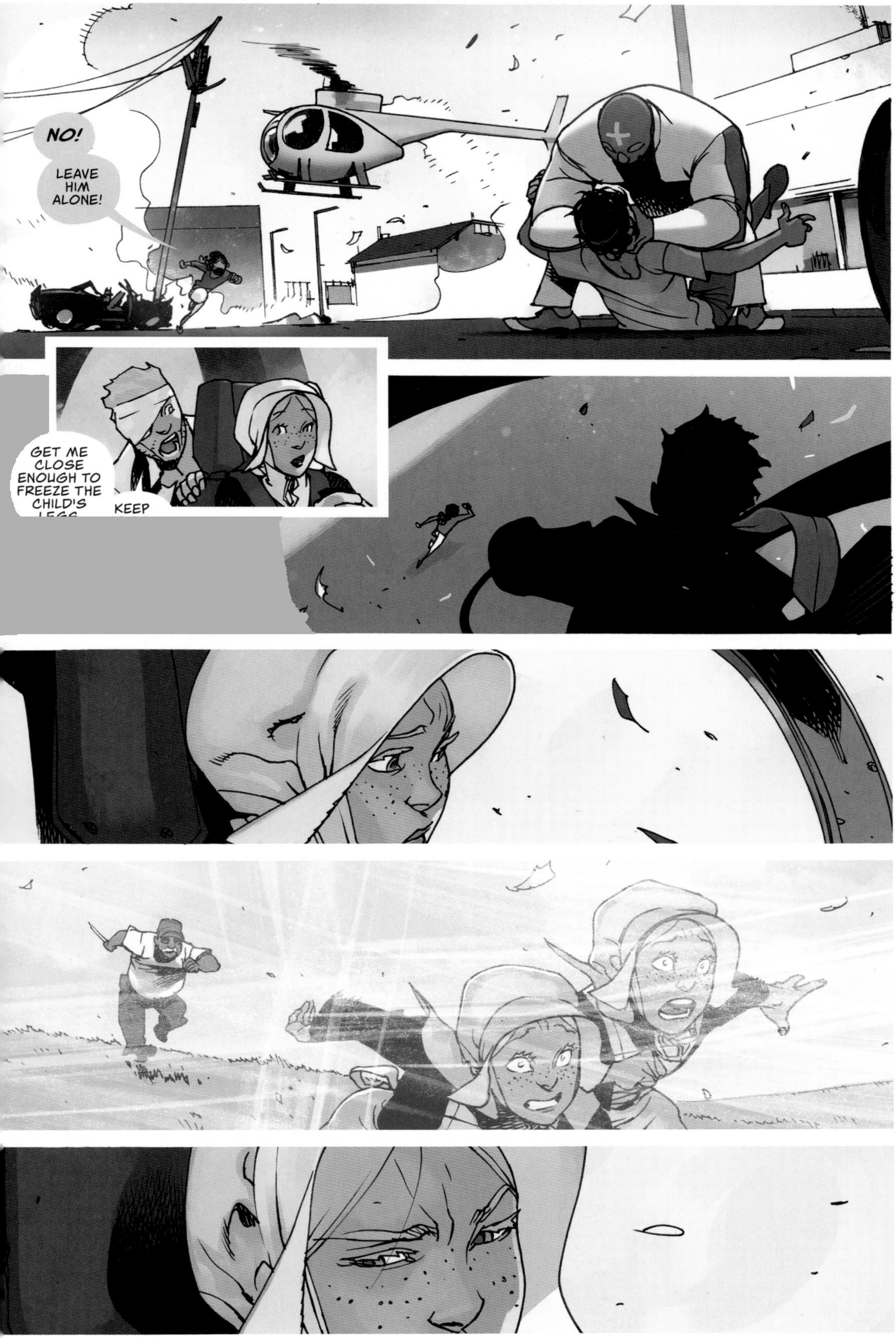
NO!
LEAVE HIM ALONE!
GET ME CLOSE ENOUGH TO FREEZE THE CHILD'S
KEEP

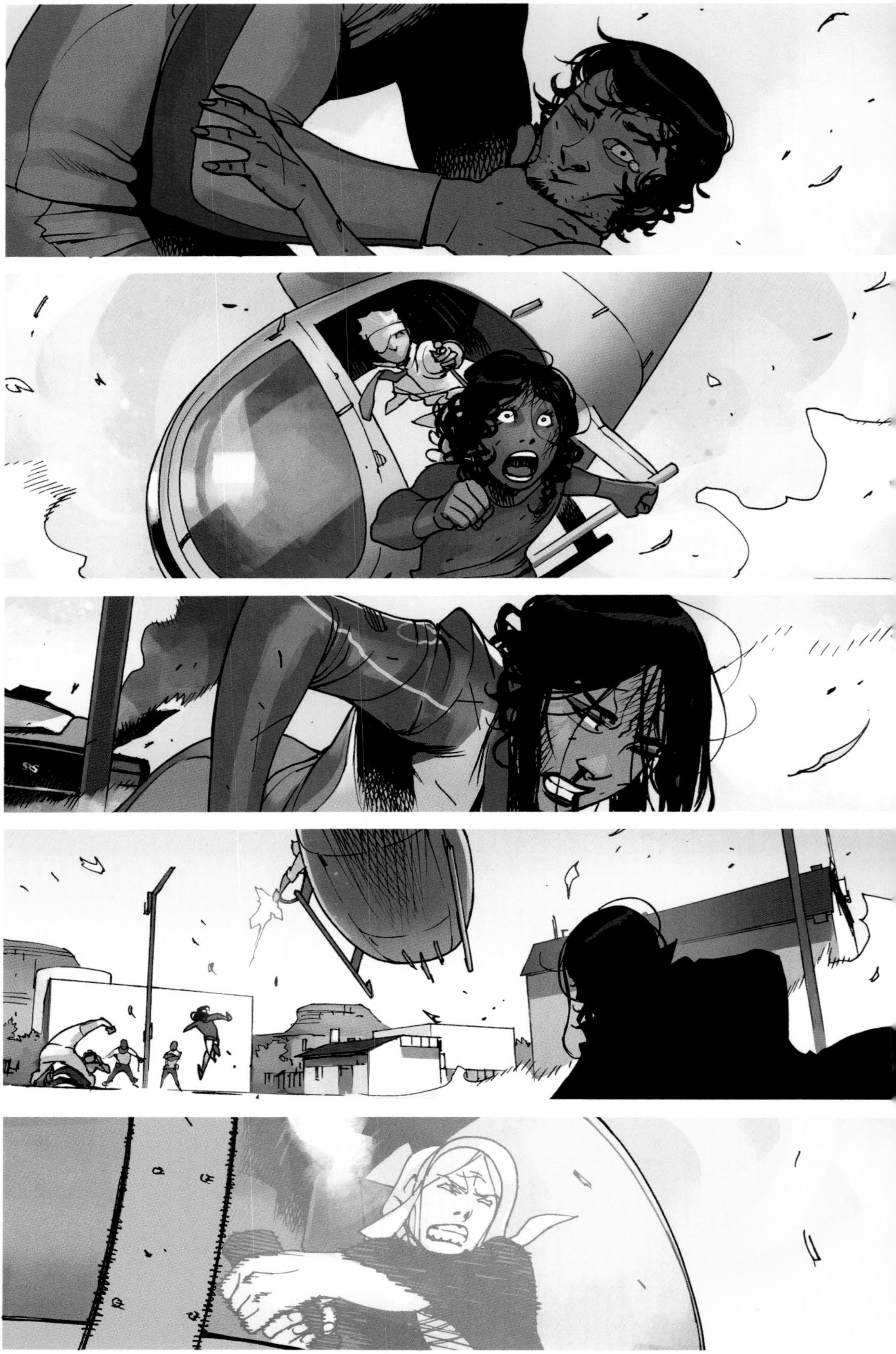

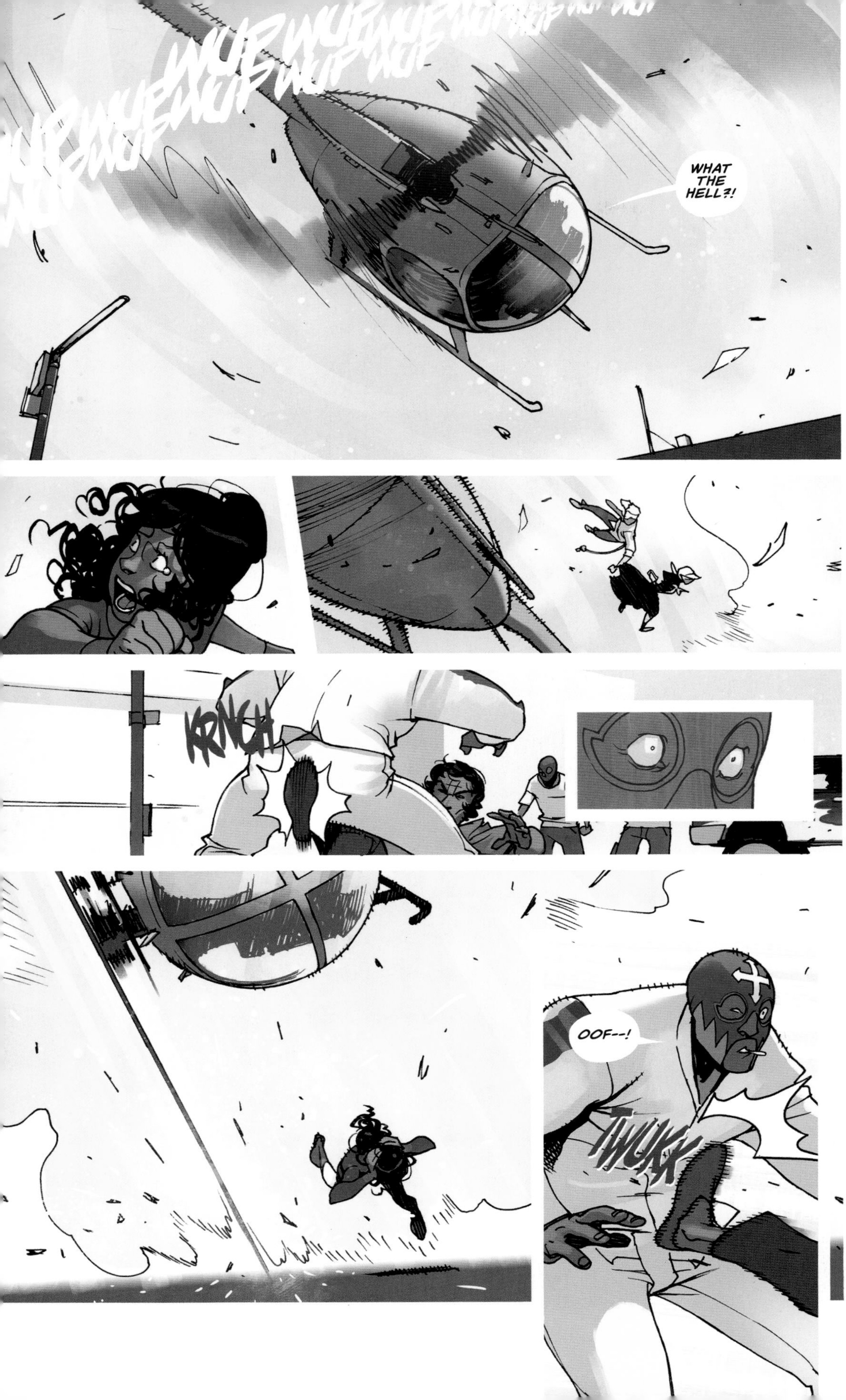
WUP WUP WUP WUP WUP WUP WUP WUP
WHAT THE HELL?!
KRNCH
OOF--!
TWUKK

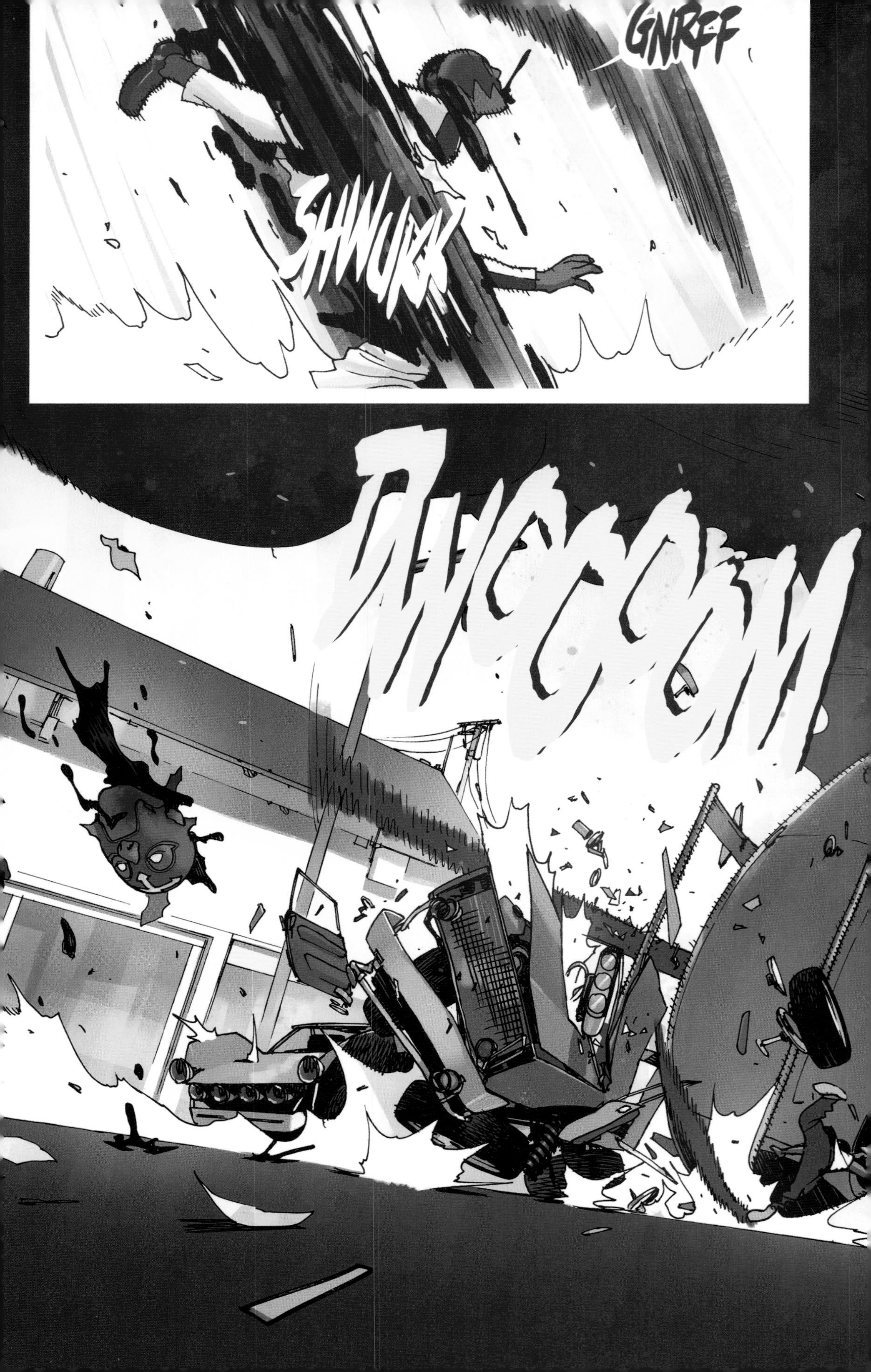
GNRFF
DWOOOOM

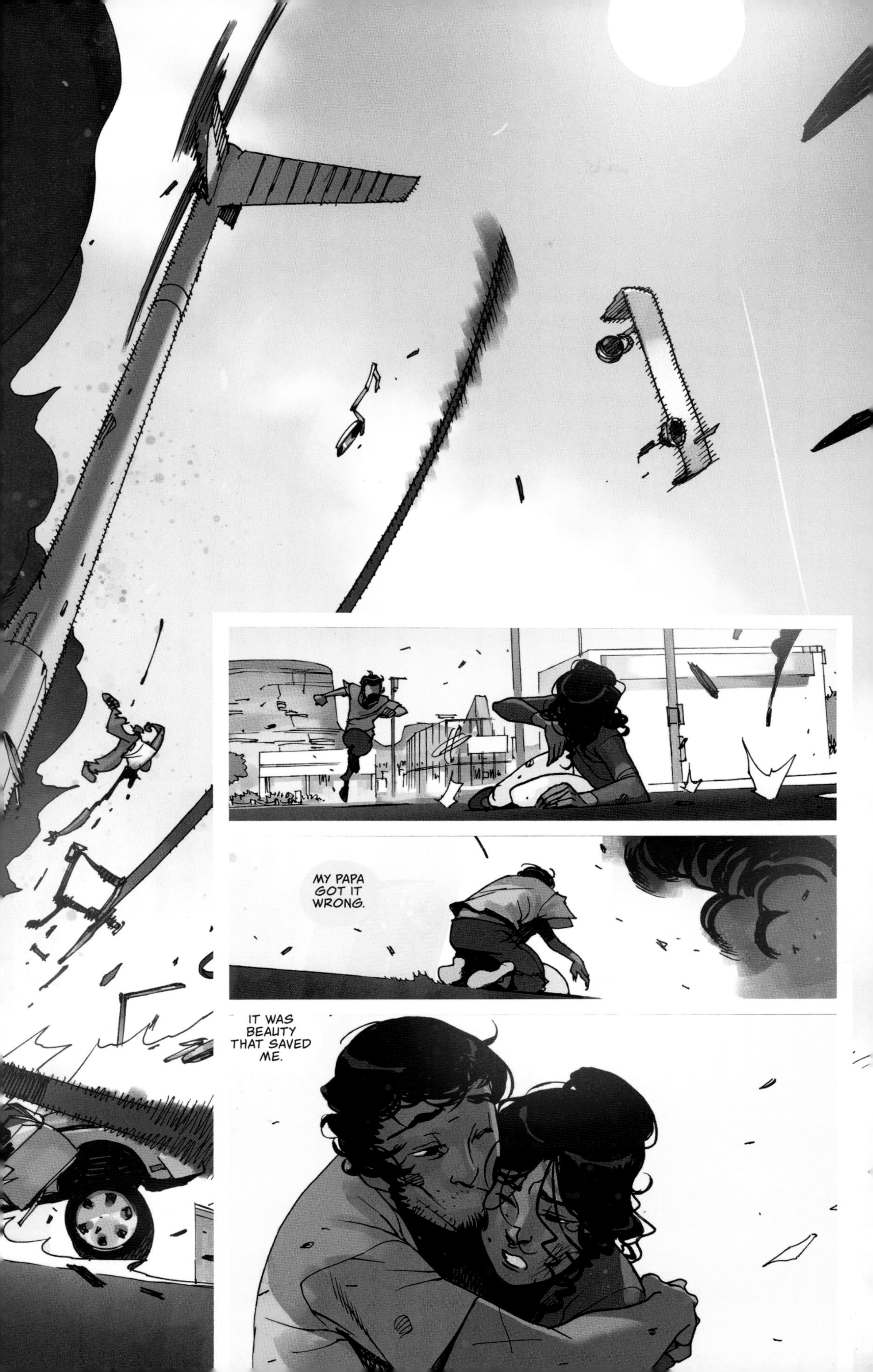
MY PAPA GOT IT WRONG.
IT WAS BEAUTY THAT SAVED ME.

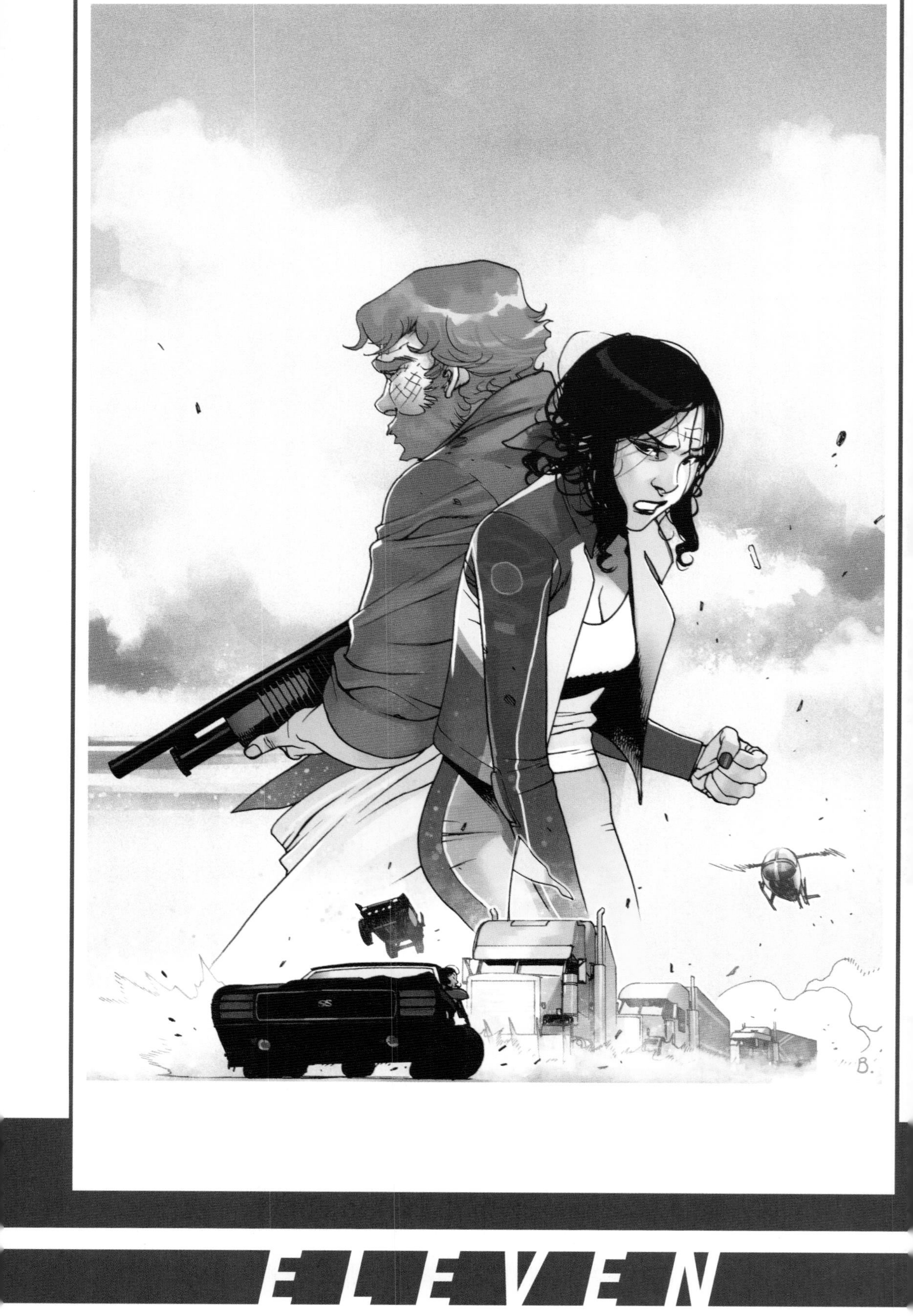

E L E V E N

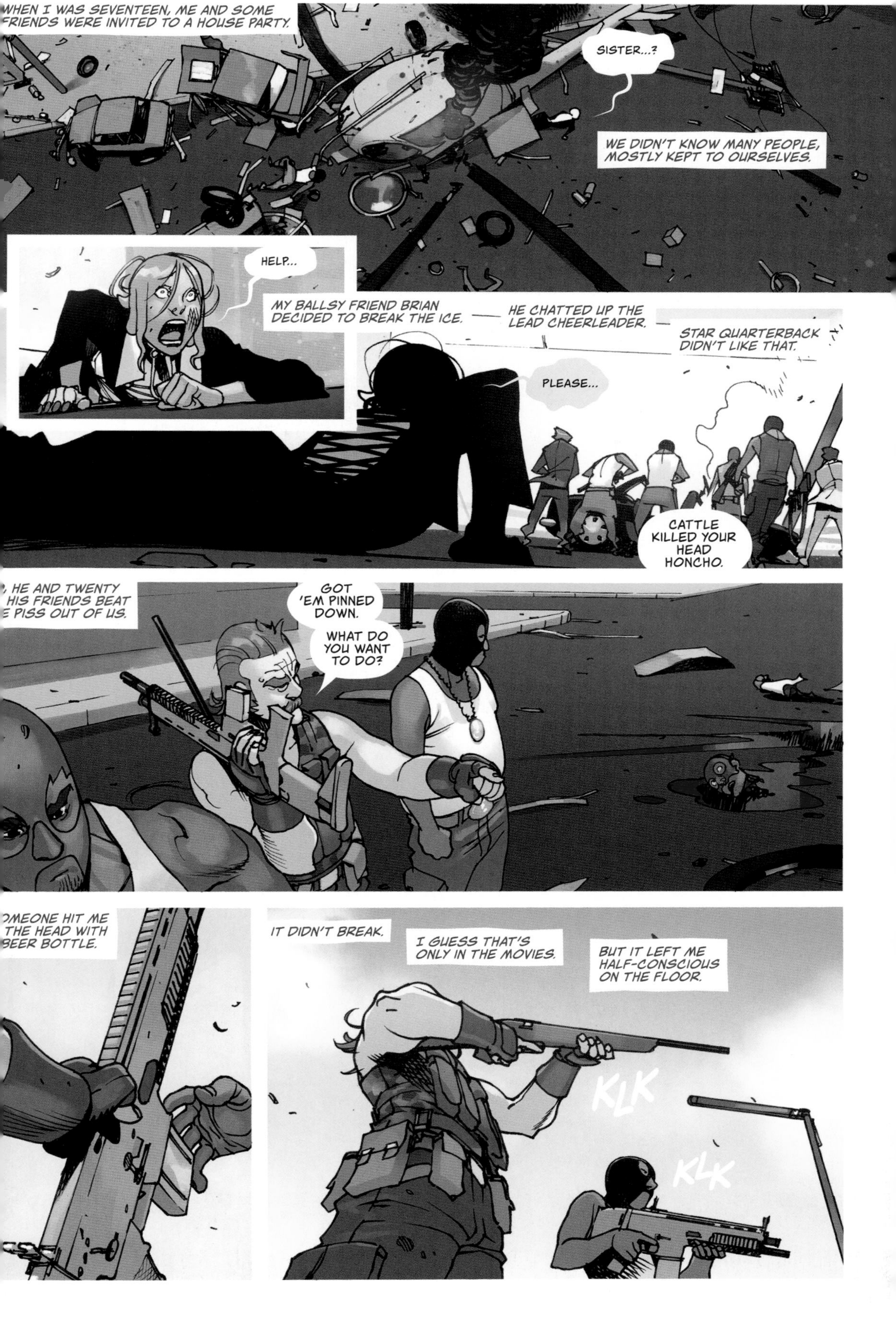
WHEN I WAS SEVENTEEN, ME AND SOME FRIENDS WERE INVITED TO A HOUSE PARTY.
SISTER...?
WE DIDN'T KNOW MANY PEOPLE, MOSTLY KEPT TO OURSELVES.
HELP...
MY BALLSY FRIEND BRIAN DECIDED TO BREAK THE ICE.
HE CHATTED UP THE LEAD CHEERLEADER.
STAR QUARTERBACK DIDN'T LIKE THAT.
PLEASE...
CATTLE KILLED YOUR HEAD HONCHO.
HE AND TWENTY HIS FRIENDS BEAT PISS OUT OF US.
GOT 'EM PINNED DOWN.
WHAT DO YOU WANT TO DO?
OMEONE HIT ME THE HEAD WITH BEER BOTTLE.
IT DIDN'T BREAK.
I GUESS THAT'S ONLY IN THE MOVIES.
BUT IT LEFT ME HALF-CONSCIOUS ON THE FLOOR.
KLK
KLK

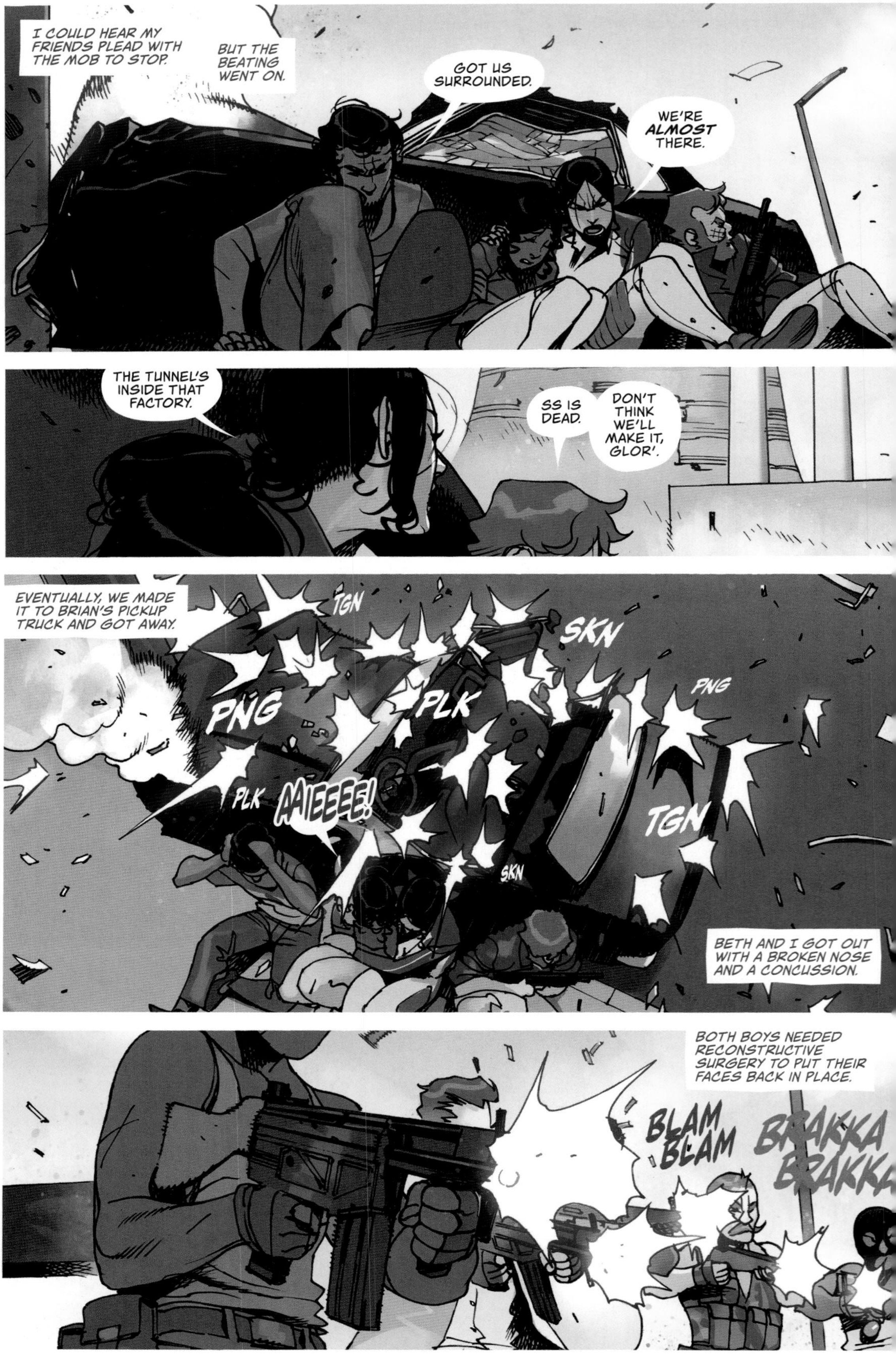
I COULD HEAR MY FRIENDS PLEAD WITH THE MOB TO STOP.
BUT THE BEATING WENT ON.
GOT US SURROUNDED.
WE'RE *ALMOST* THERE.
THE TUNNEL'S INSIDE THAT FACTORY.
SS IS DEAD.
DON'T THINK WE'LL MAKE IT, GLOR'.
EVENTUALLY, WE MADE IT TO BRIAN'S PICKUP TRUCK AND GOT AWAY.
TGN
SKN
PNG
PLK
PNG
PLK
AAIEEEE!
TGN
SKN
BETH AND I GOT OUT WITH A BROKEN NOSE AND A CONCUSSION.
BOTH BOYS NEEDED RECONSTRUCTIVE SURGERY TO PUT THEIR FACES BACK IN PLACE.
BLAM BLAM
BRAKKA BRAKKA

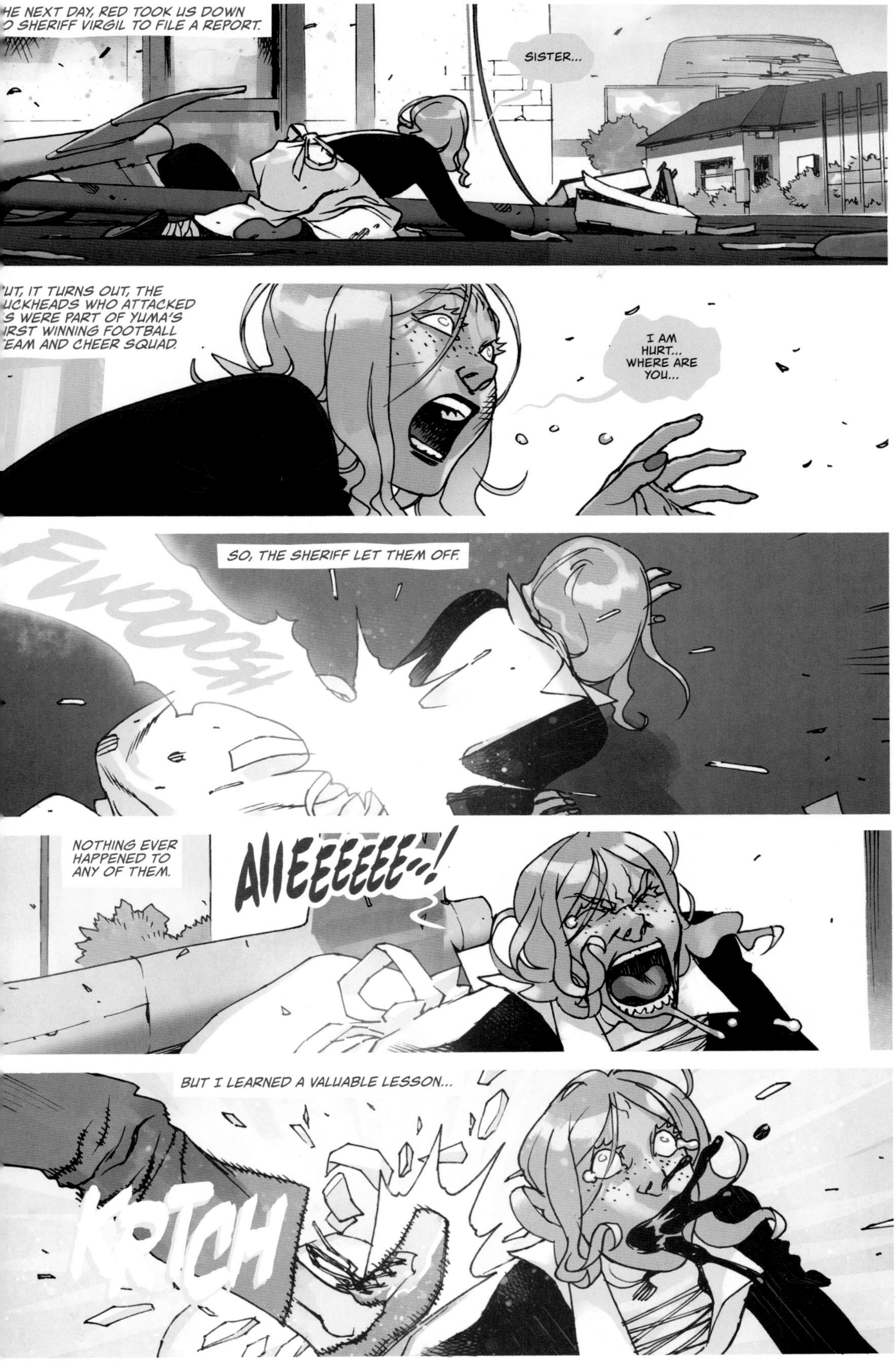
HE NEXT DAY, RED TOOK US DOWN
O SHERIFF VIRGIL TO FILE A REPORT.
SISTER...
UT, IT TURNS OUT, THE
UCKHEADS WHO ATTACKED
S WERE PART OF YUMA'S
IRST WINNING FOOTBALL
EAM AND CHEER SQUAD.
I AM HURT... WHERE ARE YOU...
SO, THE SHERIFF LET THEM OFF.
FWOOOSH
NOTHING EVER HAPPENED TO ANY OF THEM.
AIIEEEEEE--!
BUT I LEARNED A VALUABLE LESSON...
KRTCH

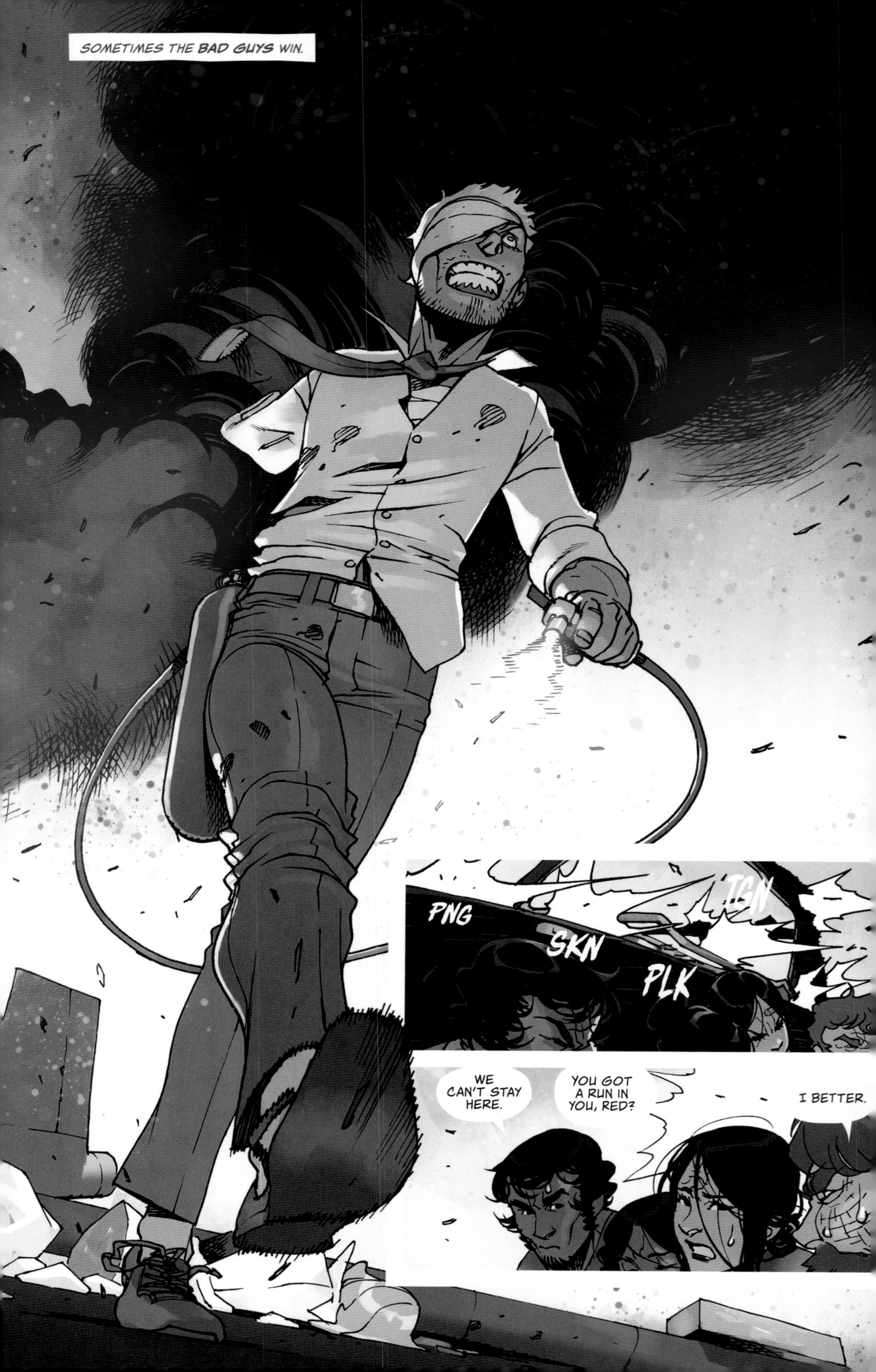
SOMETIMES THE BAD GUYS WIN.
PNG
SKN
PLK
TGN
WE CAN'T STAY HERE.
YOU GOT A RUN IN YOU, RED?
I BETTER.

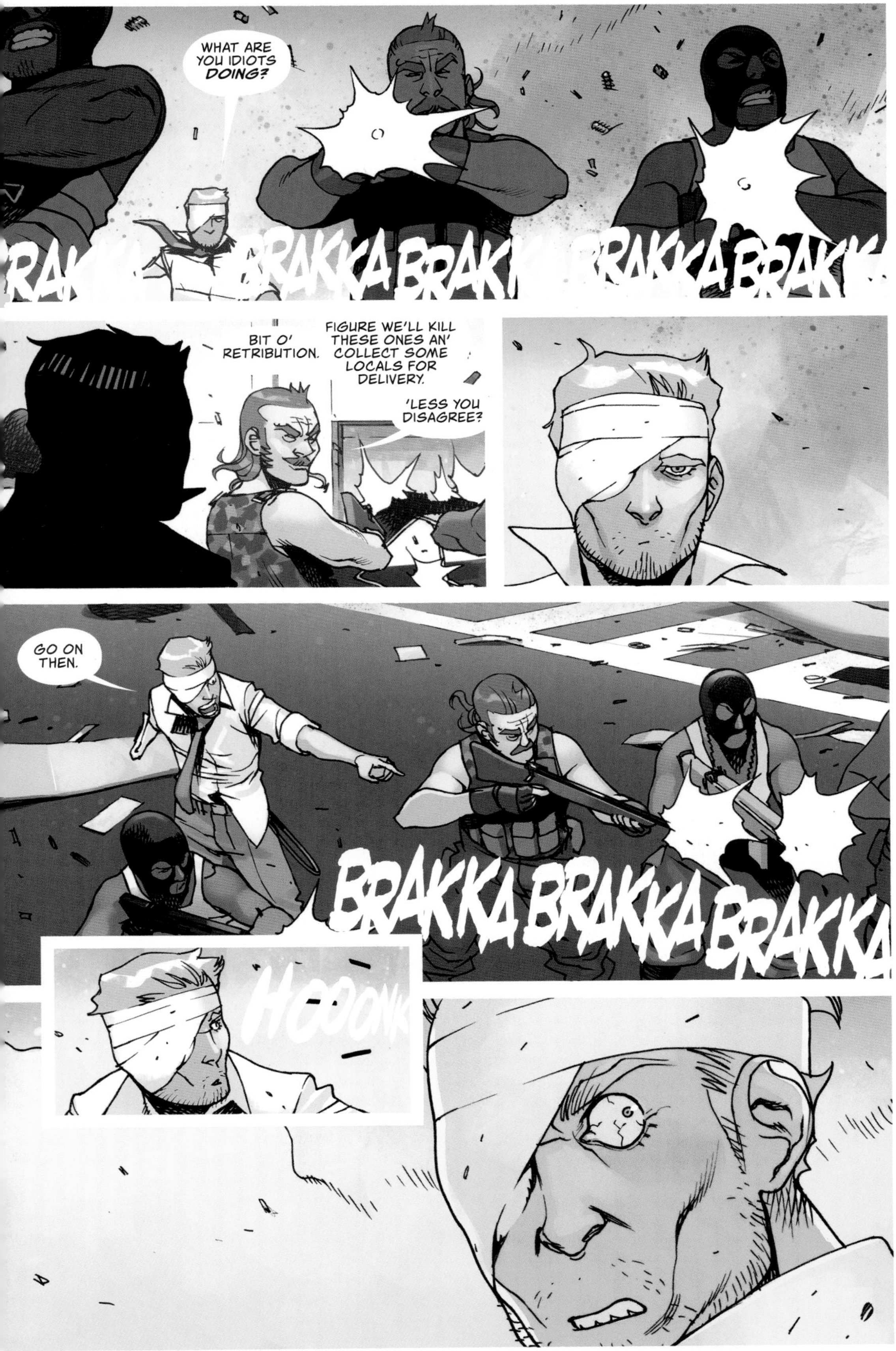
WHAT ARE YOU IDIOTS DOING?
BRAKKA BRAKKA BRAKKA BRAKKA BRAKKA
BIT O' RETRIBUTION.
FIGURE WE'LL KILL THESE ONES AN' COLLECT SOME LOCALS FOR DELIVERY.
'LESS YOU DISAGREE?
GO ON THEN.
BRAKKA BRAKKA BRAKKA
HOOONK

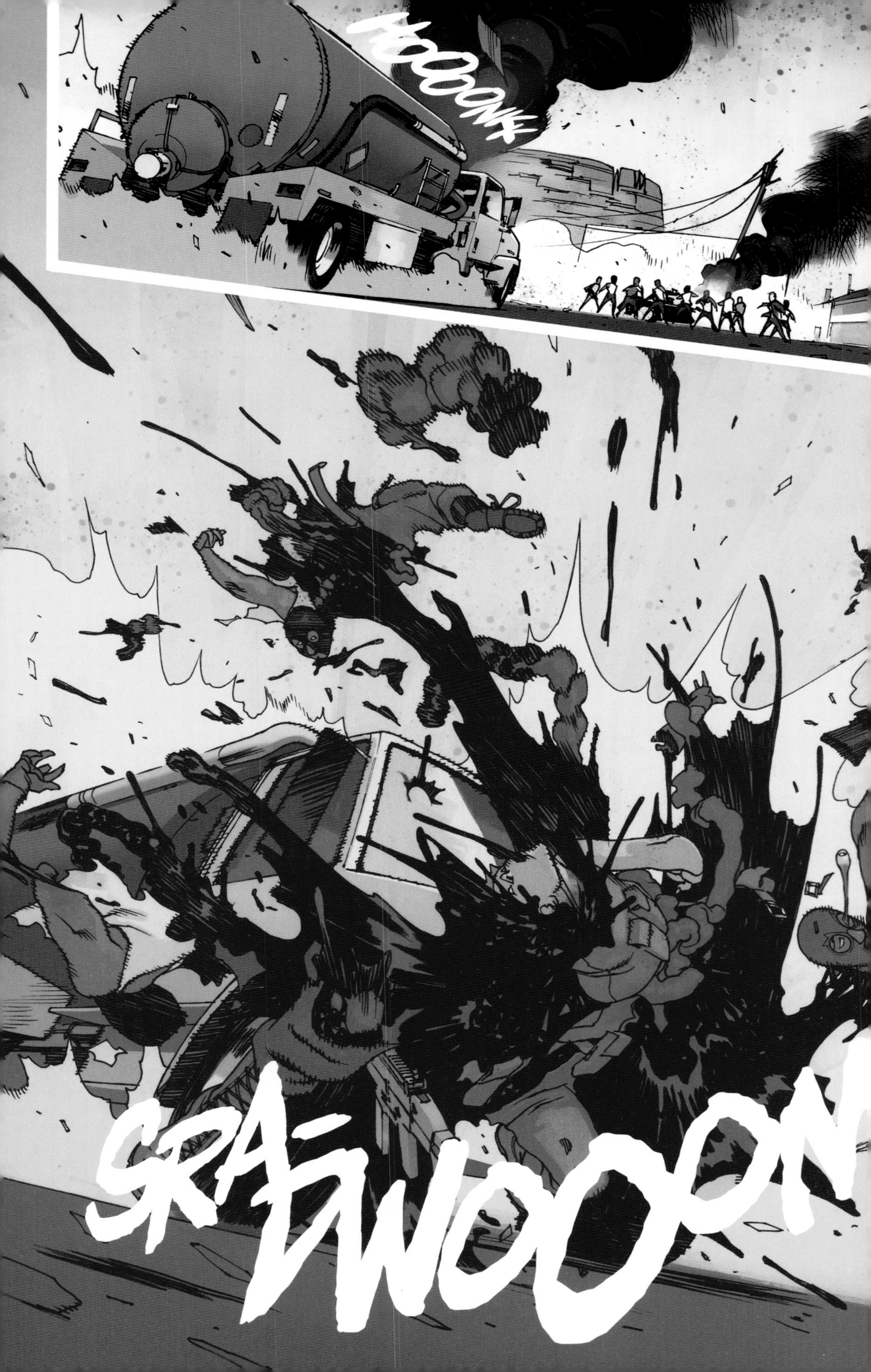
HOOOONK
GRA-DWOOOOM

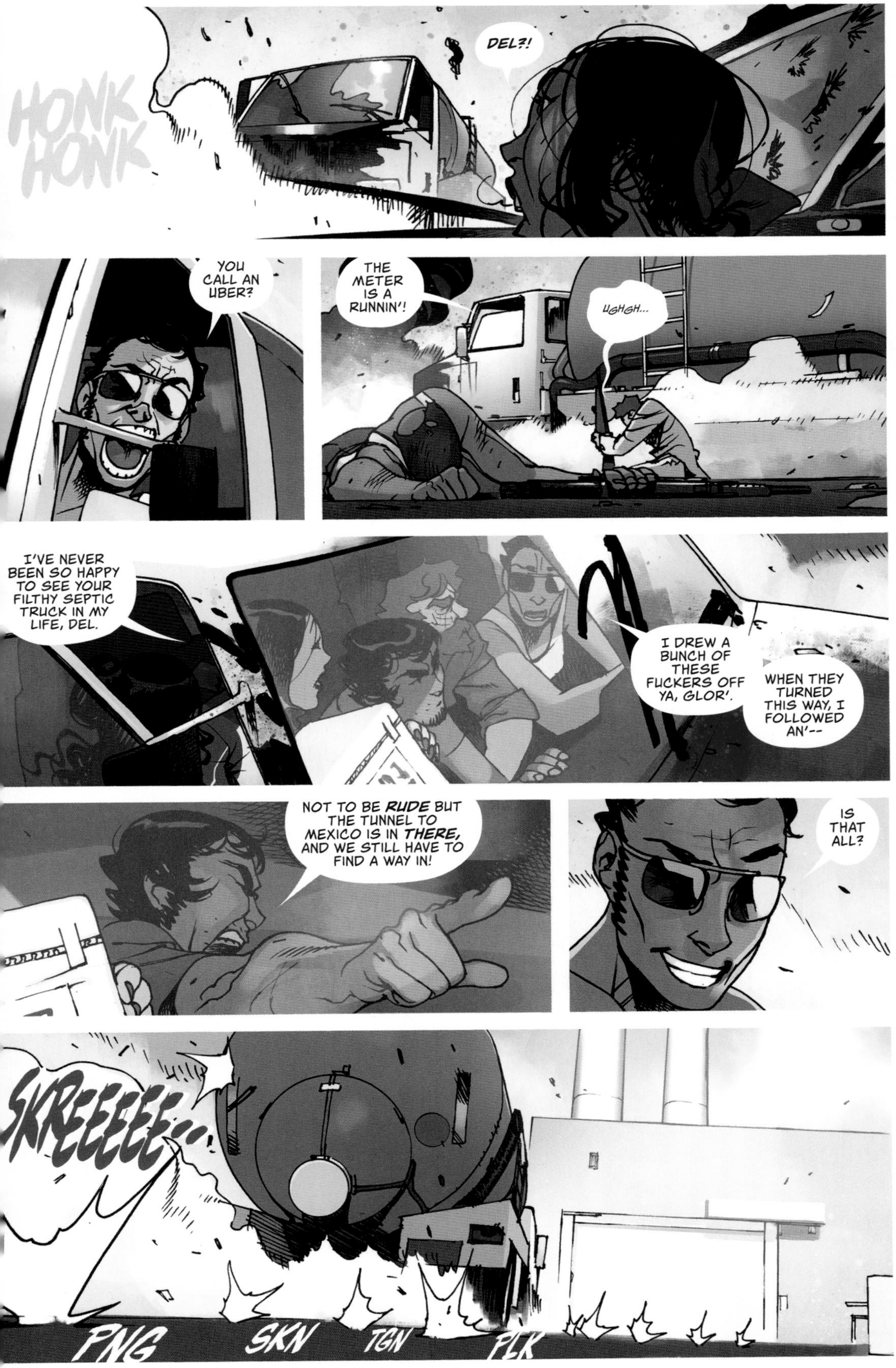
HONK HONK
DEL?!
YOU CALL AN UBER?
THE METER IS A RUNNIN'!
UGHGH...
I'VE NEVER BEEN SO HAPPY TO SEE YOUR FILTHY SEPTIC TRUCK IN MY LIFE, DEL.
I DREW A BUNCH OF THESE FUCKERS OFF YA, GLOR'.
WHEN THEY TURNED THIS WAY, I FOLLOWED AN'--
NOT TO BE *RUDE* BUT THE TUNNEL TO MEXICO IS IN *THERE,* AND WE STILL HAVE TO FIND A WAY IN!
IS THAT ALL?
SKREEEEE...
PNG
SKN
TGN
PLK

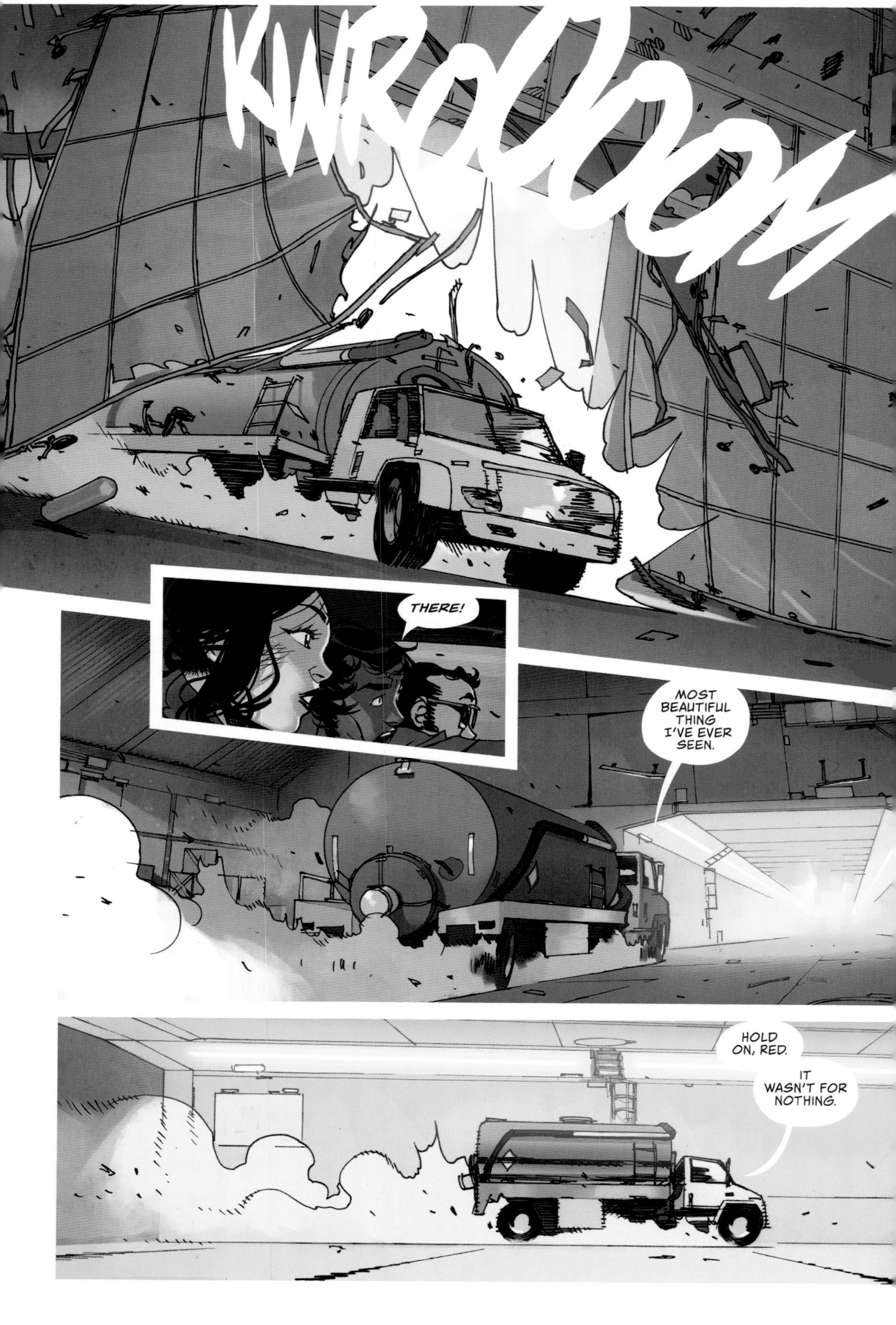
KWROOOOM
THERE!
MOST BEAUTIFUL THING I'VE EVER SEEN.
HOLD ON, RED.
IT WASN'T FOR NOTHING.

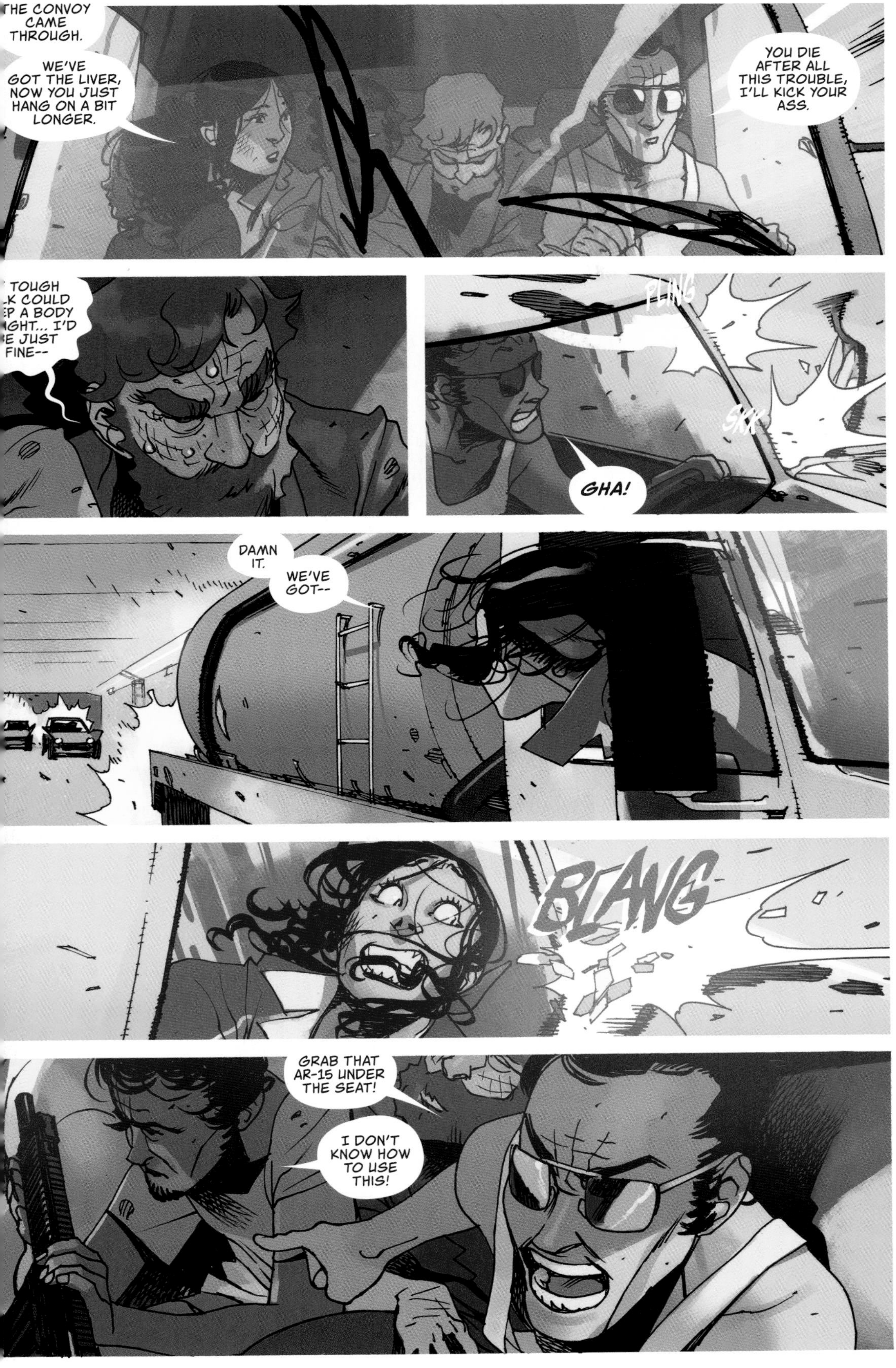
THE CONVOY CAME THROUGH.
WE'VE GOT THE LIVER, NOW YOU JUST HANG ON A BIT LONGER.
YOU DIE AFTER ALL THIS TROUBLE, I'LL KICK YOUR ASS.
TOUGH K COULD EP A BODY IGHT... I'D E JUST FINE--
PLING
SKK
GHA!
DAMN IT.
WE'VE GOT--
BLANG
GRAB THAT AR-15 UNDER THE SEAT!
I DON'T KNOW HOW TO USE THIS!

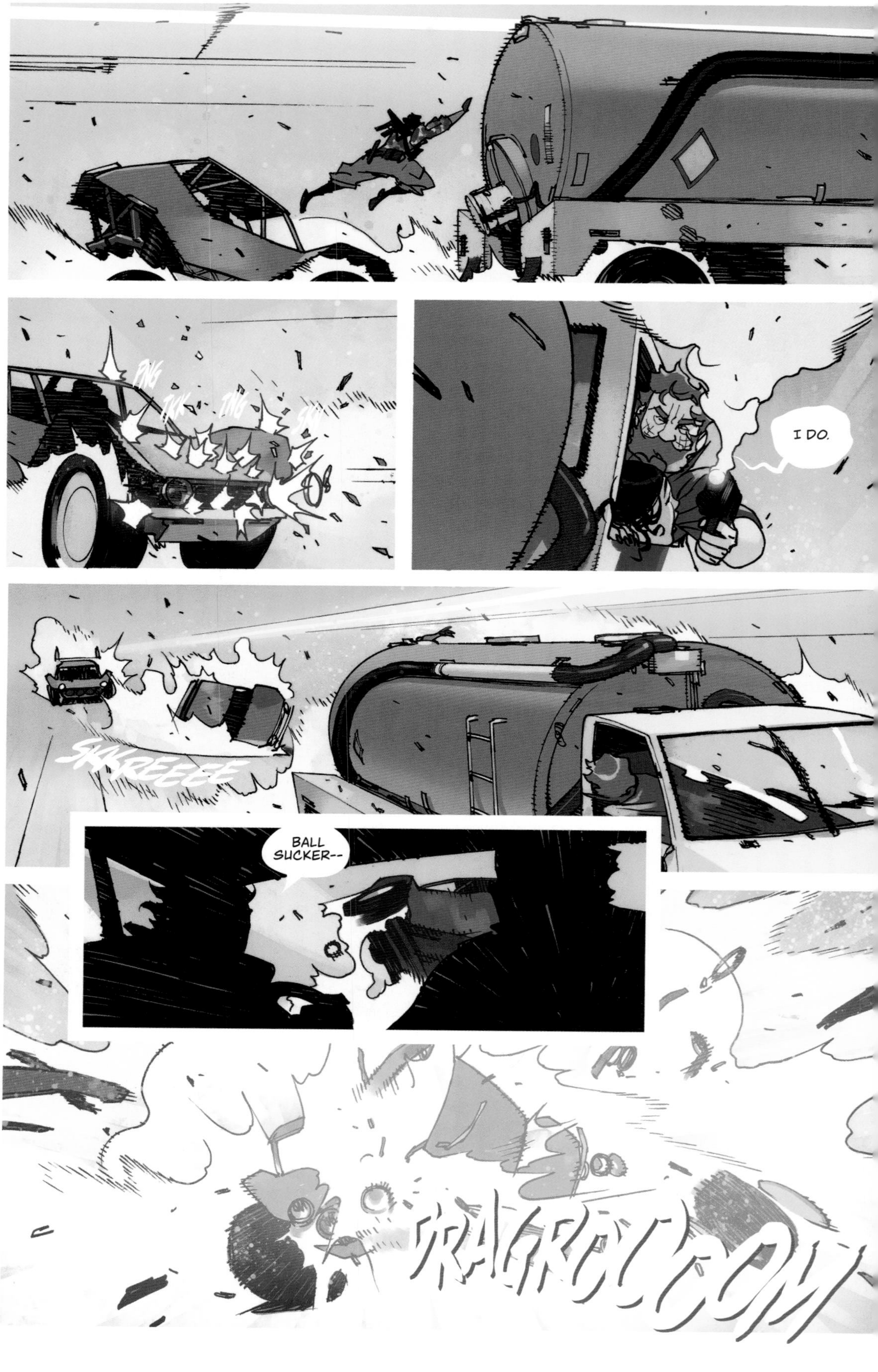
PNG
TKK
TNG
SKK
I DO.
SKKREEEEE
BALL SUCKER--
TRAGROOCOOM

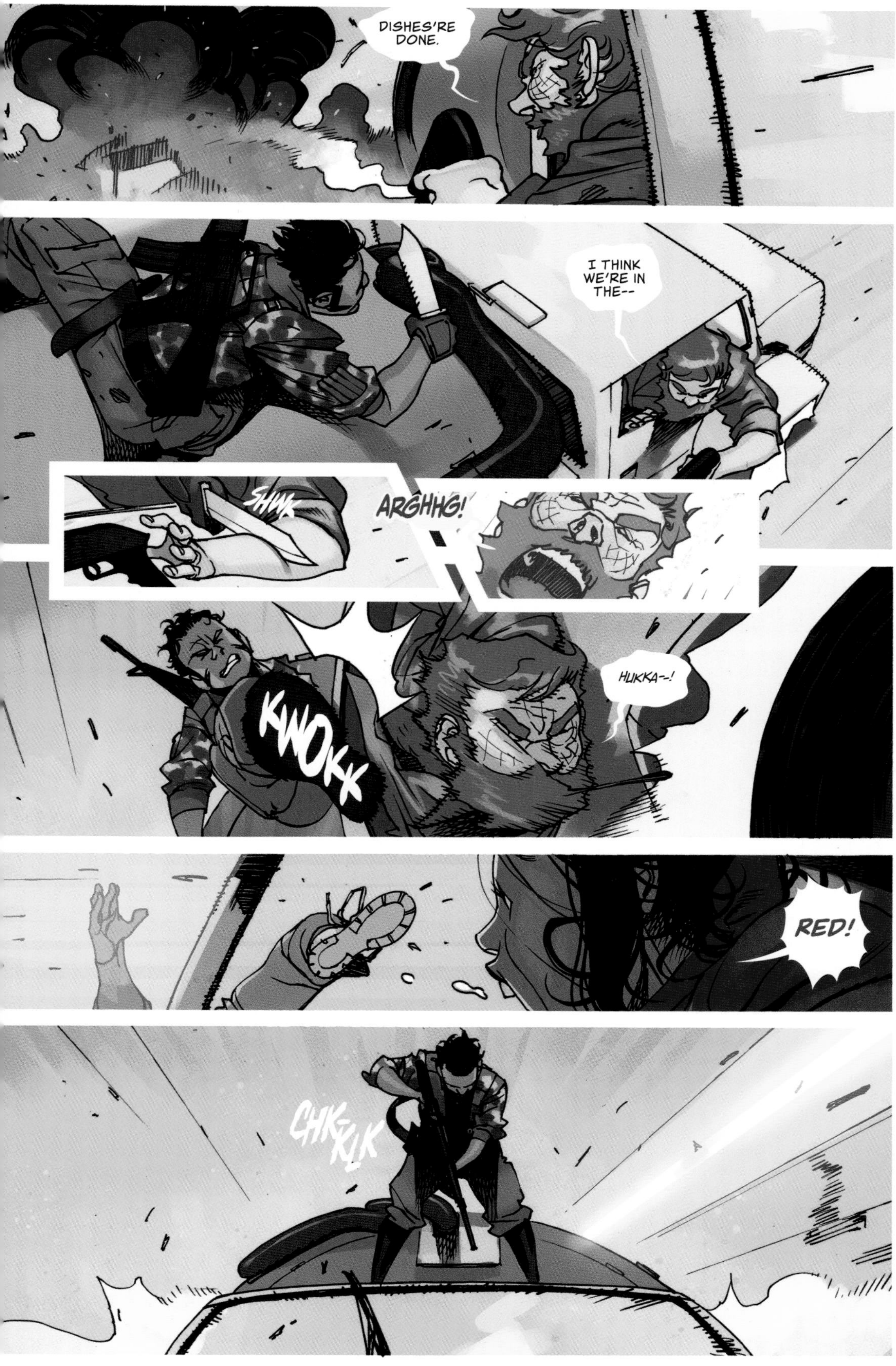
DISHES'RE DONE.
I THINK WE'RE IN THE--
SHUNK
ARGHHG!
KWOKK
HUKKA--!
RED!
CHK-KLIK

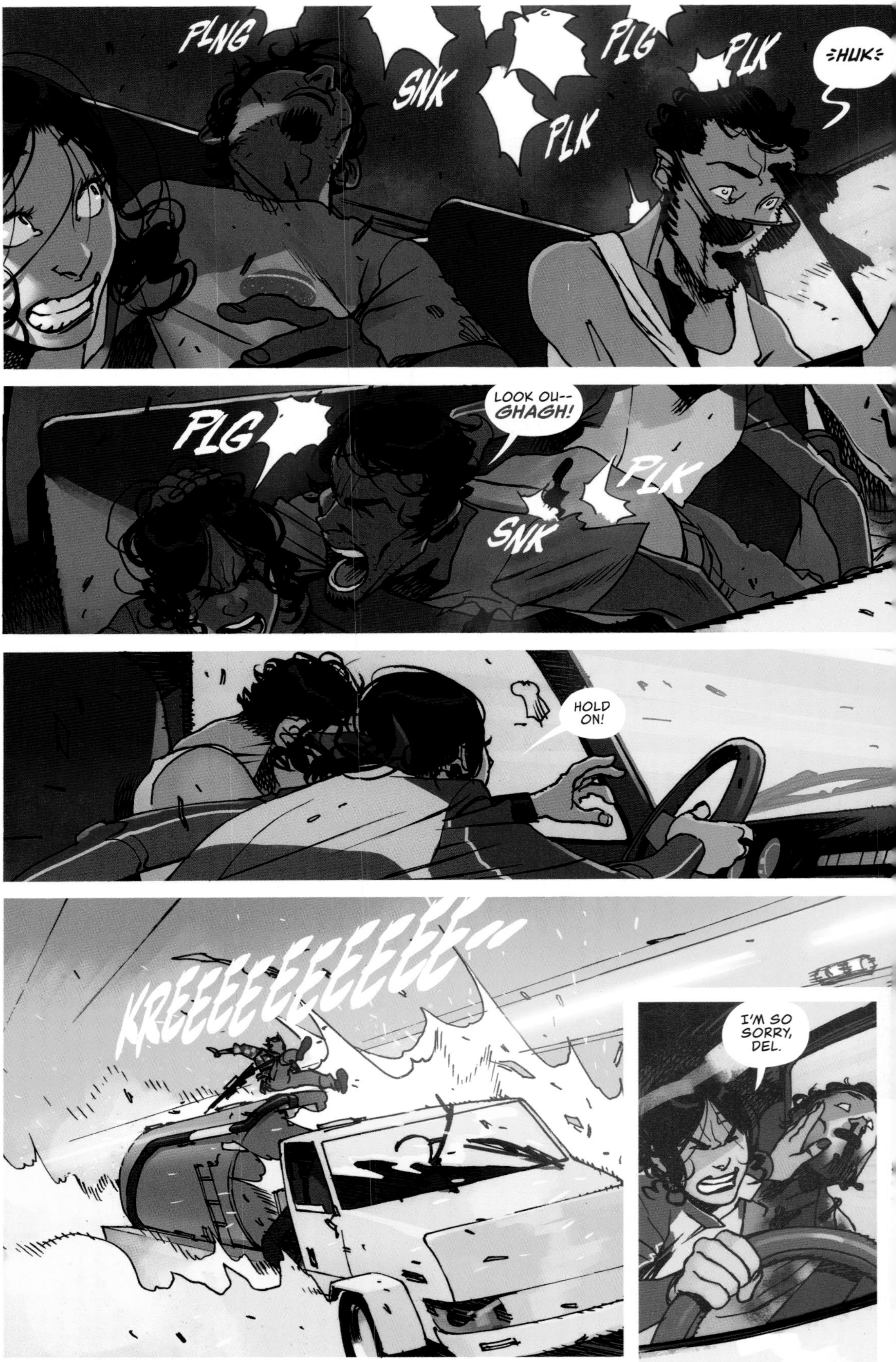
PLNG
SNK
PLK
PLG
PLK
HUK
PLG
LOOK OU-- GHAGH!
PLK
SNK
HOLD ON!
KREEEEEEEEEEEE--
I'M SO SORRY, DEL.

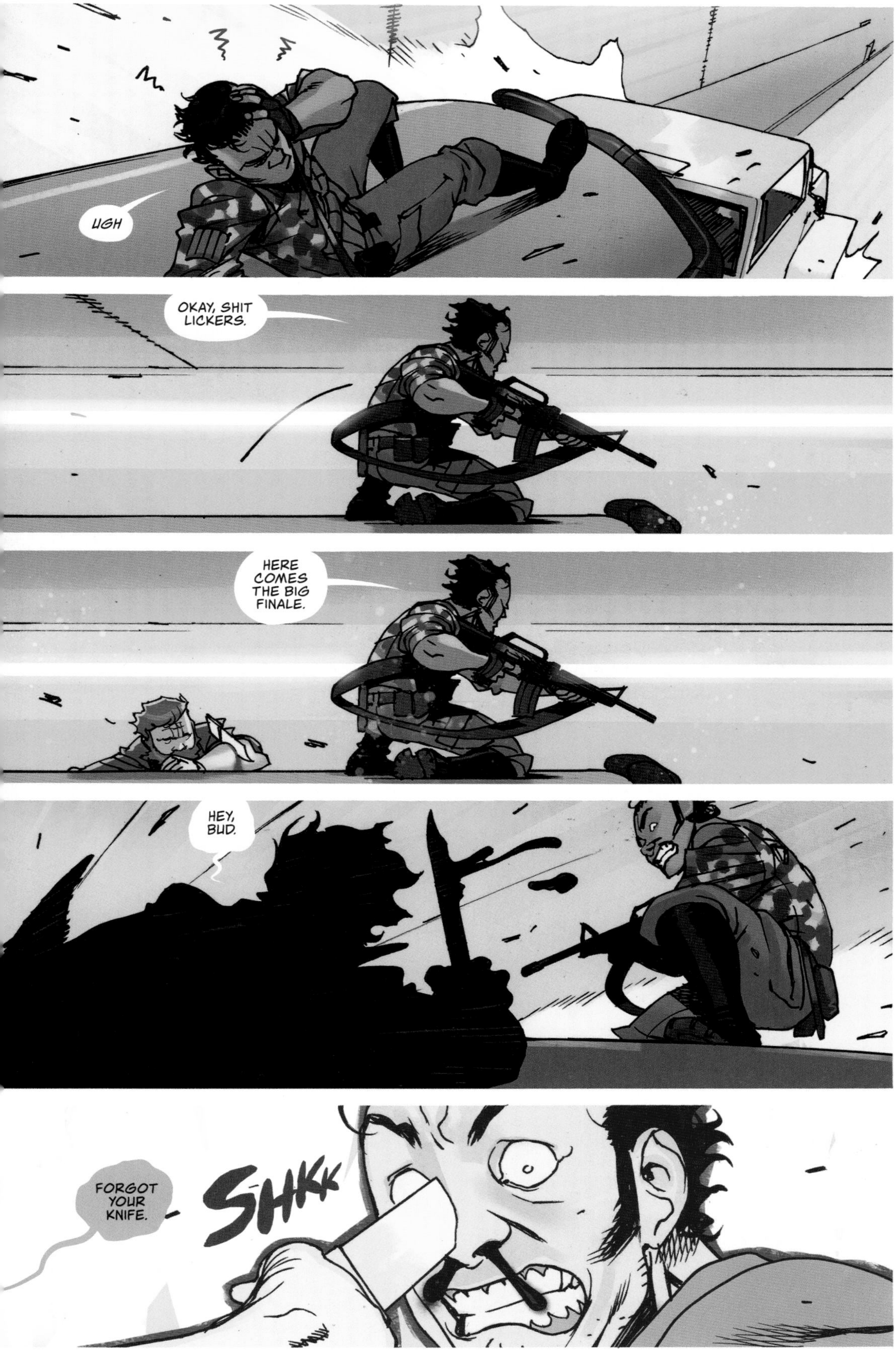
UGH
OKAY, SHIT LICKERS.
HERE COMES THE BIG FINALE.
HEY, BUD.
FORGOT YOUR KNIFE.
SHKK

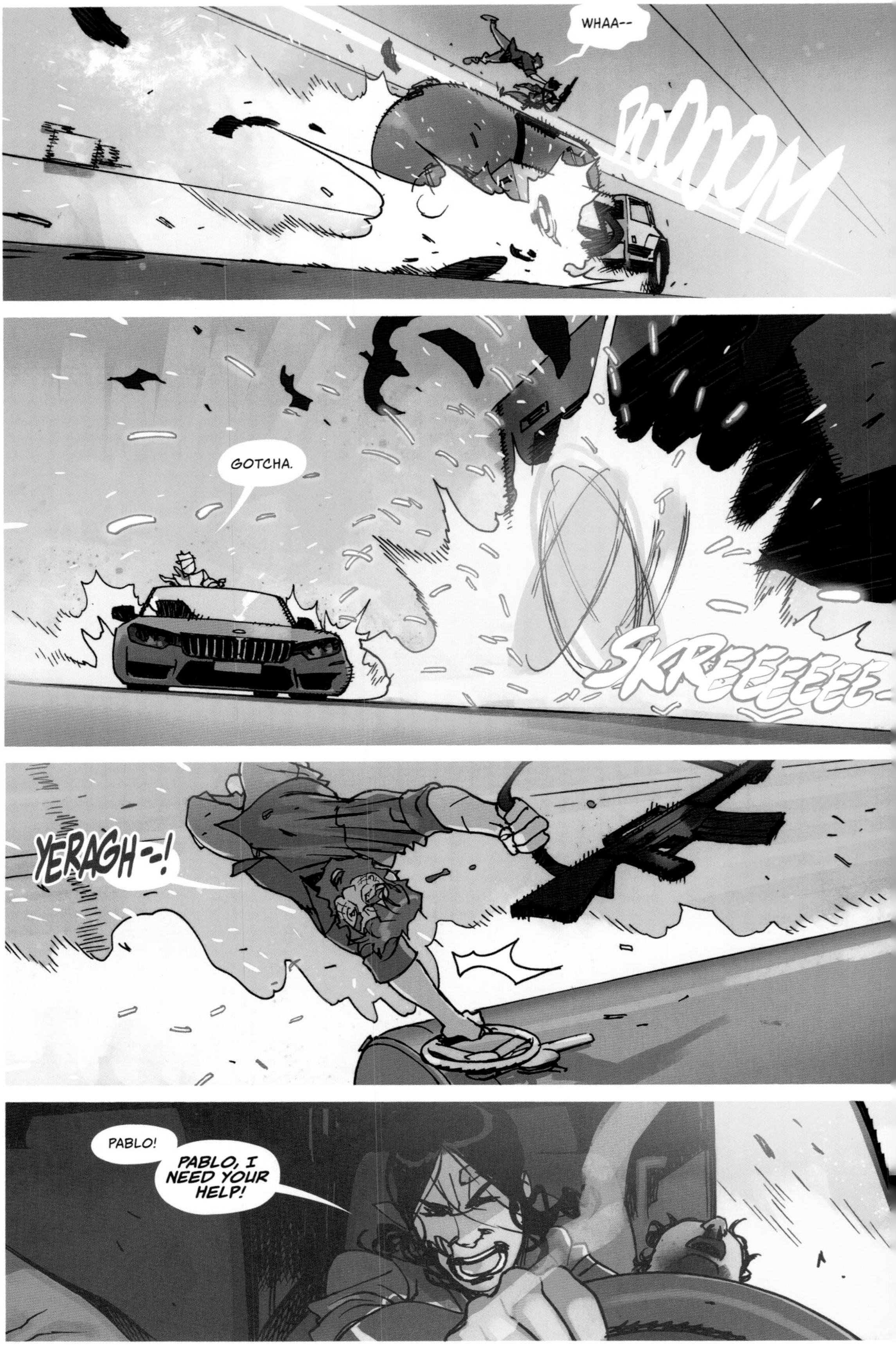
WHAA--
BOOOOM
GOTCHA.
SKREEEEEEE-
YERAGH--!
PABLO!
PABLO, I NEED YOUR HELP!

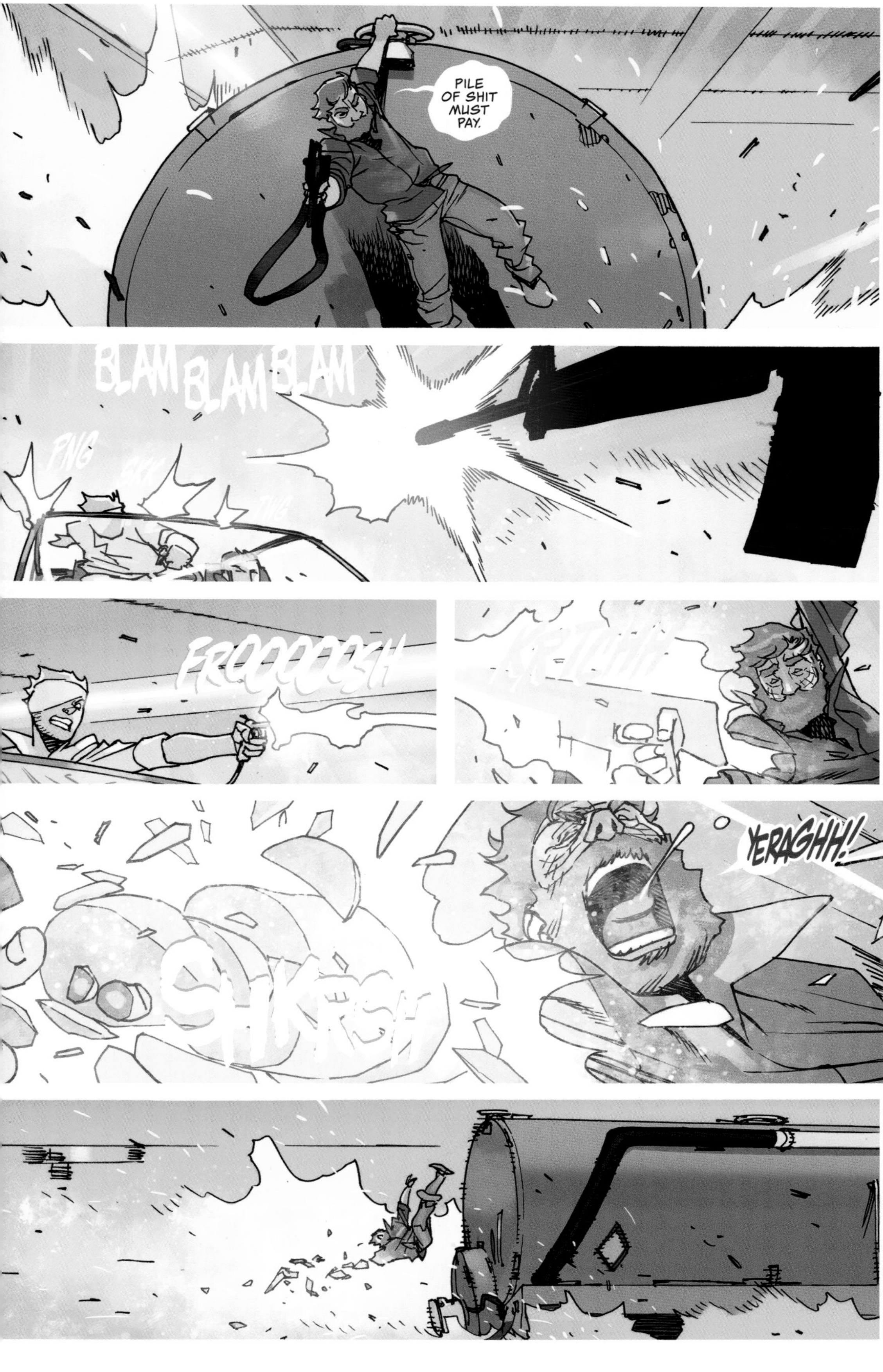
PILE OF SHIT MUST PAY.
BLAM BLAM BLAM
PNG
SKK
TWG
FROOOOOOSH
YERAGHH!
SHKRSH

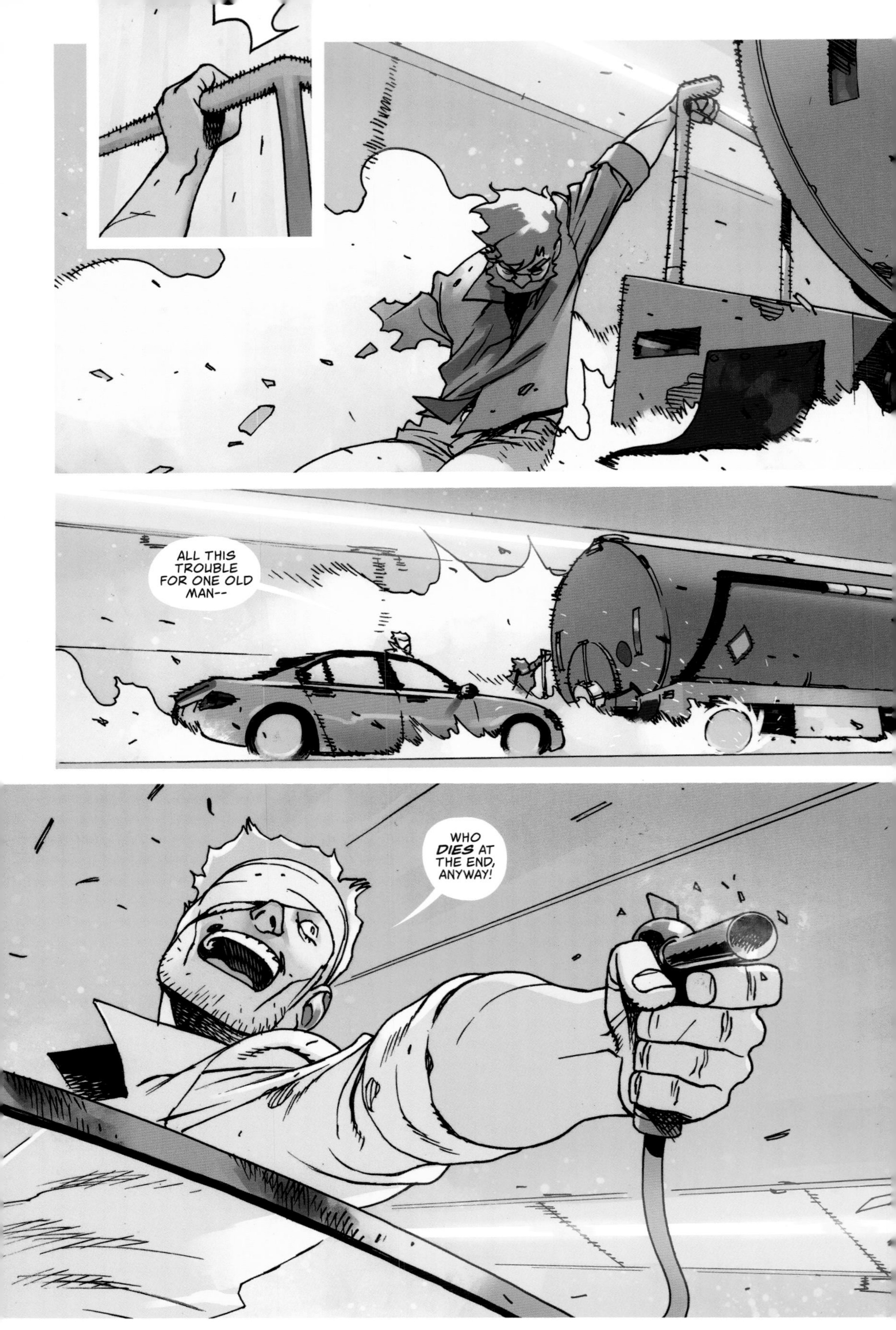
ALL THIS TROUBLE FOR ONE OLD MAN--
WHO DIES AT THE END, ANYWAY!

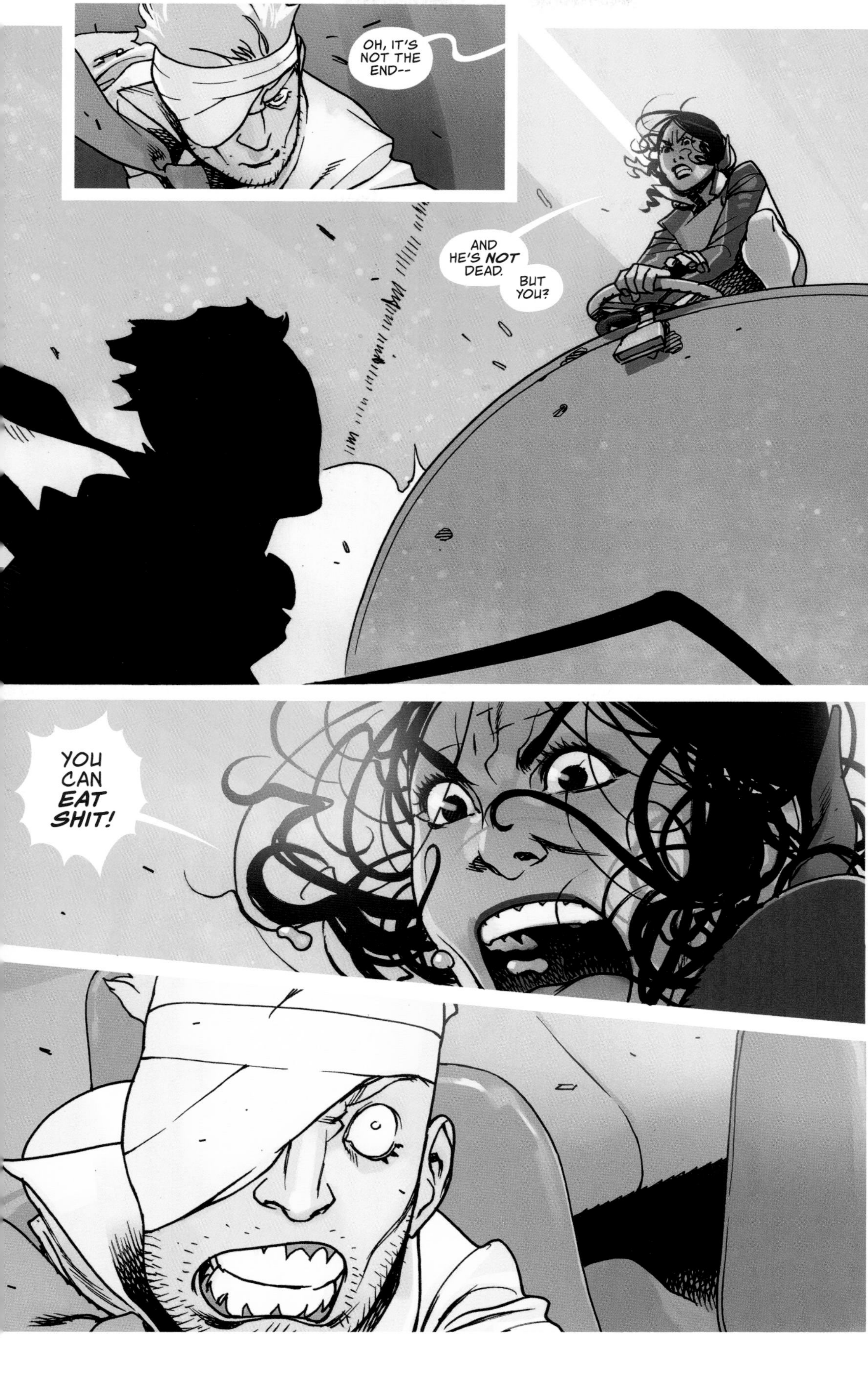
OH, IT'S NOT THE END--
AND HE'S NOT DEAD.
BUT YOU?
YOU CAN EAT SHIT!

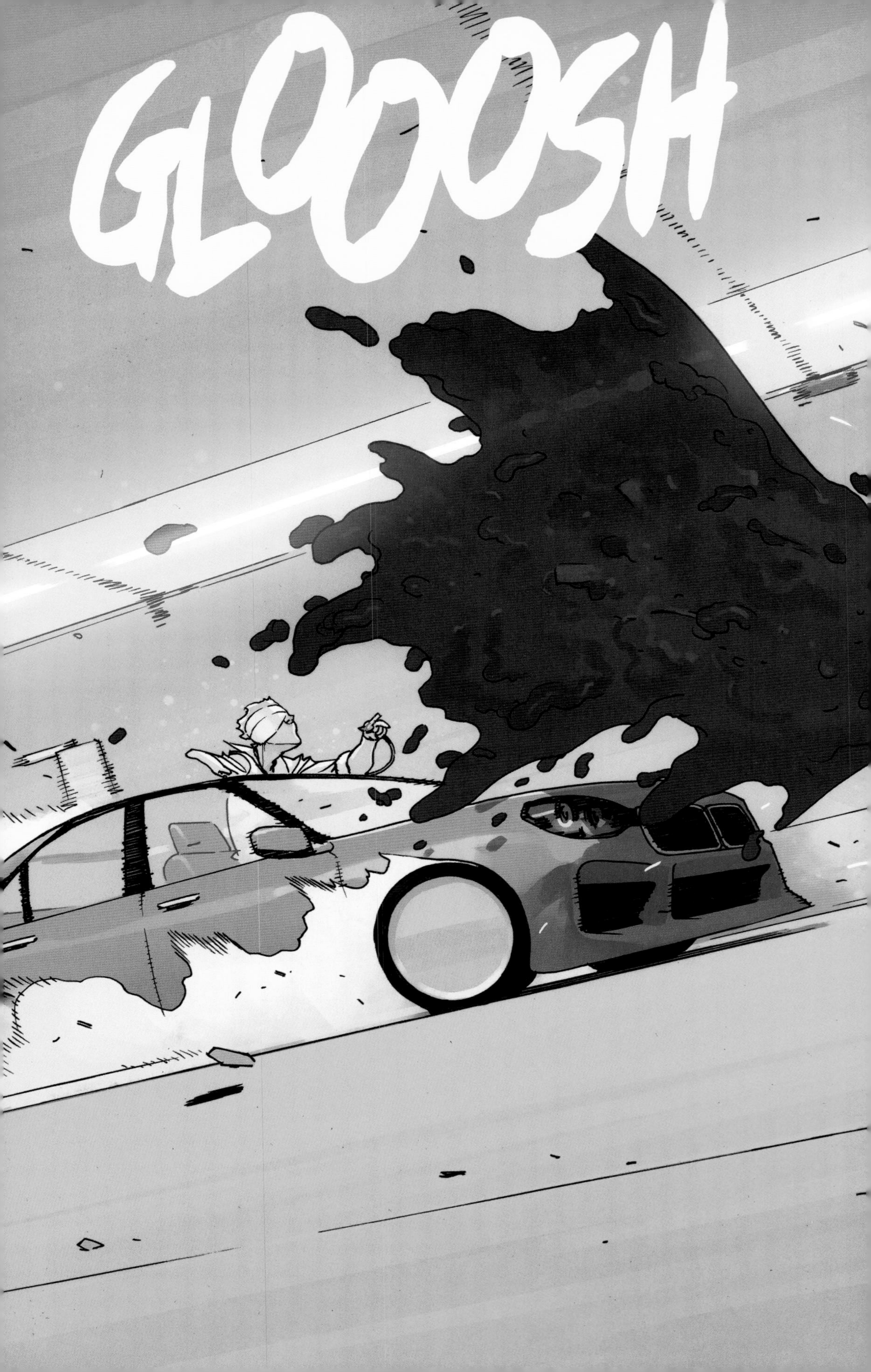
GLOOOSH

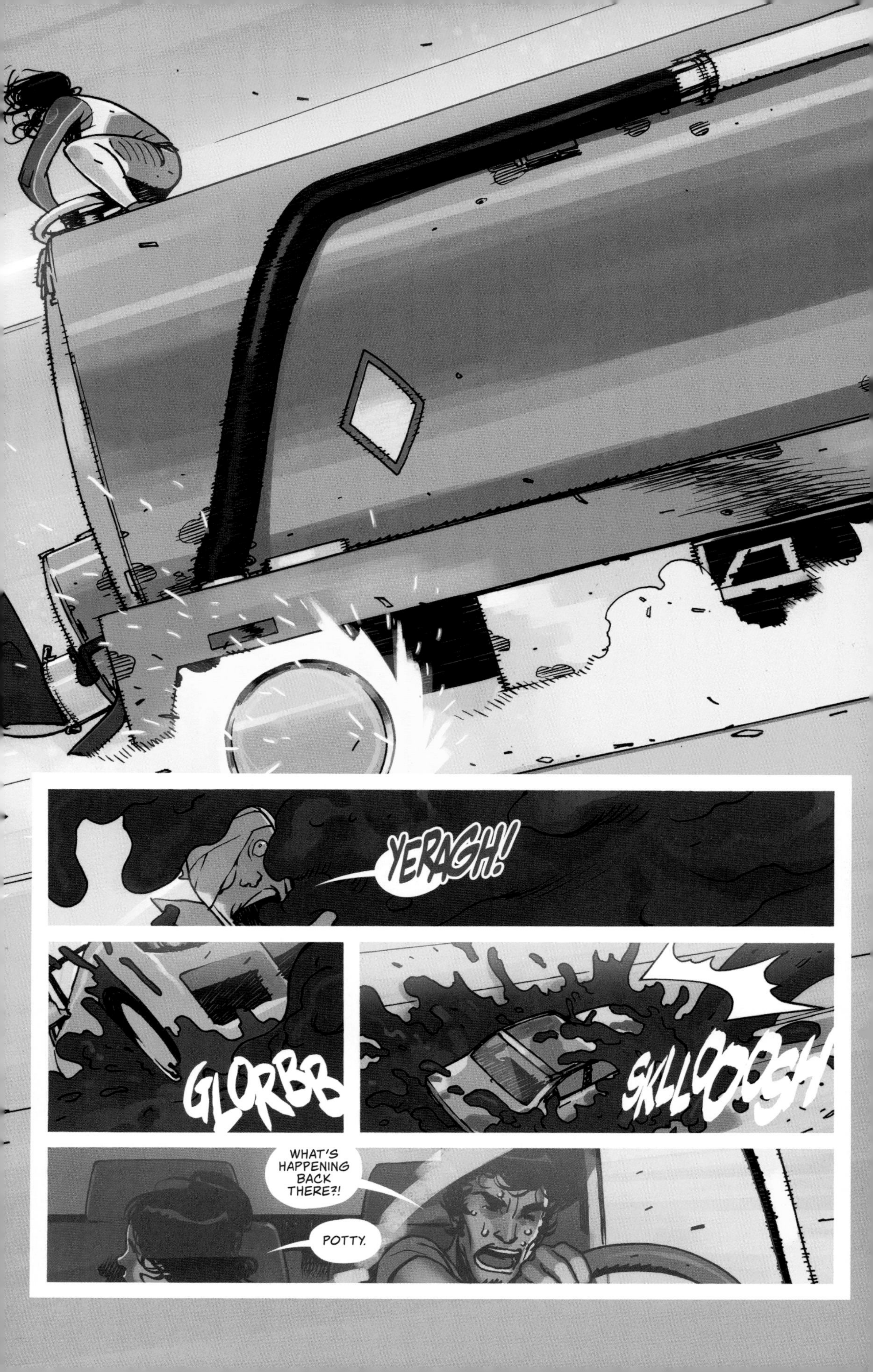
YERAGH!
GLORBB
SKLLOOOSH!
WHAT'S HAPPENING BACK THERE?!
POTTY.

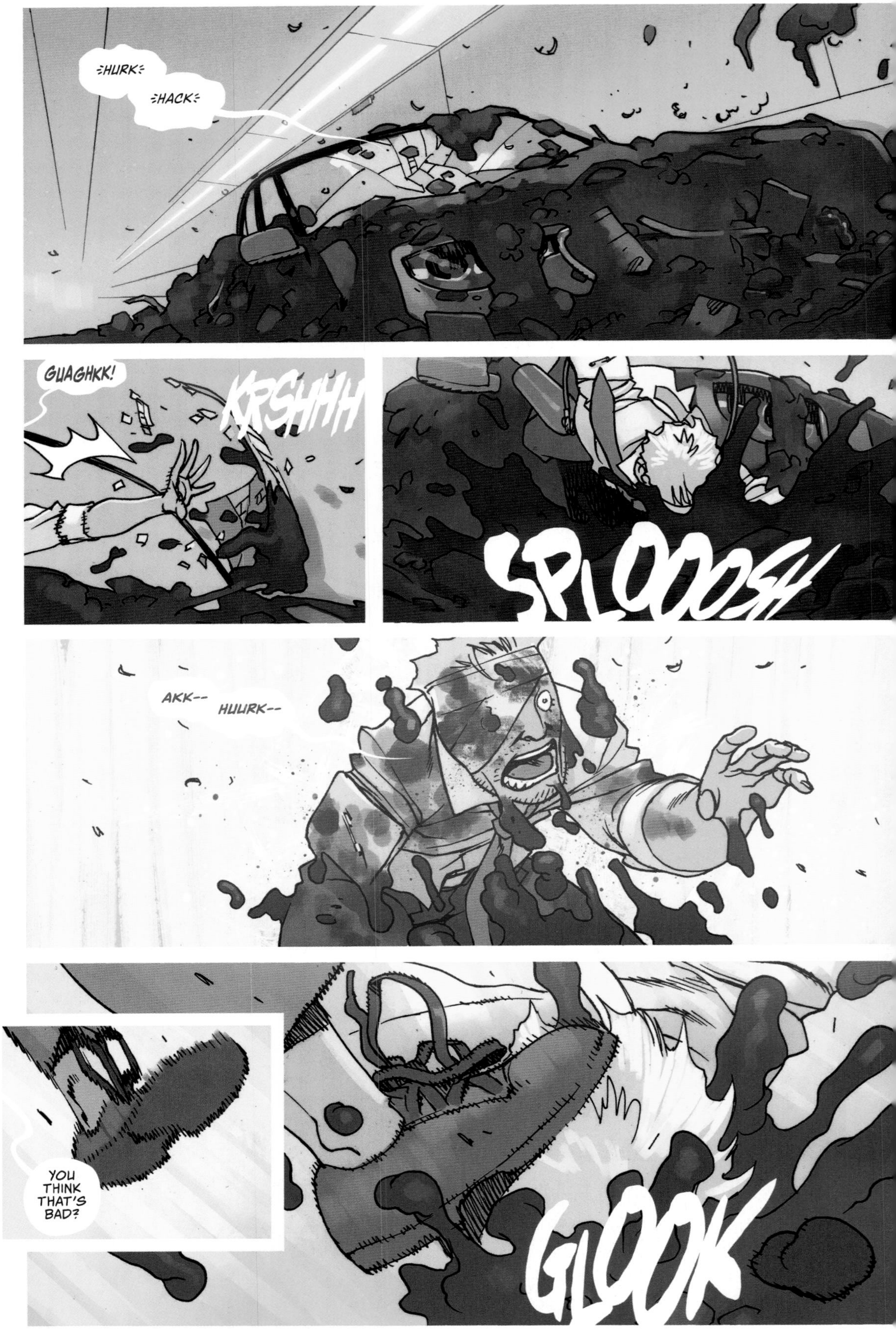

HURK
HACK
GUAGHKK!
KRSHHH
SPLOOOSH
AKK--
HUURK--
YOU THINK THAT'S BAD?
GLOOK

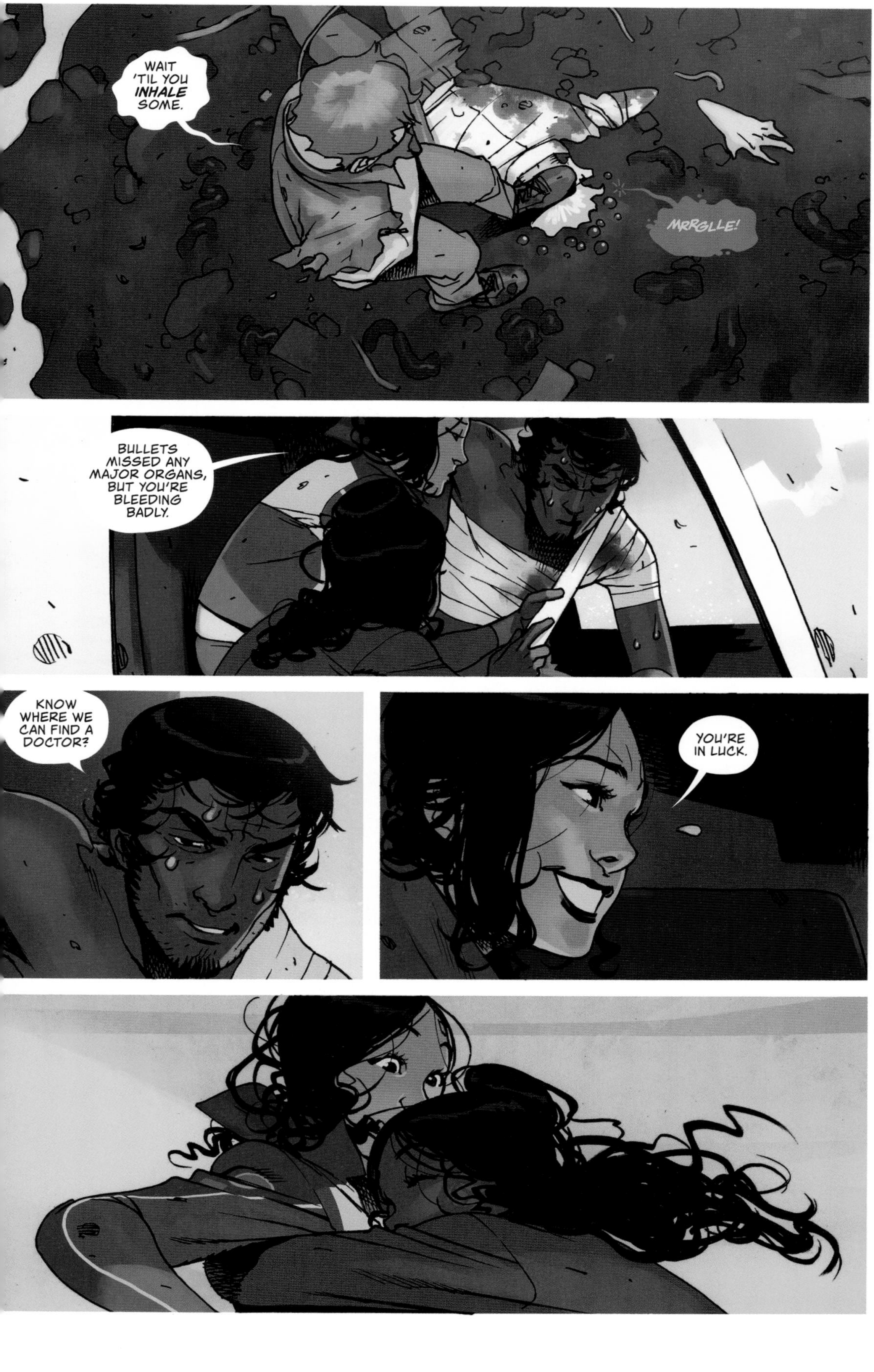
WAIT 'TIL YOU **INHALE** SOME.
MRRGLLE!
BULLETS MISSED ANY MAJOR ORGANS, BUT YOU'RE BLEEDING BADLY.
KNOW WHERE WE CAN FIND A DOCTOR?
YOU'RE IN LUCK.

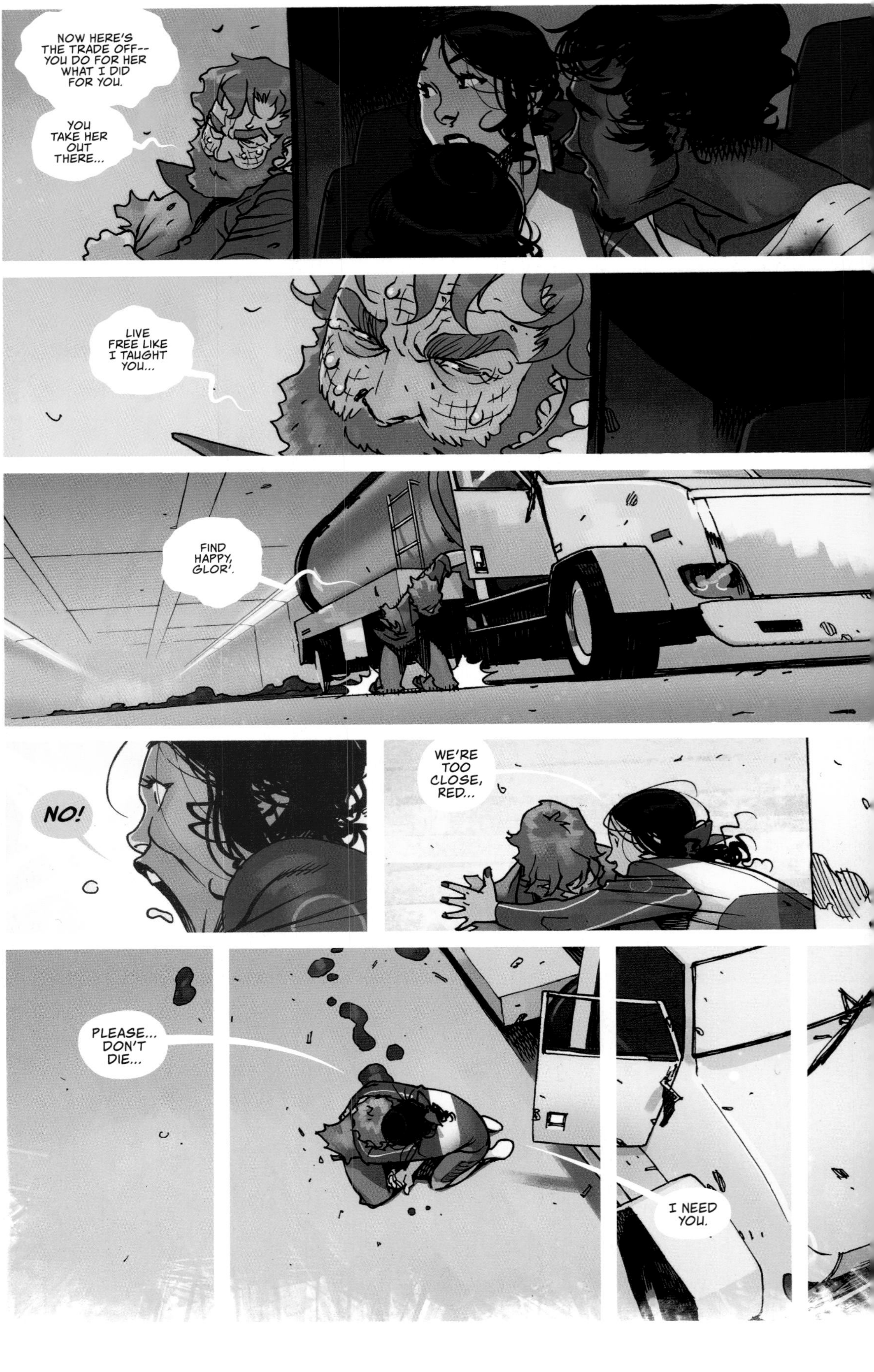
NOW HERE'S THE TRADE OFF-- YOU DO FOR HER WHAT I DID FOR YOU.
YOU TAKE HER OUT THERE...
LIVE FREE LIKE I TAUGHT YOU...
FIND HAPPY, GLOR'.
NO!
WE'RE TOO CLOSE, RED...
PLEASE... DON'T DIE...
I NEED YOU.

"MY EARLIEST MEMORY
OF RED IS BATHED IN
AMBER AFTERNOON
SUNLIGHT."

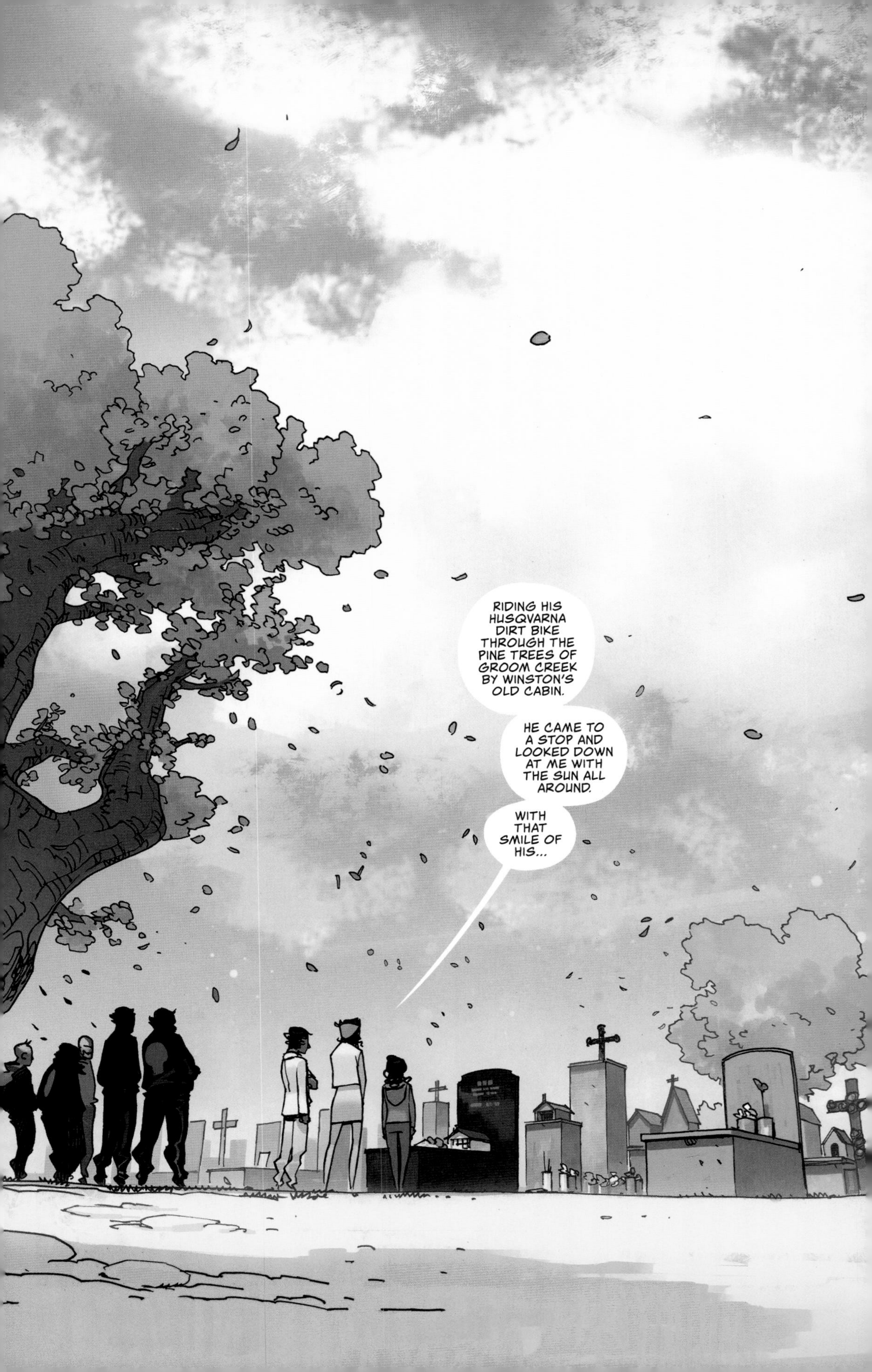
RIDING HIS HUSQVARNA DIRT BIKE THROUGH THE PINE TREES OF GROOM CREEK BY WINSTON'S OLD CABIN.
HE CAME TO A STOP AND LOOKED DOWN AT ME WITH THE SUN ALL AROUND.
WITH THAT SMILE OF HIS...

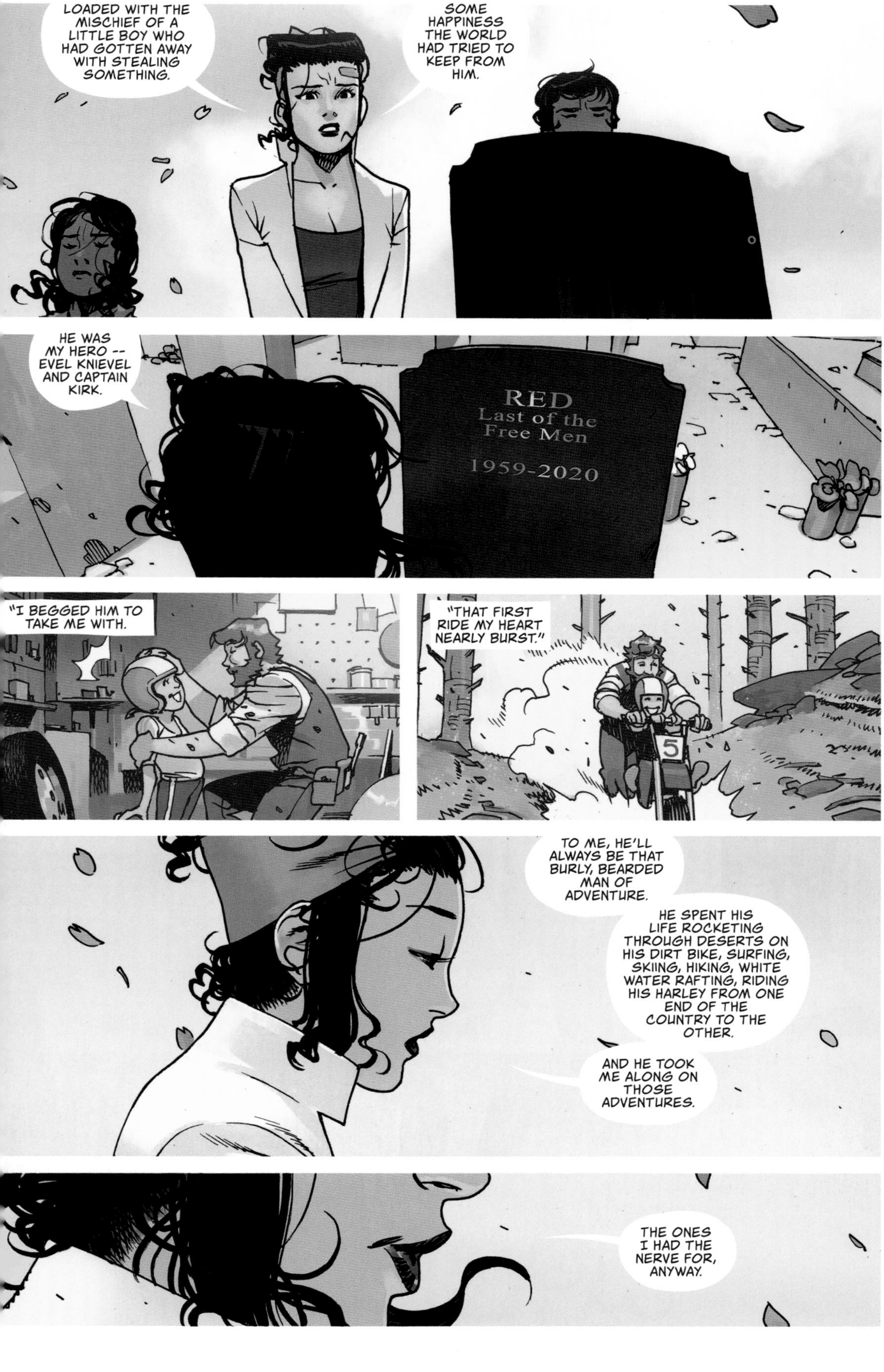

LOADED WITH THE MISCHIEF OF A LITTLE BOY WHO HAD GOTTEN AWAY WITH STEALING SOMETHING.
SOME HAPPINESS THE WORLD HAD TRIED TO KEEP FROM HIM.
HE WAS MY HERO -- EVEL KNIEVEL AND CAPTAIN KIRK.
RED
Last of the Free Men
1959-2020
"I BEGGED HIM TO TAKE ME WITH.
"THAT FIRST RIDE MY HEART NEARLY BURST."
5
TO ME, HE'LL ALWAYS BE THAT BURLY, BEARDED MAN OF ADVENTURE.
HE SPENT HIS LIFE ROCKETING THROUGH DESERTS ON HIS DIRT BIKE, SURFING, SKIING, HIKING, WHITE WATER RAFTING, RIDING HIS HARLEY FROM ONE END OF THE COUNTRY TO THE OTHER.
AND HE TOOK ME ALONG ON THOSE ADVENTURES.
THE ONES I HAD THE NERVE FOR, ANYWAY.

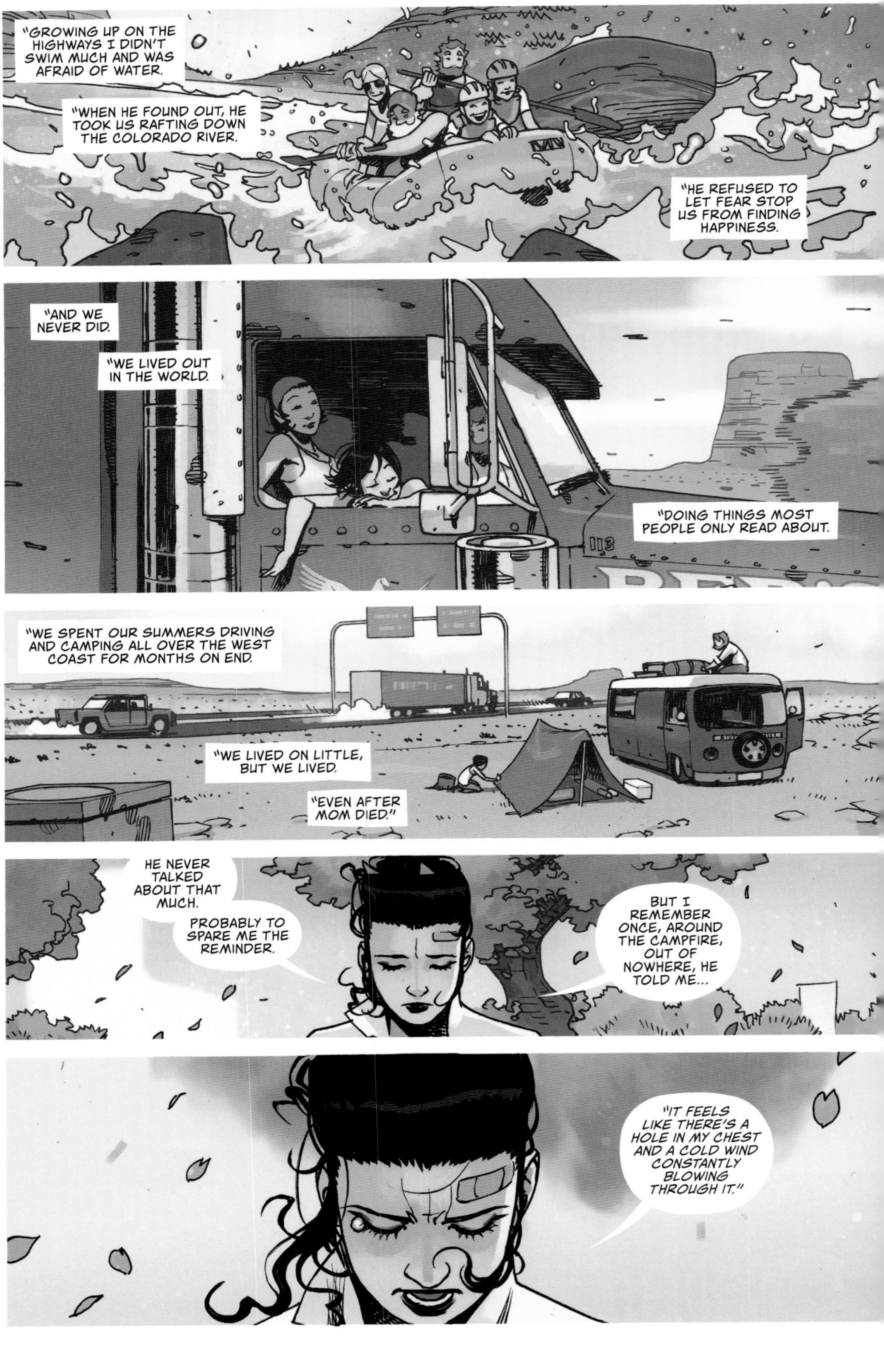
"GROWING UP ON THE HIGHWAYS I DIDN'T SWIM MUCH AND WAS AFRAID OF WATER.
"WHEN HE FOUND OUT, HE TOOK US RAFTING DOWN THE COLORADO RIVER.
"HE REFUSED TO LET FEAR STOP US FROM FINDING HAPPINESS.
"AND WE NEVER DID.
"WE LIVED OUT IN THE WORLD.
"DOING THINGS MOST PEOPLE ONLY READ ABOUT.
"WE SPENT OUR SUMMERS DRIVING AND CAMPING ALL OVER THE WEST COAST FOR MONTHS ON END.
"WE LIVED ON LITTLE, BUT WE LIVED.
"EVEN AFTER MOM DIED."
HE NEVER TALKED ABOUT THAT MUCH.
PROBABLY TO SPARE ME THE REMINDER.
BUT I REMEMBER ONCE, AROUND THE CAMPFIRE, OUT OF NOWHERE, HE TOLD ME...
"IT FEELS LIKE THERE'S A HOLE IN MY CHEST AND A COLD WIND CONSTANTLY BLOWING THROUGH IT."

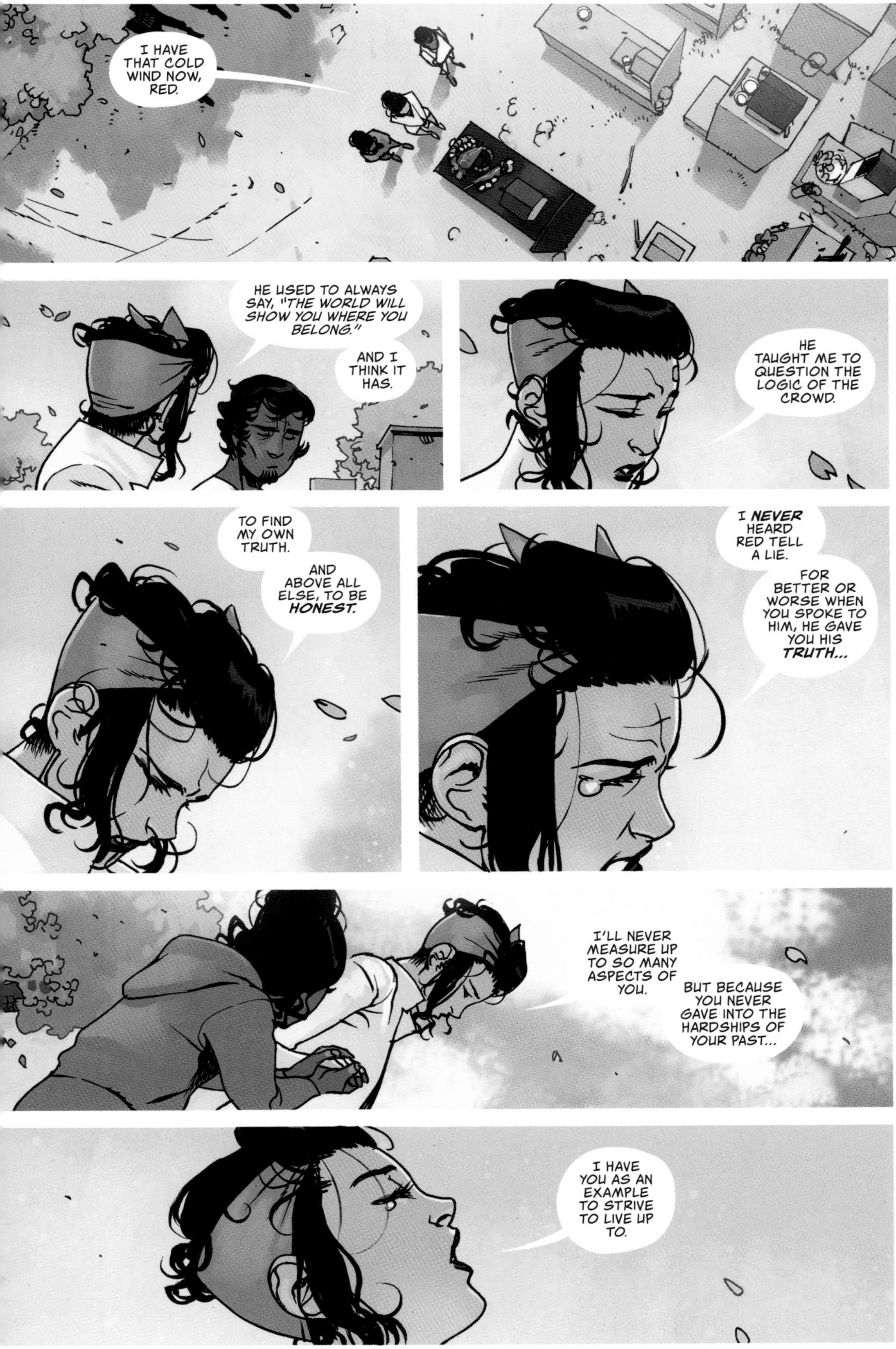
I HAVE THAT COLD WIND NOW, RED.
HE USED TO ALWAYS SAY, "THE WORLD WILL SHOW YOU WHERE YOU BELONG."
AND I THINK IT HAS.
HE TAUGHT ME TO QUESTION THE LOGIC OF THE CROWD.
TO FIND MY OWN TRUTH.
AND ABOVE ALL ELSE, TO BE HONEST.
I NEVER HEARD RED TELL A LIE.
FOR BETTER OR WORSE WHEN YOU SPOKE TO HIM, HE GAVE YOU HIS TRUTH...
I'LL NEVER MEASURE UP TO SO MANY ASPECTS OF YOU.
BUT BECAUSE YOU NEVER GAVE INTO THE HARDSHIPS OF YOUR PAST...
I HAVE YOU AS AN EXAMPLE TO STRIVE TO LIVE UP TO.

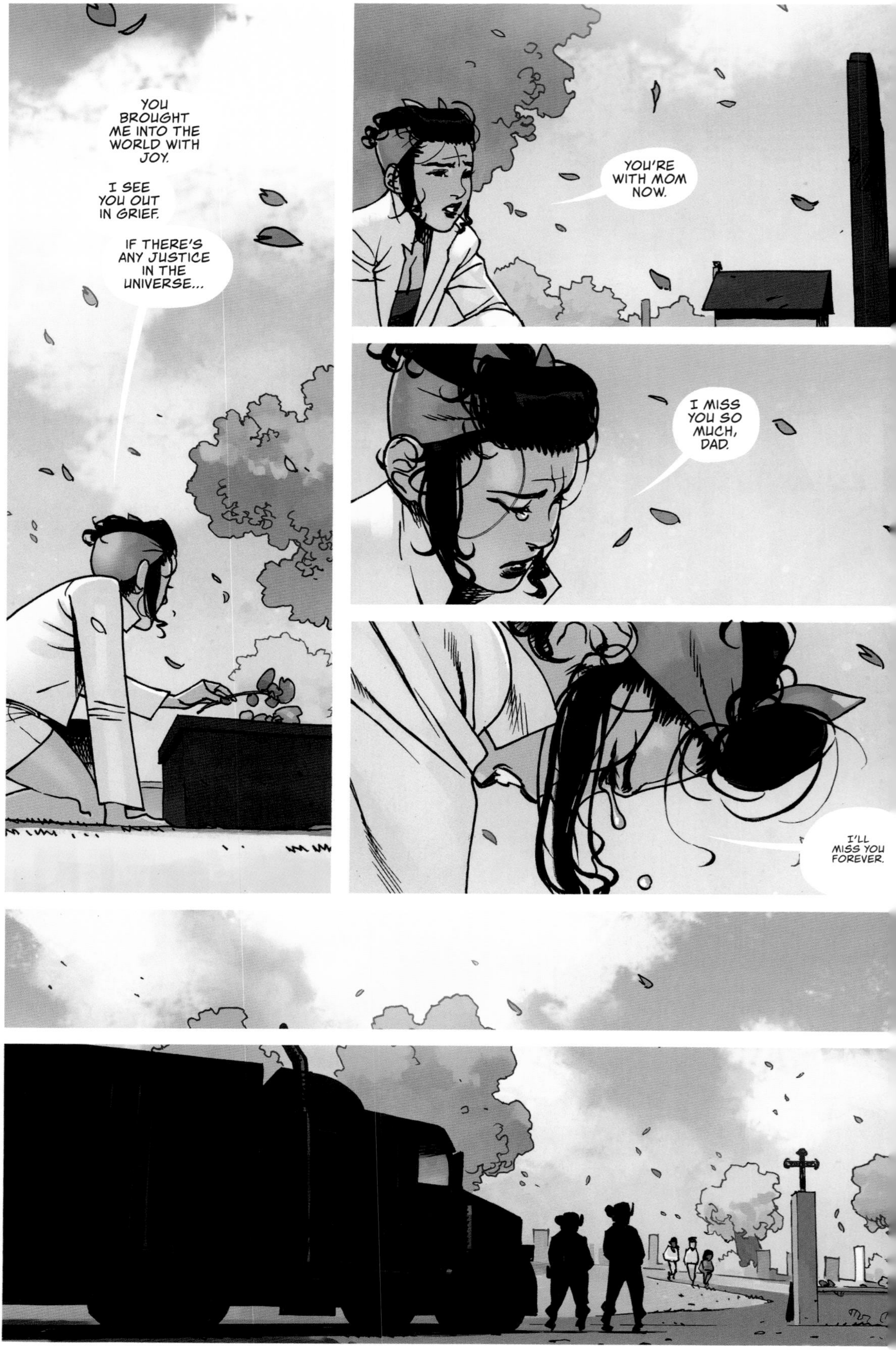
YOU BROUGHT ME INTO THE WORLD WITH JOY.
I SEE YOU OUT IN GRIEF.
IF THERE'S ANY JUSTICE IN THE UNIVERSE...
YOU'RE WITH MOM NOW.
I MISS YOU SO MUCH, DAD.
I'LL MISS YOU FOREVER.

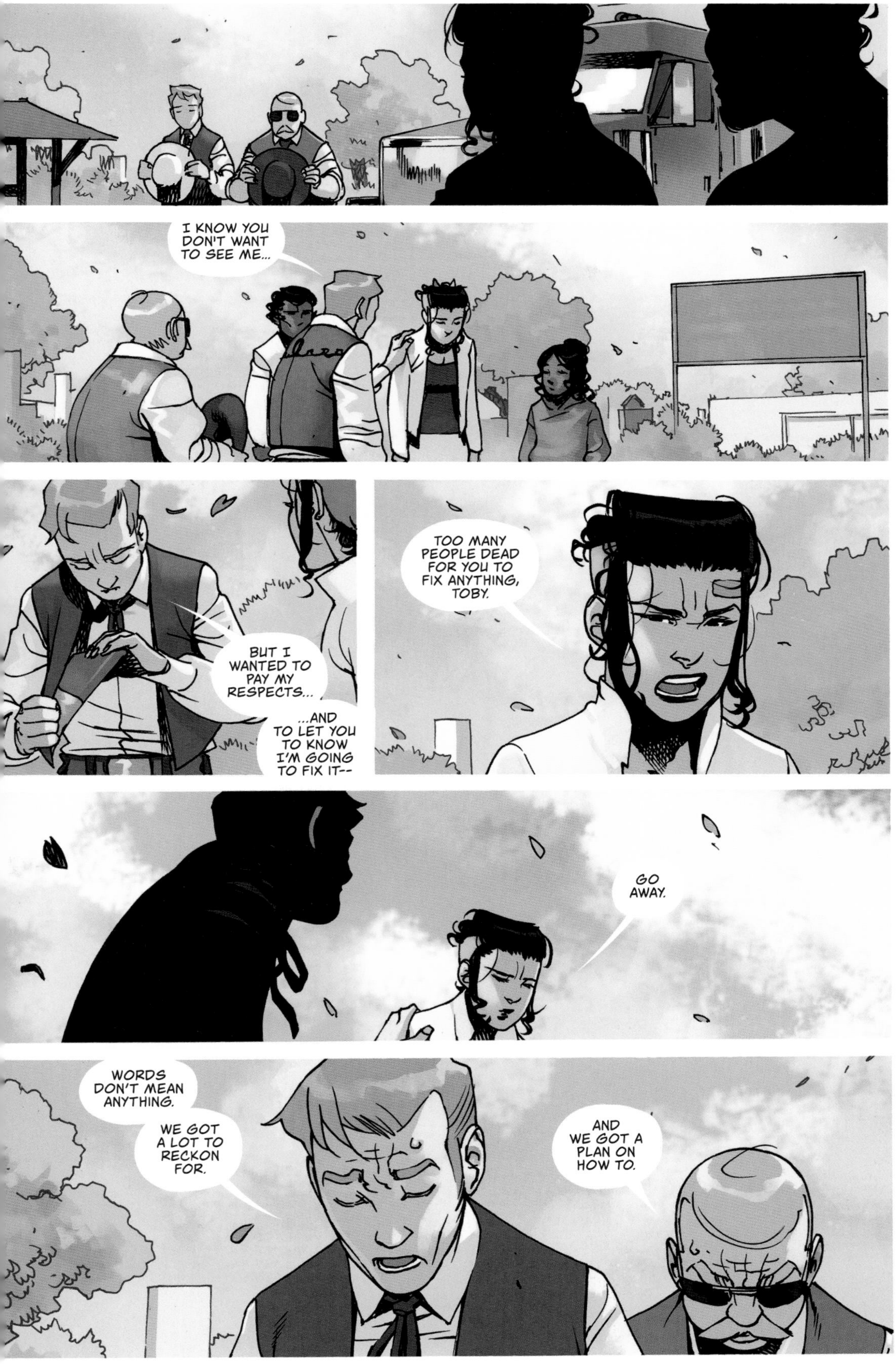
I KNOW YOU DON'T WANT TO SEE ME...
BUT I WANTED TO PAY MY RESPECTS...
...AND TO LET YOU TO KNOW I'M GOING TO FIX IT--
TOO MANY PEOPLE DEAD FOR YOU TO FIX ANYTHING, TOBY.
GO AWAY.
WORDS DON'T MEAN ANYTHING.
WE GOT A LOT TO RECKON FOR.
AND WE GOT A PLAN ON HOW TO.

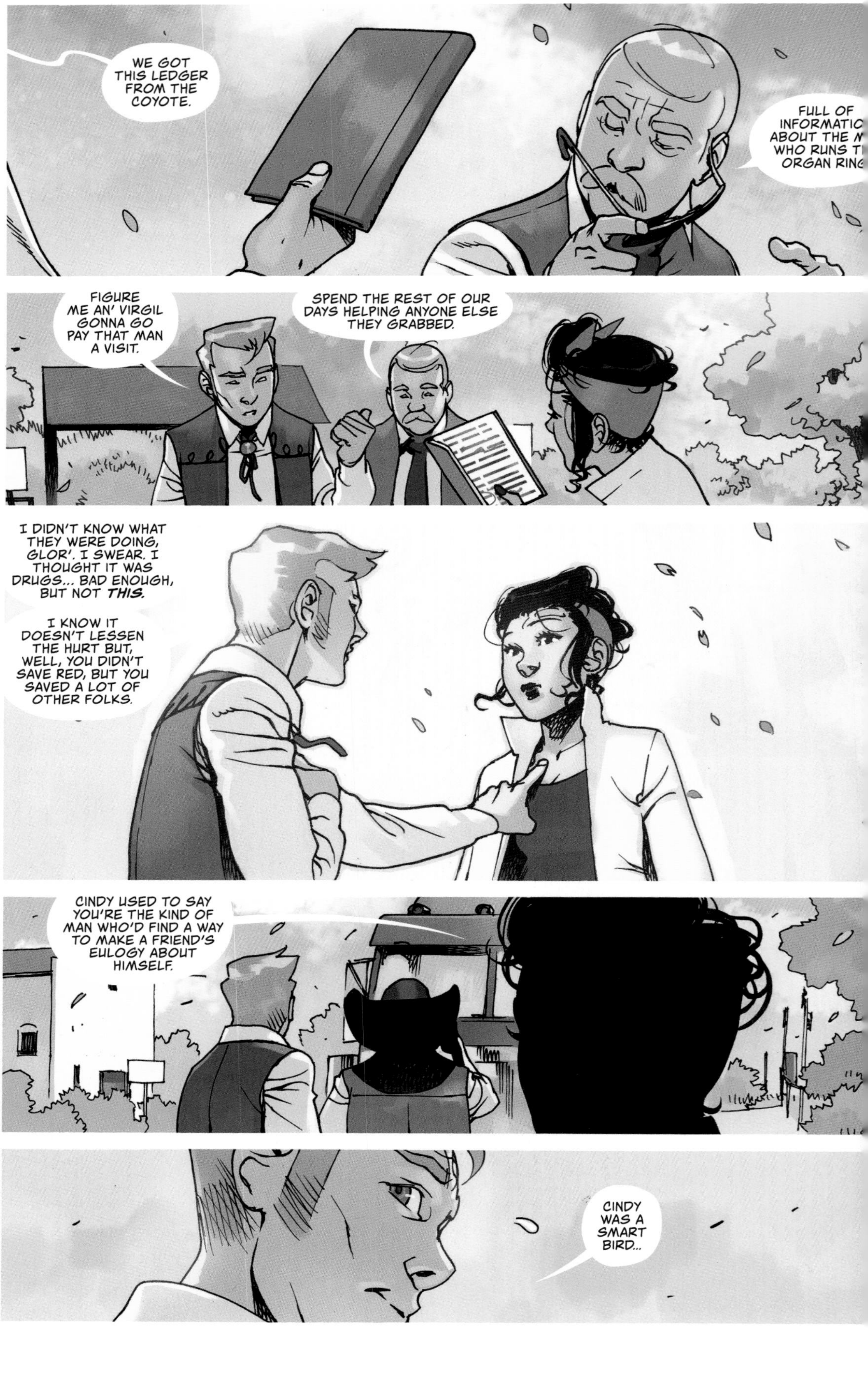

WE GOT THIS LEDGER FROM THE COYOTE.
FULL OF INFORMATIC ABOUT THE M WHO RUNS T ORGAN RING
FIGURE ME AN' VIRGIL GONNA GO PAY THAT MAN A VISIT.
SPEND THE REST OF OUR DAYS HELPING ANYONE ELSE THEY GRABBED.
I DIDN'T KNOW WHAT THEY WERE DOING, GLOR'. I SWEAR. I THOUGHT IT WAS DRUGS... BAD ENOUGH, BUT NOT *THIS.*
I KNOW IT DOESN'T LESSEN THE HURT BUT, WELL, YOU DIDN'T SAVE RED, BUT YOU SAVED A LOT OF OTHER FOLKS.
CINDY USED TO SAY YOU'RE THE KIND OF MAN WHO'D FIND A WAY TO MAKE A FRIEND'S EULOGY ABOUT HIMSELF.
CINDY WAS A SMART BIRD...

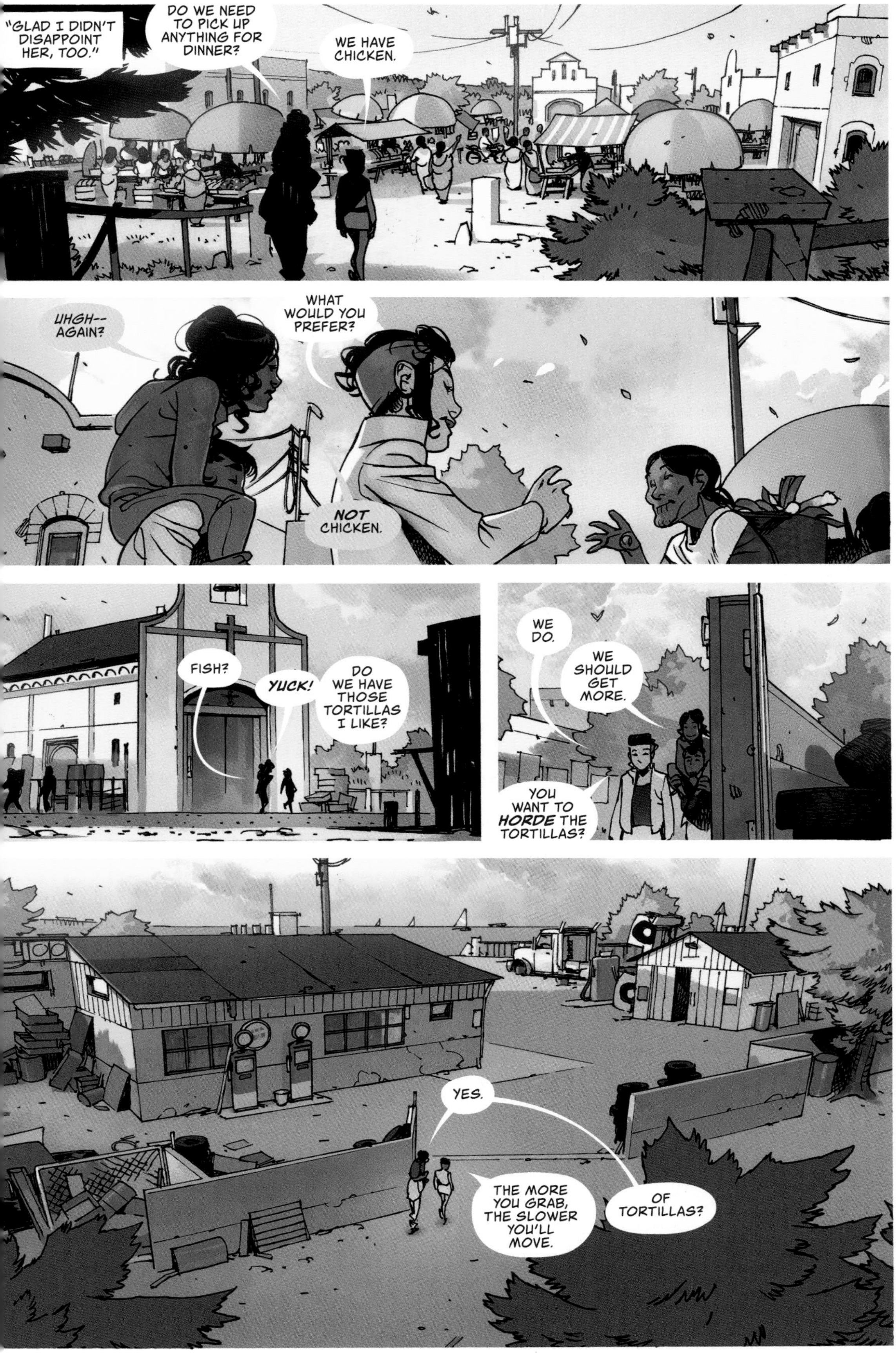
"GLAD I DIDN'T DISAPPOINT HER, TOO."
DO WE NEED TO PICK UP ANYTHING FOR DINNER?
WE HAVE CHICKEN.
UHGH-- AGAIN?
WHAT WOULD YOU PREFER?
NOT CHICKEN.
FISH?
YUCK!
DO WE HAVE THOSE TORTILLAS I LIKE?
WE DO.
WE SHOULD GET MORE.
YOU WANT TO HORDE THE TORTILLAS?
YES.
THE MORE YOU GRAB, THE SLOWER YOU'LL MOVE.
OF TORTILLAS?

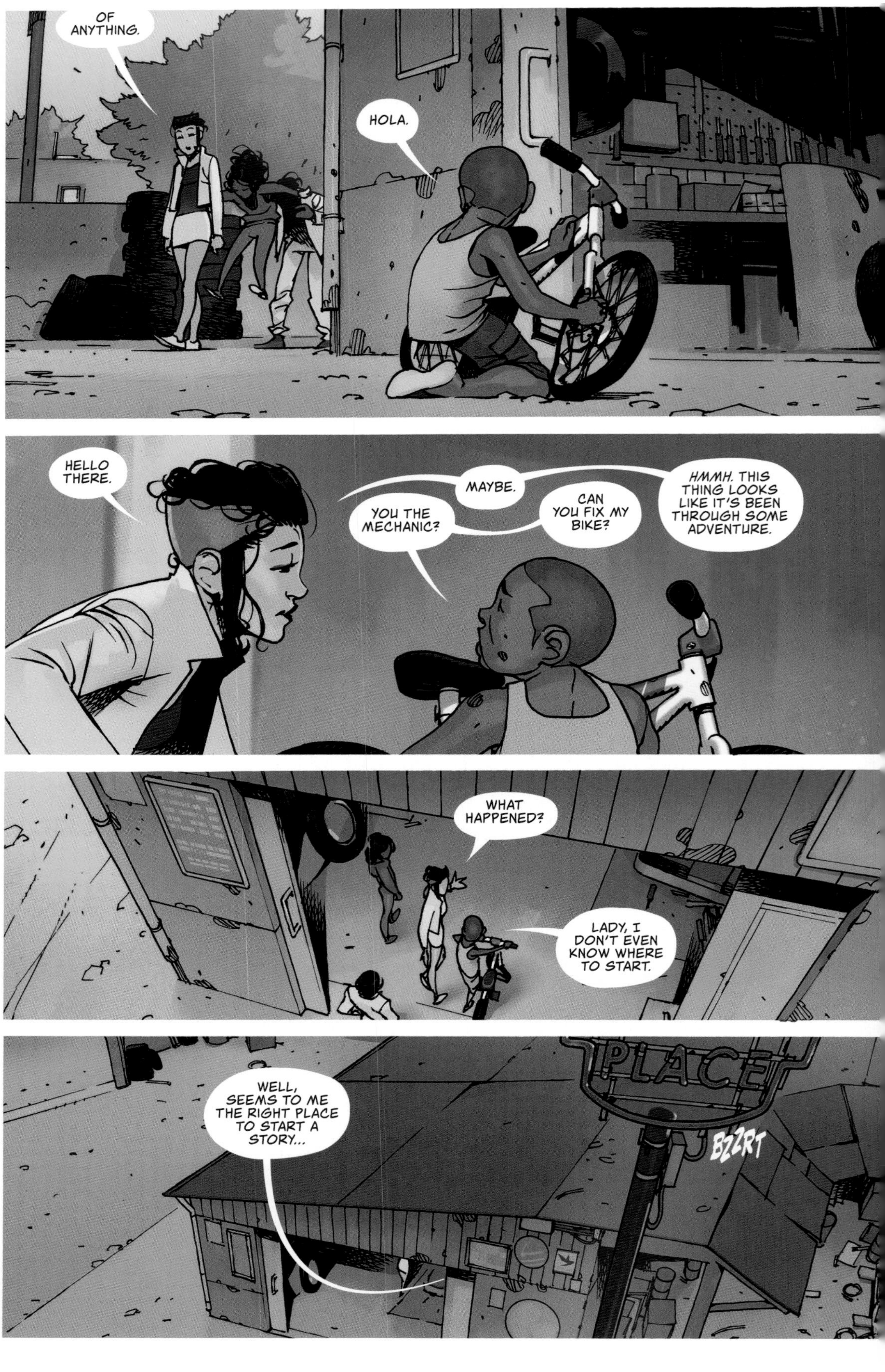
OF ANYTHING.
HOLA.
HELLO THERE.
YOU THE MECHANIC?
MAYBE.
CAN YOU FIX MY BIKE?
HMMH. THIS THING LOOKS LIKE IT'S BEEN THROUGH SOME ADVENTURE.
WHAT HAPPENED?
LADY, I DON'T EVEN KNOW WHERE TO START.
PLACE
BZZRT
WELL, SEEMS TO ME THE RIGHT PLACE TO START A STORY...

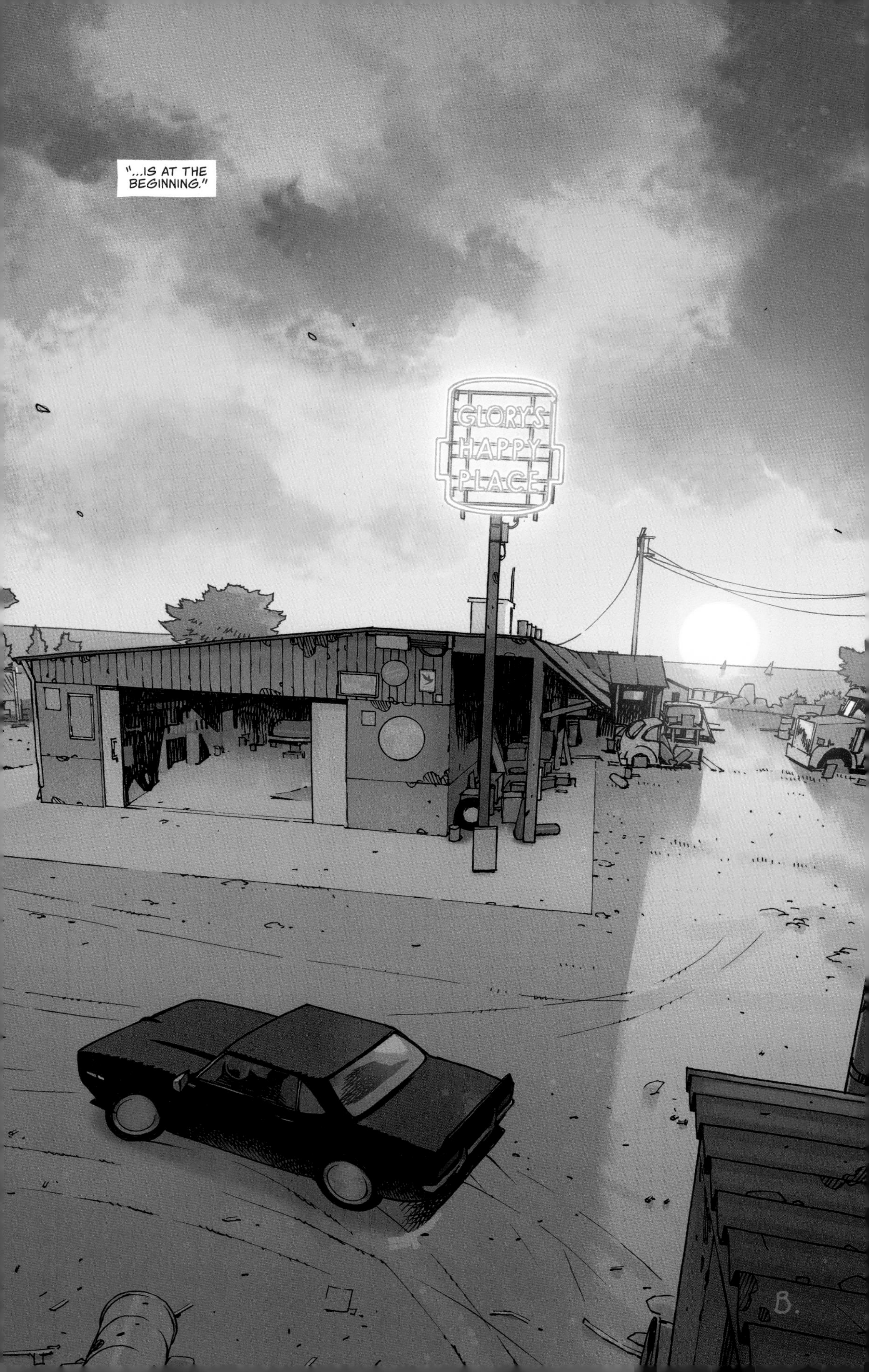
"...IS AT THE BEGINNING."
GLORY'S HAPPY PLACE
B.

COVER GALLERY

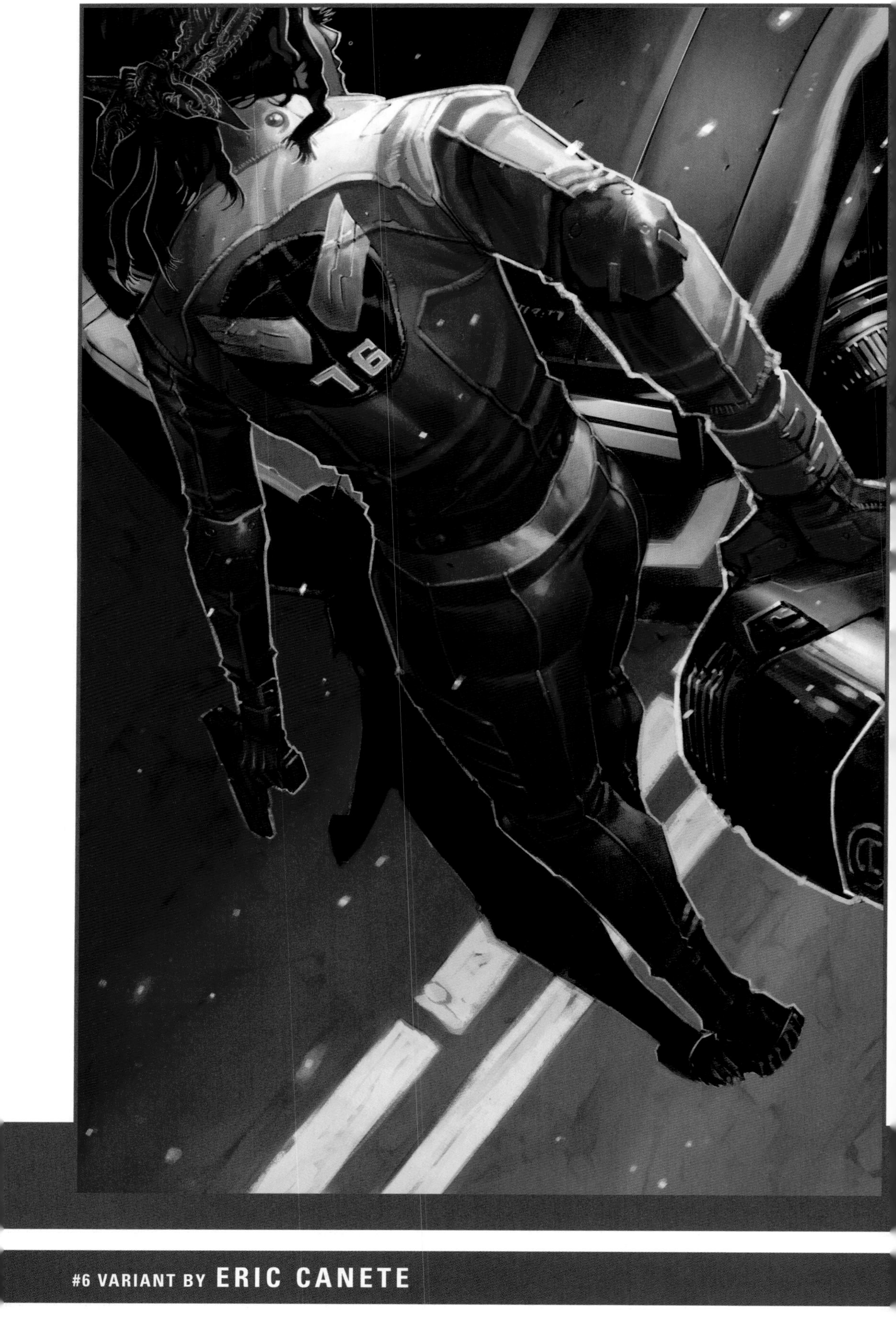
76

#6 VARIANT BY **ERIC CANETE**

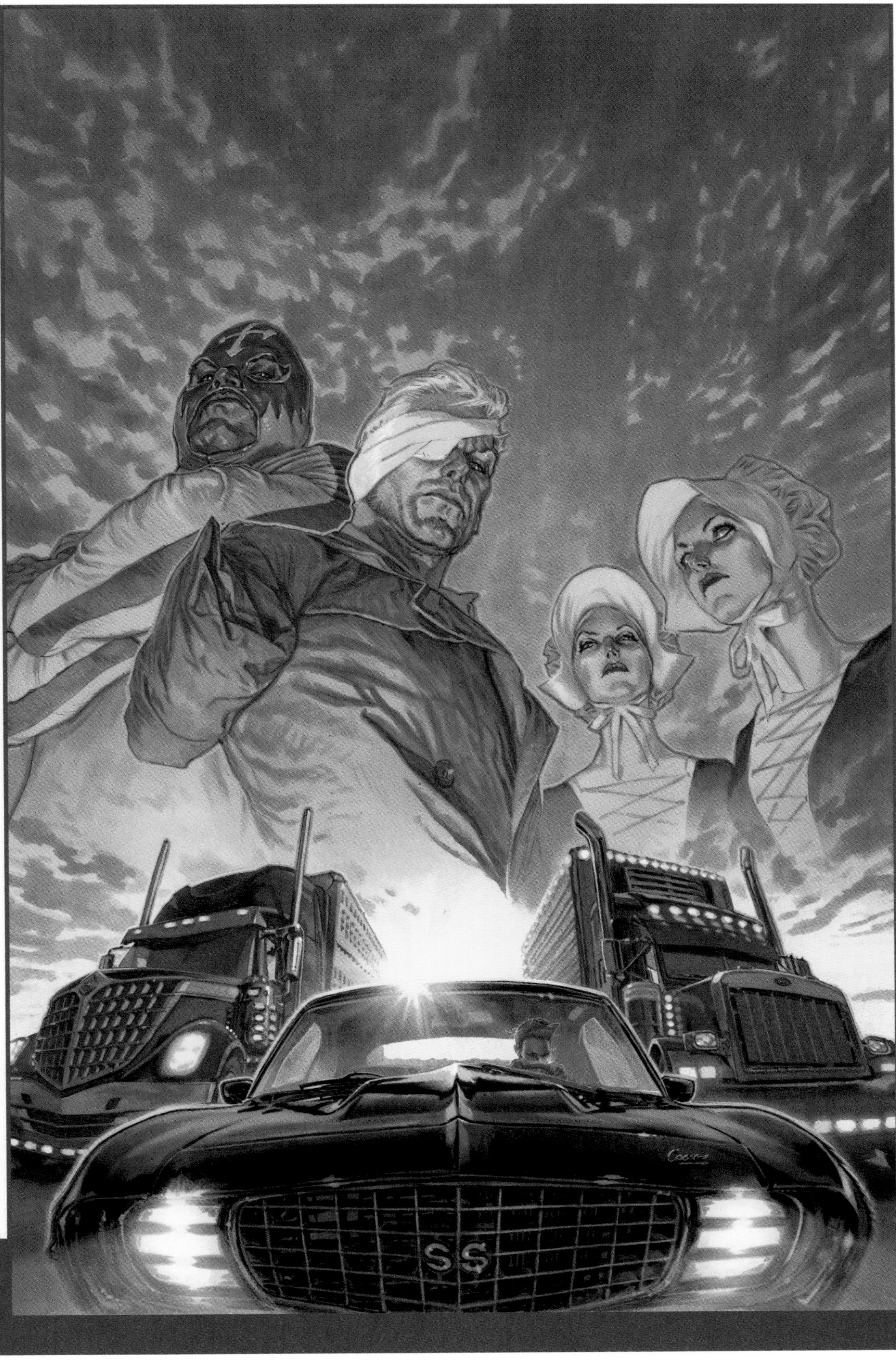
SS

#7 VARIANT BY **LEWIS LAROSA & MORENO DINISIO**

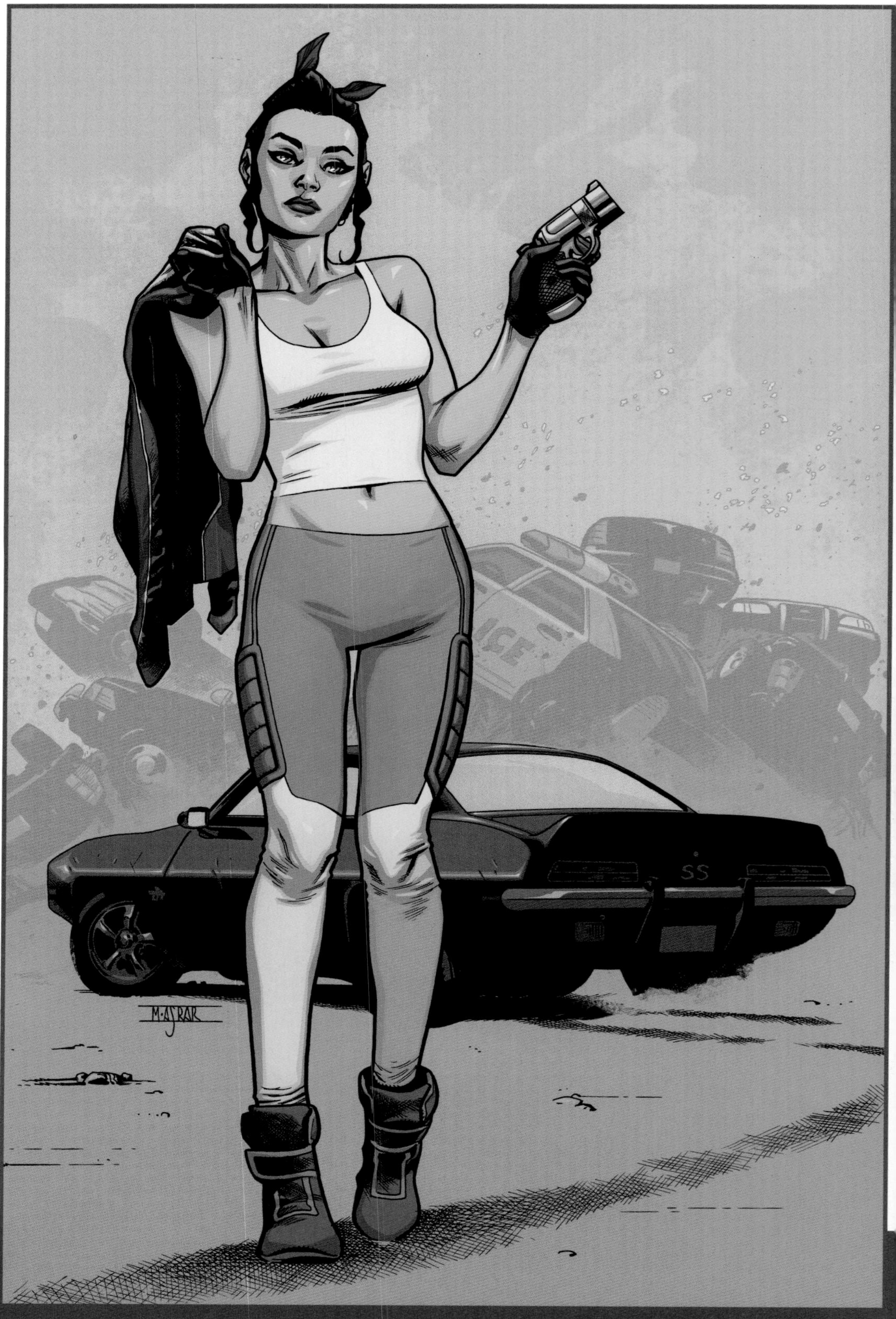
M.ASRAR
SS

#8 VARIANT BY **MAHMUD ASRAR & DAVE McCAIG**

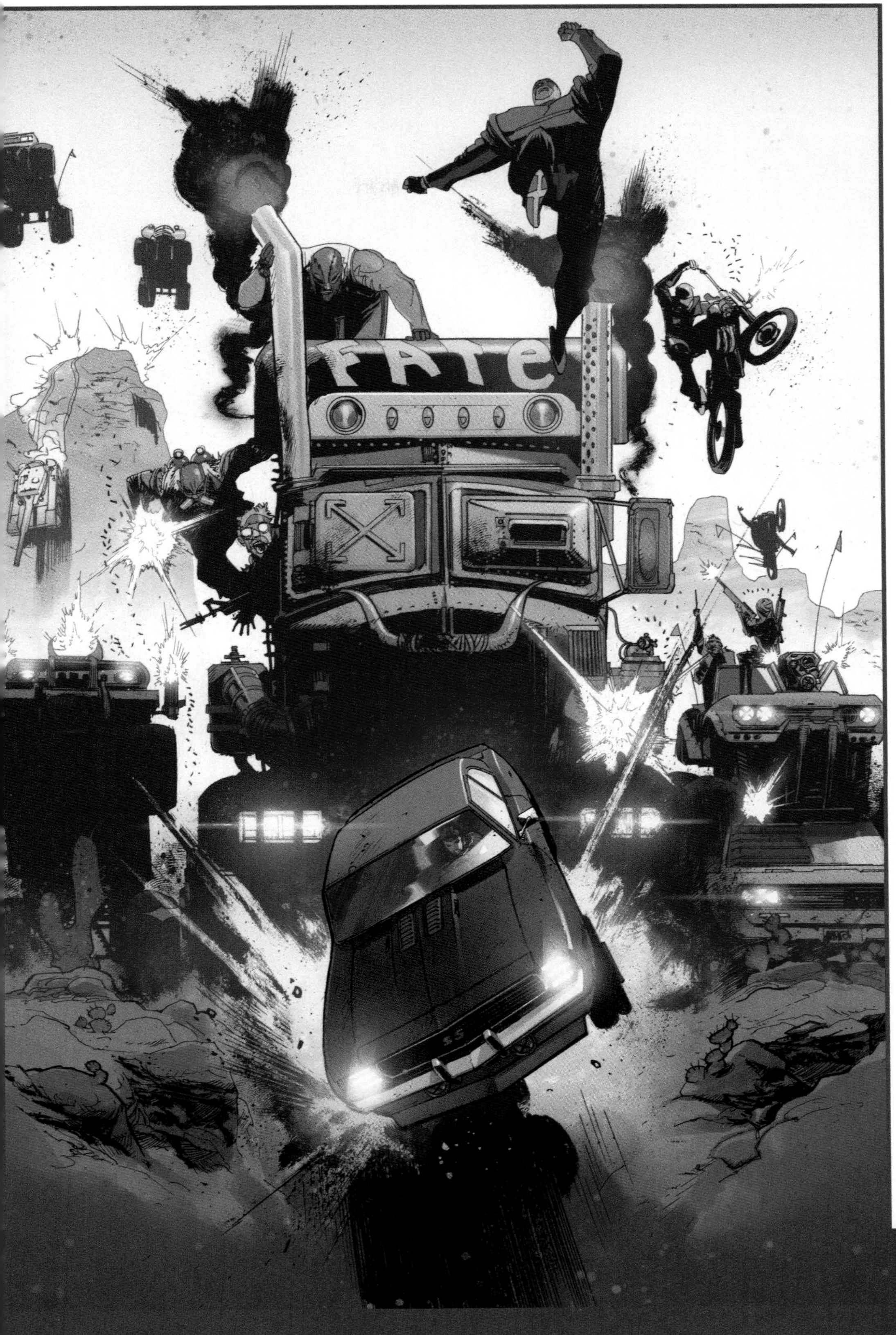
FATE

#9 VARIANT BY **SEAN GORDON MURPHY & BENGAL**

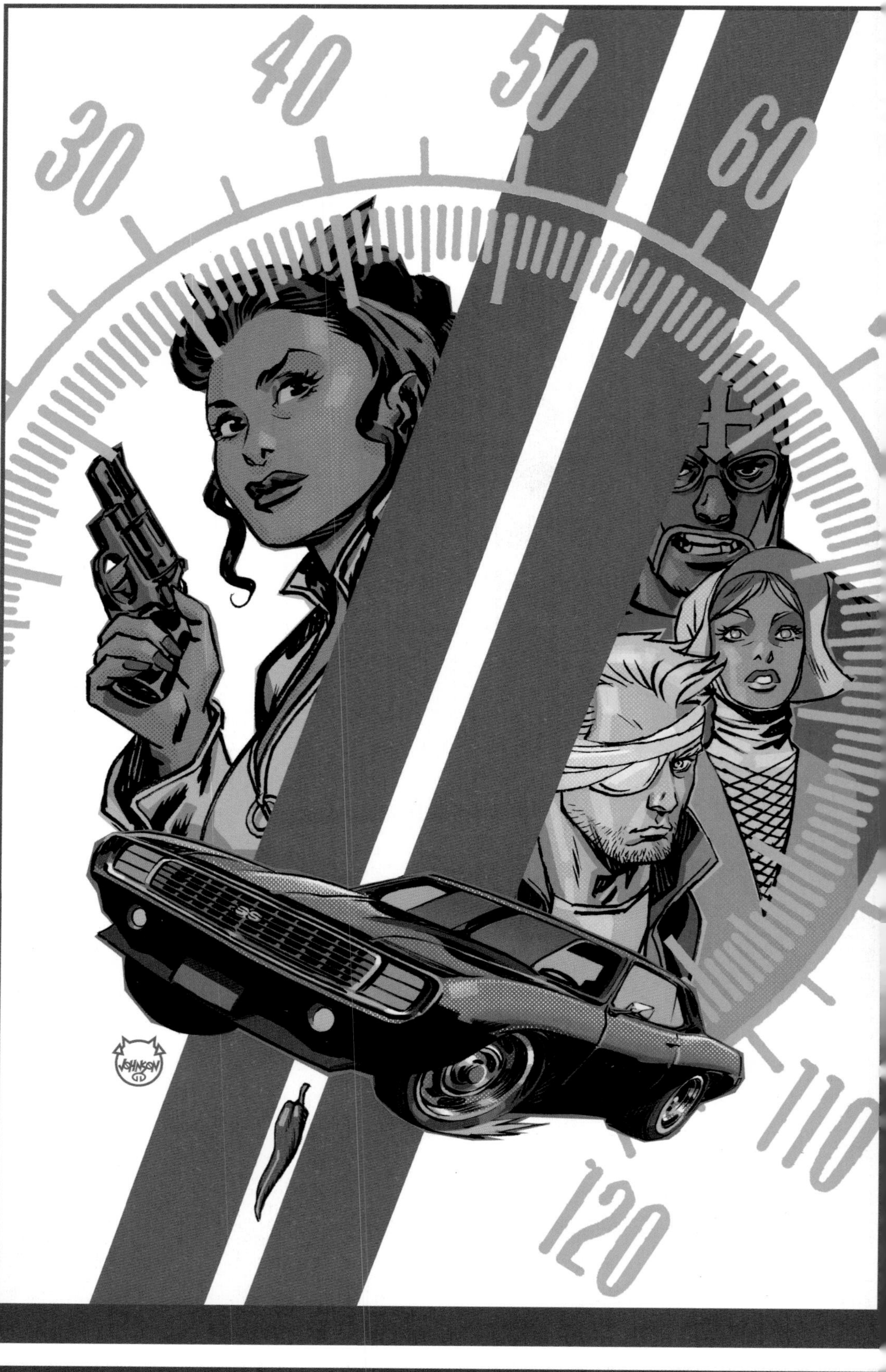
30
40
50
60
110
120
JOHNSON

#10 VARIANT BY **DAVE JOHNSON**

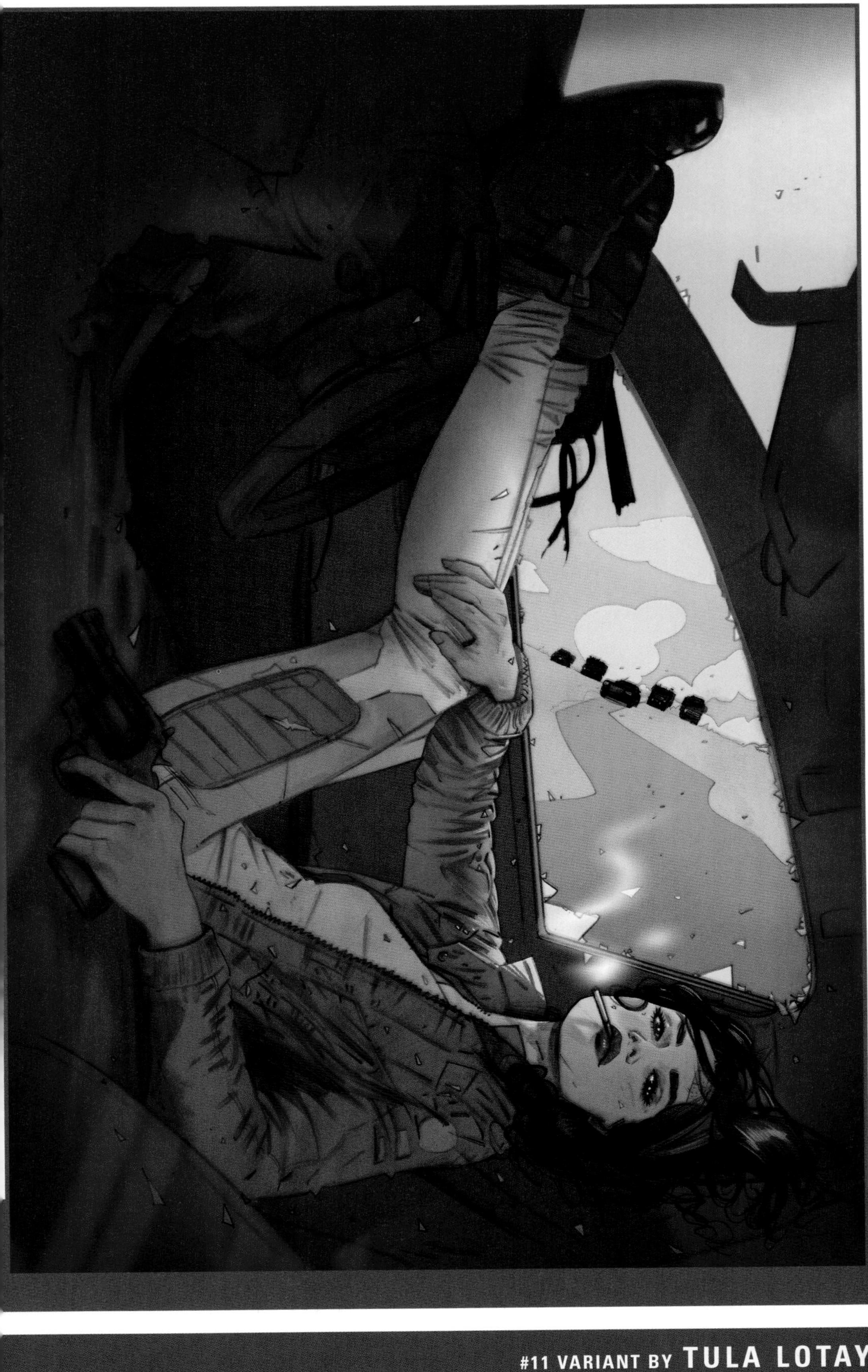

#11 VARIANT BY **TULA LOTAY**

RICK REMENDER is the writer/co-creator of comics such as DEADLY CLASS, FEAR AGENT, BLACK SCIENCE, SEVEN TO ETERNITY, and LOW. During his years at Marvel, he wrote *Captain America*, *Uncanny X-Force*, and *Venom* and created *The Uncanny Avengers*. Outside of comics, he served as lead writer on EA's *Bulletstorm* game and the hit game *Dead Space*. Prior to this he ran a satellite of Wild Brain animation, worked on films such as *The Iron Giant* and *Anastasia,* and taught sequential art and animation at San Francisco's Academy of Art University.

He currently curates his own publishing imprint, Giant Generator, at Image Comics and previously served as lead writer/co-showrunner on SyFy's adaption of his co-creation DEADLY CLASS.

After being an author for over a decade for the European comics market, **BENGAL** got the opportunity to start doing covers and interiors for DC Comics & Marvel in 2014 and started working regularly and exclusively for the American industry, on several characters such as *Supergirl*, *Spider-Gwen*, *All-New Wolverine*, and many more. In the meantime, he was already developing a longer-term, creator-owned project with Rick Remender, which became DEATH OR GLORY.